MW00573055

Traces of Two Pasts

TRACES OF

Aerith
Gainsborough

Tifa
Lockhart

FINAL FANTASY VII REMAKE

TWO PASTS

Kazushige Nojima

Translated by Stephen Kohler

Library of Congress Cataloging-in-Publication Data
Names: Nojima, Kazushige, 1964- author.
Title: Final fantasy VII remake : traces of two pasts / Kazushige Nojima.
Other titles: Final Fantasy VII remake. English | Traces of two pasts |
   Final fantasy VII
Identifiers: LCCN 2022041291 (print) | LCCN 2022041292 (ebook) | ISBN
   9781646091775 (hardcover) | ISBN 9781646096565 (ebook)
Subjects: LCGFT: Science fiction. | Fantasy fiction.
Classification: LCC PL873.5.O48 F56 2023 (print) | LCC PL873.5.O48
   (ebook) | DDC 895.63/6–dc23/eng/20221027
LC record available at https://lccn.loc.gov/2022041291
LC ebook record available at https://lccn.loc.gov/2022041292

Manufactured in the United States of America
First edition: March 2023
1st Printing

Published by Square Enix Books, a division of SQUARE ENIX, INC.
999 N. Pacific Coast Highway, 3rd Floor
El Segundo, CA 90245, USA

SQUARE ENIX
BOOKS

www.square-enix-books.com

FINAL FANTASY VII REMAKE
TRACES OF TWO PASTS

Contents

Episode 1
Traces of Tifa

The breeze over the grassy plain swept through Tifa Lockhart's hair, reminding her of home. When she'd been living in the village, her hair had remained forever tousled by the winds howling down from Mt. Nibel.

Walking just ahead was Aerith Gainsborough, who gestured widely at the sprawling grasslands and asked, "Hey, are you used to this kind of stuff?"

Tifa had only met the other woman a few days earlier, but she found her easy to talk to. In fact, within hours of first meeting, they'd already been chatting and joking like old friends.

Another gust swept the plains, sending waves rolling through the grass. Tifa turned to face the way they'd come, catching the wind at her back as she did so. The amount of distance the party had covered surprised her.

When Tifa returned to walking, Aerith had moved close to her side.

"You mean, have I ever seen endless fields like this before?" replied Tifa.

"No, I mean the walking. Hours and hours of it. First the badlands, and now grass."

"I don't mind it, I guess. It's good cardio."

Aerith laughed. "Everything comes down to exercise for you, doesn't it?"

"If I had a choice, though," continued Tifa, "I'd take a hiking trail in the mountains over this. At least that way the scenery changes as you go along."

"Right?! Ever since we left the city, it's like we've been walking in circles. It never ends! I used to dream of having a picnic in a wide-open field, but if this is all the grasslands have to offer, I think I'll pass."

"I'd say this is closer to hiking than a picnic. Picnics are about sitting down to eat and having fun."

"Does that mean you've been on one before? A real picnic?"

"Sure I have."

Tifa thought back on the days she'd spent as a child in the village.

"I mean . . . sort of," she clarified. "They were like picnics. We just used a different name."

"Yeah? What did you call them?"

Tifa's cheeks flushed, and her gaze fell as she answered, "Tea parties."

There was an amused snort. Tifa looked up in time to see a ripple of laughter work its way through Red XIII's leonine pelt. The beast—for he was a beast, at least in appearance—flicked his flame-tipped tail from side to side as he walked.

Though Tifa had accepted him as their traveling companion, she had to admit she was still unnerved by the dissonance between his appearance and his humanlike speech and intelligence.

Aerith's eyes sparkled. "Tell me more! I wanna hear all about your tea parties!"

"Sure."

But even as she answered, Tifa realized she wasn't quite sure where to begin.

Nibelheim was a tiny village at the base of Mt. Nibel. It had always been a modest community, established first as an unnamed base camp for prospectors whose gil-hungry eyes fixated upon the mountain's unique flora and fauna. Even after Nibelheim had proven itself a nominally permanent fixture worthy of a name, it was still little more than a basic settlement in the wilderness, consisting of a few households offering room and board to adventurers making their way up the mountain.

It wasn't until the community attracted the attention of Shinra Manufacturing that it started to resemble a proper village. The company was in search of a site to conduct top secret, cutting-edge research far removed from the prying eyes of the Republic of Junon, and Mt. Nibel seemed the perfect choice. It was 1960, one year following the discovery of mako energy, and Shinra was anxious to investigate all potential uses of this new resource. Construction began on the facility that would come to be known as the Shinra Manor. Next came the Nibel Reactor, a massive undertaking that saw the tiny mountain village flooded with laborers from across the country.

If Nibelheim ever achieved anything resembling prosperity, those were the years. But by 1968, construction of the reactor was complete, and the itinerants had moved on. Only a tiny research crew remained, along with a small number of civilians contracted by Shinra to maintain its new facilities. Life in Nibelheim grew quiet once more.

Over the years, the facilities' remote location became more of a drawback than an asset. As the reactor aged, Shinra saw no need to update it, instead throttling operations until the reactor was all but offline—at least in a practical sense. The village, with no other industry to fall back on, saw its population dwindle. Everything depended on Shinra. The only money flowing in came from fees paid by the company for land-use rights, barely supplemented by the wages earned by the ever-shrinking contingent of maintenance workers. Nibelheim's entire existence was tied to a couple of worn-down facilities that the company seemed ready to do away with at a moment's notice.

The villagers agreed that something had to change. They debated endlessly over ways to secure their community's future but failed to find a clear path forward. Ultimately, their voices and ideas were as fleeting as any of the angry gusts sweeping down from Mt. Nibel's foreboding peak.

"There were only four other kids around my age in the village, and they were all boys," explained Tifa. "We had our own little clique, I guess you'd say. We were so inseparable, the villagers started referring to us as the Four Fiends. Those were the friends I'd eventually start having tea parties with."

"Wait . . . But if it was you plus four other kids, shouldn't you have been the Fabulous Five or something?"

"One of those four boys was Cloud. The rest of us used to invite him along for our adventures, but he always refused—that is, if you could get a response out of him in the first place. Most of the time he straight-up ignored us. The way he acted got him into a lot of fights, until eventually the other boys were always referring to him as 'the weirdo' or 'that menace to society.'"

Tifa glanced ahead at Cloud Strife, who led the way on their journey across the grasslands. Cloud would have undoubtedly overheard her story, but he gave no sign of acknowledgment.

Tifa was born in May 1987, the first and only child of Brian and Thea Lockhart. Thea succumbed to illness when Tifa was only eight, leaving the girl to be raised by her father. What things Brian couldn't manage on his own, the other women of the village were happy to assist with. They taught young Tifa to cook and to sew, and all manner of things a village mother would teach her daughter. Nibelheim's was an old way of life, passed down over generations, all the way back to the days of the republic. Men went out to work, and women stayed behind to tend the home. Thus, a woman's lot in life was thought to hinge largely upon the man she ended up with.

Emilio, Lester, Tyler, and Tifa. They'd been the Four Fiends ever since they learned to walk. Each was the eldest or only child, and their parents were all quite close too. The four spent their days running wild around the village, roughhousing and sharing adventures—in short, growing up together. But too soon their carefree days would be cut short, the dynamic among them never to fully recover.

The death of Tifa's mother sent shock waves through the community. Tifa suddenly found herself an object of pity—someone everyone else was supposed to feel bad for. Burgeoning adolescence only complicated matters. As the boys neared their teenage years, their perception of Tifa shifted yet again. She was no longer a childhood playmate. She was a girl, and one that any of the three boys would have been happy to end up with. Their afternoon adventures were soon peppered with attempts to flirt and show off.

Still, the mood when they were together remained lighthearted, and Tifa, for her part, didn't mind the silly and somewhat flattering displays. She also knew her line and was careful not to cross it: when any of the boys invited her out alone, she responded with vague silence. She didn't want to decline outright and risk hurt feelings. Instead, she pretended not to catch the subtle invitations and shrugged off the ones that were more outright.

Around that same time, the boys began to speak of leaving the village. These were the first symptoms of a plague of wanderlust that seized upon all the young men of Nibelheim. Tifa's friends talked of joining Shinra's ranks to make names for themselves, or of moving to Midgar to strike it rich. The specifics of each dream varied, but all three converged on a single point: a triumphant reappearance in the village to take Tifa's hand and whisk her away to a better life. He'd keep her safe, each boy promised. He'd give her a future. In their eyes, Tifa was a badge of honor—a trophy to be won, proof of success and escape from a life of mediocrity.

It was Tifa's twelfth birthday. She was walking about the village in the new pair of sandals she'd received from her father. They were the latest fashion in Midgar—and frankly, a poor choice of footwear for the rough, packed dirt of Nibelheim's main square. She was concentrating intently on each small, careful step when Zander, the head of the village, called out to her.

"Well, if it isn't Tifa Lockhart! Say, you remember that litter of kittens we just had over at our place? I've been thinking you might be the perfect person to take one home, and I hear that today just so happens to be your birthday."

Tifa's eyes grew wide. Zander walked back toward his home and signaled for Tifa to follow.

"Come on," he said. "I've already cleared it with Brian. You get first pick of the litter."

She'd lost count of the number of times she'd begged her father for a cat. This was a dream come true.

Inside Zander's home, Tifa peered at the kittens asleep in their little wooden box for a very long time. Finally, she lifted a small white cat from among its siblings and cradled it in her arms.

"Hmm. Good choice," said Zander. "That one's name is Fluffy. But seeing as she's your cat now, you ought to pick a name that you fancy."

He paused for a moment, then added, "'Course, if it's all the same to you, I'd recommend you stick with Fluffy."

Cat clutched to her chest, Tifa ran home as fast as her sandal-clad feet would allow. Halfway across the square, the kitten tried to leap free. Tifa twisted to maintain her grip, and the panicked motion sent her crashing to the ground. Instead of home, Tifa's next stop was Dr. Sanq's tiny village clinic. The diagnosis was a sprained right ankle.

"One of my brand-new sandals was in pieces, and I had some pretty bad scrapes too," recalled Tifa. "One even ended up getting infected. Between the resulting fever and my sprained ankle, I was in bed for a week.

"And just to top it off, Fluffy ran away all the same. She found her chance later that week, when Dad left the door open."

"Oof," replied Aerith. "The bad luck kept piling on. I take it that means you kept the name Fluffy, though?"

"Dad felt awful about letting the cat escape, so while I was stuck in bed, he roped the entire village into a coordinated search. Zander told everybody the lost cat's name was Fluffy, so that's what everyone went around calling as they looked. It just kinda stuck. I was pretty upset that I didn't get to name my own cat, but it's not like that was Fluffy's fault."

Once Tifa's fever subsided, villagers began to check in on her. The first day, she was happy for the company. By the third, her tune had changed.

"Do they have to come by the house *every* day?" she moaned. "If they stuff me with any more snacks, I think I'm going to burst."

"You should be grateful," chided her father.

"Can't I go outside yet? I wanna help search for Fluffy. Didn't the doctor say it's important for me to get outside and gradually work my ankle back into shape?"

"I suppose he did say that," her father replied. "Okay. You win. How about we start the day after tomorrow?"

"I have to wait a whole 'nother day?"

"They need me on the mountain tomorrow. We're behind on trail maintenance for the route up to the reactor."

"I can practice walking by myself," Tifa pleaded. "I promise not to leave the village."

Her father sat in silence for a moment. Tifa could guess what was running through his mind. To a doting father, the words *I can do it myself* weren't much different than exclaiming, "Go away, Dad! I don't need you anymore!" The subtle shifts in the man's expression suggested that he was mourning how quickly his daughter was growing up, and that he was a bit cranky about it too.

When he finally spoke, his tone was gruff. "All right. You're a big girl. But don't you dare step foot outside the village. And don't overdo it either. The second your ankle starts feeling sore, I want you back home and in bed.

"And while we're at it . . ."

Her father proceeded to list off a half dozen other stipulations. Tifa nodded dutifully. She knew better than to press her luck.

The next morning, she was giddy with anticipation as her father readied himself for work. But just as he was about to head out, there was an unexpected knock at the door. The timing seemed almost contrived. Tifa's father opened up to find Claudia Strife, their neighbor—and Cloud's mother.

"Sorry to bother you so early," she said. "I'm just here to drop this little one off."

Tifa saw that the woman was holding something in her arms. It squirmed restlessly, then poked its head up to look around.

"Fluffy!" exclaimed Tifa. "Thank you so much, ma'am. Where did you ever find her?"

"Apparently she was near the trailhead, just past the gate. Actually, it's Cloud you ought to thank. He brought the poor thing home with him yesterday. I told him to go see you right away, but you know how that boy is. So here I am, bright and early."

Tifa thanked Claudia again. She took the kitten into her arms and slowly limped her way up the staircase to her bedroom on the second floor.

"Welcome home, Fluffy," she told the cat. "So Cloud's the one who found you, huh? Imagine that. I wouldn't have thought he'd even heard about my new cat."

With Fluffy's return, walks around the village suddenly seemed more of a chore than a joy. Tifa was anxious to play outside again, but on the other hand, her ankle still throbbed with every movement. The idea of working it back to health was less appealing without a lost cat to find.

Around that time, she had a surprise visit from Emilio.

"C'mon. Gotta get that ankle back in shape," he announced, holding a basket at his chest. "I brought some fruit and a thermos of tea."

"Huh? What are you talking about?"

"I'm taking you out for a walk. Let's head down to the pool at the base of the falls. I mean, technically speaking, that's still part of the village, right?"

"Did my dad put you up to this?"

"He asked me if I could come up with some way to get you more excited about your recovery. Said there were some rules, though. No leaving the village. That sorta stuff."

The boy seemed nervous, almost giddy, as if he'd decided there was some other, deeper reason that Tifa's father had reached out to him specifically. But in the time it took Tifa to get ready, there was another knock at the door. Lester had arrived, also holding a basket. Tifa couldn't help but notice a trace of disappointment in Emilio's eyes.

Though the waterfall in question was vital to the village's survival, it had never been named. It was simply "the falls." Geologically speaking, it wasn't anything remarkable—just one outlet of many for the natural spring water housed deep in the rock of Mt. Nibel.

With the two boys at her sides, Tifa made her way down to the plunge pool, gingerly testing her weight on the injured foot.

They'd arrived and were searching for a dry place to sit when Tyler appeared. Apparently, Tifa's father had had a word with all three of her would-be suitors.

"I brought sandwiches for lunch!" Tyler yelled as soon as he was in earshot. "Home-cured ham!"

Emilio and Lester cheered. Everyone knew that the best cured meats in the village came from Tyler's home. The family recipe had been passed down for generations. Even Tifa found herself smiling about the welcome surprise.

The old crew now assembled, conversation naturally turned to Midgar. To the boys, it was a place of hopes and dreams.

Up on the plates, Midgar had real schools for the city's children to attend, while kids in the slums learned to read and write from parents in the community who volunteered for the task. Thus, the four friends concluded, their own level of education was probably about the same as kids living in Midgar's slums.

For kids from the slums, enlistment was supposedly the quickest way to rise through Shinra's ranks. The three boys wondered aloud how risky that path might be. How dangerous would it be to serve in the military? What was the fatality rate, especially given the ongoing war?

The other option was money—if you could figure out how to get it. Topside, money talked. You could buy your way out of any trouble.

Even as children, the four suspected that their conversations were a jumble of truths, half-truths, and wild misconceptions. Still, the boys earnestly chattered on, and Tifa, for her part, found the strings of speculation relatively engaging. It was rather fun to let her imagination run wild, indulging in feelings of wonder and surprise about what might await in the unknown, far-off world of the city.

Tifa leaned back and listened to the boys carry on.

"After I move to Midgar, I wonder if I'll ever feel like coming back."

"Ha! You'll *have* to if you can't get used to city life."

"No way. I don't wanna be the one everyone knows came running home, tail between his legs. I'd go live in some other town."

"Well, *one* of us better come back. Otherwise, Tifa will be pretty lonely."

The boys laughed, and Tifa replied, "I'm sure life outside Nibelheim will be so exciting, you'll forget all about me."

She regretted the words the moment they left her mouth. She knew it sounded like a plea for attention, and just as she feared, Emilio and the others immediately steered the conversation elsewhere in an obvious attempt to cheer her up.

When lunch was over and they'd left the pool, the boys talked about how nice it had been to eat outside.

"That was a fun picnic. We oughta plan another one soon."

"How does that count as a picnic? We barely stepped foot outside the village."

"No, see, a picnic is *supposed* to be somewhere close to home. You're thinking of a hike."

"Well, what I'd like to try," began Tifa, "is a tea party. Doesn't it just sound so elegant?"

She'd seen photos once, of wealthy families during the days of the republic. They were pictures her mother had shared when Tifa was still small enough to sit upon her knees. The people in the shots had found a nice spot on the grasslands, where they spread out their blankets and unpacked their baskets to enjoy snacks and a cup of tea in the open air. Reflecting on the photos now, Tifa realized they must have been very old—perhaps taken by her great- or even great-great-grandparents.

"Tea party? What the crap is a tea party?"

"Beats me. But if Tifa thinks it'd be fun, count me in."

"Me too!"

Thus began the Fiends' new but short-lived tradition.

Back in the present, Tifa smiled softly.

"The three of them could never stop talking about Midgar," she said. "Eventually, it started to feel like it was me versus the city. If I wanted to keep my friends' attention, I had to compete. I started saving up to buy the kinds of clothes girls in the city wear. When I couldn't get my hands on something directly, I'd go to the villagers who knew how to sew and ask them to make the pieces I needed. I was begging the village general store to track down fabrics they'd never even heard of.

"I went all out with my baking too. I was determined to make each treat I brought to a tea party the best one yet. I don't think I've ever worked so hard before or since just to grab the attention of a bunch of boys."

"Ha! Tifa versus Midgar. I like your style." Barret Wallace let out a great roar of laughter. At some point, he'd sidled up to Tifa and Aerith, eager to catch the tale of Tifa's past.

Spring was near, and the Four Fiends' next tea party would be their last. All three of the boys had declared their intent to leave the village as soon as winter passed, and the news had Tifa feeling uncharacteristically sentimental. At the last moment, late in the evening on the day before their outing, she decided to bake a homemade cake. She briefly considered cookies, but cake seemed the more appropriate treat for a special occasion. Tifa rifled through the kitchen cabinets, jotting down the ingredients she lacked, and then raced over to the village general store—Emilio's home.

Just as she placed a hand on the shop's door handle, she felt eyes at her back. Tifa turned to find Cloud Strife.

Any encounter with Cloud would have been unusual enough. But what really astonished Tifa this time was the fact that the boy was staring straight into her eyes. Typically when she ran into Cloud, he'd look away and find some excuse to dash off. There was something different about him today.

His lips parted as if to speak. She saw them move but couldn't make out the words. Tifa tilted her head in confusion, and Cloud bolted forward.

Tifa flinched, certain he was about to ram into her. But a single step shy of a collision, Cloud stopped. He leaned in, mouth inches from her ear. When he spoke, the words were so rushed, they nearly blended together.

"After dark," he whispered. "Up on the water tower."

All Tifa could think to reply was "Okay."

Cloud nodded and sprinted off into the falling dusk, as if fleeing from danger.

Tifa, flustered both by the meeting and by what seemed to be an unnecessarily hasty departure on Cloud's part, scurried back home. She'd forgotten all about the shopping excursion.

When she walked inside, her father met her with a quizzical stare. The last thing she needed was a line of questioning from her dad, so she pretended to scowl and stomped up the stairs to the safety of her room.

Fluffy was waiting on the bed. Tifa scooped the cat up in her arms and slumped to her knees on the floor. Her heart was racing, and it wasn't only from rushing home.

When was the last time she and Cloud had spoken? It felt like months.

Ah, she recalled. *Fluffy's latest disappearance.*

The fiasco of Tifa's twelfth birthday had only been the beginning; Fluffy had run away dozens of times since. It didn't take long for Tifa to notice that the cat was actually quite reliable about coming back on her own after she was allowed to roam free for a few days. Still, it didn't feel right to ignore the poor thing, so she always went out looking. The cat had a tendency to head to the mountain, and though monster sightings were rare, they weren't unheard of.

On that particular day, there had been no sign of Fluffy in the village. Tifa decided to widen her search, and just as she arrived at the trailhead, Cloud came running down the mountain. He had to have noticed Tifa, but he refused to look her way. Only at the precise moment they passed did he finally acknowledge her presence.

"Saw Fluffy," he said brusquely. "Right after the first bend."

"Thank you."

Cloud didn't stop or accept her thanks. He continued straight on to the village. But just before he was out of earshot, he turned and shouted, "Hey! You forgetting to feed it or something? It was munching on a dead bird!"

"Of course I'm feeding her!"

Tifa stormed up the trail.

Not a minute up the mountain, she found Fluffy, tail held triumphantly high, mouth and whiskers caked with blood.

"How old would I have been . . . ?" Tifa mused to herself.

She was still in her room, thinking back on an even more distant past. Fluffy was now resting on her knees, purring happily, her eyes narrow slits as Tifa stroked the soft fur along her back.

Tifa recalled that when she and Cloud were very young, they used to spend all day playing together. Cloud's front door was right next to her own, making it easy to run back and forth between the two homes. As children, they'd had little reservation about inviting themselves in whenever they pleased.

Ah . . . That little Strife boy has a face like an angel.

That's how Tifa's mother had once described Cloud.

They'd been sitting at the dinner table—the three members of the Lockhart family. Tifa must have been six or seven at the time. For some reason, the compliment made her very happy. Almost embarrassed, in fact. Tifa's mother seemed to pick up on that fact, and she shot her daughter a knowing glance. Brian happened to catch the subtle exchange, and as Tifa recalled, he'd spent the rest of the evening in a sour mood. It was one of the few memories she had of her family while it was still intact.

At some point, she and Cloud had grown distant. For a time, she wondered if perhaps it was due to some kind of falling-out between Cloud and the other boys of the village. The obvious suspect was the accident on Mt. Nibel, shortly after the death of Tifa's mother. But even if the events of that day really had played out as everyone claimed, Tifa still felt a nagging sense that there was more to it. Cloud had been pulling away from her long before that fateful day.

She asked herself a question she'd asked dozens of times before: *When did we stop being friends?*

Tifa rose, cradling Fluffy in her arms, and crossed to the window. In the center of the square, the water tower stood lonely in the day's fading light. It didn't seem like a very covert meeting spot. Every home in the village had a view of the tower from its windows. Of course, that was probably why Cloud had asked to meet at night, once the village was asleep.

What time exactly did he want her there? Midnight seemed like a safe bet, but then again, *after dark* covered far too many hours to be certain.

In a way, the ambiguity was flattering. Perhaps the short exchange showed that Cloud believed him and Tifa to be close enough that there was no need to elaborate. The tiniest exchange would suffice to put them on the same page.

But if that were true, why did he always act so cold and indifferent?

She felt as if she could spend all day wondering and not get any closer to solving the puzzle of Cloud Strife, so in the end, she turned to more pressing matters.

"Hey, Fluffy . . . What should I wear tonight?"

Unfortunately, the cat wasn't the least bit interested in the inquiry. She leapt from Tifa's arms and burrowed into the blankets on the girl's bed.

A knock came at her bedroom door.

"Hey, Tifa?"

It was her father. When she opened the door, she found him obviously exhausted from work.

"I'm gonna turn in early today," he said. "Maintenance work on the rope bridge was pretty rough."

"Okay," replied Tifa. "Sleep well, Dad."

"Thanks."

Her father paused, a hint of confusion crossing his face.

"Is something wrong?" she asked.

"I came up here planning to ask you the same thing . . . I could've sworn you were in a bad mood when you got home."

"Dad! Even if I *were* upset, I wouldn't want you bugging me about it."

Her father chuckled back. "All right. My bad. Good night, then."
He waved and retired to his own bedroom across the landing.

Tifa turned her attention back to her closet, evaluating her choices for the midnight rendezvous. It occurred to her that technically this would be the first time she'd ever snuck out of the house while her father was asleep. Not only that, she was going out to see a boy. And *Cloud Strife*, to boot! Suddenly, it felt like one of the biggest moments of her young life had sprung upon her. Everything was unfolding so fast. She knew she was far too excited for any hope of sleep.

She settled on a pale green dress, the color of young leaves. It was a piece that Emilio had once said looked especially good on her.

Once Tifa had herself together, she waited, trying to calm her nerves. Near midnight, she peered out the window once more, expecting the whole village to be asleep. Instead, the windows of several homes were still lit, and worse, there was no sign of Cloud at the water tower.

Tifa reluctantly flicked off the lights to her own room and headed into the hallway, closing the door before Fluffy could follow. She placed an ear against the door to her father's room and was relieved to hear loud, carefree snores. With slow, careful steps, she descended the stairway, then tiptoed through the living room and was free.

Tifa emerged into the night with a gasp.

Stars. The sky was full with countless glittering stars, like raindrops suspended in the sky, ready to come falling down at any moment.

She wondered what Cloud would say to her up on the water tower. What special feelings might he confess? And if he did venture a step beyond friendship, how would she respond? Did she love Cloud? Did she like him as more than a friend? She pressed a hand to her chest as the thoughts swirled. Of course she liked him. But she felt it wasn't the kind of "like" that made you want to be together with a certain person forever.

That little Strife boy has a face like an angel.

Shortly afterward, Thea had added, *Everyone loves to fawn over Sephiroth the hero these days, but personally, I think little Cloud is going to grow up to be much more attractive.*

It was quite the compliment: Cloud, a boy from a tiny village most of the world would have trouble locating on a map, declared victor over Sephiroth, the young hero of the nation, the face of SOLDIER and Shinra's military might.

Tifa finally understood.

The reason her heart seemed to rise in her chest anytime she saw Cloud . . . The reason she grew nervous and fumbled for words whenever he was near . . . It wasn't because she had feelings for him. It was because she looked up to him. He was a beautiful, untouchable presence, like one of those countless stars glittering in the distant sky.

Tifa murmured thanks to her mother for somehow managing to guide her still, years after their parting.

The tension of the upcoming rendezvous lifted. Her steps felt light, and she dashed across the clearing to the water tower. She saw that Cloud was in fact there, and that he was sitting on the wooden platform near the top, legs dangling over the edge.

The last time she'd climbed the water tower, she'd been a small child. As she made her way up now, she prepared herself for what might come. She'd talk to Cloud normally, she told herself. The way they usually talked. Except . . . how *did* they usually talk?

"Heya."

Despite all her efforts, her greeting felt awkward and contrived.

But she wasn't alone. Cloud's announcement atop the water tower turned out to be astonishingly mundane.

When spring came, he said, he was leaving for Midgar.

She'd heard it thrice before: He wasn't going just to look for work. He wasn't like the other boys.

Little did he know how well-worn his claim truly was.

Still, the night was anything but spoiled, thanks to the magic of the star-streaked sky. Or perhaps it was because she found it rather cute how worked up Cloud was about the grand future he believed was awaiting him beyond the village.

Whatever the reason, it ignited a sudden spark. The words that next spilled from her lips came entirely on impulse.

"Just . . . promise me one thing," she began. "When we're older, and you're a famous SOLDIER . . . if I'm ever trapped or in trouble . . . "

She hesitated, then blurted out, "Promise you'll come and save me."

For a brief moment, time stood still on the water tower. She hadn't come intending to say something like that. It just popped into mind. But once the promise was sealed, it seemed to her a thing of singular importance. She'd discovered that Cloud—the quiet neighbor who had always seemed as unreachable as the stars—was just a normal boy like any other. She'd come to understand that she *did* like him. And it was that special kind of "like"— the one that ties up your heart, making you yearn to be with that person for the rest of your days.

The icy sharpness of the winds blowing down from Mt. Nibel subsided, signaling spring's arrival. Tifa's three tea party companions were soon packed and ready to head off.

The night before Emilio's departure, he showed up at her home, swearing he'd be back. "Wait for me," he pleaded. In the morning, Tifa watched as he hitched a ride out of the village on the beat-up old truck that delivered parts and materials for maintenance on Shinra's facilities.

As the truck sped off, Emilio hoisted his upper body out of the window on the passenger side, waving both arms in wide arcs until he and the truck were completely out of sight.

When Lester and Tyler's day arrived, the typical sounds of morning in Nibelheim were drowned out by the roar of a helicopter. This was a special treat provided by Shinra for new recruits: before their life of service to the company began, they were given the chance to leave their hometowns in style.

Lester offered Tifa a crisp, cheerful goodbye, along with a firm hug, before dashing off to find his seat in the chopper's rear bay. Tyler fumbled with his words and stood with eyes downcast, fidgeting uncertainly. Knowing it was almost time for the helicopter to take off, Tifa reached her own arms out, pulling him close in a friendly embrace. A few of the village's younger girls also ran up to hug him goodbye, and Tifa saw Lester watching with envy from where he sat strapped in and ready to depart.

Cloud's departure came a bit later, when the afternoons were again warm and pleasant. However, Tifa wouldn't get the chance to see him off.

A Shinra army truck rolled into the village in the dead of night, and Cloud hopped aboard with no one but his mother to wave goodbye. His processing had been delayed, Tifa later heard, on account of him not having his application papers entirely in order. As for the helicopter ride, the bulk of Shinra's forces had been dispatched to some pressing new offensive around that time. An aircraft couldn't be spared to pick up one lone straggler from a tiny mountain village.

Thus, Tifa didn't hear about Cloud's departure until the next morning. There had been no goodbye. No promise to meet again. No hug.

Her first reaction was to laugh. In a way, it wasn't surprising. That's how her relationship with Cloud had always been.

Then the laughter broke and turned to sobs.

When Tifa's thirteenth birthday rolled around, life in Nibelheim was depressingly quiet. Her father attempted to cheer her up with a great celebration, but all she could focus on was the fact that not a single card had arrived from any of the boys who had left the village.

She tried her best to bat her sadness away.

It just slipped their minds, she told herself. *They're busy with their new lives, and they just happened to forget. That's all.*

"Hey. Tifa."

Tifa shook the memories off, returning to the present. The voice was Barret's.

"What is it?"

"You all right? You got pretty quiet there."

"Yeah. Sorry. Just hung up on some old memories. Where was I again?"

"You versus Midgar."

Tifa laughed. "Right. I guess the next big thing was my encounter with Master."

The boys gone, Tifa's life consisted of reading books, sewing, and cooking. She went entire days without conversing with anyone other than her father—and, of course, Fluffy. But Tifa adjusted to the change with unexpected ease. In fact, she found she was even beginning to enjoy it.

A slower, more peaceful world had opened up to her, and it prompted another realization: this had to be why Cloud preferred to spend his time alone. He liked his quiet solitude.

Before, Tifa had felt bad for him. She'd assumed he was lonely —an assumption that now struck her as terribly presumptuous, and more than a little embarrassing. Now she understood that it was a choice. Cloud chose to block out the things that he found distasteful or troublesome to deal with.

It filled her with envy. It meant that, in a way, Cloud was her exact opposite. She imagined how different her life could be if only she possessed the resolve to stick to her own convictions and not worry what others thought. The possibilities seemed endless.

One day around that time, her father called to her from the other side of the house.

"Tifa! I can't find Fluffy. Would you go out and look?"

Tifa sighed. "She ran away *again*?"

Frankly, she felt the cat would do fine on her own. Someone in the village would most likely spot Fluffy and put out a dish of food. Or, failing that, Fluffy would scrounge up her own dinner; the cat had proven herself an adept hunter of birds and other small creatures living on the mountain.

Fluffy's fine! She'll be back before we know it!

Tifa imagined responding as such, envisioning how the conversation would play out. She'd anxiously peer at her father's face for signs of disappointment or annoyance. She'd worry about how other villagers perceived her: the lazy Lockhart girl, too uncaring to go out looking for her poor lost cat. Worst of all would be the crushing sense of guilt if anything were to happen to Fluffy.

So in the end, Tifa headed out to look.

"Fluffy!" Tifa called as she searched. "Where are you?"

Cloud wouldn't be bothered by any of that stuff, she thought. *He wouldn't care what people said.*

She checked the gaps between buildings and Fluffy's other favorite hiding spots, and it began to seem likely that the cat had wandered farther afield. With another great sigh, Tifa turned to head up the mountain.

As she ascended, she kept her gaze fixed upward, watching the clouds rolling high in the sky. Before she knew it, she'd reached the banks of the Gunnthra River. A cool wind rushed through her hair, and she turned to look back the way she came, realizing she'd forgotten all about the purpose of her hike. She scanned in a wide arc, searching for traces of Fluffy, then pivoted to look up and down the length of the river.

Tifa gasped. Her eyes had caught on what appeared to be a figure waist-deep in the water. She leaned forward and squinted, realizing it was a man. He stood abreast the surging current, an aberration in the familiar scenery of the mountain.

The man's appearance struck her as both boyish and elderly. His frame was stout, and his sleeveless attire exposed broad shoulders and muscled arms thicker than even the hardiest men of the village. His hair was gray yet full of vitality. He wore it long in the back, pulled into a ponytail—just like Cloud, Tifa realized, though the stranger's locks were quite a bit longer.

The man's feet were planted firmly on the riverbed, legs obviously straining as he fought from being swept away by the raging waters.

He must have got himself stuck out there, and now he can't move, thought Tifa.

The same thing had happened to Emilio once. It had taken all the boy's strength just to stay in one place as he cried for help. The adults in the village had rushed to the riverbank with every length of rope they could find, which they tied together into a throw line to pull Emilio to safety. That day, the village instituted a new rule: children under the age of eleven were forbidden from approaching the Gunnthra without an adult. During high-water periods, the current grew so strong that even grown-ups had trouble wading through it.

Memories flooded Tifa's mind—scenes of Emilio sobbing and wailing for help as he held on for dear life. The fear of that day gripped her anew.

"Are you all right?!" she called to the stranger. "Hang on! I'll call for help!"

Tifa made to dash down the mountain, but a burly voice roared at her back.

"No need for that, young lady! Observe!"

The man began to lift one leg slowly, confidently out of the water, extending it forward and up until the toes were higher than his head. Only his left leg remained submerged, braced against the current as the angry river battered and swirled more fiercely than ever. Tifa didn't need to be at his side to know how incredibly difficult such a feat would be.

And then, in the blink of an eye, the man's right leg snapped back down, and he bounded up out of the water to what seemed an impossible height. Tifa felt quite certain his eyes had momentarily been at the same level as hers from where she stared down the steeply sloping bank.

How could any human jump like that? she thought.

The stranger landed on the first of a small string of boulders whose heads poked above the swirling white current. He continued to hop from rock to rock, ending with one great leap that carried him all the way up the bank to land right before Tifa's eyes.

He thrust out one large, brawny hand.

"The name's Rashard Zangan. It's a pleasure to meet you."

Tifa, overwhelmed by the things she'd just witnessed, found herself unconsciously accepting the handshake.

"Ouch!" she yelped as the stranger's hand squeezed tight.

What a jerk! she thought. *What kind of grown-up plays a prank like that?!*

"Let go!" she demanded.

"Ah, apologies," replied the man named Zangan.

He hurriedly released Tifa's hand and for a moment seemed genuinely apologetic. But then he leaned in again, this time thrusting both hands out to grab Tifa's upper arms.

"Ooh! Very nice!" he exclaimed.

Tifa's feet froze in panic. She was alone with a strange man on the mountain. No one else would be near enough to hear her cries. Her mind spun as she tried to sort out what to do.

"I'd fancy a closer look at those calves of yours too. Would you mind?"

Tifa screamed internally, *Of course I'd mind!*

Fear had her paralyzed. She fought it back, and when she finally found her voice, she screamed at the top of her lungs.

"Get away from me!"

The shrill cry stunned Zangan, buying her the moment she needed to slip away and sprint down the trail to safety.

Back at home, Tifa immediately jumped into the shower, anxious to wash away the mountain dust and disturbing memory of her close encounter.

She was drying her hair, feeling somewhat recomposed, when her father returned home. Fluffy was in his arms.

"It was Zander," Brian explained. "He set out food for her at the town hall. I really wish he'd said something before you and I started searching high and low."

"I'm just glad Fluffy's safe," said Tifa.

She had no intention of telling her father about the encounter with the man on the mountain. She knew it would only land her in trouble—eventually the conversation would loop back to why she'd been near the river in the first place.

"Good point," her father agreed. "By the way . . . word is there's some wandering martial arts expert coming to stay in the village for a while. He's supposed to be real famous—travels the world to learn about other communities, and in return, he teaches exercises to ensure a long, healthy life."

Tifa's father grinned. "Sounds pretty fishy, don't you think? His first class is tomorrow morning in the village square. Whaddaya say you and I go and poke a little fun at the guy?"

"I can hardly wait."

She knew with absolute certainty that the wandering master of which her father spoke was the same unscrupulous stranger she'd encountered at the river.

News of a visitor had the whole village abuzz. Visitors meant information of the outside world—a raw, unfiltered source that excited in a way that the radio broadcasts and occasional bulk deliveries of newspapers and magazines never could.

When the appointed time came, nearly all the villagers had assembled in the main square, just in front of the town hall. Zander stood and proudly introduced the unfamiliar face—unfamiliar, that is, to everyone except Tifa. It was just as she'd predicted. The wandering martial artist that had stoked the village's curiosity was none other than Rashard Zangan.

"Residents of Nibelheim!" Zangan announced. "I appreciate you taking time out of your busy morning to attend today's lesson. I'll get right into it so as not to waste any more of your day.

"We'll be performing my very own Zangan-style calisthenics. This routine forms the cornerstone of the martial arts techniques that I, Rashard Zangan, have devoted my life to perfecting. If you memorize and perform these exercises regularly, they will help you all lead long, healthy lives. It's so effective, in fact, you might think it's magic. It'll keep you going strong until the day you die!"

At which point Zander cut in, saying, "Still kicking right up until we kick the bucket, huh?"

The quip elicited good-humored chuckles from several of the villagers. Zangan simply smiled, taking it in stride.

"All right, then," the stranger said. "Let's begin. I'd like you all to extend your arms and turn in a slow circle. This is to make sure you have enough space and won't be running into anyone else during the exercises. Please spread out if you need to."

The villagers, as of yet unimpressed, slowly shuffled out across the main square as instructed. Zangan remained in front, nodding his approval when everyone seemed sufficiently spread apart.

"Very good. Now, friends of Nibelheim, the first exercise is as follows. Take both arms and lift them straight above your head. Upper arms by your ears. Palms facing forward. Fingers pointed toward the sky. Pull yourself as straight as you can. Reach! Imagine a messenger of the heavens has dangled down to grab your wrists and is now pulling you up to paradise. Visualize yourself floating in the air.

"Slowly now. No need to rush. Once you've pulled yourself as taut as you possibly can, I want you to hold that pose. Remain just as you are!"

Tifa caught Zangan staring in her direction, a smile on his face. Flustered, she raised both arms as instructed and stretched them as high as they'd go. She envisioned herself being pulled up into the sky, rising up onto tiptoes as she stretched for all she was worth.

Many of the adults around her lost their balance. They thrust a leg out to catch themselves, after which most of them repositioned to start over. All the while, Tifa managed to hold the unfamiliar pose, surprised by her own ability. As she looked out over the main square, she caught Zangan's eye again and saw him nod in apparent satisfaction.

"You're all doing very well!" he announced. "Keep holding to the count of ten!"

Zangan began an agonizingly slow count.

". . . Eight . . . nine . . . ten!"

Tifa released the pose, breathing heavily. The sense of relief in the square was palpable. She overheard scattered mutterings from villagers disappointed that they hadn't fared better on the very first exercise.

"Again!" shouted Zangan. "Body does not waver unless mind does! And you, my friends, still tremble like newly hatched chocobo chicks!"

"Hey! Who are you calling a chocobo?!" quipped Zander, again eliciting chuckles from all across the square.

The stretching exercise began again, and again, and then again. Zangan walked among the villagers as he issued his instructions. He settled in at a new location near the center of the main square.

Tifa saw that he was still watching her intently. In fact, it almost seemed as if he'd chosen his new spot specifically to have a better view of her. She began to feel nervous, and her balance faltered slightly. Zangan grinned.

"Now, let's change things up slightly," he announced. "Both

arms up and at the sides of your head as before. But this time, I'd also like you to lift your right knee. Bring it up so your thigh is at a ninety-degree angle to your torso. Think you can do it?"

Zangan raised his own arms and nimbly lifted a knee in demonstration. His movements were so light and fluid, they seemed almost effortless.

"Is your knee up? Good. Now hold!

"If you tell yourself not to wobble, you will wobble. Instead, you must imagine yourself as a statue. Tell yourself you are made of stone. To conquer the body, you must possess a positive imagination!"

Tifa's eyes met the wandering master's yet again. Zangan seemed as pleased as ever.

"Remember, you're being pulled from the heavens!" he called to the villagers. "Reach! Allow yourself to float into the sky and be whisked away to some far-off town. Imagine you're flying off to see an old friend, and picture the look of shock on his face as you swoop in."

The villagers who lost their balance laughed away their failure. Many gave up, squatting on the dirt of the main square as the lesson continued. A few were still standing, trying to hold the excruciating pose. And among them was Tifa, an unwavering pillar supported by left leg alone.

"Now," Zangan continued, "let's add one more twist. Stay just as you are, but slowly bring your arms down. Keep them straight, so they stick out at each side. Stop when they're level at your shoulders."

Tifa followed the instructions and felt a brief sense of relief— with her arms extended to the side, maintaining her balance was far less taxing.

"Your arms now form a milkmaid's yoke. They bring you balance. Feel how much easier it is to remain steady?"

Zangan smiled and added, "But do not grow too confident. Any moment now, you'll feel the weight of your arms. Challenge yourself. See how long you can keep them aloft."

Zangan began another slow count, this time upward.

"One . . . two . . . three . . ."

Just as he predicted, Tifa's arms began to feel heavy. She fought to keep them up and was filled with sudden indignation. The fact that she was exerting herself on the stranger's behalf seemed absurd. She didn't have to do this. She could stop at any time. Why was she taking Zangan's lesson so seriously?

Without warning, an answer popped into mind. She realized she possessed the same stubborn pride as all the residents of Nibelheim. She didn't care much for Zangan, but she wasn't about to let him think less of her just because she was from the sticks.

Tifa's father had given up at some point and was now squatting on the ground at her side. He looked up at his daughter, clearly impressed at how she held each pose with impeccable balance.

"I feel like I'm seeing you in a whole new light," he remarked.

Tifa remained silent. She followed Zangan with her eyes. The martial artist was again on the move, winding his way through the square, route carefully chosen to bring him by all the village's children. As he got to each child, he'd reach out a steadying hand, using it as an opportunity to casually squeeze the child's upper arms. Then he'd crouch down low and pretend to offer pointers, poking a finger at the child's calves.

Tifa recalled the events of the previous afternoon.

I'd fancy a closer look at those calves of yours, he'd said.

She gasped softly. Suddenly, it all fell into place. A single word floated into her mind.

Trafficker.

Tifa had heard the stories. There were people in the world who sought out children with strong arms and legs—children who would make hard workers.

They were scoundrels who used honeyed words and grand promises to lure youngsters away from their homes and sell them into slavery. In the city, there were even supposed to be places that gathered up all the little orphans in the slums, raising them until they were old enough to force into lives of hard labor.

Maybe Zangan ran an operation like that.

Tifa's arms grew heavier yet. She could feel her muscles shriek in agony.

"To conquer the body, you must possess a positive imagination," repeated Zangan.

Tifa felt herself wobble. She leaned to one side, trying to compensate, but her balance was too far gone.

"Shoot!" she grumbled loudly as her right foot stomped back to the ground.

"Good! That's enough!" chirped Zangan to the assembled villagers. "Now let's move on to the left leg. Same pose as before, but this time lift your left knee instead of your right."

Like I'm gonna follow the directions of some child trafficker! Tifa thought bitterly.

She squatted down like the other villagers who had given up. Zangan undoubtedly noticed, but he pretended not to mind. He carried on with his lesson, gently coaching the remaining participants. The exercises continued one after another. Most of the villagers still standing scrambled to return to the current pose whenever they lost their balance. Occasionally, someone who had quit earlier would get back up to try again. In fact, many of the villagers did. Tifa saw that even her father hadn't actually given up. Despite frequent breaks and poor form, he still returned to his feet every few minutes to rejoin the lesson.

She began to regret her decision. Zangan's directions were clear and confident. His words carried strength. He could stir people to action and inspire them to overcome difficulty.

Tifa realized she'd never heard anyone like him before. His was a presence altogether different from the adults she'd come to know in the village. When her neighbors or even her father wanted something done, they wheedled and cajoled, then quickly escalated to shouts and threats if they didn't get their way.

In contrast, Zangan guided and encouraged. How could she have let herself believe he was the type of person to deceive young children?

She'd allowed fear and prejudice to cloud her mind. And in doing so, she'd almost missed out on an opportunity to discover a brand-new world.

"Ready for the next exercise?" Zangan called. "Careful. This one's a doozy."

"More like we're ready for it to be over!" cried Zander. Laughter resounded throughout the square. Zangan smiled and again flicked his eyes in Tifa's direction. He didn't seem like a trafficker anymore.

"Cross your arms in front of your chest," directed Zangan. "Your right hand should rest on your left shoulder, and your left hand on your right. Now bend both knees and lower yourself down like you're sitting in a chair. Don't let your backside stick out! Remain focused on your thighs. That's it. Slowly. No need to rush."

Concentrate. Focus. No need to rush.

How many times had she heard those words this morning? Tifa visualized each muscle in her body as she fought to hold the latest pose. Never in her life had she focused so intently on the movements of her body.

And then it was over.

Tifa checked the display of her phone, surprised to find that Zangan's routine had lasted all of twenty minutes.

"Very good! Let's call it a day," he announced. "I'd recommend you perform this routine every other day if possible. If you find yourself able, do it every morning. Do not rush as you perform the exercises, and do not allow yourself to take shortcuts.

"If you found today's training too intense, or if you have bad knees or a bad back, or even if you simply find it hard to stick to things over time, I'd suggest—"

"You won't find any whiners like that in this village!" shouted Zander, and the rest of the village cheered in response.

"Perhaps not. But know that I offer my teachings to all types because I, too, was once weak. There is a path to strength suitable to each of us. Allow me to help you find yours. The only tools you need to start are an imagination and a willingness to learn.

"To those of you who believe you possess those qualities, let us meet again tomorrow at this place and time. Let us make the most of our days together, for the betterment of all our lives."

"But the second day of training never came," said Tifa as another gust of wind passed over the plain and through her long hair.

"What do you mean?" asked Aerith, obviously disappointed. As

Tifa related the tale, the other woman had begun miming the exercises, lifting her own arms above her head and out to her sides. "Did something happen to Zangan? Aww. And here I was, ready to hear you go through it again so I could really get it down."

"The routine? If you'd like, I can teach you later."

"Yes, please!"

"So what happened?" came Barret's gruff voice. By this point, Tifa could tell he was all but hanging on her every word.

"Well, there was a little gathering that night. Only the adults could go. Master Zangan had invited them to sit down and listen to some of his personal philosophy. And from what I'm told, his views included some pretty heavy criticism of Shinra. He claimed the war had been driven by Shinra's desire to dominate the world and show that nothing compares to the might of mako energy. He said their roots as a weapons manufacturer meant they'd never really give up R&D. They'd always be cooking up conflict as an excuse to try out their latest inventions."

"Sounds like Zangan was right on the money," said Barret. "Those aren't criticisms. They're just plain observations."

"Yup. Honestly, my dad used to have plenty to say about the way Shinra went about things. Even the village head usually blamed Shinra every time something went wrong.

"Still, you can't exactly go around bobbing your head every time a stranger starts badmouthing Shinra. Doubly so when you live in a tiny mountain village that depends entirely on company money. Shinra's not above laying little traps to test the people's loyalty."

Aerith's eyes grew wide. "So Master Zangan was actually a *spy*?"

"No. But Zander didn't know that. He had to assume the worst. So in the end, the village provided Zangan with a nice meal and a place to spend the night so as not to cause offense, but asked him to please carry on to his next destination. At least, that's what I was able to piece together from the things I heard later on."

The night after Zangan's first and only morning exercise session, Tifa awoke in the dark to a sudden, gentle tapping sound. It was very late—or judging by the sky, very early. Dawn would soon break. The tapping noise was coming from her window, and after the fog of sleep lifted, she realized someone must be out there, beckoning her to open it.

The fact that her room was on the second story made the mystery all the more puzzling. But as she hopped out of bed and raised a hand to whisk the lace curtains aside, she had a suspicion she knew who she would find.

Sure enough, it was Zangan's face on the other side of the glass. He motioned for her to open the window, and Tifa complied, unfastening the latch and slowly pushing outward so as not to wake her father.

"Good morning," Zangan said with a grin.

"Good morning."

"I imagine you've heard the news from your father already. I'm to depart at dawn. I wish it were not so, but it is the village's desire."

Tifa nodded uncertainly.

"Before I go, there's something I'd like you to know. First of all, I'm not a trafficker."

"Huh?" Tifa felt the blood drain from her face.

"During my travels, I've noticed that youngsters tend to suspect me of being a kidnapper and older residents tend to assume I'm a spy.

"So tell me," he continued, "did I get it right? You were shooting me quite the dirty look this morning."

"I'm sorry. Please, forgive me. I shouldn't have jumped to conclusions like that."

On hearing her apology, Zangan's grin grew wider.

"Tifa Lockhart," he said. "Eyes like yours don't miss much. Surely you noticed how carefully I was observing you during the training. Allow me to speak plainly. I've taken a keen interest in you from the moment we crossed paths. I'd like to someday have you as a disciple, if it's a path you're inclined to follow.

"You possess the makings of a great martial artist—both the aptitude and the quality of mind. Your arms and legs are strong and limber. That is proof of your aptitude. As to your quality, I needed only a glimpse of what is in your heart. The key to conquering the body is a positive imagination, and one can only foster a positive imagination if she first possesses a kind heart."

"You know what's in my heart?"

"Why, of course. Don't you recall our happy encounter at the river?"

Tifa grimaced and thought, *Happy is the last word I'd choose to describe it.*

"Before your arrival, several other villagers had already walked by that morning. They all saw me, but none of them showed any concern or made any effort to call out. None except you, Tifa."

The source of his admiration seemed rather ironic. Zangan had never been in any danger or need of assistance in the first place. Tifa had only called out to him because of her own misunderstanding. She wasn't sure she liked the idea of her poor judgment being a testament to her kindness or quality of mind or anything else.

Zangan looked to the sky and said, "Daybreak is upon us. Here. I shall leave you with this book of techniques."

He produced a thin booklet from one sleeve and handed it to Tifa.

"That book describes the basic exercises needed to begin your training in Zangan-style martial arts. I've dedicated my life to devising and honing those techniques.

"The first book is divided into twelve steps that will teach you the full range of motion your body is capable of, as well as how to improve your overall strength. It prescribes specific exercises and a training routine for you to follow.

"When you've mastered the contents of that book, I'll deliver to you the second one. And when you've mastered Book Two, I'll deliver to you the third. By the time you reach adulthood, you'll wield a formidable array of martial arts techniques."

"Martial arts?" chirped Tifa. "I'm not sure if that's something I . . . "

"I'm not saying you have to think of yourself as a martial artist. The important thing is that these techniques will make you strong. They'll allow you to defeat the greatest enemy—the one that is inside you. Beyond that, how you use the physical skills you gain is up to you."

Zangan smiled and added, "To put it another way, these exercises will instill you with the willpower and perseverance necessary to obtain true strength. And it is my belief that true strength is the only weapon with which we may defeat our inner foe."

"Greatest enemy? Inner foe? What do you mean?"

"Isn't it obvious? I'm talking about your *self*. The weakness inside you. Surely you're old enough to have experienced it. Haven't you ever been filled with hopeless rage? Felt that you hated your father, or all adults, or even your friends?

"Haven't you ever screamed inside your mind that nobody understands you, or lamented that nobody recognizes how special you are, even though it's plain to see?

"We all begin to have thoughts like that in our youth. And when we let them go unaddressed, we begin to look down on others."

Tifa remained silent.

"But I would suggest that we cannot rightly judge others unless we know ourselves. Martial arts training is the ultimate method to confront your inner self and to understand it. Doing so brings you a solid basis from which to evaluate the world around you.

"To not have a solid basis is to allow your perception to be swayed by fickle things. Things like mood, temperament, or even weather. And to base your understanding of the world on easily swayed perception is to fail to understand it at all.

"My discipline offers you the chance to find your solid base.

"To see who you truly are, to conquer her and in doing so come to know the world with perfect clarity—that is what it means to study Zangan-style martial arts."

Tifa mumbled in response, ". . . I see."

But she didn't. Not really. Zangan's words seemed to her strange, overexcited ramblings.

He peered at her and continued. "You do not yet grasp the meaning of my words. But tell me, is your failure to understand a fault of mine or yours? Again, I think you'll find this a question that cannot be answered without a thorough self-understanding."

"Um . . . Okay?"

"Let's put it this way. Exercise isn't only good for your body. It keeps your mind healthy too. And there is no better exercise in this world than Zangan-style martial arts. If you're looking for a simple answer, that about sums it up."

Zangan's grin vanished, and he spoke with sudden gravity.

"The choice is up to you. I won't force it. But if you decide not to walk this path, I'd ask that you please burn the book."

"I have to burn it?"

This time, he burst into a grin so wide, wrinkles formed at the corners of his eyes.

"But of course. It does contain my greatest secrets, after all."

"Hey, Tifa," whispered Barret, leaning in close as they continued to walk the grassy plains. "How about lettin' me in on a thing or two written in that book?"

"Not a chance. Not even for you, Barret. Those are my master's secrets."

"Damn . . . Well, it was worth a shot."

Aerith turned to him, her voice teasing. "If we happen to cross paths with Master Zangan during our travels, you could always ask him to take you on as a disciple."

"Hmph. I see your game. Bet you'd have a real nice laugh over seeing him turn me down."

A low, beastlike growl came from Red XIII.

"What's the matter, Red?" asked Barret.

"I'd be obliged if Tifa could resume her story. And if *you* could keep your mouth shut."

Though Zander had determined Zangan's swift departure to be in the village's best interest, not everyone was in agreement. Many of the village's older—and more influential—residents grew quite vocal on the matter. They'd enjoyed their brief taste of Zangan's exercises and were upset they hadn't been given the chance to memorize the entire routine. Zangan had promised more to come, and now they felt they'd been cheated out of something special.

Their demands seemed simple enough: they wanted to keep practicing the exercises each morning, and they wanted a teacher to lead them. The only problem was that Zangan was long gone.

Desperate to appease the outspoken group, Zander paid a surprise visit to Tifa's home one evening. His expression was sour as he explained the situation.

"Tifa," he asked, "would you be willing to lead some morning exercises? It doesn't need to be anything fancy. Just show them the right way to do the poses Zangan demonstrated."

Tifa was caught entirely off guard. It was her father who managed to voice her bewilderment.

"Why her?" he asked.

"It was Zangan's idea. Not mine. When he left the village, he told me Tifa would make a fine instructor if there happened to be any talk of continuing the exercises. He said that of everyone in the village, Tifa had by far the best form."

Tifa blushed, yet she also felt a surge of pride on learning that Zangan had been quietly singing her praises.

"Zander, please," said her father. "We don't need another headache in our lives."

"Trust me, it's already a headache, and if we don't do something, the whole village is going to be feeling it. Please. I'm begging you. The old folks want their morning calisthenics, and they won't settle until they get what they want."

Brian snorted. He seemed to be enjoying watching the head of the village squirm. Tifa had never been certain whether the relationship her father shared with the man was one of friendship or rivalry. The way the two interacted was always somewhat bewildering.

"Well?" her father said, turning to her. "How do you feel about it?"

"All I have to do is lead the exercises? If that's really everything there is to it, I think I'd like to try."

"Oh, Tifa . . ." Her father looked as if he wanted to talk her out of it, but he held his tongue. Ever since Cloud and the other boys had left town, Brian had been voicing not-so-subtle complaints about how Tifa seemed to spend all her time lazing about the house. Perhaps the desire to see his daughter doing something constructive outweighed his distaste for this disruption in the village's routine.

He shook his head and said, "Okay, well, if you're gonna do this, do it right."

As Tifa prepared breakfast the following day, a knock came at the door. She answered it to find a villager she'd met a few times but did not know well. She was an elderly woman by the name of Monami, and as Tifa understood it, she was Zander's aunt.

The visitor's hair was pulled back into a ponytail so tight, it seemed to stretch the corners of her eyes.

"Morning," she greeted Tifa with a smile. "Goodness, I can't remember the last time the two of us talked. Zander tells me you've offered to help us out. How does two gil an hour sound?"

"Huh?"

Zander hadn't mentioned anything about being paid for this new responsibility. In fact, up to that moment, the idea hadn't even entered her mind.

"All right. I get it," Monami said. "You're thirteen years old, and we can't keep treating you like a child. Four gil an hour. That's our final offer."

"That's very kind of you, but really, the lessons aren't about making money."

"Nonsense. We want you to take this seriously, and that means you need to be getting paid. Trust me. We're gonna make you work for each and every gil."

Tifa hesitated, unsure whether she had four-gil-an-hour's worth of value to offer her fellow villagers, Zangan's endorsement notwithstanding. On the other hand, the prospect of finally having a way to earn money for herself was tempting. It would open up all sorts of new possibilities.

Monami seemed to interpret her silence another way. "Fine. Six gil."

"All right," Tifa scrambled to answer, half worried the number—and accompanying sense of guilt—might keep rising. "It's a deal. Six gil an hour."

"You know, when Brian was your age, most of his friends had left the village too."

It was morning, a few days later. Tifa and her new trainees were assembled in the village square, and Monami had begun to reminisce aloud about Tifa's parents, completely unprompted.

"But he decided to stay behind," Monami continued. "He wasn't going to risk letting his chance with Thea slip away."

"Wow. I never knew that," Tifa replied as she gently repositioned Monami's arm. Their current exercise was most effective when the chest was extended; the trainees' arms needed to be slightly back, behind the line of the shoulders.

"Y'know, back in the day, Thea was a real hot item. She could have had any guy she wanted."

It was a bit unnerving, hearing her mother described in such terms. But Tifa simply nodded, welcoming Monami to continue. She'd come to accept that listening to the elderly villagers' stories of yesteryear was just part of the job. And with lesson fees squarely in the equation, she felt responsible to make the training sessions as enjoyable and productive as possible.

"But if you want my advice," said Monami, "a fine girl like you ought to get out before it's too late.

"In fact, why not follow that Master Zangan fellow around? I bet it'd be real nice to go around seeing the world."

"I'm sure it would," Tifa replied, her tone noncommittal.

"None of that, now. I don't want to see you nodding along just to be polite. It's high time the women of Nibelheim started to make decisions for themselves."

Tifa just nodded again as she adjusted Monami's arm once more.

"The ladies of my generation didn't have that option, see? Of course, when the Strife girl came along—"

(This being how Monami referred to Cloud's mother.)

"—for a moment, it looked like things were about to change. She was always talking about heading out on her own. Hard to say if it was because she didn't like the village, or if she was just drawn to city life."

Without warning, Monami shifted to a new pose. She'd abandoned the routine and was off doing her own thing.

"Big dreams like that don't exactly fit with tradition. Folks round here have some strong opinions about how a woman's s'posed to find happiness. So when she started dreamin' of something different . . . Well, people got upset. Took it to mean she was looking down on our way of life.

"Pretty soon, nobody in the village had a single nice thing to say about her, present company included. But to tell the truth, inside I was cheering her on. I think a part of me was jealous. Could hardly fathom the idea of a woman carving her own way through life . . . It just seemed too good to be true.

"I guess that's when I first felt like things might be changing round here. Bit by bit, at any rate."

Now Tifa was helping Monami lift her knee into place.

"Keep it nice and high," she encouraged the older woman. "All the way up here."

Monami's balance began to falter. Tifa placed her hands at the woman's sides to steady her and said, "But Mrs. Strife ended up staying in Nibelheim."

"That's right. Turns out love's the one thing you can't fight. A traveler passed through town, and the Strife girl was put in charge of finding him a place to stay. Didn't take two shakes before she was head over heels. Maybe it was the air of adventure about him. Who knows?"

Monami smiled and added, "'Course, the fella did have a real handsome face. You can see it in Cloud. That boy came from two fine-lookin' parents, and he got the best of 'em both."

"He did, hm?"

"But that man of Claudia's . . . Hmph! He was like the wind. Never could settle down. One day—I reckon it was around the time Cloud would've been taking his first few steps—Claudia's man said he was gonna head off to the mountain, and that was that. Never saw him again. Some time later, a few of the villagers found his pack. Who knows what happened? Maybe he was gobbled up by a monster. You should count yourself lucky the same didn't happen to you."

Tifa shuddered. Monami had veered off onto another story—one Tifa would've been happy never to revisit.

"Maybe that's why Cloud talked you into climbing the mountain back then. I betcha he's got his father's wild ways in him."

The old woman began to lose her balance again, and this time, Tifa offered no support. Monami quickly dropped her leg to try to catch herself, but it was too late, and she toppled backward, rear end planting unceremoniously in the dirt.

"Let's try the other leg," Tifa said. "Come on. Back to your feet."

She held a hand out to Monami, only to have it waved away. With a determined grunt, the old woman rose to her feet unaided.

"Hmph. You're a strict teacher, ain'tcha? A lot tougher than that cute face of yours lets on."

"Just making sure you get the six-gil experience."

Tifa smiled to herself. She realized she was starting to get the hang of quick-witted banter.

Monami lifted the opposite leg. Once again her alignment was off. Tifa reached out to fix it, and the woman asked, "You really don't remember any of it? It must've been one nasty spill."

The incident in question had occurred when Tifa was eight. She and Cloud had slipped down a rocky slope while climbing Mt. Nibel, the impact knocking Tifa unconscious. The version of events that the village accepted—based on Emilio's and the other boys' accounts—was all she knew. It was as if the trauma of that day had pushed the memory from her mind, and the entire sequence of events had vanished without a trace.

"No," she replied. "As much as I wish I could, I really can't."

Tifa had come to appreciate the trouble with students this age: it was hard to tell if they were there to learn or to chat. When she complained about the endless gossip at home, her father laughed.

"I tried to warn you," he said. "Boy, you couldn't get me to spend my mornings with the old folks for a hundred gil a day."

They didn't listen. They were pushy. Even the better-behaved ones watched eagerly from the sidelines, nodding and chuckling about whatever bit of gossip was currently being passed around.

Tifa always had to remind herself that they weren't being mean. They just had a different way of communicating. She learned to follow their lines of conversation, lest they get upset and the lesson's mood sour.

The kinds of topics they'd touch upon never failed to surprise and rarely failed to distress. Above all else, they liked to giggle and tease about the fact that her body was blossoming into adulthood. If she was lucky, someone would notice her discomfort and change the subject, but the new threads of conversation were frequently just as bad. They'd start speculating about which of the village boys Tifa might end up with. Or, worse yet, they'd get on to the topic of Tifa's parents, casually recounting her father's past breakups or the men her mother had dated prior to settling down. To Tifa's students, Brian and Thea were just members of another generation of "young'uns," their youthful blunders fair game for idle chatter.

And at the end of the day, in the moments before sleep took hold, Tifa imagined that someday it might be the same for her. Perhaps she'd grow old in Nibelheim, reveling in memories of the past and juicy tales of the village's latest goings-on. She'd eagerly pass the things she heard on to the next pair of waiting ears, living out her days on repeat. She'd find herself a permanent fixture of the village and, eventually, one more piece of its history.

"For a while there, I wondered if I'd gotten myself wrapped up in something I shouldn't have. But as I got used to interacting with the older villagers, I realized I didn't mind their quirks so much. Everybody likes to talk and have someone to share with, and I'm fine being the one to lend an ear."

Barret laughed. "Imagine that. Our star bartender here got her start chattin' with a bunch of small-town retirees."

"Yeah. I guess I did. It was sort of a crash course in interacting with all sorts of different personalities. Fortunately, they seemed to like me. In fact, every day more and more of the village was showing up for class. We started calling ourselves the Calisthenics Club."

"Damn," said Barret, his voice mystified. "That's exactly how it went down at Seventh Heaven."

Aerith motioned eagerly for Barret to go on.

"Used to be a real quiet place, run by a guy as old as lumber. But when Tifa started tending the bar, it transformed overnight.

So many guys were pouring in the doors, you had to bat 'em away with a stick!"

"I can totally see that," replied Aerith. "Can't you, Red?"

Red XIII grunted. "I'm more interested to know what transpired with this Zangan fellow. Did he return to teach you more? I have to imagine so, from the way you manage yourself in combat."

"He did. But the story of my training is a little more involved than you might guess."

Within a month of establishing the Calisthenics Club, Tifa's daily routine had changed completely. Morning was spent guiding her students. Afternoon was dedicated to reading books and studying arithmetic. In the early evening, she'd hike up into the mountain to train in solitude, always returning home by sundown to keep her father from worrying. At night, just before bed, she pored over Zangan's booklet, committing the forms to memory and pondering each and every line for any detail she might have overlooked.

Around that time, a letter arrived from Emilio. It told of his new life in the city. He wrote about the noise, the food, and the staggering gap between rich and poor. He lamented the differences in values—the things that he'd grown up treasuring that were dismissed as provincial by the people of Midgar. Everything was new, and everything was bewildering.

I know it sounds rough, he wrote, *but whenever I'm about to lose hope, I think of you. I dream about the day I'll make it back to Nibelheim and take you away. That's why I decided to write about the parts of city life that are surprising or difficult to cope with. I want to help you be ready for when you start your new life here with me.*

The contents had Tifa fuming. Who did Emilio think he was, deciding Tifa's future all by himself?

The same day the letter came, Zangan returned. He walked into the village casually, straight up to Tifa's door as if he were now part of the community. Brian was the one to answer. Puzzled yet courteous, he acquiesced when Zangan asked permission to invite Tifa out for a day of training.

The wandering master led Tifa up to the location of their first encounter. When they reached the bank of the Gunnthra and set down their bags, Tifa looked her teacher straight in the eyes.

"Master Zangan, I've been thinking about what you said. I'd like to become your disciple, if you'll still have me. I want to become stronger."

Zangan smiled. "Those were precisely the words I was hoping to hear."

Then he paused and added, "What's wrong? You seem tense today. Irritated."

"What do you mean?" protested Tifa. "I'm feeling great."

But after a moment, she recalled her reaction to Emilio's message.

"Sorry," she apologized. "You're right. I think it's because of a letter I got from a friend."

"Tell me about this letter."

"I dunno . . . It upset me, I guess. A few months ago, he went off to the city. All my friends did. And the things he said in his letter . . . It made me want to show him that I'm better than he thinks. That I can make my own way through life."

Zangan hummed in response. After a moment, he said, "My school of fighting is not a tool for belittling others."

"Yes, Master. I know."

"No. I don't think that you do. But I suspect it is a truth you cannot grasp without further study. Here is what I propose.

"I shall test you on your understanding thus far. If it is clear that you have been diligent in your training, I will allow you to move on to the next step."

"You mean here? Right *now*?"

"Show me all the forms in the first book. You have them memorized, I hope?"

"Yes, Master."

With a deep breath, Tifa began to work her way through the physical training exercises, one by one.

When she was finished, Zangan grunted.

"Again. From the beginning."

"Yes, Master."

The second time through, Zangan began to correct her movements.

"Palms," he announced, not a minute into the first form. "Check the description. Which way are they to face?"

Tifa stopped and crouched, quickly pulling the thin booklet from her bag—it was the first thing she'd packed on Zangan's arrival that morning. She flicked through its initial pages, scanning the text.

Palms . . . Palms . . . Here it is.

Her eyes widened. All this time, she'd been doing it wrong. The palms were supposed to face *up*, not down.

"Sorry," she apologized. "I had it wrong."

"Try it again. This time as written."

She began the form again, paying close attention to her palms. The adjustment added new, unfamiliar strain to the exercises—different muscles being stretched and pulled. Tifa found herself astonished at what a difference such a tiny change could bring.

"Follow my writings precisely. Nothing is to be left to your own interpretation or desire. The training is meant to hone not only body but also mind. You must learn to abide by rules. Discipline opens the way to strength.

"By becoming my student," Zangan continued, "you stand to grow very powerful indeed. But strength alone is a dangerous thing. The more you possess, the greater your responsibility to use it wisely. That is why it must be accompanied by fortitude—the mental wherewithal to *control* your strength. Do you understand?"

"Yes, Master."

The second time through the forms, Zangan was relentless. He pointed out every tiny aberration, demanding she stop, check the text, and correct herself. She could not proceed to the next form until every detail was perfect. It took twice the usual amount of time to complete the full routine, and when Tifa was finished, every muscle in her arms and legs ached and begged for rest.

"Good," he said. "Now close your eyes and let the tension flow out of you. Focus on each part of your body in turn. How does it feel? Do you sense any pain or discomfort?"

Tifa closed her eyes and concentrated. After a moment, she responded, "My upper back. About . . . here."

She reached her right hand around her left side and touched

the base of her shoulder blade. "It's not so much painful as . . . I guess I'd describe it as a twitching sensation."

The touch of her own fingers brought instant relief.

Her response seemed to please Zangan. He hummed and nodded his approval.

"The bone there is the scapula. Your fingers currently rest on the trapezius. Surrounding that muscle, you'll also find the deltoid, infraspinatus, and teres minor. Book Two focuses on strengthening those muscles, as well as all other muscles and tendons throughout your back."

As he spoke, he produced another small booklet from one pocket.

"You'll need a sharp awareness of those parts of your body if you wish to project an air of self-assurance. From now on, I want you to walk confidently. Shoulders back, chest out, head held high. Good posture will help you not only in your training; it will define your interactions with others as you go about your life."

"Yes, Master."

"Let us not waste this opportunity. Book Two, Paragraph Two, Section One, Part One. Scapular push-ups. Shall we begin?"

Zangan lowered himself to the ground, positioning for what appeared to be a standard push-up. Tifa hurried to follow his lead.

"For this exercise, the arms do not bend. They merely support your body. Focus on your shoulder blades. Pull them apart to the right and left as wide as you are able. Then bring them back together so that they touch."

Zangan began a slow cadence. "Apart . . . Together . . . Apart . . . Together . . ."

She'd never done a push-up like this before. It was hard to even imagine the motions he was describing. She struggled, experimenting with the muscles in her back, trying to figure out how to pull her shoulder blades away from each other.

She lifted her head to watch Zangan. The line of his shoulders curled and straightened, over and over in rhythmic, almost-hypnotic motion.

It reminded her of Fluffy, and hesitating, she decided to say as much to Zangan.

"My cat sometimes moves like that."

"Indeed," Zangan replied. "There are many things we can learn from our feline friends."

Tifa turned her attention back to her own shoulder blades. Her back moved slightly up and down as she attempted to copy the curious movements she'd idly observed in Fluffy, and after a few more attempts, she began to understand the sensations that Zangan spoke of.

Apart. Together.

Zangan rose to his feet and observed as Tifa continued the exercise. Several repetitions later, he announced, "Very good."

Tifa slumped to the ground, exhausted and surprised to find herself breaking out in a light sweat. How were scapular push-ups so demanding? The range of motion was tiny!

A chuckle came from Zangan.

"Don't be too surprised," he said, as if reading her mind. "The muscles in our backs are some of the body's largest. Flexing them gets your blood pumping and your temperature elevated. It's a surefire way to work up a sweat."

When they finally reached the end of the second book, Tifa was drenched in sweat and panting hard. Never in her life had her shoulders felt so sore.

"Good," Zangan said. "If you have any questions, now is the time."

"Yes, Master," she replied. She knew she should—and *did*—have questions, but her aching back and the drumbeat of her pulse in her ears made it hard to arrange her thoughts.

When she failed to say anything further, Zangan announced, "Very well. Then let us proceed to Book Three."

"Already?!" The word was out of Tifa's mouth before she could stop herself. Every muscle in her body seemed to scream in protest.

But Zangan simply continued.

"The third book focuses on the muscles of your chest and abdomen. You must hone your front just as you hone your back. First is the pectoralis major, which can be roughly divided into three parts: upper, middle, and lower. The ideal method of strengthening differs by part. I will proceed to demonstrate the basics of each now."

Tifa did her best to suppress a sigh as she responded, "Yes, Master."

"Your general coordination and understanding of your own body is quite impressive, particularly given your age. Am I correct in assuming you've had no past training in sports or martial arts? If not, your ability suggests a great deal of natural talent. Treasure that talent, and be sure to cultivate it."

"Yes, Master."

Strength flowed back into her limbs. Zangan's careful praise seemed to pull the tension from her body, allowing her a moment to relax and recover from her fatigue.

"For now, concentrate on building your muscles. You needn't use any equipment. No barbells or dumbbells—especially not now, while you're still young and growing. When you've reached adulthood, you may choose to use them if you wish. But one of the greatest advantages of the regimen I've developed is that it does not require anything more than an open space and your own body.

"I will guide you, as I guide all my disciples, in a manner that most suits your natural self. Thick, bulky muscles have no place on you, Tifa. Your assets are your core strength, speed, and sharp reflexes. Let us focus on techniques that make the most of those innate qualities."

Zangan looked directly into Tifa's eyes and asked, "So, have you had enough? Shall we quit for today?"

It struck her that Zangan was the first person she'd ever respected with all her heart. She knew she would bear any hardship to keep from letting him down.

"No," she replied. "I'd like to keep going."

"That's the determination I'm looking for. Good."

His expression softened, and he added, "But let us call it a day. Feel your exhaustion now, and remember it. This will be your baseline. Practice each day until you reach this point. In the future, we'll have plenty of time to discuss ways to break beyond your limits when the need arises. But there's no reason to rush into that yet. What matters now is persistence. Dedication. Building good habits."

They set out down the trail toward the village. As they walked, it dawned on Tifa that Zangan's final question had been a test. In fact, the entire time, he'd been pushing and prodding to see how she would react. The thought did not upset her, and that itself struck her as unusual. Had her father done the same, she would have been furious, refusing to speak to him for several days.

When they reached the village, she saw Zangan to his lodgings for the night.

Zangan nodded to her in parting and said, "Please pass my regards along to your father."

Tifa walked across the square to her own home. A familiar aroma of spices wafted from the open windows. She realized that her father was already in the kitchen preparing dinner, and that the menu that night was one of her mother's old signature dishes.

While a favorite of Brian's, it was a meal that Tifa didn't much care for, so it rarely graced the dinner table.

"I'm back!" she announced as she opened the door.

Her father turned to wave from the kitchen. "Welcome home, kiddo."

"Are you cooking what I think you are?"

"Sorry. Couldn't help it. Been dying to have some these past few days. Don't worry, though. I whipped up something else for you."

His voice was overly chipper, and his eyes searched her face for traces of annoyance regarding his choice of meal. A wave of remorse washed over Tifa. She hated that tone of voice. She hated that apprehensive look. And she finally understood that the dynamic between her and her father was entirely of her own making.

"I was becoming a whole new person," Tifa recalled to her friends as they traversed the grasslands. "My body was getting stronger, and I was in better control of it. I had goals and routines. I was growing up. I guess, for the first time, I felt like my life was in order, you know?"

"I hear ya," Barret responded. "You get so wrapped up in your training, everything else just fades away. Feels nice to say to hell with the world and focus inward, doesn't it?"

Tifa shook her head. "No . . . Sorry, but that's not how it was for me at all. It was more like . . . I was finally free of all my own little hang-ups and childish expectations. My eyes were open to the needs and feelings of the people around me."

Barret shrugged and offered a sheepish, "Well, different strokes for different folks . . ."

"From then on, Master Zangan began to visit more often. He was still wandering from place to place, so it was hard to know exactly when he'd show up, but he seemed to pass through Nibelheim to see me every two months or so.

"I continued to lead the Calisthenics Club, and whenever Master was in town, he'd sit in and offer pointers. It made me so happy when he complimented my students. It felt like he was praising me."

At some point, Tifa began keeping a daily log in a notebook. During one of Zangan's visits, she presented it for his perusal.

The log included questions that arose during her individual training. Near the back, she recorded details about each of the Calisthenics Club participants. One villager still suffered the effects of an old injury to his left leg. Another found it difficult to raise her arms above her head. Yet another had a bad back. Tifa noted the things each student excelled at as well as the areas that needed more work. There were general evaluations of stamina, memos about family history, notes on friendships and feuds with other villagers, and cautious reminders of specific topics to avoid in conversation.

Tifa wrote about anything and everything that came to mind regarding her students: work-arounds she'd tried and their degree of success; other ideas she'd thought of but had yet to implement; exercises to focus on; forms to master.

Zangan studied the log for a great deal of time. Finally, he peered back up at her and said, "Remarkable, Tifa. This is the very embodiment of Zangan style."

He snapped the notebook shut and handed it back with an approving nod.

"Tell me, is your father home?"

"I think so."

"I'd like to stop by to say hello. In fact, if it's not a bother, I'd like to sit and visit for a while."

"We'd be delighted to have you, Master."

In truth, she was speculating wildly about Zangan's motives. For the briefest moment, she was concerned. But she knew the training was to thank for her new and much more grounded relationship with her father. If anything, Zangan's visit would be a very welcome one.

Brian Lockhart received the wandering master warmly. There was no longer any trace of the mistrust he'd once harbored—the concerns that the outsider might prove to be a dubious influence on Tifa, and the revulsion he'd once struggled to conceal about the way his daughter referred to the stranger by title of "Master." He now saw Zangan as an upstanding mentor, responsible for helping Tifa to grow up healthy in both body and mind.

Once they were seated, Zangan wasted no time.

"Mr. Lockhart," he said, "I'm here to ask for your cooperation in a matter involving Tifa."

Both father and daughter stiffened slightly.

"Your daughter has incredible talent," Zangan continued. "Even more impressive is the willpower she exhibits through her dedicated training regimen. The great bulk of Tifa's accomplishments have been made in the absence of in-person instruction— that is to say, she's needed no outside influence to maintain her motivation. That's a trait I've found among only the brightest of my disciples. And that is why I would propose . . ."

Here he looked Tifa in the eyes, and Tifa's trepidation reached a new peak.

". . . that starting tomorrow, she begin Book Five."

Tifa felt her cheeks flush hot. This was it. This was the moment of truth. The first four books covered basic movements and exercises. The fifth, as Zangan had once explained, marked the beginning of actual strikes and combat techniques.

"I'd be honored, Master!"

"But there's a catch. Mr. Lockhart, in order for your daughter to further her training effectively, she will require a sparring partner—someone to stand against her in mock combat. Would you be willing to take on that role?"

Zangan lowered his eyes and added, "I come to you personally because of a certain past failing. A promising student of mine, for whom I did not find an appropriate person to spar with, took it upon himself to practice against monsters in the badlands instead. My mistake cost that boy his life, and I swore I would never allow such a tragedy to occur again."

Brian's eyes displayed obvious concern. But when he opened his mouth, it was concern of a very different nature than what Tifa had anticipated.

"Mr. Zangan, sir . . . I'm happy to do anything I can to help my daughter, but I'm hardly a capable fighter. Would Tifa have anything to gain from a sparring partner lacking any experience?"

A chuckle came from Zangan. "I'm sure you'll have your share of scrapes and scuffs until you get the hang of it."

"Now I'm even less confident . . ."

"To be perfectly clear, both student and partner must perform each motion earnestly, as if the fight were real. Attempting to go easy on each other is a recipe for greater injury. But you should find yourself able to absorb the blows without harm by preparing some simple defensive equipment. Even makeshift gear fashioned from items around the home will suffice."

Tifa saw her father glance in her direction, eyebrows raised. She stared back at him, her own eyes pleading.

"All right," announced Brian. "I'll do it. Tell me how to proceed."

Elated, Tifa jumped from her chair and flung her arms about her father's neck—a simple display of love and delight she probably hadn't shown him in years.

"Thank you, Dad! You're the best!"

Over the next several hours, Zangan demonstrated to Tifa and her father the basic punches and kicks described in the fifth book, as well as how to defend against them, before departing the village.

Most surprising, perhaps, was how Brian took the instructions about fashioning equipment to heart. He immediately proceeded to draw up detailed plans. A skilled handyman and meticulous in his work, he'd soon readied an array of professional-looking gear above and beyond Zangan's specifications.

And thus Tifa's training continued, more intense than ever. She practiced with her father at home, and when time allowed, off the beaten paths of Mt. Nibel, where they were unlikely to be seen or interrupted by other villagers.

Zangan's next appearance in Nibelheim came three days prior to Tifa's fifteenth birthday. Excited to show off her progress, she immediately set about demonstrating the movements described in the fifth book, her father dutifully catching each strike. As with each previous book, Zangan allowed her to finish before directing her to start again from the beginning, this time with painstaking analysis and correction of unfavorable habits and deviations from the text.

"Very good," he announced when she'd completed the final section to his satisfaction. "Now, how would you feel about ending the day's training with a match against me?"

Tifa hesitated. "Against *you*, Master?"

"Do not worry. I'll not strike back. I'll only evade and deflect. Go ahead, now."

Brian scrambled to untie the bracers on his arms.

"Master Zangan!" he interjected. "Here. Use the equipment I've made. We'd be devastated if anything were to happen to you."

Zangan clutched his sides and roared with laughter. When he'd calmed himself, he hopped backward lightly and extended a fist in Tifa's direction. His hand uncurled, palm upward, and he flicked his fingers for her to approach.

To Tifa, he seemed to have morphed into a completely different person. Gone was the soft visage of her teacher, replaced by the steeled chin and commanding gaze of a confident fighter.

"Here's your chance, you ignorant little hick. Come at me."

She could hardly believe the words coming out of her teacher's mouth. Anger surged, and she readied herself to strike.

Her father called out to her, urging caution, telling her to breathe and calm her mind. But the first words were hardly out of his mouth when Tifa launched herself at Zangan. She threw a right punch with all the momentum of her sprint behind it. There'd been no move like this anywhere in Zangan's teachings.

Just as the blow was about to land, the master flicked one massive hand up, catching her fist in his palm.

He snorted. "Is that the best you can do? I've felt stronger breezes over the grasslands."

He clamped his fingers down over Tifa's fist and thrust his arm forward, releasing his grip at the last moment. Tifa went stumbling backward, then tripped and landed on her backside.

"Have you forgotten your footwork too? Book Five, Paragraph Three, Section Three."

Tifa scrambled back to her feet, jaw clenched, and approached again. This time, she brought both fists in front of her face, forearms ready to guard against any strike as she inched forward.

Gauge the distance to your opponent. Enter striking range cautiously and deliberately. Book Five, Paragraph Three, Section Two.

She followed the footwork ingrained in mind over hours spent sparring with her father.

Circle slowly. Always clockwise.

"Ah. It's nice to see you finally taking this seriously. Now show me what comes next."

Zangan began to circle slowly too, keeping Tifa at his fore. He brought both arms up in a tight guard.

She wasn't seeing any opening. She decided to try her luck anyway. With a loud yell, she darted in and unleashed a flurry of blows on Zangan.

Not one of her attacks connected. Zangan weaved and deflected, not a trace of exertion on his face.

Still she persisted, darting in and out until exhaustion finally dictated that the bout was over.

She stepped back, panting heavily and barely able to stand. Zangan placed his palms together and bowed deeply. Tifa's mind was whirling with so many thoughts, she couldn't even think to return the sign of respect.

On the way back to the village, Tifa's father invited Zangan to stay for dinner—an invitation that was accepted with delight.

The wandering master possessed a voracious appetite, and he scarfed down Brian's meal, along with several of Tifa's homemade cupcakes for dessert.

But Brian had another reason for asking Zangan over. After

the meal, he presented their guest with an envelope containing a small token of cash—money he'd saved up as thanks for the time and attention paid to Tifa.

Zangan regarded the envelope with surprise, only accepting after some hesitation.

"Just this once," he said. "Know that I will refuse any further offers. I don't ask for remuneration from my disciples. In fact, if you'll permit, I'd like to donate this gil to a certain organization with which I am involved."

"Please. It's yours to do with as you like. Although, I have to admit you've got me curious. What kind of organization is it?"

"A sort of . . . volunteer initiative, I guess you'd say. We work to ensure a future for the children of the world. Our range of activities is quite extensive, so it's rather hard for any of us to settle on a name. Usually, we simply refer to it as 'the association' or 'the network.'"

"Dad. Master. Please," interjected Tifa, desperate to steer the conversation elsewhere. "I'm sure this network is very special and all, and I'd love to hear more about it someday. But Master Zangan is leaving the village in the morning. Before he goes, I need to know what I did wrong in our match. Why wasn't I able to hit you? It was like you knew exactly what I was going to do next. How?"

Bemused, Zangan responded, "I could tell you, but I think you'll find the answer is actually quite obvious. You might wish you'd have taken a moment to work it out yourself."

"I'll live with it. Please tell me. I have to know."

Tifa's father eagerly interrupted, "Hang on! I think I can answer why. It was because you got her all riled up, wasn't it? The name-calling was all a ploy!"

Zangan laughed. "Partly. Once Tifa's mind was clouded with anger, she forgot half the things she's learned. But there's more to it."

"Why wouldn't I be mad?" protested Tifa. "A teacher I look up to suddenly sneering at me and saying awful things . . . At first I was surprised, then I felt hurt and sad. It was only after that that I got angry!"

Her words seemed to hit home, as Zangan's face twisted with remorse.

"You're right. It was not an honorable way to fight. I wouldn't be pleased to hear that you'd tried the same thing on someone else."

"I most certainly wouldn't!"

"Still, I was surprised at how effective it was . . . I thought you'd manage to land at least *one* blow."

Zangan coughed and straightened in his seat.

"The tell was your line of sight. I knew precisely where you'd strike next by where your eyes were focused."

The revelation stunned Tifa into silence.

Next to her, her father groaned, "Of course. How did I miss it?"

And Zangan laughed. "There I go again, indulging a favorite disciple instead of making her find the answers for herself."

Immediately, she wished she'd made the effort to figure it out. It was just as Zangan had predicted, and that only made the sting of regret all the worse.

"But let us set that aside," her teacher said. "Tifa Lockhart, allow me to present you with a gift, in celebration of your upcoming birthday."

He turned and reached to the back of his seat, on which hung his traveling bag—his knapsack, as he called it. After rummaging around inside for a moment, he again faced Tifa, now holding a single leather cord of the same color and material as the bag.

"This cord is a surprisingly useful item for a traveler," he explained. "It comes in handy in all sorts of ways. Its only limit, really, is your imagination. Perhaps, with some thought, it might even make a formidable weapon."

Zangan held the cord out to Tifa. "Go ahead. Take it."

He smiled and added, "I recommend you accept with your *left* hand."

Tifa peered into her mentor's eyes with uncertainty. He nodded reassuringly, a touch of amusement showing in his rugged features.

She timidly reached over the table. Zangan's free hand snapped out like a coiled snake. She felt his burly fingers curl around her forearm, and before she could react, he'd skillfully wrapped the cord loosely around her wrist—once, twice, and then he released his grip to tie the ends into a knot.

What was once a cord was now a simple, unassuming leather bracelet.

"Consumed by emotion," said Zangan. "That was the state in

which you found yourself when I goaded you on. It was what allowed me to catch your fist in my hand and proceed to easily deflect each and every one of your strikes. Your anger blotted out your hours of training and robbed you of your carefully honed techniques. It wiped my teachings from your mind—including the importance of showing your opponent respect and gratitude after a bout.

"Anger is no sin. In fact, at times it may prove an incredible source of strength. But you must always be the one in control, not it.

"Tell me, Tifa," Zangan continued, "do you recall the piece of wisdom I shared as I presented you with the first book? Who is your greatest foe?"

". . . Myself."

"And do you now appreciate what a formidable enemy she is?"

"Yes, Master."

"When you find yourself on the brink of defeat, I want you to glance at your wrist. Touch the cord and remember the lesson you've learned today."

Tifa peered at the loosely-wrapped band and gave an obedient nod.

"I know it's not the most fashionable accessory. Still, I'd ask you to keep it on at all times. As you progress through your training, a day will come when you no longer need that cord. When it does, you are free to remove it, and to instead carry a memory of it in mind."

The next morning, Tifa and her father saw Zangan off at the entrance to the village.

"I trust you haven't forgotten what I said about your line of sight?" asked Zangan.

"Of course not, Master."

"Good. Your speed is unmatched. If you can learn to keep your eyes from betraying you, I suspect more than a few of your strikes may slip past me next time we spar."

"Do you really think so?!"

"It depends on you."

Zangan peered up at the sky and said, "Allow me to propose a goal. In half a year's time, I shall return to test you again. And on that day, if your fist manages to strike true, I will confer upon you the full status of initiate."

"Initiate . . . ?"

Tifa fumbled over the word. It definitely *sounded* like something important—and something to be proud of—but she had no idea what Zangan meant. She glanced at her father, who peered back, equally confused.

"It means I will share with you the full host of secrets. You will know all there is to know about Zangan-style martial arts. In addition, I will begin working with you to develop your own unique fighting style."

"Wow . . ."

"Indeed. But a word of caution: it will be no simple process. I shall see you in six months' time. Until then, be diligent in your training, my young student."

"I will!" Tifa replied.

And her father's words overlaid her own. "She will!"

They'd chirped their responses in unison like eager schoolchildren. Tifa's father lowered his gaze and ran a hand through his hair, embarrassed by his own overzealous reaction. Zangan and Tifa regarded him with wide eyes, then glanced at each other and smirked, finally erupting into laughter. Eventually, Brian couldn't help but laugh too.

Over the next few months, Tifa trained harder than ever, determined to excel on the test promised late that fall. But the arrival of summer marked a sharp drop in the amount of time she could spend with her father. Monster sightings were growing more frequent on the mountain, leading to the formation of regular patrols—groups of villagers scouting out the mountain to keep an eye on this troubling new development.

As one of the village's three designated representatives for communications with Shinra, Brian had a great sense of responsibility to the village and was among the first to volunteer to man the patrols. Consequently, the sparring sessions with his daughter grew few and far between.

Though the residents immediately informed Shinra of the changes on the mountain, the company's only response was an order to continue monitoring the situation and to send regular reports about any new types of monsters encountered.

Unease prevailed in Nibelheim. Still, short of abandoning their homes and livelihoods, the residents saw no other option but to obey.

With each passing day, the patrols' reports grew more terrifying. And then, the unthinkable: dragons sighted near the summit.

Throughout all Nibelheim's history, there was no record of any monsters like that. Panic gripped the residents. A sense of dread pervaded every activity.

Zander convened an emergency meeting of the Nibelheim town council—which consisted of himself along with the three representatives. In addition to the patrols, they determined, a neighborhood watch was needed to ensure the village's safety. A base camp would be established at the trailhead to deal with any monsters that wandered near. Watch members would need to keep an eye on the sky as well: Kimara Bugs were known to inhabit the mountain too. Sightings had always been rare, but it was a monster capable of flight, and given recent developments, no degree of caution was too great.

The calm, easygoing atmosphere that had long defined life in Nibelheim was gone.

The constant state of alert quickly wore on the villagers. Hardest hit by exhaustion were those on watch at the base camp. On September 18, the watch members determined more hands were needed, and participation shifted from voluntary to mandatory. Every able-bodied man and woman twenty years or older would be assigned to rotating shifts at the base camp, unless they were otherwise involved in duties crucial to the community's survival.

Mt. Nibel's next surprise came the following day. The first patrol returned from the mountain shaken and breathless. The appearance of dragons on the mountain was disturbing enough, but nobody in the community was prepared for what came next.

The patrol members described a creature that walked on two

legs. It had the appearance of a man. Yet it was, without any doubt, a monster.

What in the world was happening up on the mountain?

If nothing else, the link to Shinra and its facilities was clear. The company continued to ignore Zander's many appeals for help—a reaction that seemed terribly odd, *unless* the proliferation of monsters was less of a surprise to Shinra than it was to the villagers. Zander concluded that Shinra must have some clue as to the reason. But whatever information the company possessed, they weren't sharing it.

If the residents of Nibelheim hadn't been busy fighting for their own survival, they might have been storming the facilities, demanding answers.

Tifa, for her part, was recruited to assist with meal prep. A makeshift kitchen area had been set up at the base of the water tower in the main square, manned by rotating shifts of the village's women. Each morning and afternoon, they prepared food for the patrols and neighborhood watch.

Given the circumstances, Tifa was happy for the assignment. It provided a chance to see and speak with many of the elderly residents she'd grown close to; Calisthenics Club practices were on indefinite hold due to the situation on the mountain.

The day of her first shift, she returned home in the afternoon to find her father away. A note rested on the kitchen table: *Went to the town hall.*

Brian had only just returned that morning around breakfast time, after pulling yet another midnight patrol shift. When he'd walked in, she'd noted his sagging shoulders, the heavy bags under his eyes, and the gauntness of his cheeks. Since the patrols began, he'd been losing weight at an astonishing rate.

How long is this going to go on? she wondered to herself.

She'd heard that some of the other families were even beginning to talk of packing up whatever belongings they could carry and leaving town.

After finding the note from her father, she went to her room and sat for a while, staring off into space, Fluffy cradled in her arms. Lately, she felt aimless, and her days were peppered with these idle stretches of time.

After a while, the cat began to squirm, and her mouth found the bracelet on Tifa's left wrist. Fluffy had been chewing away for several seconds before Tifa noticed.

"Fluffy! You know better than that!" Tifa chided.

She set the cat down on the floor and anxiously examined the cord. It seemed to be okay, but . . .

"No. *I'm* the one who should know better," she said.

Tifa stood and took several deep breaths.

"Book One, Paragraph One, Section One, Part One."

She began to rehearse the forms one by one, announcing the names of each section as she progressed and accompanying each movement with a short, sharp shout.

She was partway through Book Four when her father again returned home. She heard his footsteps on the stairs, followed by a knock at her door.

"Tifa? You home? Could you be a pal and help me with the door?"

She opened up to find her father holding a large cardboard box, which he immediately dumped into Tifa's arms.

"You remember old Margo, yeah?" Brian reached an arm up to wipe the sweat from his forehead. "Apparently these were some of her daughter Yasmin's favorite outfits when she was younger."

"They're for me?"

"Yup. Margo said she saw you across the square the other day and thought the clothes would be a perfect fit. Yasmin and I grew up together, you know. I had a peek inside the box, and man, it took me back. She was a great friend. The kind of person who always brightens your day the moment she shows up."

"Ha ha! All right. Thanks, Dad. I'll take a look."

"If you find one you like, go ahead and wear it around town. It'll make Margo's day. All this talk of monsters has been hard on her."

"Will do."

Tifa paused, then asked, "Hey, Dad . . . Are you getting enough sleep?"

"Just one more thing, before I forget. Then I'll go hit the sack. I swear."

"What is it?"

"The day after tomorrow—the twenty-second. Shinra says they're sending an investigation team. I think it was our latest report that finally put their butts into gear. Y'know, about the monster that looked almost human. And I'm willing to bet a whole lotta gil that this team they're sending isn't just for appearances. Mark my words. They're gonna send SOLDIERs."

SOLDIERs.

Suddenly, she was atop the water tower again, twelve years old and heart beating fast during a midnight rendezvous with Cloud Strife.

More than two years had passed, and she hadn't heard a word from him. She'd believed the memory was sealed away deep inside, where it could no longer threaten to overwhelm. Her cheeks flushed hot. She scrambled to push her father out of her room and slammed the door.

"Tifa?!" called Brian from the other side.

"Sorry, Dad! 'Night, sleep well!"

Tifa herself spent a sleepless night tossing and turning in bed as she counted off every conversation or interaction with Cloud that she could recall. There were fewer than she'd hoped. In fact, it was startling. How could she grow up next door to someone and know so little about him?

But what she lacked in quantity she made up for in clarity— nearly every memory she possessed of Cloud shone clearly, an intricate crystal figurine. Each time she viewed one, she did so carefully, examining every facet in painstaking detail with her mind's eye, before placing it back on its shelf ever so delicately, so as not to disturb it or let it be altered in any way.

Alone in her room, eyes closed, Tifa went over the memories again and again. Only one, she found, was dark and dull, its contents impossible to decipher: the incident on the mountain when she was eight years old.

Beyond Mt. Nibel rests the land of the dead.

At least, that was the tale as told in the village. So in the hours after Tifa's mother passed away, leaving her family reeling with grief, that was the legend Tifa clung to. It was her anchor of hope in an awful world.

It was that belief that led Tifa to the base of Mt. Nibel and sent her running up the trail. She was certain she'd be able to see her mother again if she could just make it to the other side of the peak.

The village boys close in age had hurried after, anxious for Tifa's safety. But when the weather began to turn, Emilio, Lester, and Tyler hesitated, and one by one, they fled back to the safety of the village.

As they ran, they called to Tifa. They begged her to turn around too. But Cloud, they said, urged Tifa to press on. Emilio and the other boys saw them disappear up the trail, and beyond that, it was anyone's guess what exactly happened. At some point, Cloud and Tifa must have slipped off the trail and gone plummeting over a ledge. Cloud got off lucky: scraped knees and a couple of bruises. But Tifa bashed her head on the way down. It would be a week before she regained consciousness.

Emilio and the other boys had already rushed down the trail yelling for help, and theirs was the story that spread around the village. The grown-ups organized a search party to locate the two stranded children, and after Tifa was carried back, Cloud didn't offer any contradiction to the tale as told.

It was strange, though. When asked why he'd encouraged Tifa to climb, he just shrugged his shoulders and said, "I dunno."

Tifa had no memory of any of it, but she knew her decision to keep climbing the mountain didn't rest on anyone else. She *wanted* to be there. So when she woke up and learned what had happened, she apologized profusely. The villagers took pity on her, knowing she'd just lost her mother, and focused all the blame on Cloud instead.

In time, they'd forget the good fortune—the fact that Tifa suffered no lasting effects beyond the lapse in memory of an already-grief-stricken day—and retain only the bad. The unbearable week of uncertainty as Tifa lay unconscious in bed . . . That was an event forever etched in the village's collective memory.

They began to speak of it as a scandal rather than an accident, twisting it into a mark of shame that both Cloud and Claudia were forced to bear. Even to this day, the villagers spoke of the Strife family with a hint of coldness and reserve.

But to Tifa, the story didn't add up. For as long as she could remember, Cloud hadn't wanted anything to do with the Four Fiends as a group, almost as if out of principle. Why would he suddenly tag along with them to the mountain?

On the other hand, Tifa had never spoken to Cloud about the incident, and he'd never tried to refute the other boys' version of events.

A part of her felt that Cloud had been trying to protect her, as if he'd stepped in to take the blame so she wouldn't have to. But why would Cloud do that? Surely he had a reason. There had to be *something* more concrete than his indifferent claim of "I dunno."

Maybe enough time had passed that she could finally bring it up. Maybe the next time she saw him, she'd find a moment to ask. And maybe that day wasn't so far away.

As Tifa prepared breakfast the following morning, her father came downstairs and idly picked up his phone, which normally sat unloved on the table. When he looked up, he was grinning.

"They're here!"

She knew immediately what he meant. The cell signal. Anytime a convoy of Shinra personnel neared town, there was a dramatic improvement in reception. Tifa assumed they traveled with some kind of equipment to boost the signal, but at any rate, it meant that, for a brief stretch of time, the villagers could enjoy the crystal-clear phone calls and lightning-fast connection speeds that city folk took for granted.

"Do you think they skipped the village and went straight up the mountain?" she asked her father.

"I doubt it. They said the team would roll into town tomorrow and rest for a night before beginning the investigation early the next morning. Zander's been yapping nonstop about how he's gonna throw the biggest welcome party they've ever seen."

"Then why's the signal already strong?"

"Beats me. Maybe they sent in an advance party to scout things out first."

Brian ate quickly and hurried out for the morning patrol. Once Tifa cleaned up, she headed out too: she had a double shift on the meal line that day.

She found the main square buzzing with excitement. Most of the other villagers had already heard the news of Shinra's plans to send an official investigation team, which brought hope and helped to ease the tension that had been mounting over the past weeks.

Within about three hours' time, the meal line had made enough sandwiches to cover breakfast and lunch for everyone on watch or patrol. The morning shift was over, and Tifa had until three p.m. to spend as she wished, after which it would be time to prep dinner and midnight meals for the overnight crew.

She decided to relax at home, first electing to take a shower. Afterward, she headed to her room, where she picked up her cell phone for the first time in what felt like days. But she quickly set it down again, realizing the only person she actually wanted to talk to was someone whose contact information she didn't have.

Her attention turned to the box at the foot of her bed—the clothes offered by their neighbor. She slid it near and pulled open the flaps. Dozens of colorful outfits greeted her eyes. It lifted her mood, and she decided it might be fun to try one on.

"Hmm . . ."

She pondered over several pieces she liked before eventually choosing a tawny vest and matching miniskirt. It seemed like the type of thing an energetic young chocobo rancher might wear. Tifa turned to her own closet, grabbing a wide-brimmed hat and pair of boots to complete the ensemble before checking herself in the mirror.

Not bad, she decided.

And then aloud, "All right. It's settled."

She was grateful for the gift and the way it seemed to ease the weight of recent events.

When Tifa returned to the meal line, she found Margo also assigned to the afternoon shift.

"My, my . . . Would you look at that," the older woman said, face beaming. "Come here. Let me give you a hug."

"Huh?" squeaked Tifa, but Margo had already swooped in, wrapping her arms tight and pressing her cheek to Tifa's.

"If I didn't know better, I'd have thought Yasmin had walked right back into town. Oh, my stars . . ."

The woman trailed off, apparently unable to say anything further. Tifa wasn't sure how to respond either. She hadn't expected the outfit to make quite that much of an impression. At the same time, she was happy to have brought a smile to Margo's face.

"You'd think that girl could visit once in a while to see her dear old mother, but no, I haven't seen her in years."

When Margo finally unclasped her arms, she promised to go through Yasmin's closet once more. There were plenty more outfits, she said, and it was a shame for them to go unloved.

The women on duty gathered for a quick meeting, and the night's menu was quickly settled: meatball soup. Tifa was assigned to chopping vegetables, and as she and her groupmates got to work washing and slicing the bright orange carrots, green celery, and yellow onions, another voice piped up.

"Tifa, you look adorable!"

She looked up to find Claudia Strife at her side.

"Do you like it? I got the outfit from Margo. It belonged to Yasmin."

"I thought I recognized that skirt." Claudia smiled and added wistfully, "I wonder what Yasmin is up to these days."

"Is Cloud doing well?"

The question surprised Tifa even as it left her lips. It was the first thing to pop into her mind when she saw Claudia's face, and somehow, she couldn't help but ask. Her heart began to race in her chest as she waited to see how Cloud's mother would react.

"As far as I know."

"Do you think he's up on the mountain already?"

Claudia tilted her head. "I'm not sure I follow."

"I heard that Shinra's sending a team of SOLDIERs, and I figured maybe one of them might be Cloud, since he knows the area. The cell signal is much better today, so they must be near. I figured maybe they're already up on the mountain."

Claudia gave Tifa a puzzled look.

After a pause, she said, "Well, I can't say that I've heard anything about it. But if he *were* assigned to a job here, I doubt I'd ever know. It doesn't usually cross his mind to keep other people in the loop."

With a laugh, Claudia added, "In fact, I guess the only time I've actually heard from him was right after he left. Just a single post-card to say the on-site processing had gone smoothly and he'd managed to enlist as planned."

"That's all?!" exclaimed Tifa. "So you don't even know if he made it into SOLDIER?"

"Nope. But, um . . . What makes you think he was aiming for SOLDIER?"

Suddenly, Tifa understood why the conversation felt so dis-jointed.

"Oh. It was just something he said to me once," she explained. "He told me he wanted to be the best of the best . . . Did he change his mind?"

"Goodness. He said that to you, did he?"

Claudia returned to chopping the vegetables, mumbling "Goodness, goodness . . . " to herself several more times.

When the vegetables were all cut, Tifa's next job was to stir the pots as they boiled. Claudia was again at her side, and at one point, the woman seemed about to speak up, only to hesitate at the last moment.

Tifa sensed that Claudia wanted to ask about the accident on the mountain all those years ago. Tifa was relieved not to have to face the question. There was really nothing she could say.

When Marc Banner wandered into the main square and caught Tifa's eye, she was grateful for the interruption.

"Tifa!" he called.

Marc had been the youngest member of the Calisthenics Club—*young* being a relative term. The burly man was easily a full gener-ation her father's senior.

"The white cat with the red bandanna round its neck. That's yours, ain't it?"

"Yes. That's Fluffy."

"I saw her just now, up by the trailhead."

Marc dabbed at his forehead, slick with sweat from his patrol's hike.

"But I wouldn't go after her," he said. "She was headed up, and the mountain's no place to be right now."

He waved and headed home. Tifa, after quickly apologizing and saying she had something to take care of, hurried to her own front door.

"Don't you dare go near that mountain!" Claudia called at her back.

Tifa, without turning, shouted, "Yes, ma'am!"

"I knew I shouldn't, but when I couldn't find Fluffy near the trail-head, I started hiking farther in," Tifa recalled. "I mean, I was concerned about monsters, but I figured I could handle them. I'd fight off any bugs that attacked and run away from anything larger. That was my plan, anyway."

Aerith's eyes sparkled. "Talk about confidence."

"More like *over*confidence. I underestimated what I'd run into up there. The bugs had grown and mutated into creatures a lot different than the ones I'd seen in the past. I wasn't far up the mountain before I found myself in a real bind."

"Oh no! What happened?!"

"Some woman from Shinra showed up and saved me. She was wearing a black suit."

Aerith's eyes widened. "A suit? Was she with the Turks?"

"Most definitely. I mean, I didn't know it at the time, but looking back now, she had to be. I never got her name, though."

"You sayin' Shinra sent Turks to investigate the reactor instead of SOLDIERs?" asked Barret. "That's not what we heard back at Kalm."

"She never told me exactly what she was doing on the mountain that day. All she said was that she was looking for someone who knew Mt. Nibel and could act as a guide. I volunteered, and they must've passed word on to Zander, because when Sephiroth and his team showed up, I was the one the village sent along.

"If I hadn't gone chasing after Fluffy that day and run into the Turk," reflected Tifa, "there's no way I'd have been sent along with the investigation team."

"Typical Shinra," remarked Red XIII. "They target the youth. Take care to remember that in the future."

"What do you mean?" Tifa asked.

"When the option presents itself, Shinra prefers to work with young minds on the cusp of adulthood. Individuals who are capable yet still naive. They're easier to turn to the Shinra way of thinking."

"Well, I wish I could go back and warn myself of that. At the time, all I could think about was how proud I was to be playing such a big part."

Aerith's voice grew soft. "Do you really believe you'd have done differently if you knew?"

Tifa pondered the question and decided that, no, it probably wouldn't have changed anything. Even if she'd known the full extent of Shinra's deceit, and that the company was only using her for its own convenience, she would have still jumped at the opportunity. She'd have done almost anything for a chance to be near Cloud again.

She didn't, however, share that answer out loud. She continued walking, and after a moment of silence had passed over the group, she whirled to face Aerith with a sudden realization. Barret's and Red XIII's eyes burned holes in her back.

"Everything afterward happened exactly as Cloud described," she insisted. "Sorry, but that's all I have to say about Nibelheim."

She faced each of her companions in turn, silently demanding they accept her declaration. Barret and Red XIII nodded silently. Aerith did too, though her gaze shifted slightly to peer over Tifa's shoulder.

Tifa turned once more to find Cloud at her side.

"Whatcha talking about?" he asked.

"Oh, um . . . Just about Emilio and the guys," answered Tifa. "You know, the tea parties we used to have. That kind of stuff."

For a brief moment, Cloud stared off into the distance, his face betraying the faintest note of displeasure.

After the Sephiroth incident, the first thing Tifa opened her eyes to was a white-painted ceiling.

It was unfamiliar. She flicked her gaze about, trying to determine where she might be. When that failed to reveal any further clues, she attempted to swivel her neck as best she could.

On the wall to her right hung a clock. The time was quarter past three, though it was hard to say whether that meant afternoon or dead of night. On the left was a sheet of white fabric that cordoned her off from the rest of the room, blocking her view of anything beyond.

Tifa checked her right side once again. Positioned near the head of the bed was a strange piece of equipment. It was fashioned from metal and emitted a low humming noise. Several tiny lights dotted the surface, each blinking its own erratic tempo. A digital display read 72, and a thin tube of some sort rose from the machine toward the ceiling, where it looped over a hook on a tall stand and came back down to Tifa, vanishing inside the folds of the blanket pulled up to her shoulders.

She tried moving her right arm and found it difficult; summoning the necessary strength seemed a monumental effort. When she did finally manage to raise her arm, she saw the thin tube rise with it.

She brought her arm into view above her head. The tube was fastened once against her forearm with a piece of tape and then seemed to disappear into the back of her hand, covered by a thick white bandage stained with what appeared to be blood.

A dull ache reverberated through the arm, and Tifa began to suspect the tube was carrying some kind of fluid into her body. When she attempted to lift herself to a sitting position with her elbows, a lightning bolt of pain passed through her chest, leaving her gasping for air.

"Ngh . . ."

She'd intended to wail in agony—the pain was that intense—but the sound that left her mouth was the pitiful groan of a wounded animal. Her throat was dry and aching. For a moment, she feared she'd lost her voice altogether.

And then, as the pain lancing throughout her body came into

excruciating focus, so too did the events that had preceded it, along with the truth of her current situation.

I'm alive, she thought.

It was an unexpected discovery, to say the least. By all accounts, she should have died back there at the reactor.

She recalled with perfect clarity the twisted smile of the man she'd grown up hailing a hero.

The sound of a door opening came from somewhere beyond the veil of white fabric, and then there was a voice.

"Coming in."

It was the soft, gentle voice of a woman. The curtain parted, and Tifa saw a heavyset doctor in a white coat. Her skin was a lovely warm brown.

"You're awake. Good. It's nice to finally be able to speak with you. My name is Dhamini Oranye. This is my clinic. Now, I imagine you have a lot of questions, but I'd ask you to wait just a little longer while I check your condition."

Even before she finished speaking, Dr. Oranye had situated herself at the device near Tifa's pillow and begun tapping away on its buttons.

"Can you tell me your name and age?" asked the doctor.

"Tifa . . ."

The word left her lips as barely more than a whisper.

". . . Lockhart," she managed to add.

And then, ". . . Fifteen."

"Very good. Can you tell me, are you in pain? And if so, what part of you hurts?"

"Chest . . ." Tifa replied. "No . . . All over."

The doctor smiled. "Correct again. Can you sense where the pain in your chest is coming from? Is it on the inside or outside?"

"Outside . . ." Tifa began, then thought for a moment. "No. Not sure. Inside too . . ."

"I see." The doctor nodded. "Unfortunately, I'm afraid I can't offer you any more painkillers than you're already on. But if your pain keeps increasing, please let me know. We'll figure something out."

Tifa regarded the doctor carefully, deciding that she looked to be about the same age as her father.

Dad!

The thought struck harder than a sword blow. She felt tears pooling at the corners of her eyes. Dr. Oranye shook her head, as if sorry she couldn't help.

No! Tifa wanted to scream. *It's not about the medicine! I don't care about that!*

"At any rate," said the doctor, "I'm really glad to see you awake. Your readings are looking good too. Would you like me to explain what happened to you?"

Tifa managed a slight nod.

"You've sustained a severe laceration from some manner of very sharp object. I hate to say it, but if I had to guess, it was probably a sword. The wound stretches from your left upper chest . . ."

Dr. Oranye reached one finger to her own chest, indicating a point just below her clavicle, then slowly drew the finger down and across, stopping just below her right breast.

". . . to just about here. It was deep enough to reach bone. In fact, it managed to shatter a portion of your sternum.

"Fortunately for you, neither lung was punctured, and your other organs also appear to be safe and functioning normally. Count your blessings, hm?

"Usually, we only hear about sternal fractures when a patient's chest has been crushed by a heavy object or otherwise subjected to blunt trauma. So, in a way, you're a very unusual case. We've reinforced the damaged portion with artificial bone as well as a short piece of metal wire. You'll probably have the wire inside you for the rest of your days, barring any major breakthroughs in modern medicine. But don't worry. You'll recover just fine, and you'll go on to lead a normal, healthy life.

"While it heals, I'm going to be keeping you in a chest brace to make sure everything stays nice and stable. It'll be uncomfortable at first, but we'll loosen it bit by bit as you recover.

"Oh, and just a heads-up. Your chest is going to ache something fierce for some time yet."

Dr. Oranye bobbed her head as she spoke, her expression sympathetic.

"That about covers it. You can thank Dr. Sheiran over in Corel for the excellent surgical work. I haven't met the man, but I can see why he has the reputation he does. As for me, I'm just here to help with your overall recovery and a few skin grafts. It seemed the right thing to do—you'd have some pretty awful scars otherwise, not just from the original wound but all the surgery. Terrible for a pretty young thing like you to have to live with. I hope you'll forgive me. I had to work fast, before the incisions began to heal."

Just when Tifa thought the doctor might be done, she launched into another tangent.

"I was a little worried about infection, but luckily you seem to be doing all right on that front. Oh! And you'll be happy to know that I stuck to the best—only the latest and greatest in medical technology. Typically, these modern grafts take three or four years to fully blend in, but you're young, so it'll likely be much faster. At this point, the aching on the outside of your chest is probably mostly from the skin grafts. Feels like a bad burn, from what other patients have told me. But that'll go away soon enough. Even the color'll blend in nicely.

"Now, any questions for me?"

It was too much to take in at once—especially just moments after Tifa first opened her eyes. She was only grasping scattered pieces of the doctor's explanation.

"Right, right," said Dr. Oranye. "Take your time. I'll be keeping you here for at least another couple of weeks, so there's no need to rush. Just remember one thing. You survived. You're going to keep on living. The past is the past, and the sooner you turn your eyes to the future, the better."

"Doctor . . . ?" Tifa whispered. "It feels like . . . I've been asleep for . . . so long. What day is it? Where am I?"

"Midgar. Sector 8 slums. And as for the date . . ."

What the doctor said next didn't make any sense. Tifa's mind spiraled.

Dr. Oranye reached over to wipe the tears from Tifa's eyes with a wad of clean, damp gauze. She circled to the foot of the bed and gave Tifa's left ankle a light tap.

"Hang in there. We'll get through this together, you hear?"

The doctor left, and Tifa was alone with her thoughts of Nibelheim—visions of her home swallowed by a sea of fire; acrid black smoke filling the air to scorch eyes and lungs.

A full month had passed since the horror of that day.

"One month . . ." she whispered to herself.

A full month since her father grabbed her arm, dragging her from the raging flames to the safety of the waterfall. When they reached the pool, he thrust Fluffy from his arms to hers.

"Stay here," he ordered. "The flames won't make it down to the waterfall. There's nothing to burn. If the wind changes and carries the smoke here, I want you to lie low to the ground. Whatever happens, Tifa, you are *not* to leave this spot."

"What are you going to do, Dad?"

"Zander's dead. *Murdered.* I'm the only representative left alive. The village's safety is my responsibility."

"No! You can't go back there!"

"Look at me, Tifa. I'll be fine. Those are our friends and neighbors. They can't get out of the village on their own. Someone has to help them."

She begged him to stay, but he only shook his head and dashed up the path to the burning village. Several times he returned, always with a wounded villager on his back or in his arms. But as he laid each down and sprinted to the village for the next, Tifa saw the familiar faces coughing and blackened with soot, and she feared that their time was already at hand. Hair and clothing was singed or missing. Appearances were so disfigured, she found she had to turn away.

After a while, she saw someone other than her father coming down the trail to the waterfall, and as the figure drew near, she realized it was Zangan. He had one villager over each shoulder, and as he carefully set the bodies down, he nodded once at Tifa before sprinting back. When Tifa's father next returned, he knelt by the two villagers Zangan had saved. Their burnt, blackened mouths groaned in agony. A hand lifted as if to grab at some unseen object, only to fall limply back to earth, like a marionette whose strings had been severed.

"Dammit all!" shouted Brian.

It was the first and only time she'd known her father to curse. His sweat- and soot-stained face glimmered in the light off the distant flames, and his bloodshot eyes found Tifa's.

"They're saying Sephiroth headed up the mountain," he said. "I'm going to go talk to him."

And with one final, decisive nod, he set off up the path.

Tifa pictured him running through the burning village and up the trail to the reactor. What would he do once he got there? How would talking change anything that had happened? What was he thinking?!

"Dad!" she called.

And then her legs were pumping of their own accord. Fluffy in her arms, Tifa fled the safety of the waterfall, reaching the village just in time to see her father running past Shinra Manor.

"Dad! Wait!"

It was hard to keep up with Fluffy squirming and struggling to get free. By the time Tifa reached the trailhead, she'd lost sight of her dad altogether. Fluffy leapt from her arms with a reproachful mew, as if demanding Tifa not proceed any farther.

"I'm sorry, Fluffy. I have to go after him."

She left the cat behind at the boundary of mountain and village and pushed onward. But no matter how fast Tifa ran, she wasn't catching up.

Meanwhile, the trail was littered with the corpses of monsters— some small, some large, but all clearly downed with a single stroke from an impossibly long blade.

Sephiroth.

The name echoed in her mind. This was the man who had ended the lives of so many people she cared for.

"Dad!" Tifa shouted again as loud as she could, but there was no answer.

When she finally reached the top of the trail, she found the reactor's massive entrance wide open, like a terrible gaping maw.

"Dad? Can you hear me?!" she cried again.

She approached the steps leading up to the entrance. A loud *whoosh* passed overhead, and she glanced up to find a Kimara Bug in flight, its beady eyes trained on Tifa. It descended, hanging in the air just over the base of the staircase, blocking her only access to the reactor—and her father, who had to be inside.

Without warning, the giant insect dove. Tifa rolled to evade, then spun to counterattack without hesitation. One punch to its gut. Her fist sank deep into the monster's soft underbelly, and its wings faltered, sending it crashing to the ground. Tifa leapt into the air, twirling and tucking one knee to her chest. As she descended, she thrust the opposite leg out, landing with the heel of her boot in the giant insect's abdomen.

Everything happened fluidly, without thought. She'd chained her movements form by form, just as described in Zangan's writings. The crushed, defeated insect lay as proof of her prowess.

But there was one thing her training hadn't prepared her for. She breathed deeply, returning from the single-minded focus of combat to find herself covered from head to toe in juices from the Kimara Bug's ruptured insides. It clung to her hair and soaked into her clothing. The smell was horrendous.

"Eww!" she exclaimed.

She could feel panic setting in, but she heard a shout to one side and just managed to hold her fear at bay.

"Tifa . . . !"

It was a man's voice. It seemed familiar, but she couldn't quite place it. Whomever it belonged to, it wasn't her father.

"Dad!" she cried, suddenly remembering her search.

"Dad! Are you there?!"

"Tifa?"

This time she heard a woman's voice. She felt a finger poke at her cheek, but no one else was around.

"Who's there?!" cried Tifa.

She frantically spun in a circle, and when she again faced the reactor, another monster stood before her, as if it had appeared out of thin air.

This one exhibited a disturbingly *human* form.

Tifa shrieked, and as she did, the earth beneath her began to quake.

"Tifa! You're having a nightmare! Wake up! Come back to me!"

The menacing maw of the reactor pulled away into the distance and was replaced by blinding light. Tifa squeezed her eyes shut, unsure if the light was real or imagined. After a moment, she squinted her eyelids open just a sliver to check.

"It's okay, honey. You're safe now. Nothing here will hurt you."

The dream was gone, replaced by Dr. Oranye's concerned face. At the doctor's back was a bright light. Daylight. Sun was pouring in from the window in the wall to the right of her hospital bed.

Tifa noticed the window's lace curtains swaying gently in a slight breeze.

"It's morning?" she managed to ask.

"Seven o'clock. That's not real sun, mind. It's from the sun lamps."

"Huh?"

"That's how we get light down here in the slums. Shinra's got giant electric lamps affixed to the underside of the plate. When you're well enough to walk again, you can go out and see them for yourself."

Dr. Oranye smiled and said, "Anyway, enough of that. It's time for your checkup. Could you start by telling me your name and age? And today, how about naming your hometown too?"

"Tifa Lockhart. I'm fifteen years old. I'm from Nibelheim."

"Do you remember who I am?"

"Dr. Dhamini Oranye."

"Very good. Can you tell me if you're experiencing any pain right now?"

"Um . . . My chest hurts, and there's a tingling in my wrists and ankles."

"That's to be expected. I'm sorry to say, though, that you'll have to bear it for a while. We need to start weaning you off these painkillers."

Dr. Oranye leaned close, peering into Tifa's eyes.

"There's something else I'd like to ask, just out of personal curiosity. Do you remember anything about the injury that landed you here?"

"Are you asking who it was that attacked me? I'll never forget. Not for as long as I live."

"Is that so?"

"It was Sephiroth. As in Sephiroth, SOLDIER First Class. He cut me down with his sword at the mako reactor above Nibelheim."

Dr. Oranye nodded, but the gesture was hesitant and couched in doubt.

"Could I ask you a favor, then?" the doctor inquired. "Would you please promise not to talk about it, at least for as long as you're here in my clinic?"

"Why? Why can't I talk about what happened to me?"

"I'd sooner not have my practice caught up in any kind of trouble."

Dr. Oranye bowed her head apologetically. As she did, Tifa felt a surge of anger in her chest.

"What do you mean, *trouble*?"

"As far as I know, Shinra isn't aware you're here. I've accepted you as my patient, and I feel it's my duty to keep looking after you until you're back on your feet. But that's as far as I can go. I'm already toeing the line. I don't know anything about your background, and based on what you've said, I'd rather not learn any further details about the incident that put you here.

"I just can't afford to have Shinra thinking I'm an agitator, you see? If I want to keep providing my patients the best possible care, I need to show support for the company. Otherwise, I'll be cut off from all the latest drugs and equipment. And if that happens, the residents of the slums are the ones who really suffer."

Dr. Oranye looked Tifa in the eyes once more and implored, "Please tell me you understand."

". . . Yes. I understand."

As if she'd had any choice. She still lay nearly comatose, wrapped in bandages and with tubes snaking from her body.

"Doctor," she asked. "When will I be able to leave?"

At the question, Dr. Oranye's face flushed with embarrassment. It seemed the matter was even more complicated than the doctor had let on.

"I've got three conditions before I can discharge you from my care. First, I need to see that the grafts are taking properly. They need to be at stage three or above. Second, I need you rehabilitated enough that I'm confident you can go about daily tasks by yourself. And third . . .

"Third . . . there's the question of payment. I'll need to ask you to reimburse the clinic for your treatment as well as your stay. I'd have to run the numbers to be sure, but I'm afraid you're looking at a sum of about . . ."

The number that next left Dr. Oranye's lips was one Tifa had never imagined in terms of gil. It sent a shiver down her spine.

"I . . . I don't have that kind of money. In fact, I don't have *any* money . . ."

"Yes, I figured as much."

The doctor fell silent and gazed pensively out the window. After a moment, she murmured, "I imagine you don't even have a place to stay after you check out."

A sense of doom washed over Tifa. She'd lost everything, only to wake up in an unfamiliar, far-off place. She had nothing left, and now she was being told she had *less*; she was stuck in a massive hole of debt.

"Well . . . Let's just take it one step at a time," said the doctor. "First, we'll concentrate on your skin and on getting those muscles back in shape. The grafts should work themselves out as long as you keep eating healthy, and I'll have my son, Rakesh, come by to get you started on some rehabilitation exercises."

That was how Tifa met Rakesh. Their initial encounter came three days later, and Tifa could immediately see the resemblance—the young man had inherited his mother's hair and warm brown skin. Also familiar were the contours of his well-shaped nose and the pleasant ring of his voice.

"Hey. You must be Tifa," he said with a smile. "I'm Rakesh Oranye. Mom says I'll be in charge of your rehabilitation program. Here. I got you a little gift, just to kick things off."

Rakesh gently gripped Tifa's wrist and pressed a soft rubber ball into her palm.

"Whenever you've got time on your hands—and I'm willing to bet you've got a lot these days—you can use this to flex your fingers. It'll help bring back the strength in your hands and forearms.

"Just make sure to back off and let yourself rest if your wrists ever start to hurt."

He reached over and placed a ball in her opposite hand too. "There you go. Now you've got a matching pair. Go ahead and try them out. Flex both hands."

Rakesh brought his own hands to the sides of his head and mimed a squeezing motion with a goofy smile. Tifa couldn't help but giggle.

"You've got a beautiful laugh.

"All right," he said, suddenly all business. "Let's put our minds to this and get you out of that hospital bed as soon as we can."

Tifa gave what she thought was an energetic reply, but Rakesh must have spotted the uncertainty clouding her eyes. Sharp perception seemed to be another quality he'd inherited from his mother.

"You're worried about the money, aren't you? Mom mentioned it was an issue. No promises, but I think I might have a way to help you there too.

"See, Mom used to live topside before some bad luck sent her tumbling down here. But I'm a slum kid, born and raised. I know the ropes, and I've got connections."

Rakesh smiled triumphantly, but Tifa had only understood about half of what he'd said, so the explanation did a poor job of dispelling her worry.

"Anyway, that's still a long way off. You'll just have to trust me."

And she knew it was true. What other choice did she have?

The excruciatingly tight brace she'd found clamped about her chest on first regaining consciousness had since been substituted for another, slightly-less-suffocating one. But she wasn't fully recovered. Not yet. The bone still needed much more time to heal.

Undeterred, Rakesh dove right into her new exercise routine. Tifa could tell from the movements he selected that he was doing his best to find ways to regain her strength without undue strain on her chest. They began with the grip exercises and moved on to leg movements and basic stretches.

"You've lost a lot of muscle mass lying in bed, but there's not much we can do about that now. Once you're all better, you'll be able to build it back slowly. At this point, our goal is to reclaim a level of basic functioning. Your muscles have forgotten what it's like to flex and move, so your strength is gonna be low. And after a month without use, your nerves will be a little rusty at carrying signals, so your coordination's gonna feel off too. We have to train both of them back to health—muscles *and* nerves."

Rakesh circled to the foot of Tifa's bed, where he lifted her ankles and calves, shaking each joint gently to ease the stiffness of time.

The rehabilitation sessions had been going on for nearly half a month when Tifa made an unexpected observation.

It was a particularly warm afternoon, and sweat was beading on Rakesh's forehead as they worked. He lifted a forearm to wipe it away, then shucked off his jacket.

"Whew. Sure is hot today, huh?"

The short-sleeved tee underneath revealed an attractive, lightly muscled physique. Tifa's eyes followed the length of one well-toned arm, stopping at the wrist. Rakesh was wearing a bracelet. More precisely, a single leather cord had been wrapped loosely around his wrist and tied together.

Tifa lifted her own wrist into view. Zangan's gift was still there. Hers had darkened a little with time, but there was no doubt: it was the same type of cord.

Tentatively, she asked Rakesh, "Are you a friend of Master Zangan's?"

Rakesh gave a puzzled stare. Eventually, he nodded his head thoughtfully.

"Right. I forgot that you missed that part." He fell silent for a moment, then continued. "I'm a disciple of Master Zangan's, just like you," he explained as he continued to raise and lower Tifa's leg, gently bending it at the knee. "But wow . . . You must not re-member anything following your injury."

"It's mostly a blank," replied Tifa. She shook her head. "Actually, it's pretty much *all* a blank."

There was a vague memory of Zangan shouting, begging her to hang on, his voice faint as if coming from a place very far away. And there was a fleeting image of nurses hurrying about a room, along with a male doctor, his brow furrowed with concern. She assumed the man had to be Dr. Sheiran—that other doctor Rakesh's mother had mentioned when Tifa first woke up in the clinic.

What few traces she had were blurry and fragmented. They could have passed for dreams if the people around her now hadn't convinced her otherwise.

Rakesh cleared this throat. "The first hospital handled the re-construction work on your sternum. The surgery went without incident, but your condition hadn't stabilized. From what I un-derstand, the doctor in Corel recommended you be admitted to a bigger facility—somewhere in Junon or Midgar, where you'd have access to better treatment options.

"He made some calls, and the Research and Development Division at Shinra HQ offered you a bed, but Master Zangan wouldn't have it. A few heated discussions later, it was decided you'd be transported here. Master Zangan just happened to recall that one of his students—that'd be me—had a mom running a clinic in Midgar's slums. I guess you could say it was fate."

"Why the argument over where to treat me?"

"I mean, it's Shinra HQ. They've got some of the best medical professionals on the planet. The doctor in Corel couldn't believe Master Zangan would turn them down."

"But . . . of *course* he turned them down. It's *Shinra.*"

"Oh, believe me, I get it. Aside from his own feelings, Master Zangan said he couldn't let you wake up to that. He didn't even want to think about how you might react, waking up to find yourself in Shinra's care after everything you went through. I wish I could honestly say you're in better hands with us, but we hoped at the very least you'd be happier here.

"So?" he pressed. "Are you? Come on. Don't leave me hanging."

Rakesh flashed her a cocky smile, obviously trying to convey that these last questions were meant as a joke.

Tifa nonetheless replied in earnest. "Yeah. I'm glad I'm here."

"Here's a little advice, one Midgar resident to another. Hate on the company if you have to, but do it inside your head. Nothing good comes of speaking out against Shinra. That's rule number one in the slums."

"I'll be sure to remember that," she said. "Any other rules I ought to know?"

"More than I can count. But there's no need to hear the rest from me. You can pick 'em up as you go along. Gives you another reason to get out of this bed and back into the world, am I right?"

Rakesh loved to talk. It was just one more way he took after his mother. Over time, Tifa came to know all the ins and outs of the little clinic, as well as the story of Rakesh's father. The man had been a medical researcher and practicing doctor for Shinra; he was the one who taught Rakesh the rehabilitation techniques Tifa was benefitting from now.

But Rakesh's father had an interest that extended well beyond physical therapy. He was a biologist by training, and in Shinra's employ, he'd specialized in observing and cataloging the overall musculature of the many unusual specimens kept in the company's labs. That is to say, his focus wasn't humans, but monsters.

"He used to tell me that the basics hold true for everyone—animal, human, or monster. If the thing's got bones and muscles, it always works pretty much the same way. Kinda hard to believe we've got that much in common with monsters, huh?

"Trivial as it sounds, he left his mark. He's listed as the editor in chief for one of the better-known monster encyclopedias. And then he went and got himself killed researching some new specimen."

Rakesh laughed. To Tifa, it seemed a morbid thing to laugh about, doubly so given that the unfortunate party was Rakesh's own father. Still, she wasn't unaccustomed to such comments. She recalled that the elderly villagers in her Calisthenics Club had also often joked about death.

Scattered among the frequent rehabilitation sessions were the once-weekly fluoroscopes of her chest. Each time, Tifa stood very still while the machine recorded its images, which Dhamini proceeded to pull up on a monitor alongside the results of the previous week's scan. Tifa's eyes could flick back and forth between the two images a hundred times without any certainty about what had changed, but Dhamini would only need a brief glance. As the doctor's eyes checked the screen, she would either nod in approval or shake her head with a frown. Each week, Tifa prayed for the former.

"Ah. Looking good!" Dhamini announced one particular day, peering at yet another inscrutable pair of images. "Everything's on track."

It was the last day of November, and a thumbs-up this time was particularly exciting: it meant that the chest brace could finally come off.

"Deep breath for me, would you?" the doctor said. "Keep sucking in air until it starts to hurt. Slowly now . . . No need to rush . . ."

The familiarity of the words struck Tifa. It was that same gentle caution Zangan had urged during her initial taste of training in the village square.

Slowly now. No need to rush.

For the first time in weeks, she found she could breathe as deeply as she wanted without pain.

"Looking good," Dhamini said with a smile. "Okay, next I want you to hold your arms above your head. Reach like you're trying to touch the ceiling. Slowly now . . . No need to rush . . ."

Tifa cautiously raised her arms, fearing pain at any moment. But they continued upward until fully extended, and then Tifa was stretching up as high as she could reach, and no ache came.

"I can do it!" she exclaimed. "It doesn't hurt!"

"Congratulations, Tifa. You're healed."

Dhamini patted Tifa's head in the way a mother might praise a young child. Tifa instinctively ducked away.

"Ha! All right. I imagine you must be dying to wash your hair."

It was as if Dhamini had seen straight into her mind. The doctor and her son had regularly sponged Tifa down while she lay in bed. And Tifa was grateful to them for that kindness, but in a way, it only left her feeling more desperate for the chance to take an actual shower.

Right at that moment, there was a knock at the door. Tifa knew immediately that it was Rakesh. She hurried to pull her hospital robe tight.

"Come in," said Dhamini.

"Well?!" exclaimed Rakesh as he burst into the room. "What's the word?!"

"I'm all better!"

"Congratulations!" Rakesh smiled and flashed a thumbs-up.

What followed was the longest, most luxurious shower of Tifa's life. She hogged the booth until she began to feel a little guilty about how much water she was using. But it was heavenly to finally have her hair and skin feel truly clean again.

She relished in her newly recovered freedom of movement. But those sensations naturally led to thoughts of leaving the clinic, which in turn brought her mind to the third stipulation.

Suddenly, the joy of the shower was overshadowed by the specter of debt. Tifa gloomily turned the water off, dried herself with a towel, and changed into the new underwear, top, and bottom thoughtfully laid out on the bed by Dhamini.

The outfit was admittedly not to Tifa's taste—it consisted of a rather nondescript, baggy blouse and a skirt of perplexing middling length. On the floor rested the same ballet flats she'd used throughout her rehabilitation program with Rakesh. She slipped the shoes on as usual.

The simple act of changing left Tifa exhausted. Her arms and legs felt heavy. She sat on the edge of the hospital bed to catch her breath, but somehow even sitting required too much effort, so in the end, she flopped onto her side.

In the comfort of the blankets, she mumbled to herself, "It's gone . . . It's all gone."

The clothes she'd loved—her own outfits and the ones shared by Margo. The favorite pair of boots and the wide-brimmed hat. The photos she kept of Mom.

Her dad. And probably Fluffy too.

All her personal treasures, including Zangan's books. The staircase she vaulted up and down to get to her room. The door she'd slammed shut on her father in embarrassment. Her piano. The view from her window of the village's little square. The water tower. Even the muscles she'd built and honed over countless hours of training.

"All of it . . . gone."

Her voice broke, and on the hospital bed, in the loneliness of the clinic, Tifa quietly sobbed.

The next morning, Dhamini sat next to her bed and gently informed her that the clinic needed the bed available for other patients within the week.

"I really wish I could waive all the treatment fees," she told Tifa apologetically, "but it would be a hit we just can't afford to take. You don't need to pay all at once. I'm happy to work out installments with you."

"Thank you."

But Tifa had no idea what she was going to do. She didn't have the means pay one gil per month, much less proper installments.

Rakesh had entered the room with his mother, and when he saw the despair in Tifa's eyes, he tried to cheer her up. He had a sure lead on a job, he claimed. Better yet, it included cheap accommodations, which would help ease the sting of rent.

The reassurances did bolster some hope. But worry continued to win out.

"What kind of job is it?" she asked.

"Do you know how to cook?"

"A little. But I don't know if I'm ready to do it all day long. I feel like my muscles have completely wasted away."

Rakesh tossed a small booklet onto the bed. "Here. I thought you might like to borrow this."

He smiled. "Recognize it? Book One for students of Zangan-style martial arts."

Rakesh slowly and deliberately bent his knees and elbows, adopting the opening stance of the first form right there in the hospital room.

"I've never had a routine that just clicked the way this one does, y'know?" he said. "And the way it builds muscle is incredible. I mean, I'm sure you must know that already."

Dhamini watched the exchange between Tifa and Rakesh, obviously relieved to see the growing camaraderie, as well as the tiny glimmer of hope from Tifa. Dhamini stood and placed a hand on Tifa's shoulder. "You know what they say. The only things that can never be stolen from you are the things you learn."

With a smile and an encouraging pat, the doctor went to tend to her other patients.

It was December 4.

Tifa checked out of the clinic and stepped into the slum, nervously clutching the ID card that Rakesh had arranged for her.

"This is just a temporary card," he explained, following her out and onto the street. "It'll only permit residence in the Sector 8 slums, and you won't be able to commute topside for work. Eventually, you ought to look into applying for a proper card. In the meantime, I've put myself down as your guarantor. Oh, and it says you're from Corel. I figure you're better off not associating yourself with Nibelheim. It could attract attention from Shinra."

She thanked him yet again. In all the preparations to begin her new life, Rakesh had been extremely thorough.

Tifa took her first few steps along the packed dirt paths that served for streets in Midgar's slums. She realized it was the first time she'd been outside since the day she chased her father up Mt. Nibel. It was also her first taste of the chaos of the slums. There was uneven ground to navigate and a constant stream of other pedestrians to avoid. It was a far cry from the rehabilitation sessions. Exhaustion quickly mounted, and a storm of worry and excitement about what lay ahead left her mind feeling rattled.

Rakesh walked at her side, carefully observing her. Several times, he had her stop and take several deep breaths.

"This is so embarrassing. I can't even walk right," she said.

"Don't worry. Nobody's watching. Even if they are, they don't give a damn 'cause it's none of their business. That's how it is here in the slums. C'mon. One more breath."

She filled her lungs as full as she was able, glancing upward as she did so.

Tifa had known about the plate, but she was surprised to see it all the same. The city—or the slums, rather—had a ceiling. Steel girders crisscrossed its surface in a complex yet methodical design. Pillars reached up from the neighborhoods like slender fingers to hold its great weight. Here and there, like treasures nestled among the steel, were the massive lamps Dhamini had described, compensating for the sunlight blotted out by mankind's ambition.

Above that ceiling was a whole other city, along with several mammoth reactors to power it. Tifa turned to look outward, away from the city center, and found the base of the nearest reactor. It made the one on Mt. Nibel look like a miniature.

Back home, she'd seen plenty of videos and photographs of Shinra's city. But the images could have never prepared her for the magnitude of Midgar in real life.

Above all else were the *people*. Everywhere you looked. People,

people, and more people! Somewhere among the myriad faces, she reflected, was Emilio's. Maybe Lester's and Tyler's too. And . . . perhaps even Cloud's.

Not that it mattered. Everywhere she looked, there were so many people that the possibility of running into anyone she knew seemed terribly remote.

"Every time Master Zangan stops by, he complains about the stench," said Rakesh. "I know I'm his disciple and all, but it kinda hurts hearing your home described as a dump. When you've got this many people living in one spot, of course it's gonna get a little musty."

She'd noted that too: the onslaught of what seemed a million different smells, some identifiable, some not. There was dust. Sweat. Iron. Spice.

Still, it didn't strike Tifa as unpleasant.

"It doesn't seem to bother me so far," she said.

Rakesh laughed. "Well, inside or not, you've been living here for close to two months. Your nose has had time to adjust."

"Does Master Zangan visit often?"

"Not really. Maybe once every three or four months. But he's got a lot of disciples spread out over the slums, so even when he's in the city, it doesn't necessarily mean I'll get a chance to see him."

Rakesh reached a hand to the cord at his wrist. It seemed to be an unconscious reaction.

Tifa nodded her head toward it. "What does it mean for you?"

"This?" Rakesh held up his wrist.

Apparently, she'd been right. He hadn't realized he'd been touching it, and he was surprised to have been caught doing so.

His answer was hesitant. "Um . . . How do I put it? I mean, it's a kind of amulet, same as yours. Mine's supposed to keep me on the straight and narrow. Doesn't do a very good job, though. Life in the slums comes with more than its fair share of temptations."

They'd walked for some time when Rakesh paused and motioned for Tifa to stop too. He lifted a finger, pointing out the narrow entrance of an alleyway off the main street.

"That's where you turn to get to your new place," he said. "Take a good look at the surroundings so you remember it."

Tifa spun in a slow circle. She found a small shop nearby with crates of vegetables lined out in front. The inside was stocked with trays of meat, canned goods, and bottled drinks. A general store. Just like the one run by Emilio's family.

"You got it?" asked Rakesh. "C'mon. We follow it all the way to the back."

He led her down the narrow alley. The air suddenly stunk of fetid water.

"When it comes to the alleys, even I'll admit they smell pretty bad. But every building's gotta drain its wastewater in some direction, and better here than out onto the main street. Don't worry. You'll get used to it soon enough. It's honestly pretty amazing how the human nose learns to adapt."

Rakesh pointed again. "Look. An alley cat."

He stopped walking and turned to grin at her. "You'll see a lotta strays roaming free in the slums. You like cats?"

"Yeah."

She thought of Fluffy, who had also loved to roam free. Tifa hoped that somewhere out there, her cat was still alive and well.

"By the way, you missed out on some pretty big news while you were in the clinic." Her companion's expression was now somber, and his eyes carefully searched hers. "It's about Sephiroth. There was an official report on TV about a week ago. Apparently, he was killed in action over in Wutai. I guess that must mean they found his corpse, because before that, they were saying he'd gone missing."

She was glad to hear it. After what Sephiroth had done, he deserved to die. But the news also robbed her of something. Anger still boiled deep inside, and if Sephiroth was dead, where was she supposed to direct it?

"When Master Zangan brought you to the clinic, he gave us the gist of what happened. So I get how you must feel. But maybe this is a sign. Think of it as a chance to move on."

Tifa looked away and hummed in vague agreement. It seemed to suffice for Rakesh, who resumed leading her down the alley.

About halfway to the far end, they arrived at a spot where a small stool had been set out on the bare ground. On it sat a man. He was neither young nor particularly old, and his deeply tanned, weathered features suggested many hours spent laboring outdoors.

Deep wrinkles creased his forehead, and a large capelike garment obscured his body from the neck down.

"Tifa, I'd like you to meet the Watchman. Let him get a good look at you. You'll wanna be sure he recognizes you next time you pass through."

Rakesh turned to the seated man and said, "This is Tifa Lockhart. She's the new tenant."

"It's very nice to meet you," ventured Tifa. She couldn't fathom who this man was or why his approval was necessary just to go to and from her new home.

The Watchman only glared in return. Rakesh smiled at Tifa and stepped past the man, motioning for her to follow.

"Beyond this point, we're on Manson turf."

Rakesh paused and added, "Oh. I guess I should explain. You're now officially working for the Manson Crew."

"What's that?"

"Think of Manson as the guy in charge around these parts. Don't worry. You won't have to meet him yourself. I'll make all the arrangements for you."

"Is he dangerous?" she asked, recalling the seedy appearance of the Watchman.

"He can be. But that's just part of life in the slums. Every sector has a few bosses who've carved out their own little slices of the neighborhood. But generally, you're safer *on* a gang's turf than off it. They've got a close eye on everyone and everything 'cause they know that the more orderly they keep their turf, the less likely Shinra is to start poking around. Remember that."

Rakesh was obviously trying to paint life in this particular part of the slums as positively as he could. Still, Tifa noted how he avoided answering her question with assurances that she had nothing to be afraid of.

Another moment of walking, and they'd reached the end of the alley, which opened into a small clearing.

"Here we are," announced Rakesh.

Numerous long, large wooden boxes stood in the clearing. More precisely, they were iron skeletons—posts and beams assembled into rectangles—into which wooden panels were fitted to form the sides. The iron was obviously once painted bright red, but much of the paint had since peeled, leaving the exposed portions to rust. The lumber was old and scarred from decades of use.

In all, there were about twenty of the nigh-identical boxes, all scattered haphazardly about the clearing.

"They used to be cargo containers," explained Rakesh. "You know. For transport by truck or whatever. That's how the place came to be known as Container Row.

"In fact, these particular containers were all used to haul in materials during construction of the city. They're not much to look at now, but they represent some serious Midgar history."

Rakesh arched his eyebrows, as if indicating he'd made a joke and it was now time to respond with a laugh.

The moment passed, and he returned to a serious expression.

"Don't worry. It's not as bad as it seems. The interiors are actually pretty nice."

He led her to one of the containers. A small door was fitted into the side facing the alley. On the door was a latch, from which hung an old padlock. Rakesh produced a small key from his pocket, inserted it into the base of the lock, and turned. The shank popped open with a loud click, and he twisted the padlock free of the latch, handing it to Tifa.

"Feel free to add another lock or two if you're worried about safety. It'll make coming and going kind of a pain, though."

As he spoke, he pulled the door open and ducked inside. The door was so tiny, even Tifa had to stoop to pass through. Rakesh tugged on a cord dangling from the ceiling, and the room was flooded with harsh light. Tifa glanced up to find it came from a single naked bulb.

"The monthly rent includes electricity. Power's cheap in the city, thanks to the reactors."

Tifa was only half listening. Rakesh reached behind her to close the door and then turned her attention to the inside portion of the latch.

"You can attach the padlock on this side too. Just be careful not to lose the key. Otherwise you'll be locked in."

Inside, the place actually felt kind of like a home. The walls and floors weren't too bad, she decided, and on the far side across from the door was a small window and a vent for fresh air. On one side rested a cheap wire bed frame with a thin mattress, a simple blanket, and a cushion apparently meant to serve in place of a pillow. Farther back was a small table with a single matching chair. On the right side—looking in from the doorway—an old cupboard stood flush with the wall. In it was a small assortment of tableware.

"The furniture's all included. The trick is to not think too much about who it used to belong to. If you cook anything, keep the door and window open so you've got enough airflow. But I wouldn't recommend cooking too often. No point in risking the buildup of fumes when you can just eat at work."

Tifa looked at Rakesh questioningly.

"Don't worry. I'll get to the job. But to finish up here . . . uh . . . I put some towels and other essential stuff in a bin under the bed. And I guess that's pretty much it. Any questions?"

"What about water? How am I supposed to take a shower or go to the bathroom?"

"There's a shared area at the far end of the row. Toilets and showers are all back there. Don't worry. The water from the spigots is safe enough to drink. Filtered and everything. You can fill that guy up . . ."

He pointed to a large plastic water jug resting against the wall.

". . . so you have water at home. Probably don't want to fill it up all the way, though. Gets real heavy."

"And what about, um . . . ?" Tifa trailed off, uncertain how to ask her next question.

"Lemme guess. How much is rent?"

"Yeah."

"Fifteen gil a day."

"That much?!"

"Trust me, that's crazy cheap around these parts. And pretty soon, you're gonna be rakin' in so much cash, fifteen gil's gonna sound like peanuts. 'Course, how much you actually earn ultimately depends on you."

The way Rakesh spoke reminded Tifa once more of the stories of traffickers in the city. It was a phenomenon she'd had a vague, nagging fear of ever since she heard about it as a child—something akin to monsters and ghosts, and yet at the same time so much more *real*. Those tales of men who tricked children into lives of hard labor had continued to make her nervous well into her teenage years.

She recalled how she'd misconstrued Zangan's actions during their first encounter. What if her intuition had been right all along? What if Zangan *had* been waiting for his chance to sell her into slavery? Considering the fact that he'd been the one to place her in Rakesh's care . . .

"Oops. Sorry," sputtered Rakesh. "This probably sounds like I'm trying to sell you on some kind of sketchy gig. I promise, the job is completely aboveboard. I'll take you by after we're done here."

Rakesh turned to open the door. He led Tifa out, patiently waiting while she familiarized herself with the latch and padlock. Next, they walked to the back of the clearing, where Rakesh pointed out to her the communal spigots, as well as the showers and toilets. One full container served as the shower area, an entire wooden wall stripped away to allow free access—and visibility—of the stalls themselves. Just outside was a folding chair, in which hunched a little woman who appeared to be on the cusp of old age. A small desk stood before her, and on it rested a tin can. As they approached, Tifa peeked over the rim of the can to find it full of coins.

"This is the Waterkeeper," explained Rakesh.

"Three gil a shower," rasped the woman. "Watch out for men tryin' to sneak a peek. Ain't no separate facilities for the ladies."

Given the design, Tifa wasn't exactly sure *how* one was supposed to stay on guard.

"You got four choices," continued the woman. "Shower with your clothes on. Shower in your underwear. Shower in a bathing suit—if you got one. Or get over it and stop caring who sees what."

"Are you serious . . . ?" asked Tifa.

Surely Rakesh and the woman were playing a prank on her. They had to be, right? But the showers themselves were hardly reassuring. There were five stalls, and while they were divided from one another by thin partitions, there were no doors or other means of privacy from anyone approaching the container. This was going to be a serious issue.

Perhaps it was as the woman said, and she'd simply have to make do. Maybe the clean, comfortable standard of living she'd known in Nibelheim was just one more thing she'd lost.

Having introduced Tifa to her accommodations, Rakesh led her back through the narrow alley and onto the main street. Tifa noted that the landmark she'd picked out earlier—the general store—was now teeming with customers. The shop was tended by a young man wearing an apron. He addressed his customers cordially, seeming to know many of them quite well.

Tifa wondered again about the new job awaiting her. What in the world could it be? If it was something unconscionable, would she know how to turn it down? And if she did refuse, would Rakesh be upset with her? Would this mysterious Manson fellow be angry?

She decided that if things looked bad, she'd better communicate her refusal delicately.

Tifa continued to follow Rakesh, completely reliant on him as they traversed the unfamiliar tangle of the slums. She imagined the sorts of awful jobs the city might have that she wouldn't want to be subjected to. She didn't yet know what was normal for people in the slums, or where their values lay. All she could do for now was stick close to Rakesh, both literally and figuratively, and hope for the best.

The thought had her feeling more helpless and alone than she ever had before.

"Gil for your thoughts?"

Their small party had arrived at its next stop on the long trek across the grasslands. Tifa sat in the shade of a tree, and beside her Red XIII lounged like a large, complacent house cat, his pale eye peering up at her with curiosity.

"Just remembering my first few days on my own in the slums."

"Ah. Now that's a tale I'd be fascinated to hear."

"You sure you don't wanna enjoy the sights with the others? They look like they're having lots of fun."

She gestured in the direction of their companions. Cloud and

Aerith stood at the edge of a fenced pasture. A bright yellow chocobo had wandered near, and Aerith was chattering excitedly as she reached out to pet it.

"If you are insinuating that you'd prefer to be alone, I shall take my leave. But if you do not mind my presence, I would rather stay."

"All right. Stick around and keep me company, then."

After cutting her story off at those final days in Nibelheim, just prior to Sephiroth's arrival, she'd walked more or less in silence. The events that immediately followed were too difficult to talk about. Not to mention, there were a few things she *couldn't* share.

Still, it was nice to talk, and to let everything out to a patient ear.

"I felt like I'd lost everything," she admitted. "But the one thing I guess I did have was luck. I met a lot of good people. Many of them became very dear. In a way, I kinda miss that part of my life."

Evening was falling when Tifa and Rakesh arrived at an abandoned lot near the Sector 8 Undercity Station. She was learning that the lamps on the underside of the plate were programmed to mimic the cycle of the real sun. Evening in the slums was marked by fading light and lengthening shadows just like anywhere else.

Rakesh waved his arm over the rows and rows of mismatched railcars resting on the dirt lot.

"These cars have all been given a second shot at life," he said. "Every one of them belongs to the Manson Crew. And the first one *you* ought to know about is that blue one over there."

She found the one he was indicating. It appeared to be an old freight car. Every inch of its exterior had been repainted blue, and it was easily large enough to fit three of the wooden trucking containers she'd seen at Container Row.

Rakesh dashed ahead to the the car and slid its massive door open, climbing aboard and beckoning for Tifa to follow. She quickened her pace.

Inside the car, she was struck by a wall of heat and moisture. Sweat immediately began to form at her brow. Accompanying the muggy air was a sweet aroma that quickly had Tifa's stomach rumbling. She realized she hadn't eaten since she left the clinic.

The railcar, she found, contained a large commercial kitchen, in which three women busily worked away. One was tending a large pot on a stove burner. Another was chopping vegetables at a central counter. And the third was furiously kneading a lump of dough on another smaller counter running along one wall.

None of them paid any mind to Rakesh or Tifa.

"We call the one stirring the pot Miss Simmer. Over by the wall is Miss Roller. She's in charge of the dough. And in the center is Miss Chopper. She does the veggies."

"Are those their *real* names?"

"Ha ha! Definitely not. Even I don't know their real names."

In a hushed tone, Rakesh added, "And I'd recommend you not ask, unless they're the ones to bring it up. That goes for the rest of the people you meet in Container Row too. Personal details are kind of a touchy subject."

"Noted. So, um . . . is this where I'm going to be working?"

It didn't look so bad, she decided.

"Not quite. See, they do all the prep work. Everything they make gets carried over to a food cart, which is where you come in. You're in charge of putting on the finishing touches and, most important, selling the product. C'mon. I'll show ya."

They backed out of the railcar, and Rakesh slid the large door shut. The three women in the kitchen hadn't looked up once.

Rakesh approached the adjacent railcar. As he opened its door, he explained, "This one's the office-slash-warehouse. You'll pull the cart out of here in the morning and roll it back in at night. Today's an off day, so the cart's inside. Go ahead and take a look."

Tifa peeked inside. Sure enough, a small wheeled food cart rested at the back of the dim freight car. At its top was a sign that read *Sector 8 Steamed Buns* in big, festive letters.

"Steamed buns?"

"That's right. Yummy, fluffy pockets of white dough loaded up with nutritious veggies and mouthwatering, sweet 'n' spicy minced meat. They're the best in the sector. Maybe in the entire slums."

"Do you really think I'm up for this?"

"If it doesn't work out, no biggie. We'll find you something else. But why not go into it with a positive attitude?"

"Yeah. All right."

"Pops will show you the ropes tomorrow. If anyone knows how to sell steamed buns, it's Pops. He's been doing it for close to forty years."

"Wow . . . This cart's been around that long?"

"It's his own secret recipe." Rakesh smiled. "Oh, and Pops has me in charge of keeping the books. Want a rundown of how the compensation works?"

"Please."

"At the end of the day, we tally up the number of steamed buns sold. Twenty percent of the sales go to you, twenty to Pops, and another thirty is split among the three ladies working the back of the house. The final thirty goes to the Manson Crew. In exchange, they source all of our ingredients for us.

"One bun sells for three gil, so if you move a hundred a day, that's a cool three hundred gil. Out of that, your take home is sixty."

"Sixty gil, huh . . . ?"

It didn't sound too bad, but then again, she was new to the slums and to working life in general. She didn't have any basis for comparison.

"Remember, you're making twice as much as any of those ladies in the kitchen. That's 'cause you're gonna be the one pulling in the customers. How well we do is all up to you."

When they'd finished the tour, Rakesh accompanied her back as far as the alleyway to make sure she knew the way.

Alone in her new room, Tifa quickly set about making a few critical calculations.

"If rent is fifteen gil a day . . . and a shower costs me three . . . and I take all my meals at the cart so I eat for free . . . That leaves me with forty-two gil per day.

"And if I set most of that aside to pay the clinic, I'll be able to settle my debt in about . . ."

She ran the numbers inside her head. When she arrived at a result, her brow furrowed for a moment, and she started over. It was easy to make a mistake with large figures like these; she knew she might not have it right on her first try.

But the second attempt yielded the same result as the first.

"Sixty-six years?!" she blurted. "That *can't* be right."

Tifa proceeded to triple-check her math. The answer did not change.

How was she supposed to endure *sixty-six years* living out of a cramped, dingy shipping container, eating nothing but steamed buns day in and day out?

Tifa spent the night tossing and turning, plagued by worry. When the soft gray at the window signaled dawn was near, she was still wide awake. She stood decisively, grabbed two towels and a change of clothes, and headed out.

Just like the day before, the Waterkeeper was on duty, sitting quietly at her desk. Tifa dropped three gil into the tin can: Rakesh had thoughtfully provided a small advance to cover any immediate expenses.

"I'd like to use the showers, please," she said.

"You're sure you're ready?" rasped the Waterkeeper, her eyes arched to indicate she was asking after Tifa's *mental* preparedness.

"I'll wrap one towel around me and keep it there until I'm done."

"Ain't gonna be anyone else coming by at this hour," the woman replied. "But if your luck don't hold and someone *does* show up, I'll shoo 'em away. Go on. Get to it."

"Thank you. I really appreciate it."

"Gonna cost you another two gil, though. That's the lookout fee."

Tifa's jaw almost dropped. After a brief reflection, she decided it was probably worth the cost. She fished another two gil from her pocket and dropped it into the can.

The woman chuckled. "A young thing like you must have one hell of a story to wind up on the Row. But then again, I s'pose that's true for the lot of us. And if you're gonna live out your life in the dregs of Sector 8, you might as well be able to enjoy a nice, relaxing shower."

Tifa decided she was grateful the woman had offered to play lookout at all. But as she stepped into the shower—which was surprisingly hot—her thoughts weighed heavy.

The dregs of Sector 8. That's my home now.

With some difficulty, Tifa found her way back to the station area and located the abandoned lot, cluttered with decommissioned railcars.

Her partner-to-be stood outside, awaiting her arrival. He was a small, old, pale-looking fellow, but his most notable feature by far was his outfit: a bright red shirt and matching red trousers. Age had left his dark hair peppered with silver, and he wore it cropped close against the scalp.

He scratched at his head with one hand and stared as she approached. Tifa could almost *feel* his eyes as they swept up and down the length of her body.

"Congratulations. You pass. Now let's get a move on."

The man ambled toward the second railcar Rakesh had shown her: the "office-slash-warehouse."

"Call me Pops," the man said. "Your name is Tifa, right? You wanna stick with that, or should I think up a street name for ya?"

Pops abruptly turned, and she felt his eyes again, wandering their way down.

"Lessee . . . A good name for you would be . . ."

His gaze lingered at her chest. It made her want to bring her arms up, as if to cover herself.

Instead, she blurted, "Tifa's fine. Just Tifa, please."

"You sure?" The man's shoulders slumped. "Pity. I coulda come up with somethin' real catchy."

He resumed walking toward the railcar. When he arrived, he threw the sliding door open. The door rumbled noisily along its track.

"Let's get the cart out. Chop, chop."

Despite his phrasing, he remained by the door, apparently not intending to help. Tifa walked past, grabbing hold of the cart where it lay at the back of the railcar. She expected to struggle as she tried to wheel it out. However, the cart was surprisingly light, and she maneuvered it through the doorway with no trouble at all.

"Next we gotta load up the goods. Wheel 'er over to the kitchen. They'll have today's batch ready and waiting."

Apparently, all of this was going to be Tifa's responsibility and hers alone. She pulled the cart alongside the door of the all-blue railcar. Just inside the entrance, she found large containers full of finely-chopped vegetables and other garnishes, as well as rows upon rows of semicircular white hunks of dough. There was also one giant pot full of a thick, tangy ground-meat mixture—the seasoned, slow-cooked concoction that would serve as the heart of the dish. She lifted each container onto the cart, taking particular care with the pot, which was heavy and hot to the touch. Pops made no motion to help load the ingredients either.

Inside, the three kitchen ladies continued to labor away. Tifa offered a cheerful greeting, but they remained silent and kept their eyes on their work.

"Good. You'll get used to this routine real quick," said Pops. "Now, give 'er a pull."

The wooden poles at the front of the cart were fashioned in the shape of an *H*—two parallel bars jutting straight out from the body of the cart, connected with a crossbeam. Tifa ducked under the crossbeam and positioned herself to roll the cart along behind her, bearing the load on her hands and stomach.

It wasn't unfamiliar work. In Nibelheim, Tifa had occasionally transported items around in much the same fashion, using a small handcart. The handcart had always been around, parked in the same corner of the village for as long as she could remember. Once, when she was very small, she'd hopped into the back for a ride around the main square. Had Tyler been the one pulling her along, or was it Lester? She couldn't remember.

Loaded up with the day's offerings, the Sector 8 Steamed Buns cart had grown considerably heavier. Tifa leaned forward, feeling her abs tighten as she pushed. A dull ache began in her chest and slowly spread outward.

"You all right?" Pops said, peering at her face.

He seemed genuinely concerned. Perhaps he was friendlier than his initial impression had led her to believe.

"You're lookin' pale," he remarked. "You get any sleep last night?"

"Not really," admitted Tifa.

"Aw, c'mon, now. We're *countin'* on you! We're supposed to move five hundred of these things today!"

"Five?" chirped Tifa. "Um . . . I don't mean to be rude, but . . . Yesterday, I was told we were aiming for *one* hundred."

"If you're only selling a hundred buns a day, this ain't the line of work for you. The last girl was able to do a thousand, no sweat."

"A *thousand*? In one day?!"

"What else? Look. It's your first time, so we're settin' the bar low. Five hundred."

"A thousand buns in one day . . ." Tifa murmured to herself. It was hard to even visualize that many steamed buns.

On the other hand, if she *could* hit numbers like that, she'd be able to pay off her debt much faster than she'd imagined. Instead of sixty-six years, this whole ordeal could be behind her in less than seven.

Seven years still seemed like a long time, but it no longer felt impossible.

"I can do it," she said. Then, looking at Pops, "Five hundred. A thousand. I'll sell them as fast as we can make them."

Chin up and jaw set, Tifa wheeled off toward the station. Suddenly, the cart was feeling a whole lot lighter.

"Honestly, looking back, I can't believe it got me so fired up. But that tiny glimmer of hope was more than I'd had before."

Tifa glanced at Red XIII, who was still lying in the grass beside her. His face was turned away, but when she watched closely, she saw a faint, stifled trembling from his withers to the base of his tail.

"Are you *laughing* at me?!" she demanded.

"Not at all," replied the beast, but she could hear the quaver in his voice too. "So tell me, did you end up selling a thousand buns?"

"Wouldn't you like to know!"

As Tifa rolled the cart into the area outside the Sector 8 Undercity Station, Pops directed her to set up shop on the end farthest from the platform. Apparently, Sector 8 Steamed Buns had a regular spot—and as far as Tifa could tell, it wasn't exactly a prime one.

Next, Pops explained, she needed to chock the wheels. Tifa complied, noting that he still wasn't lending a hand. He seemed intent on having Tifa experience every step of the process herself.

Then it was time to prepare the workspace. First, she had to pour a little water into the base of a steamer pot and set it to boil. Next, she needed to heap piles of the chopped vegetables and other available garnishes onto several large platters, which were then set out in plain sight for customers to choose from. Finally, the large pot containing the meat needed to be hefted up onto the other stove burner; it was to be kept over low heat at all times so its contents would be piping hot and ready to go.

The water in the steamer began to bubble. Pops had Tifa place the day's first hunks of dough inside to get them started, and then set out a stack of the light brown wax paper that she would use to wrap and serve each finished bun.

"You gotta calculate backward," explained Pops. "Work smart so the first buns are finished steamin' the moment we open. C'mere. That's where you stand."

Pops pointed to a spot right at the center of the workspace; when customers approached the cart, Tifa's face would be the first thing they'd see.

"Check the little drawer for gloves," Pops added. "You're gonna want 'em. Just wait until you pull your first bun out. You'll see."

"Now, get one piece of wax paper flat in your left hand and plop a bun on it. It's gonna be hot. Don't drop it. Hold the bun down with your left thumb, and use the knife in your right to split it. Careful not to cut all the way through. See? Now you've got a pocket for the fillings. The whole thing flaps open and shut like a little mouth. You got it?"

Pops's instructions continued rapid-fire, with no pauses to ask questions or catch up. Tifa fumbled through the motions, a bun in one hand and the knife in the other.

"That's the way. There's your pocket. Now, you gotta stuff a piece of lettuce in first, and then ladle on a scoop of the meat.

Not too much liquid, ya hear? Then the customer's gonna tell ya what kinda garnish he wants. He gets to pick three. Slap those on, pinch the paper shut to close the bun, and hand it over.

"Some customers'll order two or three, but you still gotta make 'em and hand 'em over one at a time. If they're plannin' to take the order home, they'll bring their own bag or box. That's not our responsibility. Just listen to what they order, make it, and hand it over."

He watched Tifa pour her first ladleful of the minced meat.

"Nah, now that's too much liquid, see? You gotta get the proportions right, or else the sauce overpowers the rest and we end up lookin' like a cheap knockoff of our own recipe."

The meat was already on the bun. There wasn't much to be done about that, so Tifa finished out the instructions, adding garnishes and pinching the bun shut.

"Try it," ordered Pops.

She took one bite, and then another. A tangy sweetness spread across her tongue, and the chopped vegetables gave a satisfying crunch between her teeth. She'd never eaten anything like it, and yet the food was somehow familiar and comforting.

"It's delicious," she said.

"Reminds you of home, don't it?"

Tifa's eyes widened. "That's exactly what I was thinking. It really does. I mean, it's the first time I've ever eaten a steamed bun, but . . ."

"It's my ma's secret recipe. Doesn't matter who you are or where you came from, it'll always take ya back to your younger years. If you ask me, it's almost magic."

Pops roared with laughter, and Tifa felt as if she were seeing a whole new side of the man—one she could have never predicted based on their initial encounter.

She'd just finished setting up when the station area came alive with people, many of them eyeing the food carts set up along the fringe. Soon there were droves of them, enough to leave Tifa aghast.

Here was another lesson about life in the slums: eating out was the norm. A general lack of running water at home meant that, for many, cooking wasn't an easy option.

And of the slums' many culinary offerings, those that could be eaten on the go—like Sector 8 Steamed Buns—were a particular favorite in the morning, when everyone was rushing to and fro.

"Here they come!" Pops said with a grin. "Look alive, Tifa!"

She was still gawking when their first customer flicked three coins into the jar.

"C'mon!" said Pops. "Grab a paper! Run your hand over the steam once to get it damp. That way it'll stick right to ya."

Tifa waved her hand over the steamer pot and slapped her hand against the stack of wax paper as instructed. The customer pointed wordlessly at three of the garnishes on display. Bell peppers, nuts, and celery. Tifa reached for a handful of sliced peppers but stopped short.

In her hand, she still only had the square of paper.

Bun first! she instructed herself.

Her hand whipped back to grab one and—

"Ouch!"

Pops was right. Fresh from the steamer, they were scalding hot, even *with* the gloves.

She looked down at her feet, where the dropped bun lay in the dirt.

"Sorry," she said, looking back up at the customer.

The man didn't appear to notice or care. He stared blankly at the large pot where the meat was slowly simmering.

Pops whispered, "Paper, then bun, then knife. Cut it open, pop the lettuce in, ladle the meat, add the garnish. Pinch it shut. Hand it over."

He added, "And for you, let's sneak in one more step. Before you do anything else, take a deep breath."

Tifa gasped. Of course. How could she forget about breathing? About *concentrating*?

She thought back on Zangan's lessons and drew a long, deep breath. She held it for a moment before an equally slow release.

The waiting customer turned his eyes to Tifa, interest piqued by this aberration in the food cart's snappy routine.

"Um! Sorry!" she stammered.

He smiled in return. "Keep at it, kid. You'll get there."

Tifa bobbed her head in thanks, grabbed another bun, and placed it into the other hand with its waiting square of paper.

The battle of her first day had begun.

Sector 8 Steamed Buns stayed open for business from six thirty in the morning to eight at night. Breaks were to be taken at Tifa's discretion when business was slow. However, as Pops explained, there were three rushes when she'd need to be fully alert and working her hardest: two hours in the morning, three for the lunch rush, and another three-hour block leading up to closing.

Her first morning rush was hampered by endless mistakes, but by lunchtime, she felt like she was getting into the swing of things. There was a rhythm to the work. The secret to success was finding it and remembering to breathe—just like Zangan's training. She visualized the flow of her movements: up from her feet, through her legs, across her back, and out of her hands. There was no weakness. No pain. Just a constant stream of motion.

In the end, she managed to make eighty-eight buns during the morning peak and a hundred and twenty at lunchtime. The numbers brought an intense feeling of accomplishment. She'd found the rhythm. Her persistence had paid off.

Between rushes, Tifa swapped out with Pops, tending the buns in the steamer while he handled customers' orders. Pops had set out a folding chair for them to sit and rest on, but Tifa never found an idle moment to make use of it: even in the supporting role, she found she had to be alert and watching, anticipating which passersby were likely to approach so she could have the right number of buns ready to slice and serve. For Pops, timing buns was second nature, handled almost subconsciously as he lounged at her side. But Tifa didn't yet know the signs. She observed and listened as Pops pointed out the telltale marks of likely customers.

At two in the afternoon, Pops thrust a couple of buns in her direction and said, "Here. Lunch. The first two are on the house. You wanna eat more, you gotta pay."

Tifa suddenly realized she was starving. She scarfed down her meal, inhaling big mouthfuls of air with each bite to cool off the steaming hot dough.

There had been a few starts and stops, but she felt like she was getting pretty good at the job. Her muscles were tired, but she was not in pain. Even her tender sternum seemed to be holding up.

It was the third and final rush of the day that laid her limits bare. A few minutes in, Tifa's arms and legs felt as though they'd begun to petrify. It was the sort of fatigue she remembered feeling after running through several of Master Zangan's books in succession, and she found all her will was needed just to remain in motion. For each new customer that stepped up to the cart, time stretched longer yet until the bun was finally handed over and the order complete. Dropped buns littered the ground at her feet. Drips and spills from the ladle had left minced meat splattered all across her workspace.

Finally, when Pops couldn't bear any more, he motioned for them to swap.

"I'm fine," she said. "I can do this."

To which Pops answered, "No. You can't."

He was right, and she knew it. With eyes downcast and a storm of remorse and disappointment swirling in her gut, Tifa relinquished her spot.

"You've got the talent but not the stamina," said Pops, with a hint of disdain. "It's a damn shame too. With your looks, we coulda pulled in more customers than this place has ever seen."

The words stung.

"Go on and get yourself home," he continued. "If you're ready to try again tomorrow, I'll see you in the morning. If not, don't bother comin' back. I can't afford to hold your hand forever."

Not long after Tifa made it back to her shipping container apartment, there was a knock at the door. She opened to find Rakesh.

He explained that he'd stopped by the cart in the evening to see how her first day was going and to offer a few words of encouragement. Pops had filled him in on what happened.

Honestly, all Tifa wanted to do was wrap herself tight in the blanket and bury herself in bed. But given all the support Rakesh and his mother had provided, it didn't feel right to turn him away.

"Holding up all right?" he asked. "Wanna stop by the clinic? Mom would be happy to give you a quick checkup."

"No. I'm not in any pain. I just need some time to sleep this off."

Rakesh raised his hands briefly as he responded, "Your call."

He cleared his throat and then asked, "Think you'll be able to go in again tomorrow? Pops sounded worried."

"I'll be there. It's not like I have much of a choice."

"I'm sorry, Tifa. I really wish we could waive the expense. It's killing Mom too, having to do this to you."

"I'll pay what I owe. I'm not asking to be treated differently from any other patient."

Rakesh smiled. "Thanks. You have no idea how much that means to us."

He reached a hand to one pocket and said, "Hey. Check this out. I brought you something."

It was another of Zangan's manuals. Book Two.

"I've already memorized this one, so you can have it." He placed the booklet on her bed, nodding goodbye before he headed out.

After Rakesh was gone, Tifa murmured, "I've memorized it too, you know."

She stood in the center of the tiny room and began performing the first form described in Book Two, leaving Rakesh's copy unopened on the bed.

Book Two, Paragraph One, Section One.

When she was finished, she moved on to the next form.

Book Two, Paragraph One, Section Two.

And then the next.

Book Two, Paragraph One, Section Three.

Her body followed the movements of its own accord. Everything was going to be okay. She still had the things she'd learned. No matter how much else she lost, Zangan's lessons could never be taken from her.

As always, Zangan's forms helped. They lifted her mood and focused her mind, bringing her back in tune with her body. It became clear *why* the evening rush had overwhelmed her after she'd done so well in the afternoon. Yes, she'd been exhausted. Frankly, she'd been half asleep all day. Small surprise that her body had eventually cried out in protest when she continued to push it.

It was obvious enough now, but throughout the morning and afternoon, she'd been too wound up to notice. Anxiety had masked fatigue, pumping her full of adrenaline on which she managed to get by. But by the time the third rush rolled around, her nervousness had begun to subside.

As the forms calmed her mind, she grew conscious of an unexpected smell in the apartment. After a moment, she traced it to herself: the faint tinge of meat sauce clung to her body and clothes. Suddenly, nothing was more important than a shower and a round of laundry. But to manage the latter, she'd first need to go shopping for another outfit, and before she could do that, she needed more money, and . . .

When Tifa's eyes opened, faint light at the apartment's tiny window signaled a new day. Her concerns of the previous night were still unaddressed, but she felt well rested, and it was early: not yet dawn, judging by her previous experience.

She cautiously stretched her limbs, anxious at the possibility of searing pain at any moment. When her muscles instead relished in the movement, she lifted herself from bed and began to perform a few gentle squats. No problem there either.

On a whim, she decided to lift one knee, holding the first pose that Zangan had demonstrated in the village square all those years ago.

"It'll keep you going strong until the day you die."

She repeated Zangan's words, quickly following up with Zander's quip.

"Still kicking right up until we kick the bucket."

The memory lightened her mood. Today, she told herself, she'd make it to the end of the third rush.

Just like the morning before, the far end of Container Row was quiet and empty, save for the Waterkeeper waiting patiently in her rusty folding chair.

Tifa had plunked three gil into the can and was halfway inside the shower container before she spotted the difference. There were still five stalls, but one on a far end was now concealed behind a large blue curtain. Bold yellow letters were painted on the fabric: *LADIES*.

Wide-eyed, Tifa leaned back out of the container to glance at the Waterkeeper. The old woman was grinning from ear to ear.

"Four gil for the special shower."

"Is . . . Is this for *me*?!"

The woman waved the question off.

"Four gil," she repeated. "And if, say, you wanna shower twice a day—once in the morning and once at night—I'll cut you a deal. Only five gil per day, paid up front each morning."

It sounded almost too good to be true.

Mentally, Tifa noted the implication about the Waterkeeper's authority: apparently, the price to use the showers was whatever the woman decided.

"All right," agreed Tifa. "I'll be right back with the other two gil."

"By the time you get back, the whole Row's gonna be awake and heading to the showers," said the woman. "Go on. Get in there and freshen up. Consider it an introductory discount. One day only."

The second day of work flew by. Tifa made it all the way to closing time, and when the dust had settled and the day's sales were tallied, she'd sold nearly four hundred steamed buns.

It was a start, but not a triumph. Not yet. Pops appeared to concur, judging by his expression as he finished the tally. The last girl could sell a thousand a day. That's what he'd said.

Even so, Pops gave Tifa a cursory nod for finishing out the day.

"It all hinges on the rushes," he counseled. "Morning, afternoon, and evening. Three peaks per day. That's a total of 480 minutes in which we gotta do the bulk of our business.

"Now, 480 minutes works out to 28,800 seconds. You sold just shy of four hundred buns today, which means each one took you seventy-two seconds on average to make. That's over a minute per bun. Tell me, how fast are you gonna have to go if you wanna break a thousand?"

Tifa panicked for an instant, but then she saw that the calculation was quite straightforward.

"One bun every 28.8 seconds."

"Bingo. Now, we'll still sell the odd bun or two outside of peak hours, so let's round it off. Say, thirty seconds each."

"Two buns every minute?"

It was more than double her current speed. Was that even possible?

"Here's some advice. When I see you workin', I see a country girl movin' at a country pace. But you live in the city now. You gotta adapt to the city's tempo. Don't think; just *do*."

Pops looked her up and down and added, "Figure that out, and you'll go far. If I was a bettin' man, I might even say you've got fifteen hundred a day in you."

Tifa fumbled with the numbers in mind. In order to hit fifteen hundred buns a day, she'd have to make one bun every *twenty* seconds. Three buns a minute might be a feat possible to accomplish once or twice, but Tifa seriously doubted it was a pace she could maintain for hours on end.

When she expressed her misgivings, Pops scrunched up his face.

"The faster you get, the more customers we're gonna have *outside* of the rush too. Think about it. When a guy's walkin' by, lookin' for a bite, how do you think he makes up his mind? What's the deciding factor?

"Besides us, there are six other carts in front of the station. You've got our Sector 8 Steamed Buns, sweet 'n' spicy and guaranteed to have you thinkin' of home. But then there's the lighter, easy-on-the-spices Sector 5 Steamed Buns and the perk-you-up Sector 6 Skewers. Then you got them fancy-pants Slum Sandwich guys; the Veggie Soup shack for the health-conscious crowd; the thick, savory Rice Porridge boys for the heavy eaters; and, last but not least, the new cart on the block, the Spicy Noodle joint.

"Now, sure, folks have their likes and dislikes. But the number-one thing they're lookin' for is *speed*. Most of 'em will settle for whatever, just as long as the cart's got a line and it's movin' fast. Can't have no line at all—that's a whole other problem. The cart that wins is the one that pulls customers in twos and threes and keeps churnin' through 'em."

The explanation poured out of Pops in a hushed, excited tone, as if he were divulging the deepest secrets of the trade. Tifa couldn't help but lean in close, eyes wide and head nodding.

"Problem is," Pops announced, abruptly leaning back, "every cart here knows it, and we're all playin' to win. So we turn to one last trick to pull ahead of the pack. Sex appeal. You get a cute girl servin' up the food, and doin' it fast, and that's just enough to tip things in your favor. *Now* do you see why I picked ya?"

"You chose me for the job because you think I'm *attractive*?" Tifa hesitated. "I'm . . . I'm not sure that's . . ."

"No need to be modest. Between that sweet little face and that youthful quality you got about ya . . . C'mon. You know what I'm talkin' about. You're all grown up, and at the same time . . ."

Pops flicked his eyes from Tifa's feet to the top of her head.

"Anyway, maybe you're flattered, or maybe you think I'm a pig. Frankly, I don't care. Woman or man, when the name of the game is sales, looks are key. You're walking proof. I've never seen anyone make steamed buns so slow and *still* keep the customers flocking in."

Pops looked Tifa in the eye. "So if you can learn to work fast, I ain't jokin' when I say we could hit fifteen hundred a day."

"In the end, he had me on board. I mean, I'll admit I was a little repulsed at first. I didn't like the idea that people were coming to the cart because of how I looked. But at the same time, there was a satisfaction—almost an enjoyment—in seeing my numbers get better by the day.

"I'd try out little variations, shaving off a second here and a second there. I arranged the garnishes differently so I could reach the popular ones just a bit easier and practiced with the knife so I could cut faster. Like I say, it really reminded me of the Calisthenics Club and Zangan's training routines. I think I just enjoy that kind of stuff. It's easy for me to get wrapped up in a new challenge, setting new personal bests until my execution's flawless.

"I was starting to come around on Pops too. He wasn't one to mince words, but he didn't strike me as a bad person. As far as he was concerned, if you were good at your job, that was all that mattered. You always knew exactly where you stood with him."

Red XIII let out a deep, breathy rumble, somewhere between a house cat's purr and a lion's chuff.

"Your story is making me hungry," he announced. "I'd have liked to try one of those steamed buns."

"They were amazing! Although, to be honest, I never found out what kind of meat Pops was using to make them. I was kind of afraid to ask."

"Perhaps I'm not so hungry after all."

Tifa shrugged her shoulders.

"So," continued Red XIII, "did your efforts pan out? Break any records?"

"I did! About four months into the job—I remember, because it was just before my sixteenth birthday—I sold one thousand and *three*. That was a pretty good feeling."

"I imagine it was."

"And then my birthday arrived, and it was the first time in my life I didn't have anyone around to celebrate with. That left me feeling pretty down.

"But," Tifa continued, "things were about to get better. I didn't know it yet, but I was about to make my first real friend in Midgar."

It was Wednesday, the week following Tifa's sixteenth birthday. Wednesdays were her off days—the only day of the week that Sector 8 Steamed Buns wasn't open. Tifa had stopped by Dhamini's clinic for her monthly checkup.

It was a familiar routine. First, Dhamini would ask a few basic questions about how Tifa was feeling. Next, she'd palpate the grafts to see how they were healing. Last came the photographs.

As Dhamini had explained, the techniques used in Tifa's treatment were new and exciting. The medical community was eager for case studies, particularly ones with photos demonstrating the healing process over time.

But no matter how often Dhamini reassured Tifa that her face would always be out of frame, the idea that countless unknown doctors and researchers would be seeing photos of her bare chest was terribly unsettling.

"This discoloration—these black-and-blue patches," Dhamini said, pointing to several spots on Tifa's chest, "will fade over time. In fact, compared to the day you checked out of the clinic, they've already started to blend in with the rest of your skin quite well. I bet you've noticed."

Tifa had to agree that the grafts were starting to look much better.

"But," continued Dhamini, lips suddenly pursed, "this spot over here isn't looking so great."

She slid a finger across a portion of Tifa's solar plexus.

"If it doesn't take, you might end up needing another minor graft."

The doctor furrowed her brow and continued. "I wonder if it's because of that wire buried underneath . . . You know, the one they put in at Corel to help reinforce your sternum."

"I see . . ." replied Tifa.

"No need to rush into a decision right now. Let's just continue to keep an eye on—"

A loud yell cut Dhamini short.

"In all my years . . . !"

Tifa could tell it had come from the other side of the clinic. All the same, she scrambled to pull her top back on. Dhamini, for her part, calmly thanked Tifa for coming in, apparently unsurprised by the outburst from this other, unseen patient.

Tifa was on her way out of the examination room when Rakesh called out, "Tifa! Perfect timing! Think you could give me a hand?"

"What's the trouble?"

"We've got another patient in the back. Truth is, she's in need of a procedure a lot like yours, but she's absolutely refusing to go through with it. Think you could talk with her for a second? I just wanna show her it's not as scary as it seems. It might help her out, seeing someone who's been through the same thing."

Tifa hesitated. "I'm not sure I'd be very convincing . . ."

"You'll be great. I know you will." Rakesh smiled. "Oh! Just be sure not to mention *how* you got your injury. I'm told the lady likes to gossip. One of those people who seems to know everybody else. Probably best not to mention your new job either."

"Why can't I talk about my job?"

Rakesh hesitated. "Umm . . . Well, she's from Sector 7, see? The fewer people there are that recognize you, the better. Especially when it comes to people outside our sector. Easier to keep a low profile that way."

Rakesh's smile returned, and he motioned for Tifa to follow. "C'mon!"

His explanation had seemed a little forced, and Tifa still didn't know exactly what she was getting into, but she went along nonetheless.

Inside the back room, on the same bed Tifa had occupied half a year earlier, an elderly-looking woman was facedown in a hospital gown. The gown was partially open, and strips of bloodstained gauze ran across the woman's back, suggesting several long, narrow wounds.

Dhamini stood at the bedside, her usual cheerful demeanor nowhere to be found. When her eyes caught sight of Tifa, they all but begged for help.

"Tifa," Rakesh began calmly, "I'd like you to meet Marle. She had an unfortunate run-in with a monster and has some pretty nasty scratches to show for it. My mom is trying to recommend a skin graft, but—"

"Oh, just sew me up and get me out of here already!" groused the woman on the bed. "I don't need you trying out your newfangled treatments on me."

She glared at Tifa, eyes like daggers.

Dhamini cleared her throat. "Marle, I know it sounds frightening, but in the long run, you're going to be much happier with the graft. Given about five years to blend in, you won't be able to tell you were ever wounded."

The doctor motioned toward Tifa and added, "This young lady is another one of my patients. She had the same operation about six months ago, and you'd be amazed at what a difference it's made. Take a look at these photos."

Tifa swallowed.

In Dhamini's hands were several printed photographs. Photos of Tifa's chest.

"What are you showing me that for?! Get it out of my face! It's *indecent*!"

Dhamini returned the photos to a manila folder with a pained smile.

"Tell her what it was like, Tifa," said Rakesh. "It only hurt at first, right?"

"That's true. It wasn't so bad after a while."

Rakesh continued to prod. "And what about now? Any itchiness or discomfort?"

"No. None at all."

Tifa's right hand slid over to her left wrist, where it gripped the leather cord tight. She was trying very hard to remain pleasant.

"Enough," said Marle. "I don't need the sales pitch. How about you and your mother give me a moment with Tifa so she can tell it to me straight?"

Dhamini and Rakesh exchanged a glance. After a moment of clear hesitation, Dhamini nodded.

"All right," the doctor said with a pointed look at Tifa. "But I'd ask you to limit your conversation to details of the treatment itself. The clinic has certain standards of patient confidentiality to think about."

Doctor and son shuffled out of the room, and Tifa was left alone with the stranger.

"Flashing around photos of a woman's chest!" spat Marle. "Who do those two think they are?!"

She glanced back at Tifa, and in a much gentler tone continued. "Sorry about that, dear. Just an old woman's grouchings. I don't mean to make this any more embarrassing for you than it already is."

"It's fine. Really."

In truth, Tifa was elated to know someone else understood how she felt. "I guess I'm still kind of processing it all . . ."

"So what happened to you, anyway?" Marle asked, raising a brow. "Monster attack?"

"Um . . . That . . . probably falls under Dr. Oranye's standards of confidentiality."

"All right. Then tell me using a *confidential* voice."

Marle grinned. It was mischievous, sweet, and disarming all at once.

"It was a sword," whispered Tifa. "One in the hands of a very bad person. But I'd better not say any more. If his . . . *associates* found out I'd talked, I could get into a lot of trouble."

It wasn't a half bad answer, she decided. Sufficiently vague, but specific enough to ward off any digging.

"Bless my soul," replied Marle. "So you're on the run, are you? Sorry to hear it. I take it that means you didn't grow up in the slums."

"Not even in the city."

"Any family?"

"None."

"You poor, poor thing. How old are you?"

"Sixteen."

"How are you getting by? Working the Wall Market?"

Wall Market. Tifa didn't know much about the place, but she'd heard the name often enough. It was how other residents of the slums tended to refer to Sector 6. The neighborhood seemed to have a seedy reputation.

"No! Nothing like that!" she exclaimed.

"I see you've heard of the place. Here's some advice. A pretty girl like you could make a killing in Sector 6. But make no mistake. Whatever shop you're working for, they're making twenty times more than what goes in your pocket. Wall Market sucks you dry and throws you out.

"If you go in there knowing that, that's one thing. But don't let anyone try to tell you the Wall Market's something it's not."

"Thank you. I'll be okay. I know it's not for me."

"Maybe not. But if you don't learn to stand up for yourself, someone else may convince you otherwise."

"I know how to stand up for myself."

"Oh, I doubt that. You're the kind of girl who doesn't like to make waves. The teeniest bit of pressure, and you'll fold like a cheap suitcase."

As much as she hated to admit it, she realized Marle was right.

"I can tell," continued the woman, "because I'm the kind who likes to put the pressure on. Be glad I'm one of the good guys."

Marle grinned and began to roll onto her side, only to cry out in sudden pain.

"Are you all right?!" exclaimed Tifa.

"I suppose that's what I deserve for telling a fib."

There was a knock, but Rakesh didn't wait for a response. He opened the door, obviously glad for the excuse to step back in.

"Are you in pain?" he asked Marle.

"What do you think?" Marle grimaced. "Get on with the surgery already. I'll take whatever fancy treatment it is you used on Tifa."

"You're sure?"

"No, I'm not. So you'd better hurry before I change my mind. Oh, and Tifa? Come by and see me, would you? Nobody I know is gonna make the trek over to Sector 8 just to watch me lie in a hospital bed, so I could use the company."

Roughly three months had passed. It was another Wednesday, and Tifa was at the clinic visiting Marle.

All attempts to dig into Tifa's past ceased after that initial encounter. Their conversations instead focused on Marle's past and on the ins and outs of life under the plate. The woman had taken Tifa under her wing, intent on tutoring her in the ways of the slums from her hospital bed lectern.

Tifa learned that Marle had once managed a number of apartment buildings in Sector 7, which she'd been forced to give up when Shinra forcibly rezoned the land underneath. A search for new property to manage took her near the perimeter wall, which was where she ran into the monster that tore up her back.

"I think it was fate's way of saying I shouldn't stray too far from the heart of town. A personality like mine's meant to stay right in the thick of things."

That was the sort of headstrong confidence typical of Marle. She liked to talk of adventures she'd had around the slums as a girl of fifteen, and of her glamour days working in Wall Market.

Tifa also learned that she was a prominent figure in the Sector 7 neighborhood watch.

More than anything else, she was grateful for Marle's compassion. The woman seemed compelled to console the lonely girl driven from her hometown and left desperate for affection. She certainly didn't seem like the devious gossip Rakesh and Dhamini made her out to be.

At the end of every visit, as Tifa prepared to leave the clinic, Marle would ask the same question.

"Made any friends yet?"

And Tifa would always give the same vague reply.

"I think so."

She was careful never to imply that the new friend in question was right there before her eyes.

But their friendship came to an abrupt and disappointing end with Marle's discharge from the clinic. Tifa arrived at one of her scheduled checkups only to be told by Rakesh that the bed in the back room had been freed up a few days earlier.

"She was looking good and seemed ready to go home ahead of schedule," he explained. "Told us to give you her regards the next time you stopped by."

And that was it.

Tifa found herself back in an endless cycle of work, with nothing in particular to look forward to on her days off. Thursday through Tuesday, she manned the cart from morning till night. By the time the cart was emptied out, wiped down, and rolled back aboard its derelict railcar, it was usually eight thirty.

On her way home, Tifa typically stopped by the general store or another roadside cart, procuring something inexpensive for dinner—anything for a break from the monotony of steamed buns. Back at the container apartment, she ate and then ran through as many of Zangan's forms as she could complete without a sparring partner. Then it was time to hit the showers.

After that, there was nothing to do but wait for the cycle to begin again. Tifa lay in bed, basking in the pleasant exhaustion of a rigorous workout, but sleep's arrival was inevitably frustrated by fragmented thoughts that forced their way into mind. On better days, she'd imagine Nibelheim as it used to be, before the mountain was plagued with monsters. It left her feeling terribly alone, but it also seemed another, equally important sort of exercise. She *had* to remember. It was her duty not to forget the sights and sounds of the village, and the happy days she'd spent there, and the smiling faces of her friends and neighbors. The memories of that terrible, meaningless loss, and the anger that accompanied it, needed to be kept fresh.

But why? To what end? Thoughts of the future left her feeling bleak and depressed. How many years until she was free of the shackles of debt?

"When Marle checked out and our visits came to an end, I took it pretty hard. It felt like there was nothing left in my life. Just day after day of selling steamed buns with a big fake smile. Instead of going out to have fun, I'd spend my Wednesday evenings alone and in a daze. Whenever payday rolled around, I'd set aside part of my earnings and take it to the clinic.

"I mean, I could see that I was chipping away at the debt. At a thousand buns a day, I had enough to pay back about fourteen thousand gil each month. And by that point, breaking a thousand buns wasn't even a big deal anymore. Between that and the decision to keep my living expenses modest, I was actually managing to save up a bit of money."

Tifa smiled for a moment, leaning close to Red XIII to whisper about the purse she used to keep in the storage bin under her bed. From the very first day she was paid, she'd made a point of always setting aside a small portion to stash away.

"The routine was wearing on me, though," Tifa admitted. "Sometimes I'd let a complaint slip while working the cart. Pops would just laugh. He'd tell me we were nothing more than a couple of cogs in the unstoppable machine of Midgar, and that we had to keep turning whether we liked it or not. But I could never laugh it off the way he did."

Red XIII growled in apparent empathy.

"It got better, though," continued Tifa. "Wait till you hear about my seventeenth birthday."

The lunch rush was over, and Pops had just swapped with Tifa so she could get some downtime. She was arranging a few extra buns in the steamer when she noticed a new customer draw near.

"I'll take twenty-two of your finest Sector 8 Steamed Buns, please. Top 'em with whatever you recommend."

"Twenty-two?!"

Pops's voice shot up a full octave. If Tifa hadn't been just as stunned, she might have laughed; she hardly ever saw Pops lose his cool.

She glanced at the customer. He was a young man with a round, open face and a thick torso padded with fat and muscle. If she had to guess, he was probably the same age as she was.

"You heard right!" said the customer with a wide grin. "The order's to share."

He pointed in the direction of the tracks, where a man and a woman leaned against the chain-link fence, absorbed in their own conversation. Their faces struck Tifa as particularly memorable; they seemed very Midgar-esque. Both appeared to be slightly older than their roly-poly companion.

"One for each of them," explained the customer, "and twenty for me."

He seemed very proud of this fact, and Tifa couldn't help but giggle. His eyes met hers, and he raised a hand to flash a confident thumbs-up. Tifa responded with a smile and a quiet nod. She edged over to Pops, intending to help with the massive order.

"Oh, and if you could put them in here, that'd be swell."

The customer held up a large wicker basket, steadying it against his chest, or maybe resting it on his stomach. Tifa wasn't sure. He waggled the basket from side to side.

"I hear you guys make a mean steamed bun," he said. "Melts-in-your-mouth goodness. I figured I had to try it for myself."

"Much appreciated," said Pops. It was his perfunctory response for every compliment.

"I'd also heard you've got a real cutie working here," continued the customer. "Frankly, the rumors don't do her justice."

"Thank you," replied Tifa with a practiced smile. But it quickly broke into another genuine giggle; the customer had turned his attention to the pot of meat sauce and was leaning in, nostrils flared to take in the sweet aroma.

"Say, what kind of meat is that?"

Pops began to answer. "This? It's—"

But the customer inexplicably shushed him.

"Wait! Wait! Don't tell me! I bet I can guess!"

"Sure. Take a shot."

Now even Pops was smiling. Tifa began slicing steamed buns and filling them as usual, fighting down unbridled laughter. As she finished the first, she placed it carefully into the provided container.

The customer immediately buried his face in the basket, loudly sniffing away. When his head popped back up, he looked like he was in heaven. Tifa found herself strangely flattered.

It wasn't uncommon for customers to leave the garnishes up to Pops and Tifa. Pops had always instructed her to respond by using whichever veggies were selling slower than usual. But for this particular customer, Tifa was determined to serve the best steamed buns she could make, complete with her favorite combinations of toppings—even if it meant risking a scolding later.

Surprisingly, when she glanced at Pops's hands, she found him doing the same. His fingers zipped back and forth in a lively, intricate dance, plucking generous helpings of each garnish from the display platters.

The customer stood mesmerized by the sight.

Tifa watched carefully, waiting for the precise moment that Pops finished off a bun to dart her own fingers in, mimicking his practiced movements as best she could. They went on like that, perfectly synchronized, one person grabbing the next bun and spooning on the meat while the other added the garnishes, until it began to strike Tifa as less a dance and more akin to one of Zangan's combat training forms.

Strike. Evade. Strike. Evade.

The comparison elicited another laugh that she couldn't quite suppress; Tifa snorted, then stole an embarrassed glance at the customer, who she found grinning and bobbing his head to the rhythm of their movements.

Work at the cart had never felt so fun. The minutes flew by, and before Tifa knew it, she and Pops had already finished the twenty-second bun and piled it atop the others in the wicker basket. The customer took another whiff of the sweet aroma wafting up from the container held to his chest, then happily bounded off in the direction of his friends. He stopped before he reached the pair and, apparently unable to wait a moment longer, pulled one steamed bun from the basket and took a great big chomp. His round chin worked up and down in exaggerated motions, and after he'd thoroughly chewed and swallowed his first massive bite, he turned to look at Tifa and offered another energetic thumbs-up.

Tifa unconsciously returned the gesture, and then, to her even greater surprise, she saw Pops doing the same.

"That right there is a good customer," said Pops. "Gotta take extra-special care of the ones like him."

"Something tells me he'll be spreading the word about Sector 8 Steamed Buns."

"That too," replied Pops. "But I'm talking about the experience. Patrons like him . . . How do I put it? They remind me why I got into this business. There's a simple joy in bringin' a smile to a customer's face."

The portly customer had now reached the fence, and he and his two friends were happily munching away. When the other man—the one who looked to be the oldest—finished his bun, he reached toward the basket for another, only to have the basket's owner grab his arm and frantically wrestle him away. Meanwhile, the woman snuck a second bun of her own, turned her back to the others, and surreptitiously scarfed it down.

Tifa had to agree with Pops. The sight of the three rekindled warm, happy feelings she'd almost forgotten she possessed.

"Anyhow . . . No time to stand around," said Pops. "Those buns aren't gonna steam themselves."

The reality of the transaction sank in. They'd gone through twenty-two buns in a matter of minutes. Tifa would need to get more cooking right away if they were to have any ready for the next customer.

"Yes, sir!" she replied.

As she turned her attention back to the steamer, a drop of liquid rolled down her cheek. It took a moment to realize it was a tear and not a bead of sweat. Tifa wiped it away with the back of her hand, blinked, and murmured to herself.

"That's weird . . ."

There was another emotion lurking in her chest. She realized she was jealous of the three by the fence for the deep friendship they obviously shared. Their simple interaction had shown her just how lonely she really was.

Several days later, Tifa was heading home from work. Traversing the slums after dark was as unnerving as ever. She walked with her muscles tensed, wary of every sound and movement.

"Hey!" called a voice at her back. "Hey, you!"

Tifa whirled around, shoulders hunched defensively.

What she found was a very pretty young woman with a slender face and sharp nose.

"I knew it was you!" exclaimed the woman. "You work for Sector 8 Steamed Buns, right?"

Recognition finally dawned. It was the woman who had been leaning against the fence—one of the three friends who had "shared" the massive twenty-two bun order.

The trio had been by the cart a few times since, sometimes together and sometimes not. Tifa would smile and exchange a few words, but that had been the extent of their interactions following the spectacle of the first encounter.

"Oh. Hello," replied Tifa.

"My name's Jessie," said the woman. "Jessie Rasberry."

As the woman introduced herself, she placed a hand on one hip, cocked out confidently to the side.

"Nice to meet you. I'm Tifa Lockhart."

"Oh my gosh! Your name is as adorable as you are! Tell me, how old are you? Seventeen or so?"

"Sixteen."

"Aha! Well, it's nice to finally get to speak to you outside of work."

"Yeah. I guess so."

"Um . . . Is it just me, or am I getting some serious please-leave-me-alone vibes?"

"No! Not at all! I just . . . Well . . . Actually, yeah, you're probably right."

Truth be told, the thought of having a conversation with Jessie had her over the moon. Everything about the woman was so cool. So confident. But Tifa had no idea what to say to her, or how to say it.

A touch of worry crossed Jessie's face. "Sorry. I didn't mean to make you uncomfortable. I'll let you get on your way. See you at the cart?"

Tifa nodded and mumured an apology. She turned away, resuming the trek back to Container Row. After a few moments, she glanced back over her shoulder. Jessie was standing in the road, watching her go. When she saw Tifa glance at her, she smiled and gave a tiny wave. Tifa bobbed her head slightly in response and continued on.

She was very nearly at the alley turnoff when she spotted a suspicious character coming down the street. There was no mistaking the attire or the attitude. The man wore a button-down shirt with a loud pattern, and his shoulders swung from side to side with every step.

He was a tout.

Marle had warned Tifa to avoid the type, and Tifa had once seen Rakesh jokingly mimic the distinctive swagger—an imitation she now knew to be incredibly accurate.

Even Pops had advised her to stay away. Apparently, he'd once been a tout himself, years and years ago. He told Tifa that if anyone ever bothered her to simply say she was under Manson's protection, and they'd back right off. In the rare event that those magic words *didn't* scare someone away, she was to run like hell.

Tifa veered to the edge of the street and attempted to ignore the man. The tout, however, had clearly noticed her. He cut across the street, making a beeline for Tifa.

"Hey, baby," he began. "Ever thought about putting those looks of yours to work? It's easy money. All you gotta do is sit and look beautiful."

"No, thanks. Not interested."

She tried to slip past, but he was quicker on his feet than she expected.

"Whatcha lookin' at the ground for? C'mon. Lemme see that gorgeous face of yours."

The man reached for Tifa's chin. She quickly leaned back, and the fingers passed through empty air.

She was still reviewing Zangan's forms every night, without

fail. The tout didn't look particularly tough, and she estimated she'd regained more than enough muscle to take him. With each passing second, she saw another easy opening for a punch or a kick.

But she recalled Pops's warning. Touts didn't take no for an answer. They'd keep coming back until they got what they wanted. Better to minimize the interaction.

Try not to leave a lasting impression, he'd said. *And if all else fails, remember the magic words.*

An abrupt shout cut her deliberations short.

"Hey! What do you think you're doing?!"

Tifa hardly had time to turn—and the tout barely had time to react—before Jessie came barreling in, leaping up at the last moment, leg extended to connect with the man's cheek.

He yelped and hit the dirt with a thud.

Jessie was back on her feet in a flash, shouting "C'mon!" as she grabbed Tifa's hand and dragged her down the nearest alley. They didn't slow until they'd turned several corners and were deep in the tangled web of Sector 8's backstreets.

Finally, when there were no sounds of pursuit, Jessie stopped and released her grip. Between heavy breaths, she said, "All right. Let's get you home. Where do you live?"

Tifa had no clue where they were or how to get back. She fumbled to describe the general store on the main street and the alley she always turned down to get home.

"You mean . . . you live on Container Row?" asked Jessie.

"Yes. That's the place."

"Wow. I wasn't expecting that. But don't worry. I can still take you."

She didn't wait for Tifa to respond. Jessie trotted off down another alley, and Tifa hurried to follow.

As they walked, Jessie confirmed that the guy she'd knocked over was indeed a tout. To be precise, he was connected to Don Corneo. And Don Corneo, Jessie explained, was the guy who controlled the Wall Market.

"I dunno if I'd call him one of Corneo's goons, though," laughed Jessie. "That'd be a little too generous. He's about as low in the pecking order as you can get."

Still, his job was to find girls to work in Corneo's clubs. He lacked muscle, but he was plenty persistent.

"The reason I'm telling you all this is to warn you," said Jessie. "Wall Market? Steer clear. Anything connected to Corneo is a definite no-go. You got that?"

"Okay."

"Not to go all mommy hen on you or anything. I'm guessing you've at least heard of Sector 6."

"Just a little. Everyone says to stay far away."

"For good reason too."

"Hey, um, Jessie . . . ? Are you . . . Do you study some kind of martial art or something?"

"You mean the jump kick? Not too shabby, huh? Used to be part of my repertoire for action scenes. That was the first time I've actually managed to get my heel to connect."

Jessie's grin widened as she said, "Truth is, I'm an actress."

"Like a *movie star*?!"

"Well, currently I'm on a little bit of a hiatus."

"It all makes sense . . ."

"What, are you saying I'm so extraordinarily beautiful that showbiz is the only line of work I could be in?"

"Yeah."

"Well, look at you, with all the big compliments! You better cut that out before you make me blush!"

Jessie squealed with delight. Her laughter was so infectious, Tifa began to giggle too.

"Anyway, is this starting to look familiar?" Jessie asked. "We should be pretty close by now."

Sure enough, the next alley onto which they emerged was the one that led to Container Row. Somehow, all the twists and turns had brought them back.

Tifa hurried past Jessie, exclaiming, "Thanks for the help! I can make it from here!"

"No problem. But, um, I'd be happy to see you all the way home. It can't be that far, right?"

"Oh, uh . . ."

In truth, Tifa wasn't sure she wanted Jessie—or *anyone*, really—to witness her living arrangements. She was in her second year of slum life; she'd had plenty of time to grow aware of just how bad she had it. For a while, she'd even toyed with the idea of moving, abandoning the option only when she realized it would mean that much longer before her debt was paid off.

"C'mon!" exclaimed Jessie. She pushed ahead of Tifa once more, leading the way down the alley.

Soon they'd reached the checkpoint, where the Watchman sat on his stool. When he saw Tifa, he mumbled a greeting and shifted to one side to allow them to pass.

"Wow. You've got a security guard and everything . . ."

And then the moment Tifa feared had finally arrived: they were standing at the door to her container.

"Well . . . this is me," she said sheepishly.

She undid the padlock and lifted the latch.

"Ooh! How retro!"

Jessie's comments held no trace of derision, but even so, they had Tifa sinking deeper and deeper into embarrassment.

"Mind if I take a peek inside?" her new acquaintance asked. "I mean, if it's not too forward. I'm dying to see what you've done with the interior."

"All right."

Jessie darted through the open doorway, filled with glee. Tifa followed and reached for the cord to turn on the light. The apartment was more or less the same austere setup as the day she moved in; if there was any change to speak of, it was the smattering of new clothing she'd acquired, all out on hangers in plain sight.

"Um . . . When did you move in? Yesterday?"

"A year or two ago. I'm planning to move again someday, but I figure this is good enough for now."

"And you're all by yourself? No mom or dad in the picture?"

"My parents aren't around anymore."

"Oh. Sorry . . ."

Jessie's gaze wandered over the contents of the apartment.

"Huh. I take it the shower and restroom must be outside," she mumbled to herself. "Guess it makes sense. Containers aren't exactly built with plumbing in mind."

She turned back to Tifa and asked, "How much does this place run you?"

"Fifteen gil per day. I like to shower a couple times a day, so that adds another five. In total, it works out to six hundred gil. Oh, but I don't have to pay more when there's an extra day in the month. Just a flat six hundred per month."

Jessie furrowed her brow, hesitating before she finally asked, "Is there something in particular that's keeping you here?"

When Tifa decided to open up, it wasn't because she wanted help. She just wanted someone to listen. Just that alone would make all her hard work bearable. And for whatever reason, Jessie seemed like a person she could trust.

"I'm working off a debt," she confessed.

"Ah . . . " Jessie nodded, as if everything had fallen into place. "Got a long way to go?"

"Four years, give or take."

"Wh—?!"

Jessie flumped down on the bed in shock. It took her a moment to recover, but once she did, she looked up at Tifa and patted the spot beside her.

"Come have a seat. Tell ol' Jessie all about it."

Tifa obliged. She took a deep breath, formulating her thoughts, and began with the climax: the tale of a certain SOLDIER, name left unsaid, who'd gone psychotic and set her hometown aflame. From there, she kept going right up to the present day, allowing her emotions to rage like wildfire as she jumped from one event to the next.

As she spoke, she felt pangs of regret. What was she doing with her life? How had she allowed the past year and a half to slip by? She was focusing on her debt, treating it as some sort of refuge, when in reality she should have been tracking down every scrap of information on Nibelheim she could, to bring herself closer to the truth.

By the end, tears were streaming down Tifa's cheeks.

Jessie's words were gentle. "Wow . . . You've been through so much . . ." She smiled and patted Tifa on the back, adding, "I think we can definitively say that Tifa Lockhart is the hardest-working person anywhere in the slums."

The praise felt warm. Tifa sniffed and reached a hand to wipe away her tears.

"It doesn't sound to me like you've been avoiding your past," continued Jessie. "If anything, you've been doing exactly what you should to keep yourself safe.

"I kinda pride myself on staying abreast of Shinra's atrocities, and I haven't heard *anything* about Nibelheim. That says to me that the company's not just keeping quiet; they're actively covering the incident up. Which means if you don't step carefully, you could be vanished in the middle of the night or worse. Promise me you won't start digging without talking to me first, okay?"

Tifa hesitated before nodding.

"I'm not saying you should give this up. We just have to play the long game. You deserve justice, and your dad deserves revenge so he can rest in peace."

Justice. Revenge. It was a step beyond uncovering the truth and more than Tifa had dared hope, but once Jessie brought the notion up, she couldn't get it out of her head. Tifa's right hand anxiously tugged at the cord on her left.

"Why are you being so nice to me?" she asked.

"Call it a motherly instinct. Or don't. That'd be embarrassing. I just hate to see a person in need.

"And if I could help you with the debt, believe me, I would. I'm not exactly rolling in cash, though."

Jessie reached an arm around Tifa and pulled her close. Tifa sagged against Jessie's shoulder, exhausted now that the story was out.

"Where one fails, many prevail," counseled Jessie. "Together, we can take on the world."

Thus began a time of happiness and growth. Tifa would spend one or two nights a week with Jessie. At times, Biggs and Wedge were there too—those were the names of the two friends who also visited the cart. Wedge was the one with the big appetite.

Tifa's circle of acquaintances grew, as did her knowledge of the slums. Jessie introduced her to several restaurants that were safe to eat at even after dark.

Her wardrobe began to flourish too. Jessie brought by items she thought might look good on Tifa, and she shared tips and tricks from the world of show business: how an actress should carry and project herself onstage. The effects were dramatic. Even Tifa could see how much more confident she appeared. Biggs in particular was in awe; he admitted that when they first spotted Tifa at Sector 8 Steamed Buns, she'd reminded them of a small, frightened animal.

It was Tifa's seventeenth birthday. She'd just finished wheeling the cart back into its railcar and was handing the day's earnings to Rakesh. Pops sauntered off into the night, whistling to himself, just like he did at the end of every workday.

She was about to follow when Rakesh stopped her.

"Hey, Tifa?"

Something was obviously bothering him, and she found herself unconsciously on guard.

"I dunno how to say this, but . . . it's your new friends. Word is, they run with a real sketchy crowd."

"You mean the neighborhood watch?" Tifa's response came sharper than she intended.

"For them, the watch is just a cover. They're Avalanche."

"Avalanche?"

It wasn't the first time she'd heard the name. If anything, it was hard to avoid talk of Avalanche in Midgar; company broadcasts often mentioned the group, describing it as an anti-Shinra organization bent on disturbing the peace, responsible for acts of violence all over the world. Supposedly, it was under the command of a mysterious individual by the name of Elfe.

"Well, so what if they are?" retorted Tifa. "They're not bad people."

"It isn't a question of how you feel. In Shinra's eyes, they're terrorists, so you need to cut ties and stay far away. If you got caught up in one of Public Security's raids on the group, I dunno what I'd do . . ."

On the way back to Container Row, the Watchman informed Tifa that she had guests.

That's odd, she thought. *Who could it be?*

She traversed the rest of the alley nervously, craning her neck as she neared the clearing. Leaning against her apartment's outer wall were Jessie, Biggs, and Wedge.

When they spotted her, Wedge called out, "Welcome home!"

And Jessie dashed over for a big hug and an enthusiastic "Happy birthday!"

No sooner had she thanked them than Biggs piped up with the reason for their visit. "Listen . . . We know you've got work again tomorrow, but we thought maybe you could spare a couple hours to unwind."

His tone was cautious, and the other two watched Tifa intently, feeling out her response.

"There's no home-cooked birthday dinner," apologized Wedge. "But we've got a whole mountain of snacks you can munch on!"

"More important, there's something we'd like to take you to see," added Jessie.

"Really? What is it?"

Jessie grinned, and all three guests responded in unison, as if they'd planned the whole conversation in advance. "You'll just have to come and find out!"

Tifa didn't have a clue what she was in for, but then again, she figured she didn't have any reason to decline.

They wound their way through the slums for roughly thirty minutes before arriving at an abandoned home near the city's perimeter wall. The building, nestled in a sprawling scrap heap, looked ready to collapse at any moment, but when they stepped inside, Tifa found the interior clean, if bare, and far roomier than she would have expected. A crowd of eight was already assembled inside, and she had the impression that others were likely to arrive too, though for what purpose, she still couldn't say.

Several faces were vaguely familiar, possibly from occasional patronage at Sector 8 Steamed Buns, or perhaps from a passing introduction made by Biggs or Jessie.

When it looked as if everyone had arrived, Jessie raised her hand to draw the room's attention.

"Hey all!" she announced, then scurried over to lead Tifa to the center. "I'm sure some of you already know my good friend Tifa Lockhart. And I'd just like to say that today, believe it or not, happens to be her seventeenth birthday. So how about we give her a nice, warm welcome?"

Biggs began to clap, and others quickly joined in. Several of the strangers cheered and shouted their best wishes. Wedge brought his fingers to his mouth for a long, trilled whistle, only to be shushed by another patron. Apparently, they had to be careful about making too much noise.

"Thank you. Thank you all," said Tifa, turning from one face to the next, offering each a slight bow.

An older man—easily the eldest in the room—cleared his throat and said, "Well then. Shall we get started?"

Everyone grew quiet, shuffling toward the back of the room and taking a seat on the floor facing the whitewashed wall.

A small desk was carried to a spot just behind the seated audience, and on it was placed an unwieldy device that Tifa recognized as an old film projector. There had been one much like it in Nibelheim.

So that's what we're here for, she thought. *They invited me out for a movie night.*

Sure enough, the room's lights flicked out, and a beam of light shone from the projector, filling the white wall. Tifa saw a landscape in monochrome: a wide shot of a barren wasteland. In the center stood a lone young man who stared into the camera and began to speak.

"Hello. I'm Yuri Romana, mentor of planetology. Today, I'd like to speak to you about your relationship with our beautiful world. I'll unravel the mysteries of the planet's inner workings and show how it links us all.

"I'm sure some of you will have heard these things before. If so, I ask that you please bear with me. There's much to be gained in repeating the basics. In fact, it is my firm belief that it is the only way for us to overcome the oppression we face and successfully instill future generations with a firm understanding of our one and only home. It is up to each of us to find our own words and voices to express the true nature of life."

For the next half hour, the man on-screen described the flow of life between the planet and its occupants. When a person passed away, the body degraded and returned to the soil. But the *spirit* was reabsorbed into the lifestream, becoming one with the planet.

This spiritual energy continued to course throughout the planet, deep under its surface, bringing vitality and strength. Ultimately, portions of the lifestream would siphon off to become new life that populated the surface. Life came in all shapes and sizes, and in all things was life. Life was eternal, and the planet was our precious, irreplaceable vessel on which we traversed the infinite cosmos.

The film ended, and once the lights were on and the projector put away, the other audience members quickly filed out.

Jessie motioned Tifa to the door, and the party of four retraced their steps home. At a fork in the road, Wedge and Biggs split off, and then it was just Tifa and Jessie, walking in pensive silence.

Jessie cleared her throat and asked, "So, what did you think?"

"It was . . . I guess the best word I can come up with is *mysterious.* I always assumed that when you die, you're gone. Goodbye. The end."

"Do you know who first proposed that belief?" replied Jessie. "It was Shinra. They claimed to have scientifically proven that there's nothing after death."

"Before Shinra came to power," she continued, "the people of the republic used to believe in heaven and hell, and that the gods determined which one you went to based on how you lived your life. But long, long before that, in the very distant past, people had the teachings of planetology. They understood about spirits and the lifestream and tried to live in harmony with the planet."

"Wow. I had no idea."

It occurred to Tifa that if Jessie really believed in the things described in the film, she wanted to believe them too. But that didn't make them any less strange and hard to accept.

"I guess what I wanted to say is that . . . at least from the way I see it, your dad isn't really gone. He's just returned to the planet. And since our spirits are linked to the planet too, if you take the time to respect the planet and to listen to the things it tells us, you'll always be in touch with your dad."

Jessie looked down at the ground and shrugged. "I dunno . . . I just thought maybe you'd find that comforting."

They'd arrived back at Container Row and were standing side by side in the quiet night.

"Nibelheim will always be with you. And your dad will be too."

Jessie reached up and took both of Tifa's cheeks in her hands. The palms felt warm against her skin.

"You're not alone."

Tifa brought her own hands to Jessie's wrists.

"I know. I've known it since the first day you walked me home."

Jessie's eyes widened, and she scrambled backward, whipping her hands to her own cheeks.

"Hey! What did I tell you about making me blush?!"

Tifa giggled and said, "Thanks for seeing me home again. See you later?"

Jessie nodded and dashed off, hands still at her cheeks. It wasn't until she was out of sight that Tifa recalled Rakesh's comments. She'd meant to broach the subject, to find out whether Jessie truly was involved with Avalanche.

Tifa shrugged. Did it really matter?

Resting on the grass outside the chocobo pasture, Tifa continued telling her story to her shaggy companion.

"After that I started going to screenings fairly often. There were lots of different films with narration on different aspects of the planet's plight.

"The location changed every time; you never knew where the next screening would be held until the morning of. If Shinra caught wind, they'd try to shut the thing down or harass the attendees, so we had to maintain secrecy.

"After a while, I started to believe that the philosophy could help me. I thought planetology might . . . No, I *wanted* it to be able to free me from the burden I'd been carrying."

"And just what, pray tell, is that supposed to mean?" growled Red XIII. His eye had narrowed ever so slightly.

"Since the first day I woke up in the slums, I'd been telling myself I had to hang on to my father, the villagers, and the truth that only I knew. I couldn't allow myself to forget any of it.

"Whenever I was struggling to keep up with the day-to-day of my new life or found myself laughing with my new friends, I'd realize I was letting that duty slip from my mind, and I'd feel cold fingers of guilt creeping up on me.

"So when I heard the films' message . . . When Jessie reassured me that my father and my friends were still with me, inside of the planet, it was like a tiny part of that burden had been lifted. I felt like maybe I wasn't obligated to preserve those memories all by myself."

"Planetology has many interpretations," rumbled the beast. "Mine is rather different from yours."

"Yeah. Later on, I started to see things differently. But at the time, that was how I felt. And at the time, I was grateful for it."

Tifa was at the cart, skimming the froth from the simmering pot of meat, when Pops posed a rather unusual question.

"You're from Corel, right? You heard about the explosion at the reactor?"

"Um . . . Yeah. That was quite some time ago, wasn't it?"

"A year or so. Lately, rumor's been goin' around that it wasn't an accident after all. They're sayin' Avalanche was behind it. That's why Public Security's been swarmin' the slums. They're huntin' down agitators. Not that the reason for the crackdown particularly matters. If not Corel, they'd find some other convenient excuse. They always do."

Tifa tried to appear unconcerned, but she found her hands shaking so badly that anything she skimmed with the ladle ended up right back in the pot.

Pops gave her a hard stare.

"Don't you let yourself get dragged into it."

Nearly a month passed without any word from Jessie. It was by far the longest they'd gone without seeing each other since growing close.

As concerned as Tifa was, she didn't have any way to get in

touch. Jessie had always been the one to show up on Tifa's door-step or wait outside the railcar lot after work. Once or twice, Tifa had tried to ask where her new friends lived; Jessie's answers were vague, and she was always quick to change the subject.

And then, one day, Tifa awoke from deep sleep to a hurried knocking at the door. She could tell immediately that something was amiss. Even the air was thick with tension.

Tifa lurched up from bed, fumbling with the padlock. When she finally had the door open, Jessie was leaning in against the frame, blood streaming down her forehead.

"I'm sorry," blurted Jessie. "I'm really sorry. I swore to myself I wouldn't come to you for help . . ."

"What are you talking about?! We're *friends*!"

She yanked Jessie into the apartment and quickly shut and locked the door.

Given how hard Jessie was panting, she must have sprinted all the way to Container Row. She slumped to the floor, back resting against the side of the bed.

Tifa waited patiently for Jessie's breathing to calm. When it had, she said, "You're Avalanche."

"Bingo," replied Jessie, her voice still soft and airy.

"And Biggs and Wedge? Them too?"

"Right again."

"Is that why you wouldn't tell me where you live?"

The questions came out sharper than Tifa intended. A surge of anger threatened to rise, and she had to consciously battle it back down.

"You were safer not knowing," replied Jessie. "Public Security could show up at any moment—just like they did tonight."

"Is it the reactor in Corel? Were you involved?"

"Ooh. Someone's stumbled onto some juicy gossip. Where'd you hear about that?"

"I'm not a child. Don't treat me like one."

Jessie flinched, then clutched at her side with a stifled yelp, her face contorting with pain.

"What's wrong?! Have you been shot?!"

"Jumped off a roof. I don't think anything's broken, but the landing sure wasn't graceful."

Tifa was already up and yanking the padlock from the door. Jessie sensed what she was planning and pleaded with her to stop. It was exactly what Shinra would be hoping; they'd be watching the clinics and hospitals, waiting for injured targets to show up.

Still determined to find some way to help, Tifa rifled through a drawer, pulling out a small vial of painkillers. She handed it to Jessie and then grabbed the large water jug, explaining that she'd be right back.

Container Row was deathly silent. Tifa had come to understand that this was a place for folks who had hit rock bottom. All the residents of the Row had enough problems of their own without poking into anyone else's business; a young woman showing up in the middle of the night, bloodied and out of breath, didn't even merit a curious peek from the windows.

She was more concerned about the possibility of Shinra troopers. Tifa eyes darted around nervously as she waited for the jug to fill. When it was about as heavy as she could manage, she lugged it back, the weight making her hurried steps awkward and uneven.

Inside, Jessie had slumped to the floor, where she lay motionless.

Tifa scrambled to her side, leaning close to check for breathing.

"Don't worry. I'm not dead," croaked Jessie. "Not yet."

The following morning, Jessie was more or less her usual cheerful self, minus the occasional pained grimace when she shifted her weight. Tifa was hesitant to leave her friend alone, but it was a workday, and Jessie seemed to be doing well enough.

But when the morning rush was over, Tifa put her newfound acting skills to the test: she doubled over, moaning of a sudden pain in her stomach.

In nearly two years, she'd never called in sick or asked to leave early—except, of course, that very first day on the job. Pops was thus bewildered. He scratched his head and begrudgingly allowed her to take the rest of the day off.

Tifa made straight for Dhamini's clinic, where she continued the act.

After an agonizingly long sit in the waiting room, she was summoned to the back to see Dr. Oranye. The story was simple enough: Tifa claimed to have stumbled and slammed her torso into a large, dull object. The pain had been intense, though it wasn't quite as bad this morning as it had been last night.

Dhamini listened patiently, declaring that the suffered injury was unlikely to be a fracture.

"For the time being," she said, "let's just manage the pain. I'm prescribing an analgesic, but it's rather potent, so don't rely on it too heavily. Only take it if the pain starts to get overwhelming. Spend today and tomorrow resting; if you don't see improvement by then, or if things starts to feel worse, it may be a sign that there's internal bleeding. In that case, I'd recommend you bring the patient by so I can look at her myself."

Tifa's mouth fell open. Dhamini smiled and winked.

"It was a clever story, but there's a conspicuous lack of bruising to substantiate it. I *am* a doctor, you know."

Tifa's cheeks burned. With a great deal of trepidation, she managed to drag her gaze up to meet the doctor's. Dhamini regarded her with concern.

"There's a lot going on in the world these days," Dhamini said. "Take care not to get dragged into something you might regret."

Disoriented and upset, Tifa rushed from the clinic and all the way down the street to Container Row. When she arrived at her apartment, she found the latch down but the padlock missing. Her blood chilled, and she scrambled inside.

Jessie was gone. The only trace that the woman had ever been there was a single folded letter on Tifa's pillow, along with the padlock and its key.

Going to lie low for a while, it read. *Thanks for the help, and sorry about the door. Didn't want to lock you out of your own place.*

The strength drained from Tifa's body. She yelled into the dingy apartment, "If you're gonna drag me into this, don't drop me halfway!"

Then she was burning with rage again, punching and kicking the empty air, each strike accompanied by a shout of frustration.

Eventually, Tifa tired and, seeing nothing better to do with herself, decided to head back to the cart and finish out the workday.

Her return just preempted the evening rush. The difference was stark. Pops's fatigue was evident, and he greeted her with a wide smile. Here, she felt appreciated.

From the dinner rush all the way through to closing and cleanup, she worked with more determination than ever before.

Life was again work and nothing else. The days flew by, and before Tifa knew it, her eighteenth birthday was drawing near.

She was making her way home from work one evening when she found a throng at the entrance to the alley for Container Row. Its members gaped and strained their necks at something beyond the turnoff. As she reached the edge of the crowd, she heard whispers all around.

"Sheltering a terrorist," they were saying. "Someone on the Row. I heard the trooper mention Avalanche!"

Cautiously, Tifa began to cut her way through.

Up ahead, she heard a woman scream, "I told you! I don't know nothin'! Been ten years since I seen the boy!"

Tifa recognized the voice almost instantly. She began shoving people aside, fighting her way down the alley. Onlookers yelped and shouted in protest, but she paid them no mind, pushing and pushing until finally she was ahead of the crowd.

Near the Watchman's post, three Shinra troopers stood over a cowering Waterkeeper, weapons trained on the woman as they continued their interrogation.

Tifa saw another figure sprawled facedown not far from where she stood. She recognized its crumpled cape; it was the Watchman. She stepped forward and crouched at his side.

When the old man saw her, he rasped, ". . . Aisha. Don't let them hurt Aisha."

She'd never heard the name before, but she knew immediately that he was speaking of the Waterkeeper.

Tifa stood, glaring at the troopers. One finally seemed to notice that she'd pushed out in front of the crowd.

"Halt!" he shouted, rifle swiveling. "Hands where I can see them!"

The weapon gleamed in the alley's yellow light, its small black muzzle threatening death. One bullet was all it would take.

The hairs at the back of Tifa's neck stood on end. Her knees trembled violently. What was this feeling? This *rush*?

"This a friend of yours?" snarled the trooper. He was looking at the Waterkeeper.

The woman's shouts grew frantic. "I've never seen her before in my life! She's ain't got nothin' to do with this! None of them do!"

The trooper turned back to Tifa and adjusted his grip on the rifle. The corners of his mouth curled into a wicked sneer.

Tifa's fingertips trembled.

Somewhere from behind the crowd, a shout erupted.

"Officers! Over here! He's escaping down the main street!"

The trooper nearest the Waterkeeper slammed the butt of his rifle into the old woman's skull, sending her to the ground. He and one of his partners pushed past Tifa, heading for the street. The assembled crowd cried out in fear and pressed against the alley walls to make way.

The remaining trooper took a few menacing steps forward. He jammed the barrel of his gun into Tifa's breast.

Humiliation and rage seized her. Before she could process her own actions, the toe of her boot was against his chin, and his neck had snapped back with a cry of pain. The trooper fell backward onto the dirt. His bulky helmet rolled away, leaving his face exposed.

He was young. Maybe even younger than she was.

The revelation left her frozen, but someone grabbed her arm from behind, pulling her away. Tifa plopped down onto the ground, rear end first, as the shadow of a man darted past. When it reached the trooper's—the *child's*—side, it drew one hand across his neck in fluid motion. Blood gushed out in rhythmic spurts, and a strangled gurgle escaped the youth's lips.

Tifa recognized the assailant as the Watchman, saw the gleam of the knife blade in his hand. The terrified cries of the onlookers escalated to sheer panic.

That was the moment when Tifa blacked out.

When she next opened her eyes, Rakesh was sitting on a chair at her side. She was in her own bed, in her own apartment on the Row.

She bolted upright, gasping, "The boy! The . . . the *trooper*! What happened to him?!"

"The Watchman carried him off. Don't worry. He'll take care of the body."

She wished she hadn't asked.

"And the Waterkeeper?" ventured Tifa.

"She's at Mom's. Gonna have some bruises, but nothing life-threatening."

"Thank goodness . . . I hope he was able to get away."

"I'd say the odds are good, given that he was never here in the first place. Shinra must've had some lousy intel. The guy's Avalanche, though. They got that much right."

"I heard someone shout that he was fleeing down the main street."

"That was me. I was just improvising, trying to get the troopers' attention off you. Things were going great until . . . Boy, I don't think any of us saw that kick coming."

"Me neither," answered Tifa. "I guess I just couldn't hold it in anymore. My body acted all on its own."

"It was sure something . . . I feel like I've finally witnessed what it means to be truly strong."

There was a hint of awe in Rakesh's voice. Her actions had left a deep impression.

"I don't think Master Zangan would have approved," she said.

"Zangan," snorted Rakesh. "You know the thing that gets me? For all his sage advice, he's never around when you really need him . . ."

Rakesh trailed off for a moment, then piped up with, "Hey, maybe you ought to think about taking a shower. It might help you calm down."

She didn't have the energy to argue, so she swung her legs over the side of the bed. Her knees were still shaking. It was no longer the adrenaline-induced trembling of staring down a rifle; the magnitude of the day's events had caught up with her, and her legs didn't seem up to the task of carrying this monumental new weight.

More upsetting was the thought of Rakesh seeing her tremble. She pivoted back, sliding her legs onto the bed and under her blanket once more.

"What's it like outside?" she asked.

"Everyone's gone. No troopers. No rubbernecks. Nothing. Manson's people will get in touch with Shinra's, and with any luck, we'll all go on like none of this ever happened."

He grimaced, his next words more spat than spoken.

"Fucking Avalanche. See why I warned you? I told you they were trouble."

Tifa didn't answer. Her fingers curled tight around the leather cord as she swallowed her anger.

"Hey, Rakesh?" she finally said.

"What is it? I'm here for you. You can tell me anything."

"I think I'd like to be alone now."

Rakesh's dismay was plain. Tifa briefly wondered why he'd hoped to stay, but she decided she didn't really care. At that particular moment, she didn't want to have to think about anything at all.

"The choice to engage in combat, or even to train in martial arts . . . These are decisions inextricably linked with death. By raising your fists, you implicitly accept the possibility that you may one day take someone's life."

Tifa paused, running a hand through the long, soft grass. "It sounds so obvious now. But before that night, I'd never really thought it through."

"Based on your story, it doesn't sound like *you* were the one responsible for the young man's demise," rumbled Red XIII.

"That's what I tried to tell myself. But I was only running from the truth. Before you fight, you first have to make peace with death. You have to go in knowing that you or your opponent might not make it out. I wasn't ready to do that, so I shouldn't have struck him in the first place.

"The way I see it, whatever you're fighting for had better be important. Otherwise, all you're left with after victory is a crushing sense of regret. Death is too high a price to pay for some minor satisfaction."

"Hmph. You humans are certainly adept at overcomplicating things."

"Yes. We most definitely are. And me more than most."

The following day was a workday. Tifa didn't even contemplate asking for time off. Work was her one solid reality in a sea of uncertainty. If she abandoned her routines, she risked being swallowed up, mind sinking deep beneath the dark, churning waves.

But when she traversed the alley on her way home that evening—and every subsequent evening—she couldn't help but see the young trooper lying there in the dirt, blood still spraying from his neck. His final, choked gurgles looped through her mind, echoing across the alley walls.

She wanted to get out. She wanted to leave the Row far behind. It was no longer the vague, shiftless longing she'd once divulged to Jessie, but an urgent, pressing need.

The next time Rakesh was counting out her pay in the office, she broached the subject.

"I've been thinking about a new apartment . . ."

Rakesh's eyebrows shot up. His discomfort was plain to see.

"I mean, I don't have to live on the Row forever . . . Do I?" she asked.

"Of course not. Once you're done paying off the debt, you're free to live wherever you want."

"Why Container Row? Is it your mom? Does she want to keep me nearby?"

"More like Manson. It's one of his rules."

"What does Manson have to do with it? Don't get me wrong, I'm grateful for the job, but why should that mean he gets to decide where I live?"

"It's complicated. See, Mom's clinic owes money to Manson, and when you couldn't cover your treatment, she fell behind on payments. Manson agreed to leave the clinic be if you and I were willing to work for him to pay off the debt.

"One of his stipulations was that he gets to choose the job. Another was that you stay on Container Row. Manson takes these agreements seriously. If you break the rules, there's gonna be blood."

The revelation had Tifa aghast.

"You mean the money I'm paying you isn't going to your mom? It's going to *Manson*?"

"Ultimately, yeah."

"Why didn't you tell me?"

"What difference does it make? The amount you owe doesn't change. And besides, when you checked out of the clinic, you didn't seem to care about the details."

"I *trusted* you. I thought you were acting in my best interests!"

Her fingers were clenched tight around the leather cord.

Rakesh smiled. "I am. And I'm gonna keep looking out for you. Just keep your faith in me, and everything will be fine. At the rate you're selling, it'll be less than three years before you're a free woman."

He lowered his voice and added, "Or . . . there *are* ways you could work it off faster. I'd never dream of pushing you into it against your will, but . . . if you wanna talk Wall Market, just say the word."

In that moment, whatever sliver of trust she'd still had for Rakesh was gone for good.

When Tifa returned home, she yanked the storage bin out from under her bed and dug down to where the purse was stashed. When she pulled it out, she was surprised by its weight. Inside was every gil she'd managed to set aside in some two and a half years of work.

After double-checking that the apartment's door was securely latched and locked, Tifa began arranging the coins and bills in orderly stacks across the floor. Once finished, she grabbed a pen and paper, calculating the total in relation to her remaining debt.

Two years.

If things kept going as they were, she could have everything paid off in two years.

Immediately after the conversation with Rakesh, she'd been fuming. She'd wanted to demand a breakdown of her treatment expenses to see how her debt had been calculated. But now that she'd had time to think it over, she wasn't sure it was worth stirring up trouble. She'd taken the number at face value, accepted it as gospel for years. At this point, what did she stand to gain from kicking up a fuss about it, or challenging the lies about where her money was going or Manson's incomprehensible rules?

There were things she probably should have done, and things she shouldn't have. But she decided she'd live with—and *accept*— the consequences of her actions.

Just two short years until her life was in her own hands again. The goal brought her strength. She'd climb out of this debt all by herself and show them that she would not be beaten.

Tifa smiled at Red XIII.

"It takes me time to make up my mind, but once I do, I'm unstoppable. My sales at the cart were stronger than ever, and I kept earning, saving, and making payments. Wednesdays were devoted to training and review of Zangan's techniques. Honestly, the rigid, repetitive days no longer bothered me. I felt like I could march on like that, right up until the end."

Red XIII reacted with a gentle huff. "An attitude that certainly befits your personality."

"That's how I saw it too. I mean, I won't lie . . . Sometimes I dream of leading a life of glitz and glamour. But if I have to choose, I'll take quiet and predictable over exciting and uncertain any day of the week. Just a nice, hot shower and straight to bed, y'know?"

"And yet your newfound predictability was short-lived."

"Huh? How'd you know?"

"I've begun to notice a pattern to this story of yours."

There was a certain young man who stopped by the cart every few days for lunch. Tifa had come to recognize his face, but their interactions were always brief, lasting less than a minute, tops. Whenever he approached, Tifa smiled and nodded, as she did for all their regulars. Usually, he'd return the greeting with his own gentle smile and then watch with interest as Tifa completed his order with her quick, practiced movements.

One particular day, he accepted the finished bun with a comment that took her by surprise.

"The big eighteen, huh? Congratulations."

Tifa's hands froze, the knife buried mid-slice in another bun.

"How do you know it's my . . . ?"

"I was there for your seventeenth."

Suddenly, she put it together. The planetology screening. It was the only explanation. He must have been one of the others in attendance that night at the abandoned house near the scrap heap.

Tifa's pulse raced.

"There a problem here?" snapped Pops.

It was the tone he used whenever a clueless customer lingered too long at the counter in attempt to chat Tifa up. Tifa glanced at Pops to indicate that the customer wasn't unwelcome, then returned her attention to the youth, her next words hurried and hushed.

"Do you know Jessie? Or Biggs or Wedge? The three who were with me at the screening."

The young man's expression clouded. "Yeah. I remember them," he began slowly. "People said they were with Avalanche, so I kept my distance."

Suddenly his eyes grew wide, and he stammered, "Oh! But I hope you don't think everyone who studies planetology is like that! We don't all support terrorism!"

Tifa responded with feigned relief, adapting to the conversation's unexpected turn.

"Why do you ask?" he continued hesitantly.

"They owe me."

She didn't elaborate, figuring the statement was vague enough to not constitute a lie. The man nodded and headed off without another word.

The following day, he returned. He nonchalantly placed his order, and then, when Pops seemed busy, whispered to Tifa.

"About yesterday . . . I asked a few acquaintances of mine. They say there's an apartment building in Sector 7 called Stargazer

Heights. The landlady might be able to point you in the right direction. Apparently, she's one of those people who knows everybody else."

"You did that for me?" replied Tifa. "Thank you . . ."

"No problem. But . . . I was wondering if I could maybe ask one tiny favor in return."

The young man's voice dropped further still. Tifa could barely hear it over the bubbling of the meat sauce.

"Could I get a picture of the two of us?"

She smiled. "Sure!"

The youth held a camera out to the next patron in line, who accepted with a chuckle. He then backed up next to the cart and struck a pose. Tifa hoisted herself up, leaning out over the counter to get in frame. She found herself grinning from ear to ear.

When the photo was taken, the youth exclaimed, "Great! How about one more? This time, maybe you could—"

Before he could finish, Pops thundered at their backs.

"If you're gonna keep holding up the line, you better fork over some cash!"

The wait until the following Wednesday was agonizing. When it finally arrived, Tifa made her way to Sector 7 first thing in the morning.

If she'd thought Sector 8 was a cluttered mess, its neighbor was a thousand times worse. The whole place was made up of narrow, winding alleys, most of them unpaved. Everywhere she went, the air was thick with dust. The unpredictable tangle of alleys also boasted an unpredictable tangle of shops.

Every so often, Tifa stopped to look upward, noting the location of a mammoth pillar supporting the Sector 7 plate. It was a trick she'd quickly discovered out of necessity, as a way to orient herself among the chaos.

After several stops to ask for directions and only a few moments spent wandering lost, Tifa emerged into a clearing with an old two-story apartment building that matched the description of Stargazer Heights.

Open-air corridors ran along the exterior of each level, facing the clearing. Each corridor had three doors, for a total of six units in the building. And situated next to each door was a condenser for an air conditioner, all identical; apparently they came furnished. Tifa couldn't begin to imagine how exorbitant the rent must be.

A metal staircase at one end of the building provided access to the upper corridor and units. Next to it stood a thin, almost frail-looking old woman. On Tifa's approach, the woman's eyes went wide, and she cried out in astonishment.

"Tifa!"

Tifa couldn't believe it. It was Marle! The patient she'd met in Dhamini's clinic!

How long had it been?

"Bless my soul . . . You sure took your sweet time coming over to visit!"

"I'm sorry. I had no idea where you lived."

"What do you mean?! I left my address! I told the doctor's boy to make sure you got it."

Tifa recalled Marle's abrupt discharge from the clinic. Rakesh hadn't mentioned anything about a message, and Tifa highly doubted it had simply slipped his mind. No, this was intentional.

"How's the injury?" asked Marle. "Feeling back to your old self?"

"Yes. Almost completely. The skin color's still a little off, though . . ."

Marle chuckled. "I know exactly what you mean. My back's still got a long way to go too. It's a shame, really. In my younger years, and with the right type of dress, I could have more than a few men swooning every time I walked away.

"Anyway, where are you headed? If you've got business in Sector 7, I'd be happy to make introductions."

"This is Stargazer Heights, isn't it? I understand the owner of these apartments is well connected."

"You heard right. You're staring right at her."

"*You're* the landlady?! Then maybe you can help me. There's someone I'm searching for."

"And who might that be? Just give me a name."

"Well, there're three, actually. Jessie, Biggs, and Wedge."

Marle furrowed her brow.

"Biggs and Wedge . . . Yeah, I know them. Those two are on the neighborhood watch. And there's a chipper young lady who's with them more often than not. I imagine that must be Jessie."

Bingo, thought Tifa.

"They're friends of mine," Tifa explained. "We spent a lot of time together last year, but we fell out of touch, and now I have no idea where they are."

Marle's brows had pinched together so hard, her eyes were closed. What she was thinking about, Tifa couldn't begin to guess.

"Tell me something . . . How well do you know those three?"

Tifa's voice fell to a whisper as she answered, "You're . . . You're talking about their connection to Avalanche, right?"

"Hmph. Well enough, I see. And . . . ? Do they know where to find *you?*"

"Yes. They've been to my home several times."

"And doesn't that tell you something? If they haven't been by, there's probably a reason."

"I understand that. I *would* like to see them, but if that's not possible, I'd settle for knowing whether they're okay. I'd pretty well given up on ever tracking them down, but the other day, I stumbled across a lead that brought me to you. I have to at least try. If I don't, I'll regret it for the rest of my life."

"Hmm . . . I suppose I can ask around. How much time you got?"

"I don't have to get back until evening."

"Good. Let's find you a place to sit down."

Marle gestured at a side street and proceeded to explain the way to a local establishment run by an acquaintance. Tifa could wait there for a while until Marle had news.

Tifa smiled to her companion in the grass. "And that's how I got to know a little place called Seventh Heaven."

From Marle's description of the bar, Tifa had imagined a tiny hole- in-the-wall located in one of the sector's tortuous alleyways. Seventh Heaven turned out to be considerably larger.

The building was centered atop a raised foundation. A wide terrace wrapped around the exterior, furnished with several tables and chairs. By Tifa's measure, the patio alone was large enough to accommodate four Sector 8 Steamed Buns food carts. The floor space of the bar itself could probably fit eight.

She imagined the possibility: Twelve steamed bun carts, each selling a thousand buns, for a total of thirty-six thousand gil per day.

A wry smile touched her lips. With money like that, she could pay off her debt in a matter of days or weeks.

She shook her head vigorously and returned her attention to Seventh Heaven's interior. Devoid of the imagined food carts, it felt quiet and empty.

In front of her, on the table, was the tall glass of iced tea she'd ordered. The liquid had an unappealing cloudy-white appearance. The glass itself was scratched up beyond belief.

As far as she could tell, the entire establishment was run by a staff of one: the elderly man standing behind the bar counter. Both his hair and mustache were white, and he was clad in an impeccable gray suit, complete with necktie. He looked every part the gentleman, and yet his complexion was pale and sickly, like the color of the dirt in the clearing outside.

His voice was soft as a whisper. Every movement he made was so slow, it was almost painful to behold.

It seemed obvious to Tifa why the place was nearly deserted. If any other customers arrived, the man wouldn't be able to keep up. All in all, the experience offered by Seventh Heaven seemed an incredible waste of such a lavish space.

She'd been sitting for some time when Marle arrived. The woman pulled open Seventh Heaven's heavy double doors, spotted Tifa, and made a beeline for her table.

"Sorry to keep you," she said.

Marle didn't glance in the bartender's direction or even pretend to look at the menu as she sat down. She cut right to the chase.

"I've arranged to have word spread that you're looking. It may take some time, but I guarantee the individuals in question will hear about it. What I *can't* promise is that they'll respond. It's not like I can twist their arms."

"I understand. Thank you."

It wasn't the breakthrough Tifa had hoped for, but it was a step forward, nonetheless.

In a low voice, Marle continued. "From what I'm told, the timing's not great. Avalanche's leadership is in chaos. Shinra's sensed it, which is why they're going all out with the raids.

"As it is, the different cells have no way to coordinate. They can hardly meet up without worrying about troopers kicking the door down. So they go on doing their own thing, operating as a bunch of splinter groups while Shinra tries to stamp 'em out, one by one."

"I see . . ." murmured Tifa.

She recalled the night Jessie showed up with blood streaming from her forehead. Had her friend been on the run ever since, desperately trying to stay one step ahead of Shinra's troopers?

"Oh!" exclaimed Marle. "I suppose it's obvious, but my guarantee does come with one caveat. Your friends won't be getting your message if they're already dead."

Marle kindly offered to walk Tifa back to the station. On the way, she talked about Seventh Heaven and its obvious lack of clientele. The man at the counter, she explained, was the bar's owner and manager. Folks in the neighborhood called him "Old Monty." For years, he'd hawked cocktails from a roadside stand not too unlike Pops's steamed buns cart, until he finally realized his dream of building a real shop.

From the day it opened, Seventh Heaven was a hit. Lately, however, Monty had begun shortening the hours, eventually scrapping evenings altogether.

"He had a real cutie of a bartender working for him," explained Marle. "But the girl up and quit. Started dating a Shinra employee and moved topside. Old Monty put out notices for a while, trying to find a replacement, but good bartenders are hard to come by.

"Worse yet, Monty started having health troubles. He's a lot younger than he looks, you know. Same age as me, in fact."

Marle sighed.

"So there's no one left who can mix drinks?" asked Tifa.

"Oh, well, I wouldn't say that. Monty's about the finest bartender there is. It's just that his joints can't keep up with the work anymore. He's too stubborn to admit it, but if something doesn't change, he's going to lose the place. He's still payin' off the builder for the construction costs."

"That's a shame. It has such a lovely atmosphere."

"Doesn't it, though?"

They were nearing the station. Marle abruptly stopped and grabbed Tifa by the arm, her voice low and furtive.

"Tell me something . . . Do you like making money?"

"I don't know if I've ever thought of it in terms of like or dislike . . . I earn because I *have* to."

Marle gave a satisfied nod. "Good answer. Now tell me, when's the next time you're off work? Think you can stop by Sector 7 again?"

"Wednesday is always my day off, but . . . what do you have in mind?"

"I'm thinking Seventh Heaven could use our help. How about you start swinging by on Wednesdays? *Every* Wednesday."

"Huh?"

"Don't tell me I haven't sparked your interest. I'll sort everything out with Monty. All you have to do is show up."

A job at Seventh Heaven. The prospect certainly did spark her interest. In fact, for the first time in a very long while, Tifa found herself excited.

Marle shrugged. "Of course, I understand that it's your day off. If you'd rather spend it in peace and quiet, don't let me stop you. But you should know . . ."

Her voice grew even more hushed.

". . . the previous bartender was taking home sixty percent of the night's sales. That was her deal with Monty."

Tifa smiled. "It's all right. You've already convinced me. I'll be there."

Yet even as she said it, there was a nagging feeling that perhaps she'd agreed to the proposition a little too eagerly.

Tifa's enthusiasm about Seventh Heaven quickly bled over into her existing job. All week, her steamed bun sales were stronger than ever, and Pops was in the best mood she'd ever seen.

However, Marle's opportunity did require some adjustments. With Wednesdays booked from morning to night, Tifa needed to find other windows during the week to keep up with the usual activities of her day off. Most important was her training; rather than a stripped-down set of exercises each evening coupled with a complete review of Zangan's teachings every Wednesday, she'd need to split the forms back into sections, covering one book per night.

That particular change wasn't entirely unwelcome. She'd begun the Wednesday tradition because of an excess of time. In a way, it was nice not to have empty hours, if only because she didn't have to come up with ways to fill them.

When the promised Wednesday arrived, Tifa departed first thing in the morning. She rendezvoused with Marle at Stargazer Heights, and the two headed to Seventh Heaven side by side, the morning air still crisp.

Monty was happy to see them—overwhelmingly so, in fact. The workday hadn't begun and he was already showering Tifa with praise, saying what a difference she was going to make. Marle seemed to have sold him on her two-plus years of experience at the steamed bun cart.

At any rate, he proceeded to fill Tifa in regarding the establishment.

Seventh Heaven opened at eleven. Lunchtime ran from eleven to two, with a rotating special for each day of the week. As far as meals went, the daily special was the only thing Seventh Heaven offered. Monty would continue to take care of the cooking.

From two to five was teatime. They served coffee and tea, hot or cold, along with two varieties of juice. There was also an assortment of cookies and slices of cake. The coffee and tea were prepared in-house. The juice and snacks were purchased in bulk.

From five to midnight, Seventh Heaven was a bar, serving alcohol and finger foods. With Marle and Tifa helping out, today was to be the grand reintroduction of evening hours. However, due the departure of the previous bartender, the drink menu had been significantly pared down. They'd no longer be serving the cocktails they'd come to be known for.

"It's these creaky elbows of mine," explained Monty. "Thanks to them, I can't shake worth a damn."

Marle shook her head. "I don't know why that stops you. You can still stir, can't you? Plenty of cocktails are stirred."

Monty gave her a hard look. "A bartender who can't shake has no business serving cocktails. That's my philosophy, and I'm gonna stick to it."

Marle sighed. "Smart. Tank your whole business just to prove a point."

"Um . . ." Tifa raised a hand tentatively as she interjected. "Sorry, but . . . drinks can be *shaken*?"

Monty and Marle stared at her in stunned silence.

In the end, the plan was to have Tifa waitress from opening until eight at night. She'd be taking orders and delivering drinks and food for customers seated at the tables both inside and out on the patio.

"Keep a washcloth with you," advised Marle. "Thanks to the sector's dirt roads, there's always a new layer of dust settling on the patio tables. Be sure to wipe 'em down often."

When she headed out to do so, the first thing she noticed was the staring. She felt the eyes of every passerby on the street—or square, really, given how much it widened adjacent to Seventh Heaven. In fact, it wasn't just curious passersby. Even the residents were eyeballing Tifa from their shop fronts and the windows of their homes.

"Something the matter?" Marle asked when she walked back inside. "If your jaw gets any tighter, you're going to chip a tooth."

"Just nerves, I guess . . . Is it me, or am I suddenly the center of attention?"

"Ha! What'd you expect? That's what you're here for!"

It finally clicked.

She was serving the same purpose for Seventh Heaven that she did for Pops: drawing in the crowds.

She'd more or less grown used to the idea of being on display. Still, she didn't want it to be the only role she filled. Where was the fun in that?

If she was going to stick with this job, she wanted to have Marle's and Monty's respect. She wanted to impress.

During a noontime lull, she approached Monty behind the counter and, mustering up all her courage, blurted, "I'm really sorry to say this, especially on my first day, but . . . The lunch plate? It doesn't look appetizing at all."

"No need to apologize. Believe me, I know. And it's past time to do something about it."

"I'm sure we can come up with something. I bet Marle would be happy to help too!"

"I'm starting to worry I owe Marle one too many favors as it is. But you're right. Next week, let's all have a sit-down and brainstorm ideas."

As the day wore on, the number of customers steadily grew. By late afternoon, the tables were so full, the deserted bar of last week seemed like something out of a dream. And that was only the beginning; after five was when things really picked up.

At Marle's urging, Monty announced that cocktails were, in fact, back on the menu. He stirred away as Tifa busily flit among the groups of happy drunks, dropping off drinks and picking up empty glasses.

At eight, Monty pulled Tifa aside as promised, handing her the day's pay. It took Tifa a moment to process the stack of bills in her palm. Monty had carefully counted them out: one thousand gil in total.

"This is too much!" she protested.

"Fifty percent of the day's earnings. Not one gil less." Monty smiled and added, "You know, if you stuck around till closing, you'd take home almost double that amount. Nights are where the real money's at."

It took a vigorous shake of her head to ward the temptation off. "I'm really sorry, but I do have to get going. I've got my other job to think about too."

"Understandable. I'll be looking forward to seeing you next week."

She nodded and thanked Monty again. But when she made to leave the bar, Marle's voice shot up above the clamor.

"Bad news, fellas! Tifa's headed home!"

The tenor of the room changed instantly; patrons hollered protest and gripped the sides of their heads as they cried out in dismay. Marle glanced at Tifa, a mischievous grin on her face.

Tifa drew a deep breath and announced, "I'll be back next week! I'm looking forward to a long career here at Seventh Heaven!"

She bowed her head deeply, turned, and stepped out the doors, almost floating on her new high. Seventh Heaven indeed. The joy of setting new records for steamed buns sold wasn't even close to the elation of a day working here. And on top of that, there was the *money*! A thousand gil on her first day, with the potential for double!

Ripples of laughter passed through Red XIII's copper coat.

"You're making fun of me again!" pouted Tifa. "You're not even trying to hide it anymore!"

"I assure you, that is not the case," he countered, but his voice continued to betray him.

"Look, I'll admit I was really focused on the numbers. But what else was I supposed to think? Money was the key to my freedom. All I knew was that my life was on hold until I paid off Manson's stupid debt!"

"I'm told that money tends to have a profound effect on the human mind."

"Definitely so. But setting the figures aside, the point is that I was growing into bigger and better things."

The following Wednesday, Tifa woke at dawn as always, eager for the day ahead. She was returning from her morning shower, toweling her hair as she walked, when she noticed Rakesh leaning against her container.

"Morning!" he called. "Heading out?"

"Yeah . . ."

"Gonna be away all day?"

"I'm, um . . . meeting a friend."

"Hey, that's great. Glad to hear you're being social again."

Tifa fumbled for a response, trying to appear calm. Inside, she was indignant. What did it matter what her plans were? Why was she obliged to inform Rakesh?

Rakesh must have noticed the tightness in her jaw. He held his hands up and said, "Hey, don't mean to intrude. It's your day off. Your time is your own."

"Do you need something?"

"Manson's just worried. That's all. A little bird brought word from Sector 7, and he's starting to get the impression that you might have a second job."

"Well, I don't."

The words came out a little too forcefully. Lying had never been her forte.

"If it's an honest misunderstanding, then no harm done. Still, he asked me to pass along a message, just in case."

"Well? I'm listening."

"'Don't forget. You belong to me.'" The words seemed to pain Rakesh. "That's Manson speaking. Not me. But I've got instructions to keep an eye on you, and I have to be able to say I'm doing my job."

"Great. Anything else?"

She stared him down. When he didn't respond, she yanked the padlock from the latch and slammed the door once safely inside.

In recent months, Rakesh Oranye had begun to feel like a scourge on her life. Frankly, so did this mysterious Manson character. Nonetheless, she was determined to repay her debts, no matter how distasteful the creditor. It was an issue of stubborn pride.

It helped that selling steamed buns had never felt particularly objectionable, and that she and Pops made a good team.

Still, the allure of Seventh Heaven was too great to ignore. Regular shifts there could cut months from her timeline to freedom.

Little did she know, the bar's intervening week had been a bumpy one. The moment she stepped in the doors, Marle rushed forward and clasped Tifa's hands.

"It's Monty," she exclaimed. "One moment he was fine, and the next, he'd collapsed on the floor. The doctor's saying it's his heart."

"Oh no!"

Tifa's own chest constricted at the news.

"They've got him at home, and he's hanging in there, but . . . Oh, Tifa . . . He's *devastated*. All week, he'd been talking about how the three of us were going to turn this place around."

"I'm so sorry . . ."

Tifa recalled their promise to discuss the lunch menu. When she brought the issue up, his eyes had begun to shine. It was an expression Tifa knew well; her calisthenics students had worn it whenever they boasted of their grandchildren's latest exploits.

For Monty, the grandchild in question must have been the bar itself. Or maybe . . .

"I've been holding down the fort," said Marle, interrupting Tifa's contemplations. "But coffee, tea, and the baked goodies are about all I can handle on my own. That's what I'm planning to tell the customers again today. No lunch plate, and we're only open from eleven to five."

"Only till five? Isn't that a little early?"

"Any later, and we start drawing the night crowd. I'm sorry, but I'm not gonna deal with a bunch of drunks. Not when Monty isn't here to back us up. No reason to put you through that either. Not without some more experience."

In the space of a few minutes, Tifa's bright new future had shattered to pieces. Everything about the day had been a mess, right from the moment she'd encountered Rakesh.

Still, she helped Marle prep, setting out the signboard to indicate they were open for business.

It hadn't been long when Marle announced, "Here they are."

Tifa looked at her questioningly, and Marle gestured toward the windows. "Our new regulars. Every day for almost a week. They sit outside, order a coffee and a glass of juice, and drink about one thimbleful every hour."

Tifa peeked through the panes. A large, burly man was sitting at one of the patio tables, the small wooden stool straining under his immense weight. With him was a little girl who was struggling with all her might to pull herself onto the opposite seat. She slipped and was about to fall backward, but the man—her father, judging by the delicate ease of the interaction—leaned forward to scoop her up and set her safely on the stool.

"At least one of them's not so bad." Marle grinned. "Daddy-daughter date. Barret and Marlene Wallace. Isn't she adorable? Itty-bitty thing's only two years old."

"You asked their names?"

"A nosy old gal like me? How could I not? But here's the *juicy* part: apparently, the two of them are roughin' it. No home, no inn, no nothin'. Anyway, get on out there and take their order, would ya?"

The order, as Marle had predicted, was one cup of coffee and one glass of juice. Tifa returned to the counter and prepared the drinks. She carried them out, and as she set the glass down, Marlene offered a bright "Thank you!" along with an adorable little bow.

She next set down the cup of coffee. The father—Barret—slid his sunglasses down the bridge of his nose just enough to glare over the rims. Tifa hightailed it back inside.

The next hour of business crawled by.

"We're hardly getting anybody today," remarked Tifa.

They'd had a grand total of two other two-tops. Both had ordered coffee, quaffed it, and scurried out as soon as the mugs were empty. Now it was the raucousness of her first day on the job that felt like something out of a dream.

"Far as I've seen, we've had at least five other would-be patrons that made it to the top of the stairs and turned right around. Half the sector knows you're working today, but nobody can work up the courage to come in."

The rest of the afternoon dragged on in much the same manner, until, eventually, their proposed five o'clock closing time was only an hour away.

"Hey, Marle?" began Tifa. "I've gotta be honest. This whole situation really irritates me."

"Barret? Tell me about it. He sits there all day glaring at everyone who walks by. It's pretty obvious that's why we aren't getting any customers."

"Well, that too . . . But what I mean is Marlene. I feel bad for the girl. When I took their order, I could see that her clothes are filthy."

"It's a shame. I'll give you that."

"I wonder if there isn't something we can do to help."

Marle sighed. "Listen . . . I've been sticking my nose into people's business so long, I'm a regular pro. And if there's one thing I've learned, it's that the slums've got more cheats and sweet talkers than you can shake a stick at. The second they figure you for a sucker, they'll bleed you dry.

"So by all means, be sympathetic and lend an ear. But for anything beyond that, you need to keep your boundaries firm."

"How do you mean?"

"Take the girl an extra drink. Tell them it's on the house." Marle set out another glass on the counter. "For me, that's as far as it goes. I know what trouble smells like, and those two stink to high heaven."

Tifa poured the juice, but the memory of the girl's disheveled appearance continued to gnaw at her.

Boundaries, huh . . . ? Let's say I do offer to help. How much could I actually do for them? Maybe Marle's right. If I'm not prepared to go all-in, maybe it's better not to say anything at all.

She slid a straw into the glass and headed for the terrace.

When she was just shy of the doors, Marle called from the counter, "Oh, and don't forget to tell them we close at five!"

Outside, Tifa found two of the patio stools pushed together to form a crude bed. On it slept Marlene, curled up like a kitten. It was adorable and heart-wrenching at the same time. The girl was so tiny. So vulnerable.

Meanwhile, her muscled father leaned forward on his stool, elbows on the table for a better view of the street. As usual, he was glaring at everyone who passed by.

Only then did Tifa notice Barret's hands. Or rather, his *hand.* Singular. The man's right arm ended somewhere just above the wrist, covered by a dirty scrap of cloth and a cord wrapped several times around his bulging forearm.

Fear gripped Tifa as she imagined the tale behind the missing appendage. Had he lost it in an accident? A war? Visions of violence invaded her mind.

She was locked in that moment of panic when Barret turned his attention away from the street. He lifted his hand—his *left* hand—to slide the sunglasses down his nose and stare at Tifa again.

His eyes were large, with surprisingly long lashes. They possessed a gentleness, in stark contrast with the aura of intimidation radiating from the rest of his person.

Battling her nerves, Tifa was careful to meet his gaze directly as she spoke.

"This is for Marlene. It's on the house."

She set the glass down carefully so as not to wake the sleeping girl.

"And," she added, "we're very sorry, but Seventh Heaven will be closing at five today. We appreciate your understanding."

He seemed surprised and, frankly, distraught.

"*Five*?! You gotta be shittin' me!"

To which Tifa nervously replied, "No, unfortunately, I'm not. We're having some staffing issues and are unable to serve any alcohol for the time being, so we're closing up early."

"Five o'clock . . ." he repeated, this time soft and wistful. "You gotta be shittin' me . . ."

"I promise you, I most certainly am not."

"All right. I gotcha."

Relief washed over Tifa when he didn't press the issue.

Still, she hadn't cared for the man's flippant, almost-churlish manner of speech. She wanted to say something about it but forced herself to turn and walk away from the table.

When she reached for the door handle, her eyes landed on the leather cord wrapped about her wrist, and for a brief moment, she was back in Nibelheim, days before her fifteenth birthday. Zangan was rummaging through the contents of his knapsack, finally turning back to face her with the mysterious gift in hand.

I'm the one in control. Not my emotions. Me.

When my emotions threaten to consume me, I should glance at my wrist.

By turning away from Barret, had she demonstrated control, or was she simply grasping for an excuse not to offer assistance? Rage wasn't the only face of her inner foe. Rage threatened to rob her of reason, but cowardice was equally insidious. Cowardice

whispered that sometimes it was more sensible not to act. Better
to disengage and avoid the hassle. Tifa could recall many times
throughout childhood when she'd allowed herself to be led by
others rather than standing up for what she felt was right.

"I'm better than this," she muttered to herself.

She removed her hand from the door and twirled to face Barret
once again.

The man looked up at her and grumbled, "Thought you said we
have another hour. It's only four."

"If you don't mind me asking . . . When that hour's up, where
will you go next? Where will you take Marlene?"

Barret sat in silence.

"Where do you two sleep?"

"Here and there."

"I see . . . And . . . what about clothes? Doesn't she have any
other outfits? I noticed neither of you are wearing socks. Is that
because you don't have any? And what about her shoes? The soles
are worn through!"

"Pretty standard, if you ask me. We *are* livin' in the slums."

"No. If you ask me, it's pretty bad. Even for the slums."

"It ain't gonna kill us, all right?"

Tifa slammed her palm against the table. Barret jumped in his
seat.

"*That's* the bar you set for yourself? If you're not dying, you're
doing fine? Doesn't your daughter deserve better?! She needs a
bath! She needs her hair washed! She needs clothes! They don't
have to be new, but they should at least be *clean!*"

"Daddy . . . ?"

Tifa looked over to find she'd woken the girl.

"Daddy, is the lady angry?"

"No, honey . . . We're just, uh . . ."

Marlene stared up at Tifa. Tears welled in the little girl's eyes.

"Don't yell at Daddy!" she sobbed.

Tifa tried to soothe the girl with a smile.

"I'm sorry," she said. "I woke you up, didn't I?"

Marlene just shook her head violently.

"Daddy didn't do anything wrong!"

"I know. You're right. I promise not to yell at him."

"Good."

The little girl bobbed her head in satisfaction. The motion shook flakes of dandruff loose from her tangled locks and sent a slight odor wafting through the air: further evidence of how long she'd been without a bath.

For Tifa, that was the tipping point. Her eyes turned back to Barret, this time filled with fury.

"After we close up shop, you two are coming with me to the Sector 8 slums."

"Excuse me?" snapped Barret.

Marlene regarded Tifa with obvious terror.

Hoping to spare the child additional unease, Tifa leaned close to Barret's ear and whispered, "You know why business always seems so slow around here? It's because our would-be customers are too terrified to come near the place when they see *you* sitting out front!"

She snatched Barret's empty coffee cup to take back inside. The big man flinched.

"Shit. I'm sorry. I didn't mean to cause no trouble."

At which Marlene again began to howl, "No yelling! You promised!"

Tifa looked from the girl's face to her father's again. She could hardly fathom the life they must have led to end up as they were.

When she returned to the counter and recounted the interaction, Marle was unimpressed.

"Don't say I didn't warn you."

"I know. I heard you loud and clear."

"Another busybody. Just what we need around here." Marle sighed. "Hold down the fort, will you? I'll be back before closing."

Seventh Heaven was as quiet as ever during Marle's absence. Just before five, the woman returned, storming up the steps to the patio. She stopped in front of Barret, hands on her hips, launching into a long tirade that Tifa couldn't quite make out. The burly man quickly pulled the sunglasses from his face, terrified and nodding obediently at every word.

Eventually, Marle stomped inside, Barret and Marlene trailing after.

" . . . the basement," she was saying. "I just got back from Monty's, and he gave the okay. He keeps it furnished for his personal use. It's got a bed and plumbing and everything you'll need to get by. So get your tushes down there and into the shower."

"Hold up. Just who the hell's this Monty guy you keep mentioning?"

"Remember the gentleman tending the counter last week? White hair? White mustache?"

"Yeah, I remember the old fart."

"Charming. Well, that old fart, as you so eloquently describe him, happens to be the owner."

Barret's head sank between his shoulders, and Tifa nearly burst out laughing. Every movement the man made was exaggerated. She decided that his speech and manners could use some work, but he didn't seem to be a bad person.

Marle was still berating Barret. "Frankly, Monty's been fretting about that poor girl's welfare since the day you first showed up."

"Guess I probably oughta go see him and say thanks for lendin' us the room . . . "

Marle walked to one side of the bar, making her way along the half wall that separated the kitchen from the floor. After carefully checking her footing, she took a tiny hop, shoes reconnecting with a deep, hollow thud. Then, to Tifa's amazement, a small, square portion of the floor began to sink downward. It was an elevator!

Marlene squealed with delight and ran to join Marle on the slowly sinking panel. Barret scrambled after her with a shout, scooping the little girl up into his arms before she could reach the edge.

Marle slid out of sight, and an eventual clunk from the machinery indicated that the elevator had come to a rest.

"Come on down and see!" she called from below. "All three of you!"

The square panel slowly rose back up, and Barret glanced at Tifa. Tifa shrugged and stepped aboard. Barret followed, Marlene still in his arms.

"This time *Daddy* jumps!" exclaimed Marlene.

"You got it, angel."

The large, muscled man hopped in place, landing with enough force to make the panel shudder.

The square again began its descent. For a brief moment, a cross section of Seventh Heaven's wooden floor filled their sight, and then the bar was gone, replaced by a clean, well-kept studio apartment. In one corner rested a well-made bed. Other furnishings included an expensive-looking couch, a small table with two chairs, and a television. It was a perfect little living space for two.

Marle stood in the center with her arms folded.

"Monty had always dreamed of building a secret hideout," she explained. "Guess you could say he never really grew up. All I see is a massive waste of money. Especially that ridiculous elevator. And he says he *still* isn't done with the place. Wants to add a pinball machine . . . Anyway, it's yours to use as you like."

"Now that I've seen the place, I *definitely* have to pay my respects. Where can I find the guy?"

"I think he'll manage just fine without your respects. If you really feel the need to say something, save it until tomorrow. Now, I'm serious. Get yourselves into the shower before I pass out." Marle made a show of pinching her nose with her thumb and forefinger.

"Oh, and here," she added, holding out a small bundle of clothing with her other hand. "I brought a change for Marlene. A dress and everything else she needs. I'm guessing she's no longer in diapers."

"I'm a big girl!" Marlene replied with obvious pride.

Once more, Tifa was filled with the urge to scoop the girl up in a big hug. It was a new and somewhat bewildering feeling. Perhaps their brief interactions had awakened some motherly instinct.

Marle looked at Tifa. "I'll get these two sorted. You can run along—

"Oh!" exclaimed the woman, interrupting herself. "I almost forgot. You and I have one other thing to discuss. I'll take you back upstairs."

The two returned to the square panel of the elevator. Marlene called after them as she tugged her arms free of their sleeves.

"You have to jump! Jump to make it go!"

Marle grinned, her eyes turning to slits. She hopped in place with another little thump, and the elevator began to rise.

On the way up, Tifa pondered Seventh Heaven's mysterious owner. The existence of the room was startling and the design of the elevator eccentric, to say the least. What sort of past was hidden behind the man's dapper, white-framed features?

"I'd also like to see Monty," she announced. "To express my thanks. And to wish him a quick recovery."

Marle shook her head. "Next week. He'll need a few days before he's up for visitors."

"Oh . . ."

"Don't you fret. Monty's got me looking after him. Heaven knows I'm stuck with the old coot."

Obviously eager to change the subject, Marle next asked, "What's your take on Barret? Now that we've heard more than two words out of the guy, I'm thinking he'd make a pretty good bouncer. Not to mention all the heavy boxes he could lift for us."

A snort escaped Tifa. Not one hour ago, Marle was lambasting her over the decision to take Barret and Marlene to Container Row. Now that the two vagrants were officially in Seventh Heaven's care, the woman was acting as if she'd meant to help them all along. Her infinite kindness was showing through.

"I'm the best busybody this side of the plate," sniffed Marle. "I'm not about to be shown up by a little rustic like you."

When they reached the patio, Marle took a quick glance around to make sure no one else was in earshot.

"Got a reply from Jessie," she whispered.

Tifa's eyes widened.

"She says, 'The week after next, on your day off. Wait to hear from me regarding time and place. Excited to see you.'"

Her breath caught in her throat.

Two weeks from today!

She was actually going to *see* Jessie again!

"How's that for a surprise?" Marle winked.

"Thank you! I don't know how I can ever repay you . . ."

"Enough of that. Just tell me we'll keep seeing you at Seventh Heaven. Same time next week?"

"Of course!"

She parted with Marle at the doors, glancing back once as she made her way down the street. A few would-be customers milled about Seventh Heaven's steps, obviously disappointed to find the bar closed. She wondered if they were there to see her and felt a twinge of regret at not being able to welcome them with a smile.

If only she knew how to make cocktails. They wouldn't have to wait until Monty was ready to come back; they could resume evening hours immediately.

Or perhaps it was better to focus on the lunch menu first? Soon her mind was racing, filled with ideas for how to save Seventh Heaven and dreams of what the establishment could someday be.

She was halfway down the alley leading to Container Row when she noticed Rakesh. He was leaning against one wall, near the spot where the Watchman used to place his stool.

"Welcome back," he said.

"Thanks," she replied hesitantly.

"Whatcha been up t—" Rakesh cut himself off with a shake of his head. "Sorry. Didn't mean to pry. It just slips out."

"What're you doing in the alley?"

"Manson's got me in charge of monitoring who comes and goes. Just till we find a new watch."

"Oh. Must be tough."

"Eh." Rakesh shrugged. "It's one more responsibility to balance, but whatcha gonna do?"

"Right. Well . . . good night."

Tifa was anxious to exit the situation before Rakesh launched into another tirade about how Manson called the shots and there was no getting away. She hurried to her apartment, yanked off the padlock, and shut herself inside.

When she tugged the cord for the light, she was greeted by familiar squalor. Whatever glimmer of new hope the day at Seventh Heaven had fostered, or belief in how much better things could be, the dingy apartment was here to laugh them away.

She knelt by the bed, dragging out the bin and yanking the purse free from a tangle of clothing.

She held it to her chest in silence there on the floor. She didn't need to open it. She didn't need to count the money inside. She knew exactly how much it contained. Every bill and every coin represented a sacrifice. She'd chosen a quiet existence, free from indulgence, and the effort was poised to pay off, speeding repayment of her debt by a full year.

Two years left to freedom. Two years until she was no longer bound by Manson's rules. The comforting weight of the purse in her arms brought strength surging back to her body. Tifa stood and began retracing Zangan's forms.

She hadn't seen her master for years. What was he doing? Where could he be? The forms, she knew, were slowly slipping— becoming more hers than his—and she didn't know what to make of it. She wished Zangan would knock at her door as he had in Nibelheim, unexpected and unannounced, eager to observe her progress and offer critiques.

In all that time, had Zangan never passed through Midgar? Wouldn't he attempt to seek her out? Surely he could inquire at the clinic. Dhamini and Rakesh would tell him where to find her. Rakesh had only to lead him down the main street, point out the alley to Container Row, and . . .

Tifa froze mid-form.

How had she not seen it? When Marle had checked out of the clinic, she left an address. Maybe hers wasn't the only one Rakesh had conveniently failed to relay.

She rushed out of her container and back up the alley.

"Rakesh!" she yelled.

He was still leaning against the wall.

"Whoa, there. Something wrong?"

"When Marle went home from the clinic, she left a message for me. But you didn't tell me about it, did you?"

"Marle . . . ?"

He was feigning ignorance. She could tell right away.

After a moment, his face lit up—a forced expression, if she'd ever seen one—and he said, "Oh! The older woman who had the skin graft. Yeah, I remember her. Man, that was what . . . two years ago? No message, though. I would've remembered that. She was pretty old, and you know how elderly people are . . . Months down the line, they claim to have said something when they really didn't, and then it becomes this whole big argument."

Now he was rambling. Nervous.

"Has Master Zangan been by to see you?" she pressed.

"Zangan? Um . . . Nope. Not for a long time."

"How long? When was the last time he visited?"

"Uh . . . I'm not sure. Lemme think . . ."

He was stalling, trying to whip up a story, and it wouldn't have been more obvious if he'd said as much out loud. How had she never recognized what a terrible liar he was? Anger bubbled up from the pit of her stomach: anger at *herself* for not knowing better. Right hand flew to left wrist, clamping down on the leather cord like an iron vise. Lately, she'd noticed the cord was black and full of tiny cracks.

Rakesh cleared his throat, finally answering with, "I honestly couldn't say exactly. But trust me, it's been *ages*."

Tifa's voice grew cold. "If you see him, tell him where I am. Tell him about Container Row and about the food cart. Ask him to come find me. And make sure your mother knows to tell him too."

"Yeah. Sure. Of course."

An overly sweet smile spread across Rakesh's lips. He seemed relieved, as if he'd dodged a bullet—or a fist.

Another Wednesday rolled around. Tifa had been excited to see Marlene all cleaned up and wearing her new outfit, but the news at Seventh Heaven was even bleaker than before.

Monty had passed away.

As Marle told it, his condition had taken a sudden turn for the worse on Sunday. When she checked in on him early Monday morning, he'd gone cold, and his chest was still.

Barret found some small consolation in the fact that he and Marlene had paid the man a visit on Sunday, just long enough to express their thanks for the use of Seventh Heaven's basement.

Marle reached for Tifa's hand and gripped it tight. "I'm sorry. I should have let you see him last week when you asked. I feel awful . . ."

Tifa didn't know what to say.

The old woman forced a smile. "Nothing to do now but keep our promise to the old coot . . . Let's make sure Seventh Heaven shines while it lasts."

Marle turned to get things ready for opening, and to Tifa's astonishment, so did Barret and Marlene. In the intervening week, they appeared to have divvied up the establishment's responsibilities. Barret mopped the floor with a determined grimace. Little Marlene scurried to the back and returned with a washcloth, proceeding to run from table to table wiping down each of the stools eagerly, if not necessarily thoroughly.

The girl was wearing an adorable little dress with an oversized bow at the back, a vast improvement over her tattered former attire. Her hair was thoroughly brushed and shining.

"We'll go until five again today," explained Marle. "Oh, and be prepared to stick around for a bit after closing. We've got some important things to discuss, courtesy of Monty."

All in all, business wasn't too bad. Marle joked that things had improved as soon as Barret adopted his new routine; since taking up residence in the basement, he'd begun heading out on long walks through the slums, leaving Marlene in Marle's care during business hours and returning in time to help with the close each evening.

The little girl, for her part, appeared to enjoy the arrangement. She sat behind the counter in a tiny chair, just high enough to peer out over the bar and vocally take charge of all the goings-on of Seventh Heaven.

"According to Barret, they arrived in Midgar about a year ago," Marle mentioned during a lull. "Marlene was just a babe."

She lowered her voice so the little girl wouldn't hear, and continued. "They'd been wandering from town to town. Along the way, Barret took an interest in planetology, and he kept up with it here in the slums. The believers hold quiet gatherings and film screenings, you see.

"Anyway, he says he met some woman at one of the screenings

and wanted to find her again, and that's how he ended up here. His plan was to sit on the patio every day and watch the road, hoping she might pass by.

"But here's the kicker," said Marle, leaning in closer. "The woman he's searching for? None other than Jessie Rasberry."

Tifa nodded in silence.

"Where we go from here is up to you. Help put him in touch or no, I'll respect your decision. Of course, I'll have plenty to say about it either way."

A customer signaled from his table; Marle went to tend to his order. For no particular reason, Tifa glanced at the counter, and her eyes happened to meet Marlene's. She smiled at the little girl and then impulsively puffed up her cheeks, widened her eyes, and spun her pupils in a wide circle. It was a face Tifa's mother used to pull to get her daughter to laugh. Not once in her life had Tifa thought to copy it. In fact, she hadn't recalled her mother's silly faces for years until this particular instant, when this one inexplicably popped into her mind. In any case, it sent little Marlene into a fit of giggles.

They were closing up when Barret returned. His expression was one of obvious disappointment.

Marlene ran to her father, welcoming him with a great big hug. When Barret released his grasp on the girl, Marle called, "Marlene! How about you go downstairs and watch some TV? *Stamp* will be on soon."

"Really? Can I?"

Marlene looked at her father, who smiled back and said, "Go on. Enjoy your show."

The little girl squealed with delight. She scrambled atop the secret square panel, and—while simultaneously shouting "Jump!" at the top of her lungs—leapt into the air and came crashing down on the wood with an impressive thud. She waved at the other members of Seventh Heaven's ragtag staff as the elevator descended and she sank from view.

Marle placed a palm-sized notebook on the counter.

"We'll start with you, Tifa," she said, gesturing at the well-worn notebook. "This here is Monty's life's work. It contains every cocktail recipe he ever came across or made up himself. He wanted you to have it."

The moment Tifa laid eyes on the notebook, her heart skipped a beat. She was destined to pass through this moment, like a waypoint set by fate for her journey through life. Both in size and color of binding, Monty's notebook was indistinguishable from the booklets detailing the secrets of Zangan's art.

"It must have been very important to him."

"If you can handle the weight, and the *responsibility*, it's yours."

"I can," responded Tifa.

She picked the notebook up and glanced inside. Monty's immaculate handwriting filled every page, top to bottom, interspersed with numerous hand-drawn illustrations.

"Damn," murmured Barret. "If you memorize what's in there and we open back up in the evenings, this place'd be hopping in no time. I could be your bouncer. Anyone gets outta line, I'll throw him out by the scruff of his neck."

"The three of us carrying on the legacy of Seventh Heaven . . . It might be fun."

It sounded like a fairy tale, almost too good to be true.

Barret flashed a confident grin. "You bet it would."

Marle didn't share their enthusiasm. When Tifa noticed the woman's downcast eyes, she asked, "What's wrong?"

"If only we could. There's a payment due on the property. Two hundred thousand gil by the end of the month. Monty was still paying off the cost of Seventh Heaven to the builder who constructed the place. The builder had already been more than generous, letting Monty drag out the repayment much longer than they originally agreed. But he's got his own finances to think of, and Monty's passing only made him more anxious."

"Only two hundred grand? Seems like a steal for a place this size."

"That's what we'd pay up front. After that, it's back to the original monthly installments."

"Ah. I getcha."

Barret scratched at his stubble and added, "Wish I could pitch in, but I ain't got ten gil to my name, much less thousands."

"Monty's estate will cover forty thousand of that down payment. It'd be up to us to cover the other hundred and sixty. Otherwise, Seventh Heaven goes up for sale. And trust me, it won't stay on the market long. This is prime real estate."

Barret took the news in stride. He shrugged and said, "Too bad. Marlene's gonna be sad about leavin' this place."

"And then what?" demanded Marle. "Don't tell me you're gonna start sleeping out in the open again."

"Sleeping bags ain't cheap."

"What kind of father are you?!" exclaimed Tifa.

He met their exasperation with a dismissive sniff.

"Spare me the lecture. I want what's best for the girl, same as any dad. I'd dress her up, braid her hair, make sure she's got a hot shower, and give her a big ol' fluffy bed to sleep in—if I *could*. But when you're broke, you don't really have the option.

"The one thing I *can* give us is freedom. No beggin'. No borrowin'. The second you let yourself get tied down by someone else's coin, you've lost your agency. Takin' on debt's the kinda behavior that leaves your parents chokin' back tears."

He was speaking hypothetically; he had no reason to think his words would hit so close to home. But Barret's admonishments forced Tifa to see her situation for what it truly was. No ray of hope could change the reality that she was tied down, slogging through an existence others looked upon with pity and disdain.

"My parents are dead," she replied. It was the only piece she could find to refute.

"Aw, shit. Don't tell me *you're* sinking in debt. How old are you, anyway?"

When Tifa remained quiet, Barret sighed. "I didn't mean to strike a nerve. It's just . . . Hell, it doesn't mean they're gone. Your parents live on inside the planet, y'know? You, me, we're all connected. As long as we've got the lifestream, we've still got the people that matter to us, whether they're breathing or not."

"Wrong," interjected Marle. "When you're dead, you're dead. Done. Free of your worries, and everyone else is free to stop worrying about you. Be happy that the people who cared about you will carry on your memory, and keep your planetology nonsense to yourself."

"Hmph." Barret scowled, but held his peace.

"Anyway, it sounds to me like we've reached a decision. Sorry to say it, but come the last day of the month, we'll be closing our doors for good," Marle said.

Barret nodded. "Let's go out with a bang."

The conclusion drawn by Marle and Barret, and the speed at which it was reached, left Tifa frustrated. They were talking about the fate of Seventh Heaven. About Monty's legacy. How could they agree to surrender it so flippantly?

A tiny, trembling voice interrupted her thoughts.

"No more home?"

The three adults had been so engrossed in their conversation, they hadn't heard the elevator carry Marlene back to ground level.

"No more Seventh Heaven?"

She was on the verge of tears.

Barret tried to steer her attention elsewhere. "Hey, what happened to your show? What's Stamp up to?"

But Marlene only shook her head.

"No more home?" she repeated. "I don't wanna sleep outside."

"It's all right, baby. We'll get by. Daddy'll find you another home."

"I like this one! I wanna stay here!"

Barret walked toward the panel, bending to pick Marlene up, but the girl slipped past and ran to Tifa, peeking out from behind her legs.

"Here!" she shouted again. "I wanna stay here!"

Her lip continued to tremble, and then she was past the brink, erupting into a long, loud wail.

"I have money," Tifa blurted unexpectedly. "I have the hundred and sixty thousand."

Marle and Barret stared at her wide-eyed.

She didn't know if it was right. She didn't know if it was smart to tell them about the money or to offer to keep Seventh Heaven afloat. But she found herself doing so anyway.

When they'd discussed the details and Tifa announced that she was heading home, Barret offered to walk her to the edge of the sector. She shook her head and told him it wasn't necessary, but he insisted. They needed to talk, he said. Leaving Marlene in Marle's care, he followed her out into the night.

"I'll pay you back," the burly man said. "I dunno how or when, but I'll find a way. Even if it means I gotta make the ghosts of my own parents cry."

"It's fine. Really. I'm doing it because I like the place. I want to keep working there. I'm going to learn Monty's recipes and put cocktails back on the menu. By the time I'm done, Seventh Heaven's going to be the most popular bar in the slums. It's just the kind of adventure I've been looking for."

She glanced at Barret and smiled before allowing her eyes to return to the packed dirt of the sector's streets. "I won't lie and say Marlene's crying had nothing to do with it. But all she did was push me along in the direction I was already headed.

"So . . . if you're really set on paying me back, buy a pinball machine someday. We'll put it in the corner, just like Monty wanted."

"Hmph."

She was glad for Barret's company. Putting the feelings into words helped steel her resolve. For all the times she'd calculated the months and years remaining until she was free from her debt to Manson, everything beyond was a blank. Seventh Heaven had intersected her journey right when she needed it, offering new purpose and new means to get by. Barret had the secret base under the bar, but for Tifa, the bar itself was a sanctuary among the slums.

"I got one other thing to ask," said Barret. "I hear you're a friend of Jessie Rasberry's."

She looked up with a start. "Did Marle tell you?"

"Marlene. She knows that's where I'm goin' everyday—to look for Jessie."

Tifa recalled that Marlene had been behind the counter when Marle told her of Barret's search. The little girl certainly was perceptive.

"Can you put me in touch?" he asked.

"Can I ask why? If it's about planetology, I'm pretty sure there's someone else I can introduce you to. One of the customers at my other job is a big believer."

"For me, planetology's just the front." Barret's voice grew quiet. "I'm lookin' to go deeper. I want an intro to Avalanche.

"I heard the film screenings usually have operatives in attendance. That's why I started goin'. So far, Jessie's the only one I'm sure about, and believe me, I've put out a hell of a lot of feelers. I want in, but Shinra's squeezin' so tight, the whole organization's gone quiet."

"I hear it's only gotten worse because of the news from Corel."

"That's where me 'n' Marlene rolled in from."

A chill ran down Tifa's spine.

"She and I both lost our home and family. Now Shinra's sayin' Avalanche was behind the explosion. But if you ask me, the company's the one that started it all. I came to Midgar to tear their whole damn empire down, starting with *that*."

He thrust a finger high into the air, pointing at one of the city's distant reactors.

"If somebody doesn't stop those things, we all lose. I didn't think about it till I started listenin' to the planetologists, but that's what mako reactors do. They suck up life. The planet's *dyin'*, Tifa.

"Thing is, Shinra's too much for one man to take on. I need allies. Where one fails, many prevail, y'know?"

Tifa couldn't help but smile. Jessie had used the same expression during her first visit to Container Row.

"So whaddaya say? Me lookin' for Jessie and you knowin' the girl . . . It's what Marle would call fate, don't you think?"

"Maybe so. Whether Jessie meets with you or not is something she'll have to decide. But I'll let her know you're looking."

"Good enough. Looks like I owe you another one, Tifa."

The next week passed without incident—or so it seemed. Sales at Sector 8 Steamed Buns had been as strong as ever, and Tifa was rolling the cart back toward its railcar on Tuesday night when Pops posed an unusual question.

"You still spendin' time with those Avalanche folk?"

"Huh?"

Tifa didn't remember mentioning anything about spending time with Jessie and her friends to Pops. There was the sudden and unexpected warning he'd issued about the group as a whole—she still remembered the way her hands had trembled as she skimmed froth from the pot of cooking meat. But she felt certain that was the only time their conversation had touched upon Avalanche.

"No," she finally answered. If he really knew, there wasn't much point in denying it. "I don't know where they are these days. I guess you'd say we fell out of touch."

"Good. It's for the best."

He seemed unusually somber.

"Why do you ask?"

"Just somethin' I heard. There's a meeting tomorrow night at ten. Real hush-hush. Representatives from all the different factions of Avalanche are gettin' together. Hard to say what it's about, but if I had to guess, they're probably trying to regroup and take the offensive.

"What they don't know," continued Pops, "is that Shinra's onto them. Word from topside is that the company's preppin' helicopters, special forces units, the works. They're gonna hit Avalanche so hard, it won't be comin' back."

"Oh."

"You're the best business partner I've ever had, and I don't like seein' you upset. So I figured maybe, if you happened to still have any friends who might be at this meeting, you'd wanna warn 'em. That's all."

"I appreciate the concern. But really, there's no need."

"All right, then. See you Thursday."

Pops began to saunter off. A few steps out, he said, "One of these days we'll hit fifteen hundred yet."

A surge of guilt swept through Tifa. She thought of her growing commitment to Seventh Heaven, and her arms fell slack. The cart rolled to a stop.

"I . . ." It took her a moment to gather the courage to say it. "I'm planning to quit. As soon as my debt to Manson is settled, I'll be going elsewhere."

Pops stopped walking but didn't turn. He responded with a hum, and then, "You gettin' close to payin' it off?"

"No. I'm still a ways off. I just thought I should let you know in advance."

"Fair enough. How 'bout we aim for two thousand before you go? The more you sell, the quicker you get outta here."

Halfway down the alley to Container Row, Rakesh was leaning against the wall, still manning the watch.

"Welcome back," he said.

"Thanks."

She avoided his eyes and walked quickly by.

"Hey, Tifa?" he called after her. "How about swinging by the clinic tomorrow? It's been a while, and Mom would love to catch up."

"Sorry. I've got plans."

Rakesh didn't push. "Oh. No worries. We'll take a rain check."

She was several paces away when she had the impulse to turn around and snap, "You can quit worrying about my intentions, all right? I'll stay here and work for Manson until the money's all paid back."

She twirled away and stormed off, not leaving him a chance to reply.

Every gil she'd saved and stashed away was now going to Seventh Heaven. It meant several more months under Manson's thumb, but that was fine. It was the path she'd chosen, and she was determined to work harder than ever.

It was her other problem that had her worried. How was she supposed to warn Jessie about tomorrow's raid?

Maybe Jessie already knew. Maybe she wasn't planning to attend in the first place. Still, Tifa didn't want to take the chance. There had to be some way to get in touch.

Her hand was on the padlock when the idea struck, so hard it made her gasp. It was a long shot, but surely worth a try.

Tifa hurried to the far end of the Row, where she found the Waterkeeper on duty as always. She calmed her breathing, trying to sound casual.

"Evening."

"Tifa. How's your day been? Gonna grab a shower before bed?"

"Yes, but . . . I was wondering if I could ask you something." Tifa lowered her voice. "I've heard Avalanche is planning a big meeting tomorrow at ten, but Shinra's laying a trap. I want to get a warning out."

"Why're you tellin' me? Shinra's the one that thinks my boy's runnin' around with the group. I ain't lyin' about it bein' ten years since I last seen him."

"Oh. I see . . ."

"And anyway, where'd you get yourself a dangerous piece of information like that?"

"It was someone I work with. He calls himself Pops."

Even as she said it, she wasn't sure it was a detail to be sharing. Did the Waterkeeper know who Pops was? Was it safe to be talking to her about Pops's secret?

The woman folded her arms in front of her chest. "Hmph. Yeah, I might know the guy. Still, it don't change the fact that there's nothin' I can do to help."

"Sorry," apologized Tifa. "I figured it might be an awkward topic."

The Waterkeeper pursed her lips tight. It seemed their conversation was over.

Tifa returned to her apartment, racking her brain for other options. Marle had delivered a message once. Perhaps she could do it again. Marle's method didn't seem particularly quick—it had taken days to get through and for the response to come back—but it was still better than nothing.

Was it worth risking an immediate trip to Sector 7? It was late, and the streets could be perilous. Then again, come morning Tifa would be headed in that direction anyway. Why not leave now and spend the night at Seventh Heaven?

She pulled out a bag and was about to begin packing. Almost as if on cue, there was a knock at the door.

"No need to open up," came a small voice that Tifa recognized as the Waterkeeper's. "I just came to say that our little chat jogged my memory. My boy once told me about a way to reach him, so I tried it and got through. He seemed real happy about your message. Said he'd share the news with all his friends."

"That's good to hear," replied Tifa. "Thank you for telling me."

"One other thing . . . Seems there was a message for you too.

'Tomorrow, Wednesday, nine p.m. at the birthday theater.' That's all he said."

"Huh?"

Her confusion received no reply; the Waterkeeper was already gone.

Birthday theater . . .

Tifa puzzled over the words. Tomorrow was the day she was supposed to meet Jessie, and—

Of course! The planetology screening! The first one she'd attended, on the night of her seventeenth birthday. Jessie had said she'd be in touch; the message had to be from her, asking to meet at the abandoned home used for the screening.

When Tifa went to shower early the next morning, the Waterkeeper was no more cordial than usual. It was as if the previous day's conversations had never occurred, and perhaps that was the point: as far as anyone else was concerned, they hadn't.

Tifa had dozens of questions. Most of all, she longed to know the specifics of this mysterious method of communication the woman had alluded to. How had she been able to get in touch with her son so quickly? And how had the message meant for Tifa been relayed in the process? Was the Waterkeeper able to contact Jessie too? Everything Tifa had heard about cell phones in the slums suggested that signal strength was just as bad or worse than Nibelheim. But if it wasn't a phone, what else could it be?

As she left the Row that morning, she briefly stopped at the mouth of the alley, turning to observe the jumble of shipping containers. She found herself imagining the occupants of the other units—something she used to actively avoid doing, on Rakesh's advice.

What if all this time, Jessie had been lying low here, ensconced in one of the other anonymous containers, right under Tifa's nose? The idea struck her as comical, and yet somehow within the realm of possibility.

When she arrived at Seventh Heaven, the place was alive with activity despite not yet being open for business. Marlene was running from chair to chair, furiously wiping each one down with her damp washcloth.

"Marlene might be even better at drawin' the crowds than you," announced Barret. The giant of a man was beaming from ear to ear. "The last three or four days, business has been boomin'. So much so, I'm thinkin' we could make it on mornings and afternoons alone."

Marle rolled her eyes. "Don't kid yourself. We've still got a long way to go."

She turned to Tifa and said, "Listen, about the builder. Does next Wednesday at seven p.m. work? I'll have him swing by the bar to pick up the payment in person."

"I'll have it ready."

"That's a lotta cash to carry around," observed Marle. "You got it in large bills?"

"Oh, um . . ."

Tifa hadn't considered the logistics.

"Most of it is in bills. But there are a lot of coins too."

"I can give ya a hand," said Barret. "We'll close up shop for the day, and I'll meet you at your place in the morning."

"How long are you expecting this trip of yours to take?!" griped Marle. "Marlene and I are perfectly capable of holding down the fort while you two fetch the cash."

Barret responded with a cheerful, "You got it."

"Good. Now that that's settled, let's get this place open. We've got a reputation to uphold."

Within minutes, Tifa could see that Barret was right. Business *was* booming, and just as he'd boasted, Marlene was the center of it all. The most surprising development was the number of families. The little girl's presence seemed to have solidified Seventh Heaven's reputation as kid-friendly.

That evening, as the last few customers filed out, Marle sidled up to Tifa.

"Tonight's the night, yeah? Your long-awaited reunion."

"I hope so."

"Just remember one thing. She's Avalanche. No matter how

good a person she may be, that doesn't guarantee anything about her associates. These freedom fighter types tend to have all the best intentions and all the worst ways of seeing them through. No act's too scummy if it's carried out under the banner of justice, or so they'd have you believe."

"I'll be careful."

"Then off you go. Skedaddle before I decide to lecture you some more."

"Sorry to make you worry."

"You should be!"

Marle did look about to say something more, but Tifa hurried to the doors, turning back only briefly to repeat that she'd have the money with her next week.

Jessie's proposed meeting spot was located in Sector 8, right along the border with Sector 7. Tifa knew the place well; she'd visited the lone, empty house several times when Jessie first disappeared, hoping to perhaps run into her. The surrounding lot, with its endless, towering heaps of scrap, was a familiar sight, if somewhat unsettling.

Over all her visits, she'd never encountered anything dangerous, but the landscape made her nervous all the same. Who knew what might be lurking among the jagged shadows?

The time of day didn't help. Night elsewhere in the slums was a facsimile. The sun lamps turned on and off, but it was never truly dark under the plate with its countless blinking lights. Out here near the wall, night was primal. It stirred fear and flooded the nostrils with reminders that the city and its great bulwarks were but a few fragile stacks of metal on the planet's vast surface.

A voice hissed from among the scrap.

"Tifa!"

Her heart nearly leapt from her chest, first with fear, and—after she turned—again with joy.

"Jessie!"

Tifa's long-lost friend sported a hooded sweatshirt and lightweight, cropped pants. She dashed around the stray piles of scrap toward Tifa, the light rapping of her footsteps puncturing the silence of night.

"We have to go. This place isn't—"

For a moment, Tifa couldn't comprehend what happened. The whole world seemed to explode around her. She heard a deafening roar and saw fountains of orange and yellow sparks billowing from a mound of rusted metal at her side. The sparks traced long, impossibly slow arcs through the air.

Then a hand was on her wrist, and she was being pulled forward, running, weaving among the piles of scrap.

"Stay low and zigzag!" commanded Jessie. "We gotta get back to the heart of the slums!"

There was another violent burst of staccato, and Tifa's mind finally caught up.

Gunfire.

Something unseen whizzed past. She felt a sharp sting at her cheek and cried out, whipping her free hand up to nurse the pain. Her fingers came away red and wet. Her head began to swim.

"Over there!"

Tifa heard the words, but her mind couldn't piece together what Jessie meant.

"Don't let go," she pleaded.

"I won't."

The weapons blared again, and the dirt at Tifa's feet popped and plumed. More sparks flew from the endless piles of scrap, bounding over to singe her where the bullets had missed. All around was chaos. Death buzzed through the air. She was afraid, and her stomach threatened to turn inside out.

"Stupid," muttered Jessie.

"What is it?"

"Open your eyes and see for yourself."

They'd come to a stop. At some point, Tifa must have squeezed her eyes shut. She cautiously opened them and peered around. They were huddled in the shadow of a giant rusted construction vehicle—what the years and scavengers had left of it, anyway.

"I'm guessing three with machine guns," whispered Jessie. "They must've been waiting among the scrap when you and I showed up. They don't have a shot on us now, but they will if we try to move."

The weapons had indeed ceased. Perhaps the assailants weren't quite sure of their targets' location.

Jessie sighed. "Shit. Betcha that's exactly what they want. Like waiting for a couple of birds in a bush."

"Who are they? Why are they shooting at us?"

"You heard about the joint meeting, right? The site we'd chosen is near the outer edge of Sector 6. Last night, when we got your tip, we figured the location must have leaked, so we called it off.

"Thing is, Shinra's stupider than we thought. They didn't have a fix on the actual meeting site. Just a vague tip that it'd be somewhere in the outskirts of the slums. So what do they do? They arrange teams to storm every suspicious location they can think of along the city's entire perimeter."

Jessie pointed to the sky. "Listen."

Tifa caught the distant roar of helicopters, gunfire, and explosions. Jessie was right. They weren't the only ones currently under fire.

"By the time we figured it out, I was too late. I'd sent word for you to meet me here by the wall. I'm just glad I made it at all. Another minute and . . ."

Shaking her head, Jessie continued. "Anyway, we're screwed now. It'd take a miracle to get us out of this one. Like, the kind of thing they'll write books about someday. In the musicals, the heroine always gets whisked off to safety, but reality's not so kind. You wouldn't happen to have a weapon on you by any chance?"

"Only these," replied Tifa, holding up her fists.

"Ooh! Check out Miss Confident! I'm guessing they don't work as well when the other guy's got better range?"

"Probably not. Well . . . maybe. I've never tried."

Tifa flexed an arm absentmindedly as she commanded herself to breathe.

"Um! Let's scratch that! I appreciate the willingness to try. I really do. But experimenting now would be a good way to wind up *dead*."

A slow whine filled the air, rupturing into a long, loud roar, much deeper than the staccato braying of the weapons from before. Bullets pinged off nearby metal in such numbers, they formed their own constant ringing. The cacophony held for an eternity, assaulting their minds and ears until the sound alone seemed just as capable of killing as the slugs it signaled.

When it finally paused, Jessie groaned, "No, no, no . . . They're pinning us down so they can close in. Standard maneuver. Oh, god! I can't die yet. I'm too young to die!"

She shook her head vigorously. "Okay, how's this? We make like we're throwing in the towel and watch for a chance to bolt. Got something white? A handkerchief? Anything?"

Tifa tried to think, but another fusillade filled her ears with thunder. This one seemed to stop as abruptly as it started . . . or perhaps not. She could still hear it, though muted and far off. Maybe the noise had blown out her hearing.

A strangely familiar voice yelled out in between bursts of fire. A *male* voice.

"Tifa! You hurt?!"

"No way!" gasped Jessie. "Life *is* a stage! A gallant hero swoops in for a daring rescue!"

"Tifa!" repeated the deep, resonant voice. "You still breathin'?! Answer me!"

Tifa couldn't believe it. What was *Barret* doing out here?!

"I'm alive!" she shouted back, thin and trembling. "Over here!"

"Come on out," called Barret. "Three scumbags down. Let's not be around when their friends show up."

Jessie cautiously emerged from their hiding spot behind the rusted construction vehicle. Tifa followed.

"You're a hard woman to track down."

In a small clearing roughly ten meters off stood Barret.

"H-hey! I remember you!" stammered Jessie. "From one of the planetology screenings. Barret, right? What are *you* doing here?"

"Like I said. Been searchin' for *you*. Turned the whole sector inside out tryin' to track you down."

"Great. Not only is Shinra after me; I've got a stalker too."

Tifa hardly heard them. Her eyes were locked on Barret's right arm. Fitted over the amputated wrist, and extending up most of the forearm, was the largest gun she'd ever seen. It looked like the sort of thing normally mounted on a military vehicle, or lugged onto a battlefield during wartime. Its six barrels still steamed and glowed faintly from the hail of bullets recently unleashed.

"Barret . . ." she finally managed to say. "Where did that come from?"

"This ol' thing? Just a little symbol of my resolve. I try not to wear it around town, out of consideration for the normal folk. But when the goin' gets tough . . ."

Tifa's eyes finally registered the other occupants in the clearing: three Shinra troopers, all dead on the ground. Next to one was a heavy-looking machine gun; it must have been the source of the deafening thunder she and Jessie had endured under cover. Still, it was nowhere near the size of Barret's weapon.

"Lucky for you two, these morons got cocky. Left their backs wide open when they advanced. I just hope Tifa can look past it."

"Huh?"

"It was either you or them."

"Oh . . . Yeah, I know."

"I'd appreciate it if you didn't tell Marlene."

"Don't worry. I wouldn't dream of it."

In the distance, they could still hear the blare of other automatic weapons. Helicopters darted through the undercity skies, some near the plate and others swooping close against the ground.

Jessie cleared her throat. "Think maybe we could save the conversation until *after* we get the hell out of here?"

"Good call. Tifa, let's get you home."

"You're coming with me?"

"Marle's orders. And, Jessie, I'd be obliged if you could join us. Got a few things I wanna ask before I lose you again."

As the trio made their way to Container Row, Barret explained his well-timed appearance at the abandoned house.

"You can thank Marle," he said. "Practically shoved me out the door, squawkin' about how things didn't feel right and I needed to keep an eye on Tifa. So I tailed you out to the wall. Lost sight of you for a while in the scrap heap, but our friends from Shinra were nice enough to point me right to you."

"Nice of you to wait until we were seconds from dying," replied Jessie, glowering at their new companion.

"Hey, all's well that ends well."

At long last, they arrived at the alley for Container Row. Rakesh, still at the Watchman's post, was visibly shaking when he caught sight of Barret.

"Just inviting a couple of friends over," said Tifa.

"C-cool. Don't let me stop you."

He stumbled two steps backward, pressing up against the alley wall with eyes as wide as saucers. Tifa very nearly burst out laughing. As she led her friends the rest of the way to her apartment, she realized the tension of the firefight was finally beginning to subside.

"My humble abode," she announced beside the door. "I appreciate the escort. Did you want to come inside?"

Barret regarded the container with suspicion. "Not sure if I'm gonna fit, and frankly, I'm none too excited to find out. But Jessie and me have things to talk about, and since it could get intense, privacy's probably best."

"You know, today was supposed to be *my* big reunion with Jessie."

"I'll keep it short," promised Barret.

She removed the padlock, opened the door, and stepped aside. Barret went in first, with a few helpful shoves from the girls. Next was Jessie, and finally Tifa.

"Oh, geez," groaned Jessie once they were all inside. "This place was *not* designed with three people in mind. Especially when one of them's the size of a tank."

Barret was hunched uncomfortably against one wall, and again Tifa had to stifle laughter.

"Why are you livin' in this dump?" complained the big man. "It's more depressing than sleepin' on the streets."

"It's . . . complicated."

"All right, big guy," said Jessie. "What is it you're dying to discuss?"

"I'm gonna keep it simple."

Barret lowered himself to the floor with a thud. He shifted his weight, trying to find a comfortable position, eventually settling down cross-legged.

"You're Avalanche, and I want in. Set up an intro with your leader for me. Elfe, was it?"

Jessie perched on the edge of Tifa's bed, casually drawing her feet up to sit cross-legged as well. Tifa leaned against the wall across from her, listening to the conversation.

"Oof . . ." muttered Jessie, scratching at her cheek and then the side of her stomach. "That . . . might not be as simple as you think. Lemme try to explain."

Barret leaned forward.

"As far as whether Elfe's in charge, you're right and you're wrong. In theory, she still leads the main faction—the *original* Avalanche, I guess you'd say. The only thing is . . . there hasn't been a lot of clear direction from HQ for a few years now. It's like Elfe's core group has lost its drive, or it's not sure what it wants to accomplish anymore.

"Whatever the reason, it's causing serious friction. Members have been splitting off, each with their own ideas of how to move ahead, and now we're left with a bunch of little Avalanches instead of one cohesive group. We're talking three, ten, maybe twenty members per faction. Nowhere near the manpower needed to take on Shinra in any meaningful way.

"Lately, some of us have been trying to merge back together or at least cooperate, but it always ends up in arguments that get us nowhere. Some of us are trying to take down Shinra. Others the reactors. Some talk of saving the planet but won't offer any specifics of how we're supposed to do it. And a few factions even wanna seize control of the city to run it themselves, or to try and bring back the old republic.

"Tonight's meeting was supposed to be another attempt to bring us together. Honestly, though, who are we kidding? It's never gonna happen. It's hard enough coming to an agreement when it's just me, Biggs, and Wedge."

"The hell . . . ?"

Barret wrinkled his brow.

"As *I* see it," said Jessie, "our top priority should be stopping the reactors. Whatever it takes. Blow 'em up, if we have to.

"Biggs just wants to be a thorn in Shinra's side. He's on board for pretty much anything that'll piss the company off, except he can't come to terms with the fact that ordinary people might get hurt.

"And then there's Wedge . . . Every time we talk about this stuff, he says it's up to Biggs and me, and he'll go along with whatever we decide. Problem is, we never actually decide. We go around and around in circles, talking about what we'd *like* to do.

"If the joint meeting *hadn't* been called off, they would've gone down the list, eventually asking to hear from a representative for the Sector 7 Slums Division—that's us—and I would've had to stand up and say sorry, we've got nothing. No goals, and no concrete plans to achieve them."

"So what you're sayin'," remarked Barret, "is that you need a leader. Not just Avalanche as a whole, but your little division too."

"That pretty much sums it up, yeah."

"How about me?"

Jessie snorted. "Just like that, huh?"

"Why the hell not?" groused Barret. "You gotta try *somethin'*. There ain't no bull's-eye if you never take the shot. And if you find out halfway through that you been usin' the wrong gun, you roll with it. Adapt. Ain't nobody smart enough to predict every twist and turn, anyway.

"Point is, shit don't get done sittin' on your ass. You gotta *act*. Put me in charge, and I'll whip the whole operation into shape. Just grab hold of my back, hang on, and we'll knock 'em all down. Who's in charge of your faction, anyway? You or Biggs?"

"In the Sector 7 Slums Division, everyone gets an equal say. That's our whole ideology. We love meetings and taking votes."

"Uh-huh. And look how far it's got you. Time to try somethin' different."

"I dunno . . . Weigh in on this, would you, Tifa?"

"More hands make less work," insisted Barret. "And here I am offerin' you two. Or one and a gun, anyway. It's fate."

"What about this is *fate*?!" Jessie threw her hands up in exasperation. "Ugh. Fine, you're right. We're not getting anywhere as we are now. You've got drive, or at least the blind stupidity to take the first step forward, and god knows we could use some of that. So go ahead. Show us something different."

The warm glow of evening was creeping across the chocobo farm.

"Jessie decided to give Barret a shot, and the rest is history. Not to say things weren't rocky while our iteration of Avalanche found its legs. Biggs in particular needed time to warm up to our new leader, but eventually he was swept up with the rest of us. It was hard to resist Barret's relentless drive to act."

"It sounds to me like the large one staged a hostile takeover," Red XIII said dryly.

Tifa laughed. "In a way. But Barret gave us the momentum we badly needed. For a little while, it was even enough to pull several other factions along for the ride.

"Ultimately, though, Jessie was right. The bigger the group, the more opinions to mediate. Arguments became common, deliberations started to drag on, and Barret couldn't take it. He'd fume in the corner until, *boom*, he was up on his feet yelling that the meeting was over. 'My way or the highway!'

"And one by one, the other factions chose the highway, leaving the Sector 7 Slums Division on its own again. The last time Barret exploded, he cut all ties and declared we were better off without them."

"I'm amazed at how you continue to put up with him."

"I told you. Fate brought our paths together. Just like it was fate that led us to you in that lab."

"Hmph." Red XIII stretched a hind leg up to scratch behind one ear. "Be that as it may, I'm anxious to hear how things resolved with the *other* buffoon in your story."

"Huh? Who?"

"Rakesh. Clearly, not everything with that young man was what it seemed."

The following week sped by. When it was Wednesday again, Tifa woke early, quickly finished her shower, and waited in her apartment for Barret's arrival.

She was grateful for the arrangement. The purse was heavy, and she knew she'd feel a lot more secure taking it to Sector 7 with

Barret at her side. A hundred and sixty thousand gil was an awful lot of money.

And it was a momentous step. This was the down payment for a brand-new chapter of her life. She'd be the proprietor of Seventh Heaven, and with any luck, she'd turn enough of a profit to some-day own it in full. If the slums had taught her anything, it was how to be persistent, chipping away at a debt one month at a time.

It took some convincing, but she'd managed to get Marle to agree to step away from the bar. She wanted to know Marle would be safe, free from suspicion of any ties to Avalanche. Nonetheless, Marle assured her, she'd be stopping by often to speak her mind and lend the occasional hand. In Tifa's mind, it sort of defeated the purpose of stepping away, but past a certain point, there was no arguing with the woman.

Tifa would continue to spend Thursday to Tuesday at Sector 8 Steamed Buns until her debt to Manson was settled. Meanwhile, Barret had agreed to run the bar. In two years, give or take, Tifa would be free to dedicate herself to Seventh Heaven full-time. If nothing else, the wait would give her plenty of time to master Monty's cocktails.

There was a knock at the door, and she heard Barret's gruff voice.

"Let's do this," he said.

She invited him in, but this time he elected to remain outside.

"Get this," he said as she pulled the bin from under her bed. "Shinra's little fireworks show last week? Ended up damaging prop-erty topside too, and the residents with a voice ain't happy about it. Shinra's gonna have to dial back the raids until this blows over."

His chuckle abruptly died when he realized Tifa hadn't joined in.

"Tifa . . . ? You listenin'? I'm sayin' this is our opening. Our chance to strike!"

She'd stopped listening the moment she realized it was gone.

The purse. The hundred and sixty thousand gil. Gone.

"It's not here," she whispered in shock.

"Huh?"

"The money. I kept it in a purse hidden under my clothes. But it's not here."

She flipped the bin over, dumping its contents. Clothes, accessories, and underwear spilled across the floor, but she didn't think to care.

"Yowza," Barret drawled.

"Cut it out. This is serious!"

"I'm *bein'* serious. A hundred and sixty big ones is a hell of a lot of dough. When's the last time you saw it?"

"Late last night. I checked on it before I went to bed."

"Which means whatever happened to it musta happened this morning. You been in your room the whole time?"

"Yeah. I was waiting for you all to . . . Wait! My shower! Every morning at dawn, I take a shower!"

Tifa shoved Barret from the doorway and broke into a sprint. At the far end of the Row, she found the Waterkeeper in her chair as always.

"This morning," she gasped, half out of breath. "When I was taking my shower, did you see anyone?"

"What, over by your place? Turn around and see for yourself. Can't see squat from here."

The old woman pursed her lips and began to fold her arms, but stopped.

"Oh!" she exclaimed. "But the Watchman did come by for a shower. When I told him you were in there, he said he'd come back later. Didn't wanna disturb you."

Tifa quickly thanked the Waterkeeper and made straight for the alley.

Barret caught up on the way. "Checked your place over as best I could. No sign of the cash."

"I think I know who's responsible."

When the temporary Watchman wasn't at his post, she rushed out to the main street, signaling Barret to follow. From there, they ran hard.

Sector 8 was just beginning to wake, and without any morning crowds to push through, they made good time. When Tifa finally stopped, panting hard, they were standing outside the clinic of Dr. Dhamini Oranye. Rakesh's home. If she didn't find him here, she'd check Manson's railcars.

Her hand was on the door when they heard the shouting. It was a man's voice, loud and menacing. There was a crash, followed by a woman's terrified shriek.

The door was unlocked. Tifa calmly pushed her way inside.

She heard a dull thump and a gasp, as if someone had been punched in the gut, followed by another crash and the unmistakable shatter of glass.

"Please! No more!" screamed a woman. The voice was shrill, but Tifa knew it had to be Dhamini's.

"Stop! Look, I've got your money!"

This one, breathless and laced with pain, was Rakesh's.

Barret lifted a thick finger to his lips, urging Tifa to wait and see how things played out.

"Oh, I'll be takin' it," announced a third voice. "But it don't change the fact that you're a week late."

Tifa's mind was reeling. The last voice was the most familiar of all, but it didn't make sense. What was going on?!

"See, I got a reputation to think about," continued the third voice. "If I let this slide, pretty soon *everyone's* tryin' to jerk me around."

"We aren't trying to jerk you around! I swear!"

"Oh, you aren't, huh? Then why's the payment late? Whatcha been up to this past week?"

Rakesh mumbled a response Tifa couldn't quite make out.

"Don't play dumb with me! You've been down at the races, bettin' your mother's hard-earned cash on those damn, stinkin' birds again. Cash that was s'posed to go to *me*!"

"I had a lead! It was a sure thing!"

There was another loud crash—undoubtedly some piece of medical equipment being knocked to the floor.

"Please don't break any more!" begged Dhamini. "Mr. Manson, *please*!"

Tifa let out an astonished cry. Her hands clamped over her mouth, but it was too late.

"Who's that? Who the hell've you got out there?!"

A small, pale old man emerged from the clinic's back room, clad in a bright red shirt and matching red trousers. When he saw Tifa, his jaw fell open, and he stammered her name.

"*You're* Manson?" she managed to respond.

Pops's eyes wandered uncomfortably. He opened his mouth to say something, closed it, opened it again, and finally exhaled a deep sigh.

"Guess there's no use tryin' to hide it. Wednesdays are when I take care of my *other* business."

"*You're* the one who's been keeping me tied down with these stupid rules?!"

"Hold on, now. What's this about rules?"

"Manson's rules. Rakesh told me . . ."

There was a terrible sinking feeling in Tifa's gut.

"Oh, *Rakesh* told ya, huh? Well then. How 'bout we let Rakesh explain? He's in the back, nursin' a bloody nose."

Tifa and Barret followed Pops-slash-Manson to the back. Rakesh was waiting behind the door, right eye red and swollen, a streak of half-dried blood between his nostrils and upper lip.

"Mr. Manson!" he exclaimed. "Please! At least take what we've got. I know it's not enough, but . . ."

Rakesh proffered an all-too-familiar purse.

"That's mine," said Tifa.

"I'll be takin' that," snapped Barret. He swatted the purse from Rakesh's hands and quickly put it out of reach.

Rakesh scrunched up his face, protesting with a loud "Hey!" as if he honestly believed the money belonged to him.

"Explain," demanded Tifa, her eyes locked on his. "Or if you won't, I bet Pops will."

Rakesh visibly swallowed but did not speak.

Pops sighed in exasperation.

"Kid owes me a damn fortune," he said. "Racked it up bettin' on the chocobos and just about every other kind of odds you can think of.

"Ever since then, the clinic's been shiftin' the burden onto its patients, overchargin' 'em for treatment. His mom's in on it, of course. At this point, there're too many victims to count."

"What . . . what about mine?" asked Tifa. "How much was mine supposed to cost?"

Dhamini shifted uncomfortably, still huddled in the far corner of the room.

"A third," she mumbled. "I'm sorry, Tifa. Really, I . . ."

Tifa's breath caught in her throat.

A *third* of what she'd been asked to pay.

Her right hand fumbled for Zangan's memento, pulling it tight—only for it to snap. Astonished, she felt her hand go slack and watched as the tattered black cord unraveled from her wrist and fell to the floor.

"You should be grateful," quavered Rakesh. "I was looking out for you. I lined up a decent job and made sure you'd never have to resort to the Wall Market."

Barret scoffed. "Let's go, Tifa. Leave these scumbags before they start to rub off on us."

"Yeah," agreed Tifa. "But before we do . . ."

Both hands clenched into fists. She raised them in front of her chin, breathed in, and held.

Slowly.

No need to rush.

She released, long and slow, and then . . .

Book Five, Paragraph One, Section One, Part One.

Her right jab was swift and smooth, landing square on Rakesh's jaw. He spun in place, slamming into the clinic's wall before sinking to the floor. Dhamini screamed and rushed to her son's side, cradling his head in her lap, but Tifa felt no trace of guilt or regret.

She regarded Pops calmly. "You knew all along, didn't you?"

"Yeah. But hell, I'd finally found me a real looker who could do the job right. Rakesh came up with the plan, and I kept mum 'cause I didn't wanna lose ya. I told ya, didn't I? You're the best business partner I've ever had."

"I loved working at the cart. It taught me the joy of serving customers. Even when the rest of my life wasn't going well, I could show up for work, concentrate on the buns, and forget about everything else. If you'd asked me—if you'd been fair about it, like a *real* business partner—I would've been happy to stay."

"Aw, hell," muttered Pops with a disappointed sigh. "Been livin' the criminal life too long for that. You hang on to what you have and don't ask questions."

Tifa turned her eyes to Dhamini.

"I expect I won't be hearing from you about this debt, or *anything*, ever again."

"It's our problem. We'll take care of it. Thank you for all you've . . . No . . . Sorry for everything we made you do."

"Tifa," croaked Rakesh. He pulled himself unsteadily to his feet. "You don't understand. I *love* you. That's why I—"

Book Five, Paragraph Two, Section Two, Part One.

One foot swiveled back. The other snapped high, the heel of her boot slamming into Rakesh's nose with a satisfying *crack*.

Red XIII rumbled in apparent satisfaction.

"That final side kick was precisely the resolution I needed."

Tifa smiled. "Thus concludes the story of my young, impressionable years."

"And you've grown out of those, have you?"

"I think so, yes."

His pale eye held on hers, searching. Tifa stared defiantly back.

"And Zangan?" her companion asked, turning his muzzle away as casually as he shifted the subject.

"No clue. But the next time I see him, whenever that may be . . ."

"Ah yes. Your long-overdue exam. Still eager to learn the deepest secrets of his art?"

"Not really. The next time we spar, I'll be using my own style. I intend to teach him a thing or two about leaving me alone for so long."

Red XIII chuffed, sending a ripple through his fur from neck to tail.

In the distance, Tifa spotted another wave of wind rolling through the grass.

"Better catch up with the others," she announced.

The gust arrived just as Tifa Lockhart stood. She turned into the breeze, staring out over the vast expanse yet ahead, and confidently strode forward.

Episode 2
Traces of Aerith

A erith Gainsborough slowly made her way down the length of the passenger ferry *Shinra-8*. Like her companions, she was wearing the signature blue uniform of a Shinra trooper, along with the unmistakable "three-eyed" helmet.

Being at sea was exhilarating. Aerith had never seen the ocean before, nor stepped aboard a ship. In truth, the vessel was a modest one, living out its years of service transporting passengers and cargo between Junon and Costa del Sol. But in Aerith's eyes, it was an endless source of wonders.

Her curiosity led her up and down the passageways and ladders, exploring every corner she could find. She quickly learned that the ship's clientele—wealthy socialites traveling to and from fashionable resorts—did not take kindly to common troopers nosing about the passenger decks. Their cold stares drove her back down to the belly of the craft, where disorderly stacks of cargo cluttered the hold.

The end to her short-lived adventure was disappointing, but at least she wasn't alone. Tifa Lockhart, decked out in an identical uniform, smiled warmly as Aerith descended the stairs.

"I overheard a useful tip up on the deck," said Tifa.

From the woman's gentle appearance, Aerith would have never guessed what an amazing fighter she was. Tifa was an expert martial artist, able to throw punches faster than the eye could see and unleash all manner of deadly kicks. She could even jump right over opponents' heads with ease. And on top of it all, she was *beautiful.*

In their short time together, they'd faced countless dangers and close calls. Every time, Aerith had found great comfort knowing Tifa was at her side. Everything about her spoke of a true friend.

"One of the passengers was saying," continued Tifa, "that if you start to feel seasick, you should try chatting with someone. Helps take your mind off the rocking of the ship."

"Huh. That's interesting. Are you feeling seasick?"

"Not especially."

"Oh. That's good. Me neither."

The two fell silent.

It wasn't until a moment later that the light bulb went off in Aerith's head. Tifa had a curious tendency to hint at things rather than saying them outright, so as not to impose on others. The comment about seasickness was her way of saying she *wanted* to talk.

"No seasickness here!" announced Aerith. "But, um . . . wanna chat anyway?"

"I was hoping to learn a little more about you," confessed Tifa.

"Me?"

"I'm a really good listener, you know. Used to run my own bar and everything."

Tifa leaned against a stack of cargo, plucking an imaginary glass from the air, which she proceeded to clean with an imaginary cloth.

"Come on in and have a seat," she said, miming a deep bartender's voice. "Don't think I've seen you here before. First time at the bar?"

"Oh, wow!" exclaimed Aerith, followed by a giggle.

"You from around here?" continued Tifa.

"Nope! My home's in the Sector 5 slums."

"Is that so? Pretty lively neighborhood. That where you grew up?"

"Oh, um . . ." Aerith hesitated. "That's kind of . . . complicated."

Tifa immediately cut the charade. She was good at that— picking up on how her friends were feeling.

"Sorry," she apologized. "I didn't mean to pry."

Both Tifa and the rest of their companions had already heard the most important part of Aerith's story: that she was an Ancient and the last of her kind.

"No," Aerith rushed to say. "It's okay. Really. The question just took me a little off guard. Nobody's ever wanted to hear my story, and until now, I guess I'd never met anyone I wanted to share it with.

"So . . ." she continued, latching on to Tifa's arm and sidling in close. "Still up for it?"

"If you really don't mind."

"Not at all!"

To understand Aerith, it was first necessary to understand her mother. Ifalna was the last full-blooded Ancient, her father and mother both hailing from that long-forgotten race, which once served as stewards of the planet.

Unlike her forebears, however, Ifalna had spent a significant portion of her life tied to one location: she lived secreted away among the upper floors of the Shinra Building as a ward of the company, cooperating in research meant to rediscover the mysteries of her people. Ifalna was generously supplied with all manner of comforts inside her living quarters. Still, it was a life of confinement all the same.

For a young girl, it was all the worse. All of Aerith's earliest memories took place within those four walls; she knew nothing of how she and her mother first came to live there. Socially, her life was desolate: all adults going about adult business, with only one person Aerith could call a friend.

Lonny. He was two years older, the son of their caretaker, Marielle, who showed up each day to look after Aerith and handle the cleaning and other chores.

But life for Aerith took a dramatic turn in 1992, when she was seven years old. Images flooded her mind, unbidden and refusing to go away. They overloaded her senses, an assault of landscapes,

faces, animals, and even monsters—none of which she'd seen before. The power of the Ancients, she'd later be told, had awakened within her.

Still young and lacking the discipline to control or ignore the
mysterious visions, Aerith found herself compelled to draw. She
re-created scenes on paper and even the walls of their quarters,
leaving the contents of her mind open for anyone to see. At the
time, she'd been convinced that the drawings could free her from
the constant onslaught.

"Looking back now, I understand," Aerith told Tifa aboard the
ferry. "I was a hostage, and to keep me safe, my mom was ready to
do whatever Hojo said.

"But when Hojo found out that I'd inherited my mother's powers, he got greedy. He had a backup test subject now, which meant
he could employ riskier, *crueler* methods—ones he hadn't dared
when he believed my mother to be the last of her kind. Every day
when Mom came back from the lab, I could see she was getting
weaker. Pretty soon, she was on the verge of collapse."

As Hojo's methods grew crueler, so too did his demands on Ifalna's
time. The professor and his staff seemed to have an endless list of
tasks and experiments to run, and to get through them, they kept
Ifalna in their lab longer and longer with each passing day.

Soon, she was being returned to her quarters in a wheelchair,
too weak to support her own weight. On the worst days, Aerith
would have to call the staff back at night, asking for someone to
help lift Ifalna into bed. Usually, the one to come lumbering in
was Faz.

Faz Hicks was a big man, in both frame and features. Everything
down to his eyes, nose, and mouth was, quite simply put, *large*. Of
all the lab assistants Aerith had seen, nobody else came close.

Perhaps because of that, it was Faz's thick arms lifting Ifalna from
the wheelchair to her bed more often than not. Ifalna looked like

a rag doll in his grasp, but his movements were gentle, and Aerith had always appreciated that.

At some point, Ifalna began to ask him for something to numb the pain, her voice sad and sweet. Aerith was careful never to say so, but she hated the coy tone of that voice. She wanted Ifalna to get better. She wanted things to go back to the way they'd been before.

"Please, Faz," her mother begged.

The requests must have stirred the big man's sympathy, for one day, with his back to the security camera, he fished a small vial and syringe from his pocket, wordlessly held them up for Ifalna to see, and secreted them away in a drawer.

"Nobody else can know," he emphasized in a low voice.

Later, Aerith watched as Ifalna carefully drew a dose from the vial in the blind spot directly beneath the camera. But she couldn't bear the sight of the needle sliding into her mother's arm. From then on, whenever the vial came out, Aerith ran to cower behind the couch.

To Aerith, events inside the room didn't have clear dates or a sequence. Every day blended into the next, such that she couldn't say exactly when the next big change came. She knew she was still seven. Beyond that, it was hard to say.

It was night, and she was burrowed under the covers in her mother's big bed, the way she always slept from the day she came to understand the surveillance camera and what it meant.

"Aerith," her mother whispered from beyond the duvet. "What if . . . What if we went on an adventure?"

Aerith considered this for a moment, then lowered her own voice to a matching whisper. "An adventure?"

"A *big* one. To somewhere far, far away."

"You mean *outside*?!"

The outside world. For Aerith, the prospect sparked curiosity and terror alike.

"Oh, how I've longed to go back out there again one day. . ." mused her mother.

It was a sentiment Aerith couldn't quite grasp, but she heard hints of sadness, like salty tears creeping into her mother's voice. She wanted to *see* what that feeling looked like, so she popped her head out from under the covers to peer at her mother. Ifalna sat with her face buried in the crook of her arm. The sleeves of her baggy dressing gown were rolled up to the elbows, exposing the awful red speckles—the countless scars left by day after day of secret injections.

"Without the men in white? And the needles? Would you get better there?"

"Yes, sweetheart . . . I think I would."

"If it'll make you better, then I'll do it. But how are we supposed to get away? The camera's always watching."

"Faz is going to help us."

"Why would *he* want to help?"

Ifalna paused for a moment before finally answering, "Because he's a good person."

The day it happened, everything started out normal. Ifalna was led away in the morning and brought back in the evening. This time, Faz was the one pushing the wheelchair.

"Hello, Aerith," he said in his deep baritone. "Everything's good to go. I've arranged a safe place for us to stay in the Sector 3 slums. You'll even have your very own room. It's not a large home, but it's all we'll need to start our new life."

He patted her arm and lumbered out.

Late that night—or very early the next morning, most likely— the alarm sounded. Ifalna slipped out of the bed and pressed a bundle of clothing into Aerith's arms, urging her to dress quickly. Aerith had never seen the clothes before and wanted to know where they'd come from.

"Faz," was all Ifalna said. She was hastily pulling on an unfamiliar outfit of her own. As soon as they were dressed, she grabbed Aerith's hand.

"Let's go."

"What if they catch us?!" wailed Aerith.

"Don't think about it. Just run."

Ifalna placed a hand against the door. It slid open with a *whoosh*.

"It's unlocked!" gasped Aerith. "How?!"

Her mother gave no response.

Ifalna closed her eyes for one deep breath. Then, with a decisive nod, she darted out into the hallway, Aerith in tow.

The corridor was empty. The piercing blare of the alarm filled their ears.

"Alert," announced a flat, metallic voice. "A breach in monster containment has been detected. All staff must immediately evacuate the lab . . . Alert. A breach in monster containment . . ."

Over and over, the message looped.

"Monsters?!" cried Aerith.

Ifalna didn't respond. She calmly assessed the corridor and, bearings established, broke into a brisk trot. Aerith had to run to keep pace, hand still held tight in her mother's grasp. But not a dozen steps in, she could already see Ifalna begin to weave slightly, fighting to maintain her balance. The burst of vigor as she darted from the room was all but gone.

They rounded the first corner. No staff members were in sight. Curiously, Aerith didn't sense any monsters prowling about either. All she saw was a lone cleaning cart abandoned in the middle of the foyer.

The cart's large metal frame sat atop four tiny casters. Long-handled brooms and mops poked haphazardly from a receptacle at one end.

Ifalna knelt and pressed her hands to one of the cart's metal sides, sliding it open to reveal the bottom compartment. Aerith had seen similar carts before, and all she could think was how very odd it was for the compartment to be empty. It was *supposed* to be full of rags and brushes and bottles of solvent. Even the metal shelves and dividers were gone.

"We'll hide in here," explained her mother. "I'll go in first."

Ifalna squeezed herself into the compartment, sliding as far back as she could.

"Now you," she called.

Aerith did as she was told, stooping low at the opening. Ifalna sat with her knees at her chest, arms squeezing legs tight to make space for her daughter. Aerith slipped in easily. In a way, it was almost fun. It wasn't nearly as cramped as she'd expected.

"We'll have to stay very still for a while, so make sure you're comfortable."

"I'll be okay like this."

"All right."

Ifalna slid the door shut from the inside, and the compartment was thrust into darkness. Beyond the thin metal veil, the alarm continued its incessant screeching, accompanied by the impassive looping message.

After what seemed like a very long time, Aerith sensed someone drawing near. The cart jolted slightly, and a voice from outside said, "It's me."

Ifalna replied ever so softly, "We're in your hands, Faz."

"Here we go."

The cart slid into motion, its casters emitting a low, constant churning as they rolled down the corridor floor.

"Whatever happens, don't say a word," cautioned Faz.

After a moment, Faz quietly announced that they were about to turn a corner. A while later, they felt the front pair of casters lurch and then the back. Faz explained that they had boarded an elevator.

"There will be several of these," he said.

Aerith felt a curious sensation, as if she were falling in slow motion. It made her stomach roil, and she brought a hand to her mouth.

"Mom, I don't feel good . . ." she whispered.

"Hang in there. It'll be over soon enough."

The long, slow descent came to an end, and the cart wheeled forward again, but only briefly. There was another lurch of the casters, a pause, and the falling sensation returned: another elevator, just as Faz had said. And then there was another, and yet another.

At long last, Faz's deep, gentle baritone announced that they'd reached the parking lot.

A strange, unpleasant smell seeped inside the compartment, quite unlike the filtered air of their living quarters.

"Your cart ride's just about over," explained Faz. "Next comes a truck. Hurry onto the cargo bed. I'll help hoist you up."

The smooth churning of the casters changed to a grating roar, and the inside of the cart shuddered and rattled. It was almost worse than the elevators, but fortunately, it didn't last nearly as long. The cart came to a stop, and the compartment's panel abruptly slid open.

"Quickly now," urged Faz.

The lab assistant's massive hands reached in, plucking Aerith from the cart like a package in transit. In one fluid motion, he lifted her onto the bed of a waiting truck.

"To the back," ordered Faz, already turning to help Ifalna, who he lifted just as effortlessly.

"You'll see several wooden crates. One is empty. Get inside, and be certain to remember the lid. The truck's driver is my cousin. He'll deliver you to the rail yard, where your crate and all the others will be loaded onto a freight car. The train's final stop is the Sector 4 slums. Wait for me there."

"Inside the box?" asked Ifalna.

"No. You'll need to leave the crate behind. A friend of mine will be there to ensure your safe arrival. I imagine you'll be asked to wait somewhere near the station. Follow whatever instructions you're given. You'll find more details in this letter."

Faz pulled a folded scrap of paper from his pocket and gave it to Ifalna, his hand lingering on hers even after the message was safely in her grasp.

"Aren't you coming with us?" asked Aerith.

"I have to head back upstairs and join in the search. If they find out what I've done, I stand to lose much more than my job."

The truck's horn blared, underscoring the urgency of their flight.

"Goodbye for now," said Faz. "Oh, and you'll find food and water in the crate."

"How long should we wait for you?"

"I'll be there by the last train of the night. No later."

Then, to Aerith's astonishment, Faz bent his head and kissed Ifalna's hand. She glanced nervously from her mother to Faz and back again.

"Thank you, Faz."

The words were hardly out of Ifalna's mouth before the truck lurched forward, and soon they were speeding through the parking lot, the heavyset lab assistant vanishing from sight as they rounded a corner.

Ifalna and Aerith had to scramble on their hands and knees to cross the truck bed as the driver lurched madly through the parking lot. Once they reached the back, they found five identical wooden crates, larger in size than the cleaning cart. Ifalna pried open lids until she found the empty one, then lifted her daughter inside.

"It smells in here!" exclaimed Aerith.

There had been many unfamiliar odors since they left their room, many of them unpleasant, but this one was by far the worst. Aerith didn't think she could bear to be in the box for another minute, let alone a whole train ride.

"Try not to think about it. Your nose will adjust in time."

But when Ifalna hoisted herself over the side to join Aerith, she also wrinkled her nose.

"See?!" exclaimed Aerith. "I told you!"

The crate wasn't as cramped as the cart, but they still sat nearly face-to-face. Ifalna stuck her tongue out at Aerith, and the two broke into giggles.

As Aerith shifted around to find a comfortable position, her fingers closed around a large paper bag. Inside, she found a small flashlight, pouches of dried fruit and nuts, a heel of hard bread, and a canteen. There was also a thin envelope, which Ifalna opened to reveal a wad of wrinkled bills.

"Next, the lid," said Ifalna, as if to remind herself.

With a great deal of effort, she managed to tug the wooden lid up and over their heads, squeezing it shut once more. The inside of the crate was pitch-black when she settled back down.

"And now . . . Right. The letter."

Aerith heard the crinkling of paper as Ifalna unfolded the scrap of paper handed to her by Faz.

"Could you shine the light for me?"

"All right."

Aerith fished the flashlight from the bag by touch, fumbling her fingers along the smooth metal surface until she found the switch. The inside of the crate erupted in harsh white light. She angled the beam at her mother, casting a spotlight on the woman's pale complexion. Beads of sweat glistened on Ifalna's forehead.

"Mom? Are you okay?" asked Aerith.

Ifalna ignored the question.

"I'm going to read the letter aloud," she said. "It's very important that we both remember what it says."

"Okay."

"'The Shinra Building is situated atop a structure known as the plate. Your destination is the slums, which are connected to the plate by railway. The crate in which you'll hide will be loaded onto a freight car. Once the train is underway, you're likely to observe flashes of red light inside the crate. It might happen several times, but you needn't pay it any mind. It is no cause for alarm.'"

"What's he mean about a red light?"

Ifalna sighed. "He writes as if I have no understanding of the outside world . . . though he's not exactly wrong about that."

"I'm scared. I don't want there to be a red light."

"Faz says it's nothing to be alarmed by. We have to trust that he's right."

". . . Okay."

"'After a time, you will feel the train level out. When it does, your destination is near at hand. You may hear announcements over the speakers. Before the train stops, climb out of the crate and wait by the door of your railcar. The final stop is called Sector 4 Undercity Station. When you arrive, a friend will open the door, and you must hand over the money I've prepared. Do not be afraid. Follow our friend's instructions and await my arri—'"

A sudden fit of coughing interrupted the last few words of the message. Ifalna turned away, pressing her mouth to her forearm.

"Aerith . . ." she managed to gasp in a brief interval between coughs. "The light . . . Off, please . . ."

Shortly after the truck came to a stop, Aerith felt the cargo bed rock and sway as workers jumped aboard. She heard the thumps and scrapes of crates slid to the edge and lifted from the truck. Little by little, the sounds drew nearer, and then it was their crate's turn, and they were being shoved and jostled, thrown and dropped. At one point, the crate even toppled onto its side. Mother and daughter bore the abuse in silence. Ifalna wrapped her arms tight around Aerith and kept one palm pressed against her daughter's mouth.

"It'll all be over soon," she soothed, her voice the faintest hint of a whisper.

After a while, there was silence. But they'd hardly breathed sighs of relief when a man's voice announced, "This one's goin' to Sector 4," accompanied by a loud thump that must have been his palm against the side.

The crate lurched into motion once more, other sets of rough hands and muffled voices directing it to the railcar. Ifalna and Aerith desperately braced their arms, legs, and backs against the sides of the crate and gritted their teeth.

With one final shove and a thump, the crate came to rest, and the heavy footfalls of the laborers faded away. They heard the great, heavy roar and squeal of a freight car door sliding shut. Again, for a time, there was silence.

When the train at last began to move, Ifalna switched the flash-light back on and laid it on the floor, where it bathed everything in a pale, otherworldly glow. They listened to the gentle, regular *ka-clack* of the wheels, a welcome change from the many cacophonies they'd endured since their journey began. Aerith soon began to nod off. She teetered on the cusp of sleep, briefly jerking awake once to peer at her mother. Even in the strange light, Ifalna's profile was as beautiful as ever.

Sensing her daughter's eyes, Ifalna turned and smiled.

Everything's going to be better now, thought Aerith. Her eyelids drooped, and at last she dozed. In her dreams, she found herself back in their living quarters, drawing one of her visions.

It was another of her mother's coughing fits that woke her.

"Mom? Are you okay?" she asked.

"Yes . . ." Ifalna replied hoarsely. "Just . . . a moment."

When the coughing subsided and she'd calmed her breathing, she clasped Aerith's hand.

"I think the train has leveled out. The bars of red light seem to have stopped too. We must be near the station."

"The red light was real?! Why didn't you wake me up? I wanted to see!"

Ifalna chuckled. "When we read the letter, you said it sounded scary."

"It *does* sound scary," pouted Aerith. "But I still wanted to see it."

As if on cue, bars of light swept from one end of the crate to the other, momentarily dyeing everything inside a deep crimson. Aerith and Ifalna looked at each other with wide eyes.

"It happened!" exclaimed Aerith. "Everything's red!"

"Yes. Very red indeed," agreed Ifalna.

"It's not scary at all!"

Ifalna reached for the paper bag and proposed, "How about we eat something? It might be awhile before we get another chance."

She broke off a large hunk of bread for Aerith and ripped open the pouch of dried fruit.

Aerith readily dug in.

"I wonder if this is what a picnic is like," she mumbled around a mouthful of bread.

"What's a picnic?" asked Ifalna.

Aerith swallowed and replied, "Lonny told me about them. You pack up a bunch of food, head outside, walk for a long time, and sit down somewhere to eat. Actually, you don't even have to take food if you don't want to. But Lonny says he's only read about it. He's never been on a picnic either."

"Hm. Sounds complicated. But I imagine the walking must be fun."

Ifalna held out the rest of the bread. For a moment, Aerith only stared at it. The flashlight's weak glow outlined the ragged edge where it had been torn in half.

"Aren't you gonna eat some?" she asked her mother.

"I already did," replied Ifalna. "I ate a whole bunch while you were snoring away with your mouth wide open."

Aerith suspected it was a lie. Still, she puffed up her cheeks, pretending to be angry about the claim that she'd been snoring.

She'd finished the bread off when the train began to decelerate. Ifalna coughed again but clenched her jaw tight to stifle the fit; her shoulders heaved up and down with the effort.

"I'm okay," she told Aerith when the fit had subsided.

"All right . . ."

In truth, the frequency of her mother's reassurances only deepened her concern.

A muffled voice sounded from somewhere outside the crate. It was tinny and lifeless, like the alarm's looping message in the Shinra Building.

"Next stop . . . Sector . . . Under . . . Next stop . . . tor 4 . . . city Station."

"Sounds like it's about time for us to get out of this crate," announced Ifalna.

She whacked at the lid until it popped loose, and then thrust it away. Once she'd clambered over the side, she leaned back in to help Aerith out.

The train had slowed, but it was still in motion. Aerith found that she had to plant her feet firmly to keep her balance as the railcar rocked gently back and forth.

"Wow!" she exclaimed. "This is so cool!"

Ifalna, meanwhile, clung to the side of the crate.

"Aerith, honey?" she said.

"Yeah?"

"Don't ever let go of that."

"Let go of what?"

"The way you find joy in everything."

"I won't," Aerith promised, though she wasn't exactly sure what her mother meant.

Ifalna was lifting the lid back onto the crate when she exclaimed, "Well, I'll be . . . Aerith, take a look at this!"

She pointed to a large shipping label affixed to the wood.

"What does it say?"

Ifalna read the label out loud:

> *From: Shinra Electric Power Company*
> *To: Shinra Electric Power Company*
> *Hold in Sector 4 Undercity Station Aboveground Storage*
> *HAZARDOUS MATERIAL*
> *Do not break seal during transit*

"Hey! We're not hazardous material!" protested Aerith.

"Not very flattering, is it?" Ifalna replied with a laugh.

Their light-hearted moment was broken by a piercing screech: the train had engaged its brakes for arrival. Aerith's balance faltered, and she clung to her mother's legs to keep from falling.

"Aerith, I want you to stay quiet for this next part. Leave the talking to me."

She peered up at her mother with uncertainty. The smiles and laughter of a moment ago had vanished.

When the train came to a rest and the railcar's door slid open again, it was a young woman on the other side. She looked grumpy and impatient, and was dressed in a big baggy set of overalls. Everything about her looked filthy.

Ifalna spoke cautiously. "Are you a friend of Faz?"

The stranger nodded.

"This is for your trouble." Ifalna held out the envelope they'd found in the crate.

The stranger clicked her tongue. "That idiot. I told him not to bother."

"Please. It's yours."

With a sigh, the woman snatched the envelope from Ifalna's hands and stuffed it into her back pocket.

"Off the train," she snapped. "Hurry."

The drop from carriage to ground wasn't a small one. Aerith could tell that even a grown-up would need help getting down, but the stranger was more concerned with scanning the area for onlookers than offering a hand.

"Okay," said Ifalna. "I'll go first."

She hopped down, vanishing from Aerith's sight. Aerith heard her feet thump against the packed dirt—along with a pained gasp.

"Mom!" she exclaimed. "Are you okay?"

"Did you not hear me? I said *hurry*," repeated the stranger, her tone even sharper than before.

Aerith could hear her mother apologizing as she stood up straight, her head and shoulders again in Aerith's view. Ifalna held both hands out, and Aerith quickly flung herself into her mother's arms, afraid that any further hesitation would spark another reproach from the woman in the strange, oil-smeared work clothes.

Aerith leapt with such force that her mother nearly toppled

over again. Ifalna swayed to one side, taking a few heavy steps to remain upright.

"I hear it's turned into a real shitshow up top," remarked the stranger. "You're supposed to hide in the container yard until Faz arrives."

She pointed to a part of the rail yard filled with tall stacks of freight containers.

"Careful around sundown. The place gets busy, people in and out to claim the day's shipments. Make sure they don't see you. The last thing I need is someone asking questions."

"How long until sundown?" asked Ifalna.

"Four hours, give or take."

The stranger made to leave, but Ifalna called out to her. "One more thing! Which direction to the Sector 3 slums?"

The woman jutted her chin to indicate, then hastily returned to her duties. It was clear she wanted as little to do with the two stowaways as possible.

Ifalna watched the woman go.

"Mom?" Aerith asked anxiously. "Shouldn't we hide?"

"Yes. You're right."

The stranger had reached the front of their railcar. Just before circling around, she turned to check on her two charges, scowling when she saw that they hadn't yet moved. She jabbed her finger in the direction of the container yard once more.

Ifalna held out a hand. When Aerith reached up to take it, her mother gripped tight.

"Are you ready, Aerith? This is where our big adventure *really* begins."

"Mom, why does your hand feel so hot . . . ?"

Ifalna smiled. "I'm just excited. That's all."

She began leading them to the rear end of the railcar. Aerith discovered that they'd been loaded onto the very last car of the train. When they reached the back, they paused and peered across the tracks. A squat station building sat in the distance, and Aerith could see the woman—Faz's gruff friend—walking in its direction. Ifalna waited until they saw her disappear inside.

There were other people near the building too. Judging by the uniforms, they seemed to be railway employees.

When Ifalna set off again, her daughter's hand still firm in her grasp, Aerith yelped in surprise.

"Where are we going?!"

Her mother was leading them in the *opposite* direction of the container yard. Aerith was beside herself with worry, but Ifalna would say nothing. She only squeezed Aerith's hand tighter and quickened her pace. Ahead, Aerith saw a chain-link fence, beyond which a seemingly never-ending stream of people traversed a wide dirt road.

"Mom?" she repeated, desperate for any explanation.

"See that fence? Let's climb it."

"*Climb* it?!"

The fence was nearly two meters in height.

"I can't! I've never done that!"

"We have to," coaxed Ifalna. "You don't want our adventure to be over already, do you?"

When they reached the fence, several pedestrians on the other side glanced at them, but no one stopped.

"You'll see," declared Ifalna. "This is going to be fun! First, reach both hands up as high as you can and grab on tight."

Her mother demonstrated as she spoke. "Now stick the toe of your left shoe into one of the holes."

Aerith whimpered. Why did they have to climb the fence? Why couldn't they just hide behind the containers like they'd been told?

Still, she lifted her arms and wrapped her fingers around the links, trying to match her mother's pose.

"Pull your weight up with your hands and stick your right toe into another hole."

"Okay . . ."

"Now reach your right hand higher and grab hold again. Good. Now your left hand."

"Oh!" exclaimed Aerith. "And next my feet, right?!"

Climbing a fence wasn't as hard as she'd imagined. In fact, it was kind of fun.

"Watch this, Mom!"

She scrambled up as fast as she could, the fence rattling loudly with her movements. Before she knew it, she was at the top, and there was nowhere higher to place her hands.

"Wow! Look at you, Aerith. Now swing one leg up and over."

Ifalna's words were cut short by a sharp shout.

"You there! Get down!"

Aerith turned to see a station attendant on the other side of the yard, waving his arms and running toward them.

She looked down. Her mother was still at the base of the fence.

"Mom!" she shouted.

"Hurry, Aerith! Over the top!"

"Climb, Mom!"

Ifalna's limbs began to work their way up. Each movement was agonizingly slow, and the station attendant was getting closer and closer.

"Stop!" he shouted again.

Aerith felt the eyes of the passersby, several of whom had slowed to watch the spectacle unfold.

It was all over. There was no way her mother would reach the top in time. As that thought entered Aerith's mind, she heard another shout, this time from the far side.

"Hurry!" A man, tall and startlingly handsome, had approached the fence. He reached a hand up to help Aerith over.

She hesitated. Who was he? A friend of her mother's? Did her mother *have* any friends on the outside?

"Go! Take his hand!" urged Ifalna. Aerith looked to her side, surprised to find her mother at the top of the fence, swinging one leg up and over. Somehow she'd made it—but the station attendant had also reached the base of the fence. He leapt with outstretched fingers, just a fraction of a second too late to catch Ifalna's other leg.

With one free hand, Ifalna grabbed the front of Aerith's shirt and pulled, trying to lift her daughter over the top of the fence. Aerith felt her weight shift dangerously far forward. Just as she was about to pitch over headfirst, a strong hand caught hold and carefully lowered her to the ground.

Ifalna hopped down after her, landing with a heavy thud and a gasp.

"Are you okay?" the handsome stranger asked, but Ifalna had erupted in another fit of coughs and was unable to answer.

Meanwhile, the station attendant had also begun to climb. He shouted at them through the links, "You're in for it now! Fare dodging is a felony!"

"He's right," the stranger admitted to Ifalna and Aerith. "But it happens so often that he's delusional if he thinks he can catch everyone who skips a train fare."

"Th-thank . . . you," Ifalna finally managed to say.

"My pleasure."

He slammed a fist against the station attendant's fingers, curled vulnerably around the links as he hoisted himself up. The attendant yelped and hopped away from the fence.

"Fuck off, Shinra," the stranger jeered. And then, as if the whole interaction had been the most ordinary thing in the world, he sauntered off down the street without another word.

Ifalna and Aerith were left alone in the acid glare of the station attendant, who was still panting heavily from his sprint across the rail yard.

"Could you tell us the way to Sector 3?" Ifalna suddenly asked the attendant. He and Aerith both stared at her incredulously.

"Why the hell should I tell *you*?!" he bellowed, loud enough to send Aerith retreating a few steps back.

"Good point. Sorry to trouble you," Ifalna apologized calmly, and, taking Aerith by the hand, set off down the street.

Aerith peeked back once to see the attendant still glaring, but soon they were lost among the endless stream of pedestrians, and she could see him no more.

"My, that was exciting," remarked Ifalna once they were well away.

Aerith looked up to find her mother beaming from ear to ear.

Mother and daughter trudged on for some time, traversing the Sector 4 slums. Ifalna seemed to want to put as much distance between them and the train station as possible, but as far as Aerith could tell, the station attendant had given up his chase, and nobody else seemed to be following them either.

As they walked, Aerith stared upward, overwhelmed by the great steel ceiling with its crisscrossed girders. Its size was hard to process, as was the fact that there was a whole *other* city on top of it—the one from which they'd just fled.

She thought of the great number of people up there, and of the Shinra Building, and of how just a short time ago they'd been way up there too.

"Better look where you're going. You wouldn't want to trip," Ifalna gently chided.

"Okay."

Aerith glanced to her sides. Of the many other people out and about in the slums, none were looking up. It seemed to Aerith that the plate was enough to leave anyone awestruck. But perhaps, given enough time, it simply became part of the background, eclipsed by more ordinary concerns.

There were lots of strange sounds too, most of which she couldn't identify. Sometimes, she'd hear angry shouts from among the jumbled neighborhoods. None of the other pedestrians paid any mind to those things either.

"Who was that man who helped us at the station?" she asked her mother.

"Someone who doesn't like Shinra very much, I suppose. I've heard there are a lot of people like that in the slums."

"Heard where? How do you know so much about the slums?"

"Oh, I asked around. Lots of little questions to lots of different people. I was picking up bits and pieces of information I thought might come in handy for today."

"Is that how you learned how to climb a fence?"

"It is. You'd be surprised what the lab assistants would say when Professor Hojo wasn't around."

"So they were actually good people all along?"

"Well, I don't know about that. They certainly felt bad for us, and I don't think they wanted us to stay locked up. But aside from Faz, none of them ever tried to help. Being a good person is about actions, not just words."

"Do you think Faz is okay?"

Ifalna didn't respond. Aerith waited, thinking her mother might be contemplating how best to answer, but when Ifalna next spoke, it was to say, "I'd like to rest for a moment. How about we sit down over there?"

She pointed at a small open space, around which several benches formed a loose ring.

Aboard the ferry, Aerith cast her eyes to her feet and frowned.

"The moment we sat down," she admitted, "Mom pulled out the little vial and jabbed the needle into her arm right there. I couldn't believe it."

"It must have been rough. For both of you."

When Aerith looked up, Tifa's eyes were glistening.

Mom would've agreed, she thought. *This is a truly good person.*

Back at that time in Sector 4, Aerith's own heart hadn't been nearly so accepting.

"I knew she was in pain, and that the medicine would bring relief. But all I could think about was me. I hated that she was doing it out in the open for everyone to see."

"You were young."

"Yeah. I was."

Aerith fell silent for a time. She *had* been young; of course she'd been self-centered and quick to judge. Yet she still had so many regrets, and she hated to write them off as things that couldn't have been avoided simply because she was a child.

"Oh!" she exclaimed, bringing her eyes back up to Tifa's. "Sorry, my mind kinda wandered off there . . . Want me to keep going with the story?"

"Please."

"After the injection, Mom seemed to get her energy back, and we kept walking. We must've walked for hours, only stopping every once in a while for a short break. Finally, we arrived at a sign that said 'Sector 5 Undercity.'"

"Mom!" Aerith exclaimed. "We've been going the wrong way! We're supposed to be going to the Sector 3 slums!"

"No. This is right where I was hoping we'd end up."

"But what about our new home? Faz said—"

"Aerith, we can talk later. It's going to be dark soon, and we need to hurry."

"Hurry *where*? Where are we going?!"

Ifalna did not answer. She gripped Aerith's hand tight and quickened her pace. They continued in silence for a time, though Aerith's mind was a whirlwind of questions.

Finally, Ifalna said in a low voice, "I heard a story once—one that I hope is true. There's supposed to be a church in the Sector 5 slums. Long ago, people would gather there to worship God, but now it sits neglected. Nobody visits, which would make it a perfect spot for us to hide for a while."

Aerith's eyes widened. "I remember reading about God and churches one time . . . Does God really exist?"

Ifalna considered the question for a moment. "God exists for those who believe. I'm told that the faithful sometimes feel a surge of strength after praying."

"What's praying?"

"I think it must be a little like when the Cetra speak with the planet. I don't know for certain. But if nobody visits the church anymore, I suppose that means that nobody believes in God anymore."

Ifalna smiled at her daughter. "That's too bad for God, but lucky for us."

"Are we going to wait for Faz at the church?"

Ifalna fell silent again but eventually shook her head.

"It wouldn't be right," she murmured, half to herself and half to Aerith. "I've already burdened him too much as it is."

"What about our new home?"

"It's not our home if we don't live there."

"Faz is going to be really disappointed . . ."

"Yes. Probably so."

"But you're okay with that?"

"As long as I have you, Aerith. You're all I need."

It made Aerith very happy hearing that. She still felt a little bad for Faz, and guilty that they hadn't followed his instructions. But if they *didn't* see him again, that would mean no new vials or syringes, and no more kisses on the back of her mother's hand.

"We'll have to find the station first," Ifalna announced. "To get to the church, I mean. The only directions I know begin from the platform."

"We could ask someone," suggested Aerith.

"No. I don't want anybody else knowing where we are."

Stuck as they were in the shadow of Midgar's upper level, the slums spent a long portion of each day with little light from the sun. To compensate, numerous large artificial lights were built into the underside of the plate; Ifalna explained that the people down here called them the "sun lamps." Only in the early morning and late evening did the residents feel the rays of the actual sun.

Aerith was baffled to hear it. The news also made her nervous: dusk was nearly upon them, and she felt certain that if they didn't make it to the church by then, something terrible would happen. What that might be, she couldn't say, but she knew she didn't want to find out.

"Look." Ifalna pointed. "That must be the station."

Sure enough, Aerith saw a platform, along which a waiting train was just stirring to life. The Sector 5 Undercity Station seemed much smaller than the one they'd fled; in Sector 4, there had been a proper station building and a big container yard. Here, Aerith couldn't find anything beyond the single, lonely platform. The street running alongside the station was much quieter too, suggesting that Sector 5 saw far fewer passengers.

"All right . . ." Ifalna mumbled to herself. "Where do we go from—"

Go from here, she'd probably meant to say. But the final word never made it out of Ifalna's mouth. Aerith's mother swayed, pitched forward, and toppled to the ground.

"Mom?!"

Aerith's shout drew stares from the little clusters of residents milling outside the station. But no one rushed over or made the slightest motion to seek help.

Ifalna's breathing was ragged. Aerith grasped her mother's arm and rolled her onto her back. Her skin was hot to the touch, and Aerith knew she must be running a dangerously high fever.

"Where's your medicine?" she asked. "I'll help you take a shot."

"All . . . gone . . ." whispered Ifalna.

What little hope Aerith still clung to drained away in that moment. She couldn't carry her mother. She didn't even know where the church was in the first place. What was she supposed to do now?

"Mom?" she asked again. "Are you gonna be okay?"

Ifalna's lips moved, as if trying to say something, but Aerith couldn't make it out. Aerith leaned close, waiting, but she only felt her mother's hot breath against her ear.

What should she do? What *could* she do? The panic must have been plain across her face.

When Ifalna did manage to speak again, she whispered what sounded like "I'm okay."

It was the same thing she'd been claiming all day long; it probably hadn't been true then, and it most definitely wasn't true now.

Why wasn't anyone coming over to help? Even at the Sector 4 station, there had been the tall stranger at the chain-link fence. Aerith peered around. What little interest she and her mother had garnered was fading fast; the bystanders were already looking away, returning to their own cares. Words and phrases flashed through Aerith's mind. *My mother's sick. She has a fever. Please help us. Please!* But none of her thoughts found a voice.

"I'm sorry, honey . . ." Ifalna murmured. "I didn't mean . . . to spoil our adventure . . ."

No! Stop! Aerith thought, and then her voice was spilling out in a burst of emotion.

"Don't *say* that!"

Ifalna neither moved nor responded, but Aerith heard a man clear his throat at her back.

"She sick?"

He was dressed in smeared, faded clothing.

"Help me move 'er over there," he said, jutting his chin in the direction of the station. "Can't have 'er blockin' the road."

The man didn't wait for Aerith to respond. He hunched down and slid a hand under each of Ifalna's armpits, then trudged backward, dragging the woman faceup across the dirt. In the process, Ifalna's shoes came off her feet. Aerith grabbed them and scrambled after.

"Be gentle with her, please!" she cried.

But the man continued dragging as before, his expression unchanged. When he'd propped Ifalna against the base of the station's concrete platform, he stepped back, brushing his dusty hands against his equally dusty trousers.

"Better find a doctor," he said.

"Where?"

"Hell if I know. But if it was *my* mother, I'd start shoutin'."

The man turned and did shout, in a loud voice that echoed across the station plaza.

"Any doctors round here?"

The inquiry found no response.

"Well, can't say I didn't try. Good luck, kid."

The man plodded off without another glance at Aerith or her mother.

A young, fashionably dressed couple descended the station steps. They stared at Ifalna without any hint of reserve, and Aerith heard the man whisper, "Daaamn . . . She's a goner, for sure."

"Are either of you a doctor?" asked Aerith.

The young man laughed and said, "Nope."

"Is that your mommy?" asked his date.

The two continued to fire off questions.

"Shouldn't you be trying to find help?"

"Doesn't she have any medicine you can give her?"

Amidst the barrage, Aerith recalled the lesson her mother had shared earlier that day. *Being a good person is about actions.* If there weren't any people like that here, she'd have to go elsewhere. She needed to find help.

"Hang on, Mom," she said. "I'll be right back. I'm going to find a doctor."

She ran. The worry she felt for her mother tugged at her legs and threatened to crush her altogether.

"Are there any doctors?!" she shouted whenever she saw a crowd. "Can anyone tell me where to find a doctor?!"

When she glanced back, the station was much farther behind than she imagined. She was debating whether to turn around, when the sound of laughter reached her ears. A large group of men and women was strolling toward her, obviously in high spirits.

I'll ask that group, she decided, *and if they can't point me to a doctor, I'll run back to check on Mom.*

But when she sprinted toward the group, calling out to them, the young man at the front suddenly wheeled around to face his friends. He walked backward, matching the group's pace and gesticulating excitedly as he shared some irreverent tale, oblivious to Aerith's approach.

"I told him where he could stick it," he laughed, "and guess what happened next? You're gonna love this. He said to me—"

The man jogged several steps back. Aerith scrambled to avoid him, but it was too late; her face smacked against his rear end, and she tumbled to the ground. Suddenly, the whole group's attention was focused on Aerith.

The man she'd run into declared, "Geez! What, are the orphans running night patrols now? Go to bed, kid!"

His friends erupted in laughter, and the group resumed its walk. Aerith struggled to her feet, listening forlornly as their voices faded into the distance. Feelings of frustration, sadness, irritation, and defeat welled up in her chest.

"Hey, there . . . You okay?" called another voice.

Aerith turned to find a woman watching her. The stranger's hair was gathered up into a loose half bun from which several locks had escaped, framing features that were soft with obvious concern.

"*I'm* okay," replied Aerith, "but my mom needs a doctor. Can you please help me find one?"

She realized she'd been crying and wiped the tears away with a dusty sleeve.

"Sorry. I live on the edge of the sector. I don't know any doctors around here."

Aerith thanked the woman and turned away.

As she hurried back to the station, she replayed the exchange in mind: *Are you okay?* I'm *okay.* It occurred to her that both question and answer were so automatic, they really meant nothing at all. How many times had she and her mother gone through the same exchange that very day?

"I'm sorry, Mom," she mumbled to herself.

She found her mother propped up against the platform as before, now with a blanket draped over her lap. To Aerith, the blanket seemed to prove that good people *did* exist in this place; one must have spotted Ifalna and offered what little he or she could spare to at least keep the woman warm.

Still, the pain was plain on her mother's face. Aerith's chest squeezed tight. She pressed a hand to Ifalna's forehead, quickly pulling back with a yelp. The fever was getting worse.

"Mommy . . . ?"

Ifalna's eyes stared blankly ahead, but she did respond in a tiny, trembling voice. "Aerith?"

"It's me, Mom. I'm right here."

The woman's gaze slowly swept to and fro, finally managing to find and focus on her daughter.

"This . . . is for you," she said, pulling a small cloth pouch from her pocket. "My father left it to me, whose mother left it to him, whose mother before left it to her. I'm afraid you won't find it to be of any use, but it has existed for a very long time. It connects the Cetra, linking us together."

Aerith's chest burned fiercely, and she declared, "No. I don't want it."

Somehow she knew that if she accepted the pouch, that would be the end.

"This life is over," whispered Ifalna, as if she'd read her daughter's mind. "Mommy has to . . . return to the planet . . ."

The small pouch trembled in Ifalna's outstretched hand. Finally, her fingers lost the strength to hold it, and it fell to the ground.

"Don't cry, sweetie. I'll always be with you . . . Always and forever."

"Mommy . . . !"

Another voice broke in. "Miss . . . Do you need help?"

Aerith looked up to find the same woman who had called out to her earlier, when she'd fallen. But before Aerith could answer the question, Ifalna abruptly leaned forward, grabbing the stranger's arm and uttering a desperate plea: "Please. Take Aerith somewhere safe."

The words were delivered with an intensity that was hard to believe from a woman who had moments ago been struggling simply to breathe. But once the words were out, her strength was spent. The husk once known as Ifalna fell limp against the concrete, its spirit having slipped free.

"No . . ." The word slipped from Aerith's mouth in much the same way.

In her mind, she heard her mother's reassuring voice: *Don't cry, sweetie. Mommy has to return to the planet, but I'll always be with you. We are connected.*

She knew. She knew it was true, yet her heart burned as if stung by a thousand tiny pinpricks, and tears streamed down her cheeks. A wail began in her gut, low and rising, and every part of her body quaked with agony.

She felt strong hands at her back, rubbing her, consoling.

But not a moment later, a shriek of metal pierced the quiet of the slums, and Aerith looked up anxiously to find the station in a flurry of activity. A train was pulling up to the platform, its brakes squealing as station attendants flagged it down.

"We need to go," the stranger said. She tugged hard at Aerith's arm, yanking the young girl to her feet. Aerith saw the cloth pouch from her mother lying in the dirt and hurriedly stooped back down to pick it up.

"It's not safe here," added the stranger.

The woman pulled on Aerith's arm again, urging her away from the station. Aerith recalled a similar moment, just hours ago, when she'd been tugged across the tracks toward a chain-link fence. Once more, she was being led to an unknown place.

Goodbye, Mom, she thought.

If Ifalna was right, they'd still be together. Aerith sensed that it was probably true. Even so, she would never again feel the warmth of her mother's body. She'd never feel her mother's arms wrap tight around her or have a chance to return the hug. Her mother would still exist, yes, but her life would take a new shape, swept up in another revolution of the planet's grand cycle.

She was struck by a sudden urge to return to Ifalna's side. She turned back and cried, "Mommy . . . !" but the stranger's hand pulled harder yet. The train had stopped, and its doors hissed open. Shinra uniforms spilled out: first troopers, followed by men in white lab coats.

"*Run*," commanded the woman, and when she saw that Aerith was frozen with indecision and fear, she swept the child into her arms and broke into a sprint.

The woman didn't let go until they neared the heart of the slums. Finally, panting hard from the exertion, she set Aerith down as gently as she could and asked, "Can you walk?"

Aerith responded with a single sullen nod.

"I'm sorry. I know you would've liked to say a proper goodbye."

Aerith shook her head.

"We did what we had to," said the woman, though it was obvious she was torn. "We never would've gotten you away otherwise."

Aerith let her silence be a response.

"Oh, you poor thing . . ."

"I'm not sad," protested Aerith. "Mom just returned to our planet."

"Yeah, that's what some people believe. Even so, it's still hard, right? You must be sad about having to say goodbye."

"I'm not," Aerith repeated, with another forceful shake of her head. "I'll see her again."

"I see . . . Well . . . How about you come over to my place for the time being? You can lie down and cry it out when you're ready."

"I didn't, though," Aerith announced in the cavernous metal confines of the cargo hold. "Elmyra thought that after the shock wore off, I'd cry and cry. But once I'd left my mom's side, I didn't shed a single tear."

Tifa regarded her with disbelief.

"You saw my home, right?" Aerith continued. "You and the others stopped by when you passed through the Sector 5 slums."

"Yeah. We did."

"I bet you couldn't believe all the flowers."

"It was definitely a surprise."

"The day I first showed up, the flowers were there to greet me. I could *feel* them welcoming me on behalf of the planet. And I could feel my mom too. So I didn't need to cry. All I'd left behind at the station was an empty shell. My mother was still right beside me."

Tifa tilted her head, looking more puzzled than ever.

"I know," replied Aerith. "It probably sounds really weird."

"Mysterious, maybe, but not weird."

"Thanks. I had a feeling you'd be able to accept it. That's what makes you so easy to talk to."

Aerith swallowed against the lump in her throat. Anxious to change the subject, she exclaimed, "Hey! So what did you think of my house? Pretty big, huh? I mean, at least for the slums."

"Yeah. It was really nice. Well cared for, I guess is the best way to put it. For a second, I almost forgot we were in Midgar, let alone the slums."

"Right?" Aerith grinned. "Actually, the house originally belonged to Elmyra's father-in-law. He was kind of an influential figure in Sector 5. Like Don Corneo, if Don Corneo wasn't evil."

"Is that even possible?"

"Um, never mind! Bad example!"

"Ugh, now I've got Corneo's ugly, puffy face stuck in my mind . . ."

"Sorry! Forget all about him! Try and imagine someone more . . . refined. A *gentleman*. Basically any face *other* than Corneo's."

"I'll try."

Tifa scrunched up her face with determination, but she ultimately relented with a giggle.

"What is it?" asked Aerith.

"Now that I think about it, I'm not sure I've spent much time with any guys I'd describe as *gentlemen*."

Though Aerith didn't yet know much about the slums, she could tell right away that Elmyra's home was a special place: the house and surrounding garden were brimming with life. An abundance of plants covered every bit of the terraced ground. There were even flowers! To a girl who had never seen blossom nor bud outside vase or planter, it was an astonishing sight to behold.

A walking path lazily meandered its way through the garden, sloping up and down, its packed dirt lined sometimes with stones and other times with wooden planks laid crosswise. The moment Aerith first set foot upon it, she felt as though her arms and legs were being gently caressed by unseen hands. The sensation didn't spark anxiety or fear; rather, a mellow calm seemed to envelop her heart. (Or perhaps her *mind*—it was hard to be certain.)

"Is someone there?" she asked.

As if in response, a gust of wind rushed by, sweeping fingers across her cheek and filling her with joy.

Elmyra Gainsborough glanced back to check on the girl. Aerith had learned the woman's name as they walked the long and tortuous route from the Sector 5 Undercity Station.

"Did you say something?"

"No. Nothing."

"Hmm . . ." Elmyra resumed walking, and added, "Lot of green here, don't you think? One of the few corners of Midgar still in its natural state, left over from before the city was built. When the season's right, the whole place is full of flowers. The ones you see now are just the beginning."

Aerith imagined the entire space teeming with red, white, and yellow blooms. A bright smile spread across her face.

"If anything, there's *too* many," continued Elmyra. "You wouldn't believe all the bugs they bring. I've tried to trim some of the plants back, even pulled some up by the roots, but the darn things are persistent."

"I think it's wonderful just the way it is."

"Well, you're in luck, then, 'cause I've thrown in the towel. These days, they grow however they like."

Past the fields rose a stately wooden structure that Aerith would in time come to know very well. Elmyra's home was topped with a red roof that looked like a great big floppy hat, with two triangular windows jutting out from the second story.

They stepped up onto the small patio, and Elmyra pulled open the home's large, stately double doors, beckoning Aerith inside. For the briefest moment, Aerith hesitated. Her entire day had been a long string of firsts, many of which she couldn't have begun to imagine from the confines of Shinra HQ. But this first was different. She was about to step inside another person's home. The very idea weighed on her like a dark, heavy stone.

When she mustered the courage to follow Elmyra inside, she was spellbound by what she found. Beams of real wood criss-crossed the ceiling. A wooden table and chairs sat in the center of the front room. The walls were full of windows. All of it seemed an incredible luxury compared to the cold, sterile surfaces of her for-mer living quarters. The furniture, dishware, pots, produce, and even the mops and brooms all seemed to stir and whisper, over-loading her mind and leaving her panting for breath.

Unaware of the turmoil behind Aerith's reaction, Elmyra could only smile.

"You sure are a strange one, aren't you? Anyway, I was thinking about your options as we made our way over. We got you away from those men at the station, but there's still the question of what to do next.

"You noticed the orphanage on the way, I hope? There's a whole slew of kids living there already, and the housemother would no doubt welcome you too. But the talk around town is that the or-phanage has ties with Shinra. And from what we saw at the station, I'm guessing you're not too fond of the company."

Aerith nodded vigorously.

Elmyra heaved a sigh. "If that's so, all the more reason to tread carefully. Unfortunately, I'm not exactly in a good spot to help you draw up any big plans. I've got a lot going on as it is. So . . . How would you feel about staying here with me for now? We'll ride it out and deal with the problems as they come."

Aerith nodded again.

"Then it's settled. Let me show you the upstairs."

A staircase curled up along the edge of the front room. Elmyra bounded up the steps two at a time: she seemed to have a rather impatient disposition. Aerith scrambled after her, but Elmyra's foot was already tapping by the time she managed to reach the second-floor landing.

"I'm thinking it'll be best if you stay up here."

"Okay."

"To be honest, this household gets more than its fair share of guests. If I suddenly had a little girl running around, people would notice, and it might raise a few eyebrows. Worst case, word could get back to Shinra.

"Eventually, in the mornings and late evenings, it'll be safe enough to sit with me downstairs, and I'll be sure to call you down as often as I'm able. But aside from that, could you promise to stay here on the second floor, at least for a while?"

". . . How long is a while?" asked Aerith.

Elmyra's brows knit, and her arms folded against her chest. All the laughter in her eyes was gone.

"Be honest with me. It's not just your mother Shinra wants, is it? They want *you* too."

Aerith understood the question, but she wasn't sure she had an answer. *Was* Shinra looking for her? It seemed likely, when she reasoned it out. With her mother gone, Aerith was the last remaining Cetra.

"Yeah . . . I mean, yes, ma'am."

"No need for 'ma'am,'" replied Elmyra. She seemed to think for a bit, then concluded, "If that's the case, you're better off staying hidden until Shinra gives up the search."

The idea of Shinra ever giving up seemed terribly unlikely to Aerith. She certainly didn't want to live on the second floor of Elmyra's house for the rest of her life.

Elmyra noticed her gloomy frown and tried to offer reassurance. "You won't be up here forever. People eventually give up. It's human nature."

"Yes, ma'am. I mean . . . yeah."

Downstairs, a doorbell rang. Now it was Elmyra's turn to grimace. Aerith tensed. Had the troopers found her already?

"Stay here, and stay quiet," cautioned Elmyra. She adjusted her hair and smoothed her clothing before hurrying down the stairs.

Aerith crouched on the landing, balling herself up as tight as she could.

I won't make a sound, she told herself. *They won't even hear me breathe.*

No sooner did she hear the click of the front doors' latch than a storm of angry shouts filled the house.

"Where the hell've you been?!" demanded a male voice.

Aerith nearly lost her balance; she had to thrust a hand out to keep from toppling to the floor.

"Oh, so now I'm supposed to keep you informed of my every move. Is that it?" came Elmyra's sharp response.

"*You* were the one who wanted to meet up!" raged the man. "Come by in the evening, you said! You think it's funny to keep me standing around with my thumb up my ass?!"

"I said I *might* be around in the evening. I didn't promise you a single thing. Not that it matters, anyway. You can show up day or night, and it won't do you any good."

"All I need is a signature and a fingerprint, and I'll be outta your hair. How many times you gonna make me say it?!"

"Say it as many times as you want, the answer won't change! There are rules and procedures for this kinda thing. I'm not on board unless Meguro is. You could have my signature and my fingerprint in *blood* and it wouldn't do you any good. If Meguro thinks you forced me, he'll run you out of the sector. So if you want to have a long, successful career, you'll shape up and do this the *right* way."

"Damn it all! This is bullshit!"

"Keep talking like that and I'll wash your mouth out with soap. Now go on. Get."

"Bullshit! Bullshit, bullshit, *bullshit*!"

"Last warning. *Scram.* And I'd suggest you think real hard about your behavior."

The front doors slammed shut, and Aerith heard the muffled cursing of the man as he departed.

A moment later, Elmyra ascended the staircase, looking more tired than ever.

She sighed deeply and said, "Carlo Kincaid. Real piece of work, that one. But don't worry. Most of the guys who come by know how to mind their manners."

Aerith was given the bedroom that had, until two months prior, belonged to Gabriel Gainsborough, the patriarch who built the house. Health troubles had left him bedridden for a time, eventually leading to his passing. But the room was clean and orderly, and to Aerith, at least, it contained no lingering sense of death.

"I know it's not very inviting," Elmyra had apologized after explaining, "but it's the only spare room I've got . . . Er, well, there *is* another, but it's full of clutter."

Aerith wasn't bothered in the least. Quite the contrary, the room seemed to welcome her.

That first night, Ifalna appeared at the head of her bed.

"I'll be praying for you," she said with a smile. "Praying that Elmyra comes to love you as much as I do."

Traces of fatigue still lingered in that smile—the same exhaustion Aerith had seen in her mother during their long trek through the slums.

"How were you able to come back?" Aerith asked.

"I never went anywhere at all," replied Ifalna. "You and I will always be together. We are connected."

She felt her mother's hand brush against her forehead, and finally she found peace. Aerith fell into a deep, restful sleep.

The following night, Ifalna appeared yet again.

"How was your day?" she asked. "Are you getting along with Elmyra?"

"I'm not sure . . . She made breakfast and brought it to my room. She sat down to eat with me and left me some bread for lunch. But after that, she headed out, and I was alone until she came back. And then it was time for dinner. But . . . she looked so *tired*. She didn't seem to want to talk, and if we don't talk, I don't know how we can become friends. What should I do?"

"Everything will be all right. Elmyra's in a tough spot at the moment, but I think you might be able to help."

"Help how?"

"Be with her. When she's overwhelmed and looks like she might cry, sit at her side, like you used to do for me."

"But . . . I never saw *you* cry, Mom. Did you really used to feel like that?"

"Yes, from time to time."

Aerith waved her gloved, armored hands apologetically. "Uh . . . Sorry. I should probably back up."

For the past several minutes, Tifa had been regarding her with a mystified expression.

"At that point, I still thought they were just dreams. I figured I'd fallen asleep and was talking to my mom inside my head."

". . . Now I'm even more confused. You're saying they *weren't* dreams?"

"It's something the Cetra can do. We become one with the lifestream as it courses by. And through it, we can talk to other people, even if they're really far away. At least, we can under certain circumstances."

"That's incredible . . ."

"Yeah, I guess it is, huh? But I've pretty much lost all that. If I'm in a place where the energy's really concentrated, I can still feel the connection, but the rest of the time, I don't feel anything at all."

"Huh."

"It's hard to say if it's a relief to be free of it, or if I miss it. In any case, back then that ability led to all kinds of misunderstandings with the people around me. I guess people thought I was a pretty weird kid."

It was Aerith's third day in her new home. The sun lamps were off, and the real sun was well below the horizon, but Elmyra had yet to return from her daily outing. Aerith hadn't eaten anything since noon, and that meal had only consisted of a bit of bread and soup. She was famished. She didn't know how much longer she could bear it.

I could go downstairs and look for something to eat, she thought. But she quickly shook her head. She'd promised to stay on the second floor. She didn't want to risk upsetting her host. What if Elmyra asked her to leave?

But I'm really *hungry. Maybe I could—*

Just then, she heard the click of the front doors.

"It's me," announced Elmyra. "I'll get dinner ready and bring it up."

From the tone of her voice, it was obvious the woman was in a very poor mood.

"Thank you," called Aerith, but she got no response.

She sat in her chair quietly, listening to the sounds from the kitchen—a quiet clink of metal, followed a while later by the bubbling of a pot coming to boil. When the meal's savory smells began to waft up the stairs and into her room, Aerith pulled out the small folding table from her closet, setting it up as she'd seen Elmyra do the day before.

At last, Elmyra appeared at her door, carrying a tray on which sat a loaf of warm bread and two bowls of baked beans.

"Sorry for the wait," Elmyra said.

Aerith gasped when she caught sight of the woman's face. A large bandage stretched across her right brow and down to the corner of her eye.

"Just took a little tumble," Elmyra said, her voice flat. "Nothing for you to worry about."

She set the tray down on the table, mumbled something to herself as she sat, and began eating in silence. Apparently, she had no intention to expound upon the incident.

Aerith, unsure what else to do, summoned the biggest smile she could muster and announced, "It looks delicious!"

If nothing else, she could at least try her very best to make the meal a cheerful one.

"Mmm! It *is* delicious!" she added after her first bite.

"Came from a can."

"Well, then canned foods are delicious."

"Great. Tell it to whoever made the stuff."

"Where *do* canned foods come from?"

"Some Shinra factory. Quit talking and eat, would you?"

The possibility that they owed this particular meal to Shinra quickly dampened Aerith's spirit.

Elmyra, seeming to regret the admonishment, added, "I don't like it either, but it's near impossible to get by if you swear off Shinra products altogether. I can bake my own bread, but the flour and the electricity for the oven are still coming from Shinra. You gotta compromise somewhere."

"What's a 'compromise'?"

"Means you gotta pick your battles. Now I'm serious. Less talking, more eating."

Irritation had crept back into Elmyra's words. Aerith wished things could have gone differently. But given that her efforts to brighten the mood had failed spectacularly, she figured she might as well try asking one of the real questions on her mind.

"I will," she promised, "but could you please tell me one thing? Where do you go every morning after breakfast?"

Elmyra paused, a spoonful of beans halfway to her mouth. Her gaze held on Aerith for a moment, then dropped just as suddenly as she resumed eating. Aerith hadn't been able to read anything in her expression, and she was all out of ideas about how to keep the conversation going.

She'd relented and resolved to eat the rest of the meal in silence, when Elmyra spoke up.

"Used to lug this table outside for picnics, y'know."

Her voice was gentle and forthcoming.

"Picnics!" exclaimed Aerith. "I've heard of those!"

"Well, as close as you can get to a picnic in the slums, anyway. Someplace away from the crowds, but not so remote that you'd run into monsters. Just a quiet spot to sit outside and munch on some ham and cheese sandwiches. Maybe with a beer or two to wash them down."

"Sounds like fun."

"Yeah. It was."

Elmyra's expression clouded, and for a moment, Aerith panicked. Wanting to keep the happy conversation running as long as possible, she asked, "Did you go by yourself?"

"Of course not."

Elmyra set the heel of bread back on her plate, stood, and walked over to her own room. She returned as quickly as she'd left, with a framed photo that she held out to Aerith.

Aerith immediately recognized the photo's small folding table. On one side sat a man, and on the other Elmyra. The two leaned in shoulder to shoulder, facing the camera. Aerith didn't recognize the man, but he had a stout, rugged build and a face to match. It was a stark contrast to Elmyra's thin, almost dainty figure. Both wore big, wide grins.

"Clay Gainsborough," said Elmyra. "Gabriel's only son . . . and my dear husband."

"Husband?!" exclaimed Aerith. "I know that word too! It's someone special! Husbands are special to wives, and wives are special to husbands!"

That made Elmyra laugh.

"Yeah, well, there's my special man," she said. "When he gets back home, be sure to call him Clay. He'll like that. He's good with kids. I know he'll be just as happy to have you here as I am."

"Where is he now?" Aerith asked, still peering at the photograph.

When Elmyra didn't respond, she looked up to find the woman very nearly in tears. Still, Elmyra was quick to force a smile for Aerith's sake.

"Shipped off to fight in the war. I got a letter a while back, though. He's accumulated some leave and is coming to visit. Except, well . . . He was supposed to arrive six days ago, but there's been no sign of him and no further word. I was on day three of my wait when I met you."

Everything suddenly clicked.

"That's where you've been going every day!" exclaimed Aerith. "You've been sitting at the station, waiting for him."

"That's right. Morning till evening. Just sitting and waiting, like a damn fool."

Aerith shook her head fiercely.

"I tried contacting HQ here in Midgar," Elmyra said, "but no one can tell me anything. Troop movements are classified, they tell me. I try to explain, but they just keep parroting that one line over and over."

"Your husband's a *Shinra* trooper?"

"Right again. And yeah . . . I know. I probably should've told you that up front. Sorry." Elmyra sighed. "Frankly, this whole family's more or less built on Shinra's back."

Aerith felt herself starting to tense up. She returned the photo to Elmyra.

"Don't worry. I'm not gonna hand you over to the company, and

Clay won't either. I don't know what kind of trouble you're in, but I'm not about to forget the way your mother looked at me. Far be it from me to deny a dying mother her final wish."

"Thank you," said Aerith, bringing her hands to both cheeks in an attempt to hide her worry.

Elmyra only stared at the image in the frame.

"The neighborhood was starting to resent the Gainsborough family. Shinra treated us too good, they said. That's what drove Clay to enlist; he was doing it for his family's future.

"Gabriel tried to stop him, but the son was just as bullheaded as the father. From the day Clay turned in his papers, the two never talked again. I was the one running back and forth between them, keeping the family business running."

"Did Clay and Gabriel not like each other?"

"Well, you know what they say. Sometimes fathers and sons are too alike."

That puzzled Aerith. It seemed to her that family members who were alike should get along very well. But from the way Elmyra's face softened when she spoke of her husband, Aerith had to believe the best of Clay. If he was a Shinra trooper, then maybe not all Shinra troopers were bad. Maybe Clay was one of the good ones.

"Enough about me," said Elmyra. "Isn't there anything you'd like to share? Are there things I should know about you if you're going to be staying here?"

Aerith could think of many things Elmyra probably ought to know, but she hesitated, unsure how much of the truth was safe to divulge.

She recalled her mother Ifalna's many anecdotes about the Cetra.

I am a descendant of the Cetra, she thought, trying the words out in mind. *The people the world know today as the Ancients.*

Elmyra was a good person. Aerith had no doubt of that. The woman didn't just say nice things. She acted. Already, she'd done a great deal to help a little girl who was, quite frankly, still a complete stranger.

And Aerith felt that Clay was certainly a good person too. In the photo, he'd worn the same gentle, honest smile as Elmyra.

But if she were to tell them she was an Ancient . . .

It seemed the kind of information that might change how people perceived and treated her. The scientists employed by Shinra had been desperate to uncover the secrets of the Ancients. They'd often seemed friendly enough on the outside. But peel back that layer of kindness, and Aerith feared many would turn out to be just like Professor Hojo, ready to cut off skin samples and stick her with needles and who knew what else.

"My mom and I . . ." she began, trying to choose her words carefully. "We were captured by a mad scientist. He locked us up in the Shinra Building and experimented on Mom. That's why she got sick. If Shinra finds me, they'll experiment on me too. So I want to stay. I like it here. I like the house and the garden and everything. I don't care if we have to eat canned food made by Shinra. I won't complain. Just please . . . let me stay."

Elmyra's mouth hung open. After a long moment of silence, she reached over the small table and grasped both of Aerith's hands tight.

"Is that all true? No . . . I shouldn't be asking that. Of course you can stay. I promise to do everything I can to help you feel safe here. So how about I sit down and we finish our meal?"

Elmyra took her seat, and the two resumed eating in silence.

When they were done, Elmyra said, "We're having a guest over tomorrow. It seems like a good excuse for me to cook a proper lunch. Heaven knows how long it's been.

"I like cooking, really. It just feels like a lot of trouble to go to when it's me living on my own. But now that you're here . . ."

"I like cooking too!" exclaimed Aerith. "I want to help."

"Hmm . . . It might still be a little soon to have you down on the ground floor."

Aerith slumped. But she quickly perked back up, asking, "The person coming over tomorrow, what's he like?"

"Hm? It's Meguro. One of the number twos."

"Number two what?"

Elmyra chuckled. "Don't worry. I'll explain it all tomorrow. He's coming over to talk business."

Elmyra stacked the dishes and carried them out. At the top of the stairs, she peered back at Aerith and casually asked, "Aerith, honey . . . You *do* miss your mother, don't you?"

Aerith cradled the bulky trooper helmet in her arms, running a finger up and down its sharp angles.

"At the time, I didn't feel lonely or sad or anything like that," she confessed to Tifa. "I got to see Mom nearly every night, just before I went to bed. Even on the nights she didn't appear, I knew we were still connected through the planet. That thought helped keep me going.

"And there was one other thing too: the materia Mom left me in the little cloth bag. I mean, it was kinda useless. I tried all sorts of things to get it to cast a spell or something, but it just sat there, emitting its soft white glow. Even so, having it near seemed to bring me peace."

"Sounds like it wasn't so useless after all."

"Yeah. I guess you're right."

Aerith touched a hand to the ribbon tied at the top of her long braid. Even now, her mother's materia was with her.

"And someday you'll get to pass it down too," said Tifa. "I wonder what kind of person she'll be."

It took Aerith a moment to understand. When she finally did, she replied, "You know what?"

"Hm?"

"I'd honestly never thought about that."

Perhaps there'd come a day when she *wasn't* the last surviving Cetra. She found the idea a bit surprising, and her eyes held on Tifa as she mulled it over.

Tifa fidgeted and hurried to add, "Sorry. That was a weird thing to say. Let's get back to your story. I'd love to hear more. Like, what was this 'one of the number twos' business all about?"

In an unexpected turn of events, Aerith was invited to join Elmyra and the visitor for lunch the next day. When she came down the stairs, Meguro rose from his chair and extended a hand. Aerith accepted it gingerly as she regarded the man with scarcely concealed astonishment. Meguro was a very large, very round fellow, likely much older than Elmyra and possessing bright, laughing eyes.

"This is Meguro," Elmyra said. "One of Gabriel's right-hand men, an old friend of Clay's, and my trusted adviser."

"Hello . . . I'm Aerith."

The great big man smiled at her. "Elmyra told me your story. Seems you've been through quite a lot."

Surprised, Aerith looked at Elmyra.

"It's all right. He's someone we can trust. And even if I hadn't said anything, he was bound to pick word up somewhere. When Shinra comes storming the station, people talk, and Meguro has his ways of finding things out. I figured it was best to introduce you sooner rather than later."

In truth, Aerith wasn't exactly pleased; the circumstances through which she'd arrived at Elmyra's home were supposed to be secret. Still, the cat was out of the bag, and there wasn't much she could do about that now.

"Aerith," began Meguro, "my sources tell me that your escape has caused quite the kerfuffle at Shinra HQ. The fallout has led to a string of rather unsavory crimes here in the slums: reprobates whisking young girls off the streets, hoping to make a quick gil by claiming they've found the girl Shinra is after."

Aerith frowned. "But how can they make money by kidnapping the wrong girl? Shinra knows who I am. They're not gonna be tricked into paying for someone else."

"Right you are. But when *Shinra* has its eye on something, others tend to turn their heads too. It might not be so hard to deceive an unscrupulous slum lord who's blinded by his own greed."

Meguro shifted his heavy frame to face Aerith more properly. "You must be, what, six? No . . . Seven."

"That's right. Seven."

"Mm-hmm. I have a daughter who's just your age. Her name is Ronna. So you see, these kidnappings trouble me on a very personal level."

The man cleared his throat and continued. "I'd like to propose a different course of action. Rather than hiding, why not come out into the open? You'd play the part of Elmyra's daughter, accompanying her as she goes about her day. When people see the two of you together . . ." Here, he pointed a finger at Elmyra. ". . . all *you* need to do is say, 'This is my daughter. I had her before Clay and I got married.' Explain that a relative was kind enough to raise the girl but that now Aerith's come back to live with you."

"Whoa, whoa. Hold on now," protested Elmyra. "What does any of that accomplish?"

"The goal is to show Aerith's face out in public, where your neighbors can see her. That way, they'll come to know her and recognize her as part of the community. If she lives hidden away upstairs, no one's likely to notice or care if Shinra or a kidnapper tries to make off with her. Think about it. You know most everyone in the sector. If the neighborhood believes Aerith is your daughter, they'll look out for her."

"All right, I see where you're going. But couldn't we accomplish the same thing without claiming I've had an illegitimate kid all this time? We could say she's the daughter of some cousin of mine or an orphan I took in on behalf of the House."

"The orphanage is right next door. There's no reason for them to ask you to take a child in when she could just as easily live there, which means the story would invite unwanted questions. But a daughter of one of your relatives . . . Yes. I think that could work. Seems more natural that way too. There's only one hitch."

Meguro narrowed his eyes and regarded Elmyra carefully.

"It'll hit much harder if people hear Aerith calling you Mother, just as I called Gabriel Father."

He shifted his eyes to Aerith.

"I grew up an orphan too, you see. Gabriel took me in and treated me like his own son. So, with all that said, what do *you* think of my plan, Aerith? Are you willing to live as Elmyra and Clay's daughter, at least for the time being?"

"I'd like that."

In fact, she thought it was a *wonderful* idea. As things were, she felt certain that no resident of the slums would intervene if she ever needed help—her frantic search for a doctor the other evening had made that very clear. But if she were to become the daughter of Elmyra Gainsborough, perhaps she'd be able to live in safety in the slums after all.

Elmyra still seemed to be mulling the proposal over. Aerith prayed fervently for her agreement.

"It's a solid idea," admitted Elmyra. "But Aerith's not the only issue at stake here. This would affect the Gainsborough family as a whole. It isn't something she and I should decide on the spot."

"Then take your time. I'll let you both sleep on it, and we can pick this up later. At any rate, when Aerith does head outside again, she ought to think about using a different name."

The last point sent Aerith's mind reeling. Change her *name*? She didn't like that idea one bit.

"Now, let me ask you something else," Meguro said, looking at Elmyra. "That little number above your eye. Carlo's work, I assume?"

"No use hiding anything from you, is there?" Elmyra glanced sidelong at Aerith as she replied.

Meguro responded with a triumphant snort. "The young man's proving to be quite a headache," he said. "I can't for the life of me comprehend why he believes himself a contender when a new spot opens up."

"With Gabriel out of the picture, he figures now's his chance. Gabriel was never too keen on the kid, but Clay's got a soft spot for him. Better yet, while Clay's away, it's me and you who'd give the go-ahead. He seems to think I'm some delicate little flower that'll break down sobbing and agree to anything the second he brandishes his fist."

"I suppose I'll have to make sure we're running an especially tight ship for the next while." Meguro's expression grew taut. "Clay does intend to succeed his father, yes?"

"That's why he requested leave. He wanted to be here in person to talk the process over with you."

"Goodness. Certainly that's not the *main* reason he's visiting. All this is just a convenient excuse for him to find his way back to his darling wife's loving arms."

Meguro followed his own quip with a hearty laugh, and he rose to leave.

"I'll deal with Carlo," he said. "As for the succession, I'm inclined to agree with Clay. Let's save that discussion until after he's back in town."

Aerith glanced at Tifa, trying to judge what other details might need filling in.

"After Mr. Meguro went home that day, Elmyra explained the Gainsborough family business to me. See, Gabriel built his name by organizing people. When a construction site needed manpower, Gabriel was the guy who could round up an army of day laborers on a moment's notice and set them to work. The way Shinra put it, he was a contractor."

"Yeah, I'm familiar with the type."

"It can be a shady business, but Gabriel had a reputation as one of the good ones. He was doing it for a long time too, right since Midgar was first being built. There used to be lots of competition, but as soon as the plate was finished, the other contractors used the money they made to go live topside in comfort. Only Gabriel and his men stayed in the slums.

"Gabriel saw it as a strategic move, and it paid off. See, all the infrastructure to support the plate is found down in the slums, right? So if Gabriel was the only real game in town, it meant that every major repair or new construction project in the undercity went straight to the Gainsborough family. And if you were a laborer, Gabriel's organization was the one you wanted to work with because that's where all the good jobs were."

Aerith traced a triangle in the air with her finger.

"Here's Gabriel," she told Tifa, pointing at its apex. "He was the 'number one'—the head of the family business." Aerith indicated a portion of the triangle slightly farther down. "Under him were Clay and Meguro, his 'number two' men. And below that were six others, the 'number three' men, each with their own stable of tradesmen and unskilled labor ready to assign to Clay's and Meguro's projects. Carlo, the guy who roughed up Elmyra, was a young worker Clay had taken under his wing. He didn't have any position in the hierarchy, but he was gunning to someday become a 'number three.'"

When Meguro had left, Elmyra came to stand behind Aerith and rested her hands on the girl's shoulders.

"Do you understand what's going on?" she asked. "This is a big decision. One you shouldn't rush. Most of this family's business comes directly from Shinra, and my husband is a trooper in Shinra's army. Knowing all that, are you certain you still want to stay?"

Elmyra waited patiently for Aerith's response. Her expression was serious, though not unkind. It occurred to Aerith that this was one way in which Elmyra was very different from her birth mother; she did her best to keep Aerith involved, even in difficult, grown-up matters. And it was precisely because Elmyra tried to honor her desires that Aerith felt compelled to think carefully before answering.

"Shinra's our client," continued Elmyra, "but that doesn't necessarily mean we agree with the way the company runs the world. Don't get the wrong idea about that."

Aerith would have been lying if she said that living in a home with such close ties to Shinra didn't bother her. But if that was the line she drew, it would mean she had to find somewhere else to live.

What am I supposed to do? she thought. *What do I want to do?*

She looked up at Elmyra. The woman's hands were rough and calloused, a world away from Ifalna's smooth, creamy skin. Her hair was dry and limp. She appeared haggard, and the bandage remained affixed just below her temple, the bruised skin on either side looking red and tender. Elmyra had only been at the station to wait for Clay, hoping against hope that today was the day her husband finally arrived. Instead, she'd run into Carlo, and now had the injury to show for it.

Elmyra stared back. This woman—this stranger—was determined to help Aerith along the path of her own choosing, despite all the hardships she was grappling with in her own life.

With a gasp, Aerith realized there was another, far more important question that she should have asked long ago.

"Do *you* mind me staying?" she blurted. "Are you really okay having someone like me in your home?"

Elmyra smiled. "Of course you're welcome. I'd hoped you felt that from the moment you stepped in the door."

Aerith stood and clutched Elmyra's legs in a tight embrace, uncertain how else to express the abrupt sense of relief and joy on hearing those words. Her cheek pressed against the woman's stomach, and she felt Elmyra's arms pull her in tight, one hand gently rubbing her back in large circular motions.

"I've never raised a kid before," she confessed. "And neither has Clay. But it's not like we started out knowing how to run the family business. We watched, and we learned.

"So . . . I might not always understand you, and I'm sure we'll have our bumps along the way. Might even come a day when Shinra finds you. But if they do, we'll put our heads together and come up with a solution. Clay, Meguro, me, and you. *Especially* you, Aerith."

Aerith shifted slightly, nuzzling her forehead into Elmyra's stomach.

"Do you think you'd be able to call me Mom? You don't have to mean it. I don't ever expect to replace your *real* mother."

Aerith tried the word out, face still fast against Elmyra's belly.

"Mom."

"What was that, honey? I couldn't hear you," teased Elmyra.

"Mom."

"Getting closer. Try once more."

"Mom?"

Elmyra laughed. "I can tell *I'm* going to need some time to get used to it. But . . . it might not be half bad. How's it feel for you?"

Aerith gazed up at Elmyra's gentle eyes.

"Not half bad!" she mimicked, prompting such a great peal of laughter, it seemed the air itself was dancing with joy.

That night, Ifalna appeared yet again. When Aerith related the events of the day, the woman closed her eyes and nodded, a satisfied smile on her lips.

"That's wonderful," she said. "I'm very happy for you, Aerith."

"But . . . Mom? I . . . I just want to say I'm sorry."

"Why's that?"

"'Cause . . ."

All at once, the guilt rose up and choked her.

"You needn't worry yourself about my feelings," assured Ifalna. "Focus on enjoying your new life. Did you two decide on a new name?"

"Elmyra says I should choose it for myself."

"I see. Well, be sure to put plenty of thought into it. Whatever name you choose will be the one to set you free."

"I know, but . . ."

The thought of abandoning the name she'd come to know and love filled her with immense sorrow.

"To me, you'll always be Aerith," said Ifalna. "My darling little Aerith. Nothing can ever change that."

"You promise?"

"I promise."

The vision of Ifalna wavered slightly, and Aerith called out frantically, not wanting her to go. Not yet.

"What if Clay feels differently?" she asked her mother. "What if he doesn't like the idea of me staying in their home, or gets angry when he hears where I've come from? What if he tells Elmyra to send me back to Shinra?"

"Somehow I don't think Elmyra would have chosen to marry a man like that."

"Yeah . . ." replied Aerith. Then more decisively, "Yeah. You're right."

Her worry eased, though it did not dissipate entirely.

"I wonder what's taking Clay so long to get home."

"Good question. Perhaps I should see if I can find him. Would you like that?"

"Yes. Please."

It was morning the following day. Aerith was seated at the table downstairs, a cup of tea in her hands. Elmyra was sitting too. A light rapping came at the door, and through the glass they saw an elderly man, slight of frame, his skin tanned from long hours in the sun and lined with deep wrinkles.

His name was Butch, Elmyra quickly explained as she rose from her seat, and he was one of the six "number three" men in Gabriel's hierarchy. When she opened up, she greeted the man warmly.

"Butch! Good morning! I wasn't expecting to see you so early."

"My bad," the man apologized. "Must've gotten the hour mixed up. You want me to come back later?"

"No, no. It's fine. Come on in."

Elmyra fetched a sheaf of papers—timelines and permits for one of their contracts, she'd told Aerith as she readied them that morning. Butch flicked through the pages, gave a satisfied nod, and stuffed the sheaf inside his tattered old briefcase.

"Who's the girl?" he asked.

"Ah, that's right," answered Elmyra. "I haven't introduced you yet. A cousin of mine passed away recently. Her daughter's come to live with me."

"She don't got a father?"

Elmyra, usually calm and composed, was all but tripping over her words.

"Hm? Oh, um . . . he's not exactly in the picture, I guess you'd say."

Butch turned to Aerith. She'd never seen a face so weathered and deeply lined. The man's eyes, now narrowed with suspicion, seemed two more wrinkles among the rest.

"What's your name, little lady?"

The question caught Aerith unprepared, not least because she'd been so focused on his complexion. She opened her mouth, uncertain how to answer, and out tumbled the first name that came to mind: "Ronna."

The moment the name slipped from her lips, she knew she'd screwed up. Ronna was the name of *Meguro's* daughter. Butch had to know that.

"It's nice to meet you, Mr. Butch," she continued shakily. She glanced at Elmyra, who looked just as panicked as Aerith felt.

Butch laughed. "Well, I'll be. That's some coincidence."

He nodded thoughtfully, features again relaxed and betraying no hint of incredulity. It was hard to say whether he'd picked up on Aerith's panic.

"Well, it was nice ta meetcha, Ronna," he announced, bobbing his head once at Elmyra and turning to leave. He shut the doors carefully and sauntered away down the garden path, leaving Elmyra and Aerith alone in the kitchen, hearts still pounding fast.

Elmyra clutched her head in her hands. "Oh, this is bad . . ."

"I'm sorry . . . I should've picked a name yesterday."

"No, it's my fault. Butch is always running early. I should've known to have you stay upstairs this morning, and . . ."

Elmyra's composure quickly returned. She knelt so her eyes were level with Aerith's. "What I'm saying is, I should've been prepared for this. Picking a new name's a big decision, and I'd been so concerned about leaving the choice up to you that it didn't occur to me you might need some guidance. I mean, of course you do. You're so grown up, I start to forget you're only seven years old."

Elmyra rose and grabbed a broom. She began sweeping the kitchen floor with short, agitated strokes, all the while mumbling to herself, ". . . Needs my help . . . 'Course she does . . . She's just a little girl . . . "

Aerith had seen this behavior a few times before: whenever Elmyra was upset, she went straight for the broom. Chores seemed to be her way of calming down and focusing her mind.

When the brief storm of sweeping was over, Elmyra put on a fresh pot of tea and invited Aerith to another cup.

"Our next visitor is Rodin. He's a number three, same as Butch. Comes across kinda flaky, but he's got it where it counts. He's a good kid."

"He's a little kid? Like me?"

"No, no. I just call him that because I've got a good decade on him. Anyway, Rodin's not due till sundown. In the meantime, I'd like to go check the station, just in case Clay arrives. Could you stay up on the second floor until I get back? I hate to make you hide, but I think we've both just learned a hard lesson about avoiding unexpected interactions until we're ready."

"Okay."

"Eventually, we'll get to a point where I can take you with me when I go out."

"I don't mind. Really. I like it upstairs."

"Take some time to think over that new name of yours. We'll just have to bring Butch in on our little secret. Not that Ronna's a bad name, but it's not too late to come up with something else."

Elmyra smiled and added, "I'll be thinking too. And when I'm back, we can share our ideas."

She left strict instructions not to open the door for anyone while she was gone—not even Rodin. Aerith wasn't even to respond if a visitor called out, asking if anyone was home. It reminded her of a picture book she'd once read, about a mother squirrel who warns her seven little baby squirrels to keep the door closed while she's away finding food. When Aerith recalled what happened to the baby squirrels in the story, she quickly scurried up the stairs, anxious to avoid the same fate.

Aerith had planned to start thinking up her new name as soon as she reached her room. Instead, she found herself thinking about the deep wrinkles of Butch's face. Someday, she decided, she'd like to touch them, to see what they felt like—although this spark of curiosity admittedly startled her.

She thought about Meguro's great big stomach too. What on earth had he stuffed it with for it to grow so large? If she poked it, would it be soft or hard? Was his daughter, Ronna, big and round like he was?

And if she *did* come up with a new name, would the name she'd told Butch come back to haunt her? Would Meguro be angry that she'd copied his daughter's name? What about Ronna herself? What was she like, anyway? Would Aerith have a chance to meet her someday, or maybe even become her friend?

Her thoughts wandered on like that, punctuated by moments in which she nearly nodded off, until she realized evening had already arrived and heard the latch of the front door, followed by the sunny timber of Elmyra's voice.

"Come on downstairs!" the woman called, and Aerith wondered, hope against hope, if the long-overdue reunion at the station had finally arrived.

Aerith noisily bounded down the steps, finding Elmyra at the bottom holding a large paper bag in either hand.

"Welcome home!" Aerith chirped.

"Thanks, baby."

"Welcome hooome!"

"I heard you the first time," Elmyra said with a laugh.

She set the paper bags onto the table, and Aerith peered inside to find them full of all sorts of unfamiliar fruits and vegetables.

"Got the urge to browse through the markets for the first time in ages," explained Elmyra. "Found some good deals on produce. How about you? What did you get up to?"

"I was thinking about Ronna," admitted Aerith. "What's she like?"

"Ronna's a good girl. I'm sure you'll have a chance to meet her soon."

Elmyra turned to the kitchen, placing vegetables on the shelves, while Aerith continued to ask questions about Ronna.

Aerith couldn't help but notice as the bounce faded from Elmyra's voice and the smile from her lips. Clay wasn't with her. He must've not shown up at the station after all.

When the doorbell interrupted the unhappy atmosphere, Aerith was relieved, and she suspected that Elmyra was too.

"That'll be Rodin," said Elmyra.

Rodin turned out to be a tall, skinny young man of about twenty, with big blue eyes and wavy blond hair.

"'Sup," he said as the door opened, followed by a casual nod to Elmyra.

The moment he stepped inside, his attention turned to Aerith.

"Hey, Ronna," he said. "Nice to meet ya. I'm Rodin."

Aerith was too stunned to react. He'd called her Ronna. Why?

Meanwhile, Rodin had opened the bag slung over his shoulder, producing a thin book that he held out to Aerith.

"Here. Butch wanted you to have this."

"Oh. Thank you," she replied hesitantly.

The cover of the book read *Let's Have Fun with Letters* in oversized type. Aerith's cheeks involuntarily puffed. The book covered the writing systems common in Midgar. She knew its contents well already because she'd been assigned the same primer for her lessons in the Shinra Building.

"Oh? Not your cup of tea?" Rodin scratched his head. "Sheesh. Well, don't tell Butch. He picked it out himself, and he's a lot more sensitive than you'd think."

"I appreciate the present," Aerith fibbed. "I just don't like studying."

"Ahh . . . Well, that makes two of us. I'm pretty good at reading, but ask me to write something, and . . ." Rodin exhaled loudly. "Especially if it's a big word, you know? I dunno why we can't just spell everything more simple."

"Rodin," cut in Elmyra, "could we please not put ideas in the child's head?"

She looked at Aerith and continued. "All right, um . . . Ronna. How about you go upstairs and study? The grown-ups have to talk business now."

Aerith did her very best to give a bright reply, then fled to the safety of the second floor. Having everyone call her Ronna made her feel terribly ill at ease.

Rodin did not seem to stay long. When he was gone, Elmyra came upstairs, apologizing for coming home so late, leaving them no time to discuss Aerith's name before Rodin's arrival.

Elmyra sighed. "Well, how do you feel about Ronna? Has it grown on you?"

"It's a pretty name," replied Aerith.

"Shall we stick with that, then?"

"Yeah."

Aerith paused for a moment, feeling the gentle rocking of the ferry as it made its way across the open sea.

When she spoke again, she said, "I take after both of my moms, I guess. How Elmyra and I settled on the name Ronna so easily, that's one way we're alike. I mean, there are more names out there than any of us could even begin to imagine, and who's to say one's better than any other?

"So I figured, let's just go with it. Things'll work out. Elmyra showed me how to be like that."

Tifa laughed. "But you're Aerith now, right? I take it the new name ended up causing some problems?"

"You have *no* idea . . . Believe it or not, my life has been at least as bumpy as yours."

Aerith sighed, and Tifa patted her reassuringly on the shoulder.

It was the day after her name had been decided. She woke up as Ronna, and in the morning they met with Marvin, and in the evening it was Roger, and the next day it was Bauman and then Louis.

Every one of Gabriel's number three men brought some kind of gift or treat for "Ronna." The made-up story spread like wildfire throughout the family business, and overnight she was a person of note: Ronna, a cousin's daughter now in the care of Elmyra Gainsborough, who was running things on behalf of Clay, who in turn stood in for Gabriel until the succession was formally resolved.

Soon, Aerith's little second-story bedroom had transformed from the drab monochrome of its former elderly occupant to a whimsical hodgepodge of primary colors, overflowing with children's toys and books.

Aerith was especially fond of the animal-and-plant trivia card sets gifted by Bauman. She'd secured Elmyra's permission to tack them to the walls, and she'd sit for hours gazing at the many mysterious, wonderful shapes that the planet's life took.

That wasn't to say she was less enamored with the dolls, trinkets, and other gifts; the whole experience of getting presents was new and exciting and made her heart dance with joy.

In any case, between the twice-daily meetings—once in the morning and once in the evening, the guest almost invariably one of the family business's number three men—Elmyra continued to spend the afternoons away from home. Aerith assumed she was visiting the station as always, but Rodin confided that as of late, she'd been seen walking about the slums, asking after anyone who might resemble her husband. In desperation, it seemed she'd begun entertaining the idea that Clay had in fact returned to Midgar, but that he was wandering the sector, unable to come home for some reason.

"That was the night," Aerith said.

Tifa nodded quietly at her side.

"It was dark, and I was already in bed. My mom had just come to visit—Ifalna, I mean. She looked upset but didn't say anything. She only stared in the direction of the hallway. So I got up, opened the door, and saw that the lights were on downstairs. When I climbed down, I found Mom—Elmyra—washing dishes at the sink. She was really going at it. Just scrubbing away, like she was irritated or anxious and trying to forget.

"The air in the front room was thick with the stink of dirt and weeds. And then I seemed to hear . . . Well, it was like a voice. And I could see a trooper at the door."

Young Aerith's first thought was that the trooper had been sent by Shinra to take her back. She cried out for help, but Elmyra kept washing like she hadn't heard.

The trooper looked toward Aerith. He pulled off his helmet, revealing a face she'd until then only known from photographs.

"Clay . . . ?" she ventured.

His hair was caked with mud. In fact, his whole upper body was streaked with dirt and dust, as if he really *had* been wandering the slums for days.

She tried speaking to him again. "Welcome home, Clay."

But Clay's eyes seemed to see right through her. He glanced about the room, as if unsure where to go next or what to do. Elmyra continued to wash dishes at the sink, oblivious, which was perhaps the most disconcerting part of all.

It's your husband! Aerith wanted to shout. *Your beloved Clay!*

"Mom!" was the word she finally managed to get out, but again, Elmyra failed to respond.

"Clay!" Aerith tried again, and the man squeezed his eyes shut, then brought them open wide, as if he couldn't believe what he was seeing and expected it to vanish at any moment. He repeated the motion: eyes shut, then eyes open. He did it again, and again, and again. What was he seeing? What were his eyes telling him? Finally, Clay lifted the back of one hand to rub at his brow. He sighed deeply and crouched down in place.

Aerith wanted to go to him, but her own legs wouldn't budge.

"Clay!" she shouted again.

Still nothing. Clay's knees hit the floor, and then he was lowering himself down on his side, heavy against the wood, as if all the strength had bled from his body. His lips moved, and despite the distance, Aerith thought she heard a faint whisper. She focused as hard as she could, desperate to catch the words.

Elmyra . . . I'm sorry . . .

"Clay! No!" Aerith screamed, and, turning to Elmyra, "Mom! Over here! Can't you hear him?!"

That was when Aerith's own eyes flicked wide open. She lay in her bed, yet she knew what she'd seen was not a dream. Clay had perished, and in his moment of death, he stood on that precipice where his soul joined the planet, and was given the chance to glimpse the one place in the world he wished to be most. Though Elmyra had failed to see Clay, he had undoubtedly seen her.

Aerith slipped out of bed—for real this time—and descended the stairs. Elmyra stood at the kitchen sink, scrubbing hard with her sponge. This time, no unsettling stink of grass flooded the room.

"Mommy . . . ?"

She hesitated, unsure how to deliver the news.

"Mommy, don't be sad."

Elmyra turned from the sink, her expression a mix of concern and confusion.

"What's wrong?"

"A man you really, really love just died. His heart came a long way to say goodbye. But he couldn't stay 'cause he had to return to the planet."

At first, Elmyra didn't say anything. She only stared.

"Clay? You're telling me Clay is *dead*?"

"Yeah, but you don't have to worry. He was able to rejoin the planet safely. At least, I'm pretty sure he did."

"Aerith, go back to bed."

Aerith immediately sensed the anger that had crept into Elmyra's voice. Her heart constricted.

"But, Mommy—"

"Last warning. Drop the games and get back in bed."

"He returned to the planet! He'll be connected with you always. So there's no reason to—"

Elmyra lunged forward, grabbed Aerith under one arm, and proceeded to storm up the staircase. When they reached the bedroom, she dropped Aerith unceremoniously onto the covers, stormed back out without a word, and slammed the door behind her.

The woman's anger lingered in the room, palpable. Aerith threw the duvet over her head and sobbed. But she wasn't crying because she'd made Elmyra angry; she was thinking of all the days her mom had waited faithfully at the station. In the end, she'd never had her chance to see Clay one last time.

Aerith wasn't sure how much time passed when she again felt Ifalna's presence at her side. It was strong and warm; she didn't need to lift the covers to know her mother was there.

"Mommy . . ." she whimpered.

When Aerith did decide to poke her head out, Ifalna was smiling gently. But there was something different about her this time. Aerith realized she could see through her figure, all the way to the far side of the room. It struck her as curious at first, until the horrible understanding crept in. She'd noticed the same thing happening to Clay when his knees hit the floor. As the time the planet allowed him came to an end, he'd begun to fade from view.

Now the same thing was happening to Ifalna.

"Mommy!" Aerith cried.

She scrambled upright, but already her mother's features were striped with the dark beams and whitewashed paneling of the wall. Ifalna's lips moved as if to speak but generated no sound. Aerith thrust a hand out, only for her fingers to pass through empty air and upset her balance, sending her tumbling from bed. Wincing from the pain, Aerith pulled herself back up, yelling for her mother. Ifalna was all but gone, lips still moving, sound still absent.

Then she *was* gone, and Aerith was alone.

The following day was a quiet one. Aerith woke to find Elmyra away. A simple breakfast and message sat waiting on the table.

Out for the day, Elmyra had written. *Won't be back till evening. Not expecting any guests.*

Aerith ate in silence and returned to her room. She sat at her desk and pulled open its drawer, where lay the small pouch left to her by Ifalna. She shook free the white materia inside, grasping it in her palm, feeling it ease her troubled heart as it always did. That, at least, had not changed.

Come evening, Aerith heard the faint sound of the latch in the entryway, followed by footsteps and the scraping of a kitchen chair across the floor. She gently opened her own door and crept down the stairs.

Elmyra was seated at the dining table in her usual spot facing the kitchen, yet her head was buried in her arms, and she was weeping softly.

The woman must have sensed Aerith on the stairs, for she lifted her face and turned, revealing puffy red eyes and tearstained cheeks.

"There was a letter," she said. "From Shinra . . . His helicopter, they say it crashed in a heavy forest. They say . . . They say they didn't find his body until it was too late. He wasn't anywhere near the crash site. He must've tried to walk out, but . . . Why? Where was he going? Why couldn't he have stayed where he was? Why did he always have to be so—"

A fresh string of sobs drowned her words.

Aerith carefully cleared her throat and ventured, "He really wanted to see you one last time. That's why he started walking. He was trying to get to you."

"And now you're gonna tell me he's returned to the planet. Please, Aerith . . . Enough. I can't listen to any more."

"But it's the tr—"

"Why would he go back to the planet?! *This* is his home! If he was going to return anywhere, he'd return *here*! And the reason he hasn't is because he's dead! You can tell all the pretty stories you like, but it doesn't change the fact that my husband is—"

Her words gave way to the wails of a young, helpless child. Aerith couldn't remember the last time she'd seen a grown-up cry. Maybe never. She felt as though a giant iron hand was squeezing the air from her chest.

"He *did*, though! He *did* go back to the planet!" she protested. "The planet connects us all, and that makes it okay, because it means we'll always be together!"

"Stop, Aerith. Just stop."

"But last night, my other mom faded away too, and . . . and . . . They have to have gone back to the planet! They just have to!"

After the moment had passed, Elmyra and Aerith clung to each other. For several days, they could manage little else. Still, the warmth of the mother and daughter's budding relationship was a salve that eased their loneliness.

When Butch got word of Clay's death, he was quick to realize Elmyra would need support. He stopped by to check in on the Gainsborough residence and arranged for other members of the family business to take turns doing the same. Elmyra had lost all drive to stay on top of meals and chores, so Rodin arranged to have money pooled for groceries, which the men brought by daily.

Meguro sent his condolences, unable to visit himself due to a flare-up of his own ongoing health issues. In his stead, he explained, he'd be sending Carlo to look after the household and all its needs.

The news piqued Aerith's curiosity, helping to distract from her sorrow. She recalled how heatedly Elmyra and Meguro had discussed the man and his aspirations.

When Carlo arrived, he was not at all what she expected. The young man was tall and wiry, with slicked-back hair and a restless manner. He always seemed to be fidgeting.

Given his reputation, she was frightened of him at first. But to Aerith, at least, he was exceptionally kind, and to her great surprise, he went about the chores with no trace of indignation. If anything, he seemed determined to help.

Though it was obvious Elmyra still didn't care for him, she tolerated his coming and going, ignoring him as best she could. To Aerith, it seemed to indicate just how deeply depressed the woman had become.

The new routine had persisted about a week, when one day, as Elmyra and Aerith each sat alone in their rooms, there came a great crash from the kitchen. They hurried to their doors, looked at each other, and rushed downstairs to see what had happened.

Porcelain fragments littered the floor of the kitchen, spilling out into the front room in a number too great to count. Amid the chaos stood Carlo, his head hung in shame.

"Were they expensive?" he asked.

"Honestly, I couldn't say. Gabriel gave them to us when Clay and I first moved in together."

"Damn. If they came from Gabriel, they sure as hell weren't cheap. Probably the best china money can buy . . . Aw, geez. I'm sorry, Elmyra. I really am. I got it in my head that the cabinets could use a good cleaning, and . . . I guess I just can't stand seein' things dusty."

Carlo stared up with obvious remorse. Elmyra's eyes continued to hold on the countless fragments scattered across the floor.

After an awkward moment, Carlo seemed to give up any hope of forgiveness. He stooped down, gingerly picking up the pieces one by one.

When Elmyra finally spoke, it was to say, "Carlo . . . go home."

"Please!" he begged. "Just gimme one more chance!"

"A few broken plates aren't the end of the world. What I *can't* stand is seeing you pick those pieces up with your bare hands. I'm not about to let you slice your fingers open. So get on home. I'll take care of the mess. And don't worry. I'll make sure Meguro hears how good you've been to me. 'Cause it's true. You've been a big help."

The color returned to Carlo's face so quickly, he almost seemed to glow.

Elmyra snorted. "And in the meantime, you should learn to

hide your feelings better. You won't get anywhere in this business if people can read you like an open book."

"Right."

Carlo slapped his cheeks and hardened his expression.

"Okay. I'll leave ya alone," he agreed. "But if you need anything, you call me, hear? And, uh . . . sorry about the other day. The thing with your eye."

"Don't know what you're talking about. I took a tumble and scraped myself up."

"No." Carlo shook his head firmly. "I shouldn'ta hit you. It wasn't right. Not to you or to Clay."

His voice had begun to tremble slightly, and Aerith had to do a double take. The man was crying!

"Clay was a good guy," continued Carlo. "Covered for me every time I screwed up. Set me straight. Put me on Gabriel's radar. I still can't believe that he's gone. . ."

"Get ahold of yourself," snapped Elmyra. And just then, as if the interaction with Carlo had flipped a switch in her mind, the despondent, mourning woman of the past few days was gone. Elmyra was back to her old, assertive self.

"Honestly, a grown man carrying on like that . . ." she groused. "It's embarrassing."

Carlo rubbed at his eyes with a forearm, grinned, and quipped, "Look who's talkin'."

He made for the door, still sniffling slightly as he waved a casual farewell.

When Carlo was gone, Elmyra turned in a slow circle, evaluating the state of the house.

"Pretty good work for a bunch of knuckleheads," she admitted. "But it's not quite up to my standards. I'm thinking we could do with a good spring cleaning. You feeling up to it, Aer—erm, I mean, *Ronna*?"

"Yeah!"

The world, and Aerith's mood, was suddenly feeling a whole lot brighter.

"She wasn't kidding about the cleaning," Aerith told Tifa with a giggle. "It was a full-on marathon. First we swept up all the broken china, and then we opened all the windows in the house to let in fresh air. Mom had a broom, and I had a feather duster, and we were whisking all the dust out of the house, along with all the tears we'd shed."

She flicked a hand back and forth, pretending to dust the surrounding crates of cargo.

"Mom loves to clean. She's got a whole collection of different brooms and mops. You'd probably burst out laughing if you saw it.

"She picked out one of those brooms and sawed off half its handle to make it just the right size for me. From that day on, that was *my* broom.

"The next day, we were armed with rags, wiping every window and wall and panel on the floor until the whole house shone. And *then* we moved on to redecorating! Elmyra said we could get new curtains for my room, and a bedcover too. It was the first shopping trip I'd ever been on in my life, and the first time Elmyra and I walked around the slums together. We were officially mother and daughter."

It was that very shopping trip that gave Aerith her first proper glimpse of the orphanage down the alley from home. The Sector 5 House, as it was called, turned out to be a lively place. Elmyra and Aerith were walking by when several children close to Aerith's age came running up the alley.

The moment they saw Aerith, they stopped dead in their tracks.

"You're Ronna!" one exclaimed.

At the declaration, the others began to chatter excitedly.

"No way. *That's* Ronna?"

"Is she an orphan?"

"She's adopted. Lives in her own house and everything. I wish *I* lived in a house."

"Hey, Ronna! Come live at the orphanage!"

"She's super cute."

"Why won't she say anything? Does she think she's too good for us?"

The rapid-fire comments and the children's unreserved nature had left Aerith too bewildered for words. She sought protection behind Elmyra's legs, peeking out as the children continued to shout.

Strangest of all was the way they addressed her as "Ronna" with such confidence. It felt as though she were being bombarded with the name, and she realized that she hadn't heard it for days now at home, ever since Carlo was sent away. The fact that she even had another name had begun to fade from her mind.

She was so disconcerted, she didn't notice when another child scurried up from the side to where Aerith cowered behind Elmyra. The little girl reached out to touch her braid, and Aerith yelped when the fingers brushed against her hair.

"Ayumu! Stop!" yelled one boy, clearly panicked. He seemed to be the oldest in the group. "You shouldn't tease Ronna! Don't you know what could happen? They'll come and get you!"

"I wasn't teasing her!" protested the young girl, who continued to pluck gently at Aerith's braid.

"She's telling the truth!" cried Aerith. "I was just . . . surprised. That's all. She didn't do anything wrong."

"Oh . . . Okay," said the older boy, though he still appeared uneasy.

"Hang on, Jean," Elmyra cut in. "I wanna hear more about this business of not teasing Ronna. Who exactly is going to come and get you?"

"It's what Carlo told us," the boy—Jean—whined back.

Elmyra knit her brows at that.

"Carlo told you about Ronna, did he?"

"He said if we ever make the girl living in the Gainsborough house cry, he'll find out and he'll make sure we cry twice as hard."

A long sigh escaped Elmyra's lips.

"Well, Ronna?" she said. "Don't just stand there. Where are your manners? The children living at the Sector 5 House are our neighbors."

Aerith gathered her courage and announced, "Nice to meet you. I'm Ronna. I hope we can be friends."

"Hi, Ronna!" exclaimed several of the children in unison.

And then they were all piling their own introductions on top of one another:

"I'm Sara!"

"My name's Zoey!"

"I'm Gerad."

Near the tail end of the clamor, a girl announced, "I'm Yoko!"

She pointed to the younger girl who had been so enamored with Aerith's hair. "And that's Ayumu. We're sisters."

The last to give his name was the older boy.

"The name's Jean," he said with the confident air and easy smile of a natural leader. "Anytime you wanna play, you're welcome to join us."

"Thank you," replied Aerith.

"Wanna come play right now?"

The invitation came from Ayumu. The little girl stared with such ardent expectation that Aerith began to blush. She'd never encountered so many kids her age all at once, or maybe ever in her entire life. They admittedly numbered only six, but in Aerith's mind, that seemed like an exceptionally large crowd. And they were *still* all staring at her!

Aerith was fumbling for how to respond, when Elmyra came to the rescue.

"Sorry, but we've got quite a bit of shopping planned today, and I really need Ronna with me to help pick everything out. But I'm sure she'd love to play with you next time. Sound good?"

Elmyra gently tugged on Aerith's hand, leading her away.

Aerith glanced back once. Sure enough, every pair of eyes was watching her go. The girl who'd introduced herself as Sara cautiously held a hand near her chest and gave a tiny wave. Aerith gave a shy wave back, and then all the children were waving, some with their arms outstretched and swinging from side to side. The sight filled her with joy, and she continued to glance back again and again, and to wave each time, until she could see the other children no more.

"Looks like you're off to a good start," chuckled Elmyra.

"Yeah!"

As they went about their day, Elmyra was careful to introduce

Aerith to everyone else they came across. They said hello to the proprietor of Elmyra's favorite café, and to the neighborhood doctor, and to numerous other acquaintances. Everyone welcomed Aerith with open arms and friendly smiles. And as they departed each encounter, Elmyra mentioned casually, as if it were no more than a passing afterthought, the news of Clay's death. Before the words of sympathy and regret could pour forth—before the shock could even fully register on the listener's face—Elmyra would add, "I'm heartbroken, but darling Ronna here is helping me keep my mind off our loss."

And with that, she'd bid farewell, quickly ushering Aerith out the door while the unresolved storm of empathy and panic still clouded the proprietor's eyes.

"Sorry, Aerith," Elmyra explained the first time. "I hope you don't mind me using you to cut these encounters short. I just can't bear the thought of reminiscing over Clay for hours on end. Someday it might do me good, but that day isn't today."

"Okay," Aerith had responded. "But don't forget. Right now I'm *Ronna*, not Aerith."

"Yes . . . Yes, of course. I suppose I should start calling you that all the time, so I don't slip up."

A week had passed since "Ronna's" official introduction to the neighborhood, and Aerith was at the Sector 5 House, enjoying the afternoon with the other children, when she spotted Meguro coming from the direction of the station.

He was hard not to notice: the man was clad in a crisp, immaculate white suit, quite at odds with the dull, grimy earth tones that dominated the undercity scenery.

The arrival of Meguro himself wasn't surprising; Elmyra had informed Aerith that he would be by, and Aerith had been given permission to stay outside playing at the House up until his visit.

But what did catch Aerith off guard was his entourage: at Meguro's heels, she spied a boy who must've been about ten. He was wearing loose-fitting trousers and a plain white shirt, along with an aloof, dismissive expression. Behind him was a young girl clad in a long, ankle-length skirt: a rather unusual choice in the slums, where low hems threatened to drag through the dirt. Consequently, the girl walked with each hand plucking the fabric at her thighs. It struck Aerith as an awfully cumbersome solution. Had the girl walked across the entire neighborhood holding her skirt every step of the way?

In any case, it was a very fine piece of clothing, as was the girl's blouse, which boasted intricate embroidery and elaborate lace frills at the collar and sleeves. She was even wearing a matching wide-brimmed hat. At a glance, it was obvious that Meguro and the two children were no strangers to luxury.

But why would Meguro bring along a couple of . . . ?

Realization struck, and Aerith (or rather, *Ronna*, as her play-mates had continued to chirp dozens of times over the course of the morning) let out a gasp.

The boy and girl had to be Meguro's children. And that meant the girl was . . . !

In a few minutes, she'd be standing face to face with the *real* Ronna!

Aerith hurriedly apologized to her playmates and shot off down the alley before Meguro could spot her, nearly stumbling over the wooden planks when she reached the garden.

"Mom!" she exclaimed as she burst into the house. "Meguro's on his way! And he's bringing his kids! The *real* Ronna!"

On hearing the news, Elmyra didn't look particularly perturbed.

"Hmph. Got the rugrats with him, does he? I suppose that makes sense. I wish he would've told me, though."

"What are we gonna do?!"

"What, you mean your name? Meguro's accommodating. He'll understand. In fact, he's probably already well aware that you're going by Ronna around town."

Aerith nodded, though she still felt terribly nervous.

When Meguro did arrive, he began by introducing his son, Marcellus. Meanwhile, Ronna stared at Aerith with open fascination.

Meguro continued with his daughter and then, when the in-troductions were out of the way, promptly snapped open the at-taché case carried at his side. From it, he produced three white roses. The first went to Marcellus and the second to the real

Ronna. The third he held in his hand as his eyes turned back to Elmyra.

"They're silk," he said, "though I'm very sorry to say it. Still, I felt it wouldn't be right to steal any of those precious real flowers out in the garden."

Elmyra nodded and pointed to a small frame set out in the center of the table. Inside was a photograph of Clay and Gabriel, the two so similar in appearance, it would have been easy to mistake them as brothers. Meguro and his children each took turns placing a rose at its base. That done, they stood abreast, clasping their hands before their chests and closing their eyes. Aerith watched with fascination, her mouth hanging slightly open. What in the world were the three doing?

At long last their eyes opened and fingers unknotted. Meguro turned, happening to catch Aerith's bewildered gaze. Aerith blushed and snapped her jaw shut.

"Not used to seeing people pray, I take it? My family's old-fashioned like that. Prayer is how we let the dead know we're thinking of them."

"Clay and Gabriel can hear what you're thinking?!"

At that, Marcellus snorted loudly. But Meguro shot him a stern look, and his gaze quickly dropped to his feet.

Aerith stole a quick glance at Ronna, and the girls' eyes met. It was clear that Ronna had also thought the comment quite amusing.

"It's my belief that they do," said Meguro. "Everything begins with belief. That's a truth that holds for all endeavors, and one which Gabriel was often known to aver."

Elmyra nodded wordlessly.

"Elmyra . . . My deepest apologies. I wanted to come right away, but my health hasn't been the best this past while."

"It's fine. I hear we've got you to thank for Carlo's help. He and the others took good care of us."

"He took his responsibilities seriously, I hope?"

"He's a harder worker than I would've guessed. Honestly, I was starting to wonder what got into him."

"I'm told that Carlo looked up to Clay like an older brother. Perhaps he decided he could pay his respects by doing what he could for the woman Clay loved. Come to think of it, that might be why he made your life so difficult in the first place. I'm sure he saw much less of Clay once you two were married. In his mind, it might have seemed like you were stealing his brother away."

"Hmph. It wouldn't surprise me none. I used to give Clay hell for staying out late, and nine times out of ten, it was Carlo with him at the bar. I guess in the end, I've been just as childish about this as he has."

Marcellus interrupted, tugging on Meguro's shirtsleeve with a pout, "Dad, I'm thirsty."

"And what do you propose we do about that?" his father replied gruffly.

The boy rolled his eyes, exasperated, but quickly regained his composure, politely asking their host for a drink.

"Sure thing," Elmyra responded, making for the kitchen. "My bad. I should've offered something as soon as you walked in. Go ahead and have a seat, and I'll get us all squared away."

As Elmyra pulled some glasses and a pitcher from the cupboard, Ronna hurried to Aerith's side.

"My birthday's in March," she said. "What month is yours, Aerith?"

"February" was Aerith's timid reply.

"Wow! So that makes you older. But only by one month."

"What're you calling her Aerith for?" butt in Marcellus. "You're supposed to call her Ronna, remember? She stole your name."

Ronna ignored him, smiling brighter than ever and reassuring, "I really don't mind that you took it."

The girl seemed sincere enough. But Aerith couldn't help but notice that she made no attempt to correct her brother's comment about stealing.

Aerith tried to smile back, but her throat felt tight, and her heart seemed to struggle with each beat.

Yet again, it was Elmyra who came to her rescue.

"I was going to wait until we got settled in, but since the topic's already up . . ."

She'd returned to the dining room table with a tray on which sat five glasses of lemonade. As she set a glass out for each person, she continued. "We'd decided to take your advice, Meguro. To pick out a new name for Aerith, that is. Unfortunately, before we'd had enough time to think it through, we found ourselves in a situation where a name was needed. 'Ronna' was the one that accidentally popped out."

"I've been curious about Ronna ever since you mentioned her," Aerith hurried to add, turning to look at Meguro. "I wondered what she was like, and I thought it would be really nice to meet her someday and maybe even become friends . . . Especially on that first day, it was all I could think about, so when I had to come up with a name, Ronna's just spilled out."

"It's my fault," said Elmyra. "I should've sat at her side to help pick something out. But now the whole neighborhood knows her as Ronna, and, well . . . Changing it would only draw more attention, so I think we ought to stick with it. That is, if you don't mind."

Meguro gave a magnanimous shake of the head. "Mind? Why would we mind? You've done nothing to cause offense."

"Actually, I'm flattered," announced Ronna with obvious delight. "The fact that Aerith picked my name must mean she likes it. It is a very lovely name, don't you think? My mother chose it for me."

"Too bad she *died* when you were born," Marcellus replied, bumping her shoulder with his.

All trace of emotion vanished from Ronna's face.

"Marcellus," their father broke in, his voice low and stern. "How many times do I have to tell you? I'll not have you blaming your sister. If you can't abide by that rule, you have no place in my household."

"Yes, sir."

Marcellus nodded sulkily. He restlessly fingered the straw in his glass of lemonade and began to use it to blow bubbles into the liquid, sending a spray of tiny drops careening over the rim and onto the surface of the table. The game seemed to amuse him, though Aerith watched half in horror, all but certain this was a child she could never get along with.

Still, he was Meguro's son, and Meguro was Elmyra's trusted friend. Aerith steeled herself, determined to accept Marcellus, crudeness and all.

"Well, if that's the case," announced Meguro, "I suppose we

should get used to Aerith's new name too. It's important to make these things a habit."

The real Ronna offered a bright smile and said, "Nice to meet you, Ronna."

"Nice to meet you too, Ronna," Aerith replied with a giggle. "And you, Marcellus."

The boy continued to blow into his straw.

Meguro cleared his throat. "And now, children, if you would excuse Elmyra and me, we have some business to discuss. Go ahead and play outside, but stick to the garden, please. I don't want you heading down the alley and away from the house."

"Yes, sir." Marcellus's reply was crisp.

He sucked up the remainder of his lemonade in one quick draw, and his sister hurried to do the same. When Aerith tried to follow suit, some of the lemonade went down the wrong way, and she began to cough, dirtying her own portion of the dining table with flecks of liquid.

Elmyra only laughed and urged them all outside.

When they stepped out into the garden, movement near the alley entrance caught Aerith's eye. Jean from the Sector 5 House was lingering there, curiously peering in at the yard and its home.

"Oh, look," sneered Marcellus. "The poor little orphan kids have come to play."

Jean, too far to catch the remark but aware he'd been noticed, waved his arms high above his head in greeting.

"Hey! Wanna join us?" he called.

"Ew!" yelped Ronna. "Hurry and make them go away, Marcellus. I don't want the creepy orphans next to me."

"They won't mess with us. Our dad's one of the most important people in the sector."

A sense of foreboding had begun to creep its way down Aerith's spine.

"C'mere! Come into the yard!" called Marcellus, his voice suddenly warm and friendly.

"Are you sure it's okay?" Jean asked uncertainly.

"Of course! C'mon! Let's play Tickle the Ogre."

"What's that?"

Jean stepped into the garden, signaling to several other kids waiting at his back. They quickly followed him in. All of them seemed to be from the House. Aerith recognized several from the times she'd been over to play, but there were at least two or three she didn't know.

"It's super popular in the Sector 4 Slums," explained Marcellus. "But I guess you wouldn't know it, living in the orphanage and all."

A shadow crossed Jean's expression, just for a moment. Meanwhile, the much younger Ayumu, oblivious to Marcellus's slight, exclaimed, "Sounds like fun! How do we play? Hey, what's your name?"

"Marcellus."

"And I'm Ronna," added his sister.

Aerith's tension escalated. She braced herself for the questions that were sure to come.

"Hey, that means . . . Whoa! There's *two* Ronnas!" Ayumu said, clearly mystified.

"It's just a coincidence. Nothing weird about it," announced Jean, as if he met dozens of girls named Ronna every day.

In a low, accusing voice, Marcellus declared, "Yeah. But this one's a *fake*."

He pointed at Aerith with a triumphant look and continued. "She stole my sister's name. Her *real* name is Aerith. Aerith the Name Thief. Isn't that right?"

Marcellus's expression had now twisted into a sickening grin. Aerith felt every pair of eyes trained upon her.

"I'm not a name thief!" she protested. "I didn't steal anything!"

"That's what they all say," Marcellus replied scornfully. All at once, Aerith knew she was seeing the boy for who he truly was.

"Stop it!" his sister cut in, but Marcellus pretended not to hear.

"I'm *not* a thief!" repeated Aerith.

They could say whatever else they wanted, but she refused to let them believe she'd stolen the name.

"Name thief," Marcellus continued to jeer.

"It's not true!"

Aerith's voice began to crack. She swore to herself she wouldn't cry, but the first few tears were already streaming down her cheeks.

"It's not true!" she repeated.

"Hey, aren't you an orphan too? That must be why you get along so well with these brats. Maybe you should've gone to live with them instead of worming your way into Clay's house. But I guess that's how it goes when you're a thief and an orphan. You'll take everything you can get."

Marcellus turned his nose up in an exaggerated show of disgust.

Someone, somewhere shouted, "Shut up!"

And then Marcellus was tumbling through one of the flower beds, along with someone else. It took Aerith a moment to register that it was Jean who had tackled the taller boy to the ground. They struggled for a moment until Jean managed to roll Marcellus on his back, and another boy rushed in to straddle Marcellus's stomach and pin his arms.

Aerith recognized the second orphan. Though small in frame, he was at least three or four years older than most of the others, and he went by the name of X—which Aerith had to admit struck her as a most peculiar name. Normally, X was quiet and reserved, frequently going out of his way to help the teachers at the House and consequently only free to join the other children's games on occasion.

Marcellus's snide remarks seemed to have ignited something in X. He stared down at the pinned boy with open fury.

"Quit it! Get off me!" yelled Marcellus.

"Not until you stop making fun of the House!" X roared back.

Marcellus's insults only grew fiercer. "It's a stupid, run-down orphanage! You're all poor, and you deserve to be made fun of!"

"Hit him!" cheered several of the orphan girls from the sidelines. "Punch him in the face!"

Aerith brought her hands to her eyes, terrified by the violence the other children were capable of.

Meanwhile, Ronna wailed, "Stop it! Please! Marcellus, tell them you're sorry!"

X had Marcellus's collar bunched in his fist, and he was shaking the other boy's head up and down as he continued to demand a retraction.

Marcellus would not relent.

"I'm not apologizing until Aerith does!" he snarled. "She's the one you should be mad at! She stole my sister's name!"

Meanwhile, Jean glanced nervously from the alleyway to the front door of the Gainsborough residence.

"I'm sorry!" cried Aerith. "I was wrong for using Ronna's name without asking!"

"You *stole* it! Say it! Admit that you're a thief!"

"I didn't steal anything!"

X lifted his free hand and slapped Marcellus across the cheek.

"Stop it!" screamed Aerith.

Her own cheeks stung, as if she were the one struck. She didn't like Marcellus. She didn't want to protect him. But the whole situation had gone much too far.

"X! Please!" she begged.

"I'll let him go just as soon as he apologizes. He can say whatever he wants about us, but I won't have him badmouthing the House."

With hand again raised, he repeated his demand.

"No!" growled Marcellus. "Not before the name thief!"

Aerith wanted it to be over. She'd have done nearly anything to put a stop to the awful, awful chaos. And so, between sniffles and panicked gulps of air, she blurted out, "I'm sorry. I stole Ronna's name. It was a mean thing to do to Ronna, and to you too."

Jean was the first to pull back, after which X scrambled to his feet. Marcellus, freed of his captors, swayed unsteadily as he pushed himself upright. His look of triumph, however, was plain.

"Hmph. So you finally admit it."

A thin trail of blood ran from the corner of his mouth to his chin. It seemed he'd bit his tongue in the fall. His entire body trembled, and it was clear he was doing everything he could to maintain an air of dignity.

"Now it's your turn," said Jean. "Take back what you said about our House."

Marcellus took a long, leisurely moment to sweep his eyes over Jean and the other children. The sickening grin returned, and he announced, "Stupid, run-down orphanage!"

First Jean and then X pounced, followed by other boys whose names Aerith didn't know. They were grabbing at Marcellus's clothes and taking swipes at his face. Ronna ran toward the Gainsborough home shrieking, and the solution finally clicked for Aerith too: they needed help from an adult. It was what they should have done at the first sign of trouble. She chased after, but just as Ronna set foot on the patio, the door swung open to reveal Meguro's great, looming frame.

In an instant he'd sized up the situation, and he bellowed out, voice like a geyser of steam exploding at the surface, "All of you, stop right this instant!"

It was such a departure from the Meguro she'd come to know, Aerith found herself cowering to the ground, body quaking uncontrollably. The sounds of the scuffle ceased, and Aerith knew without looking that every other child stood frozen in terror too.

Elmyra appeared at the door looking shocked, and Meguro stormed from the porch, past Ronna and Aerith, rapidly closing the distance to the other kids.

"Run!" cried a boy from the orphanage—Aerith wasn't sure if it was Jean or X.

She followed Meguro with her eyes, turning in time to see children scrambling, desperate to reach the safety of the alley and the House beyond. Only Marcellus remained still, proud and sullen. When Meguro reached him, he snatched his son's ear between thumb and forefinger and began to march the young boy back to Elmyra's doorstep. Marcellus winced every step of the way, awkwardly bent forward and loudly complaining about the pain.

"I have had it up to *here* with your behavior," Meguro growled.

"It wasn't my fault!" protested the boy. "The orphans barged their way into the yard! I was telling them to go home when they all attacked me!"

"Oh, yes," scoffed his father. "Our great and gallant savior. How very like you."

"Aerith's the one who started it!"

"I thought I made myself very clear. The name business is resolved. Ronna and I both gave our consent, and however you feel is beside the point. The matter does not concern you."

"But . . . !"

"I'll not say it again, Marcellus. You either shape up or ship out. Do you understand? Your behavior is an embarrassment to me and to the memory of your dear mother. I'll not have you drag our family name through the dirt. And the next time I hear someone attribute your behavior to the fact that you've grown up without a mother, so help me . . ."

They'd reached the doorstep, but Meguro still held the boy's ear tight as he delivered his scolding.

Elmyra placed a hand gently on Meguro's arm. "Surely that's enough."

"I suppose." Meguro released his grip on his son's ear and, turning to Aerith, said, "I'm very sorry about this. You'll have to excuse my son. I'd like to think he was being protective of his sister, as misguided as his actions were. Please allow Ronna and me to apologize on his behalf."

Marcellus's eyes bored into her. All Aerith could think about was how desperately she wanted to put the matter to rest.

"Thank you, but Marcellus is right," she said. "It was my fault. I'm really sorry about taking Ronna's name."

She looked at each of them in turn and apologized once more: first to Meguro, then to Marcellus, and finally to Ronna. Afterward, she glanced up at Elmyra, who frowned but nodded slightly.

"Well, then . . . Elmyra, we ought to wrap things up. Aerith and Ronna, why don't you two head inside? Marcellus, you stay right where you are and think about what you've done."

Once inside, Aerith peeked out the window at Marcellus. Crossing paths with the boy, she decided, must be very much like encountering a monster.

Meguro and Elmyra quickly brought their conversation to a close. When they'd finished, Meguro stepped inside the house, and she heard him saying, "I'll stop by the orphanage and lodge a complaint. The children won't be wandering near the Gainsborough home again. In fact, I'll make it clear that if any harm were to come to Aeri—erm, to *Ronna*, I'd see to it that their funding dries up overnight. That ought to drive the point home."

"No," replied Elmyra. "I should be the one who goes by to speak with them. I'm already quite friendly with the housemother, and I'd sooner not spoil things between us."

"Hm . . . Well. It's your choice and your home. But if at any time you wish to emphasize the point, all you need do is call."

All trace of the kind, gracious gentleman Aerith had come to know was gone. It occurred to her that Meguro's politeness was only a mask worn to distract from the ruthless underworld boss that lurked inside.

The implication was still dimly swirling through her mind when Ronna hurried to her side.

"It's no big deal," the girl whispered. "Think of it as me lending you my name. I'm doing it special, just for you. You can pay me back some other time."

Aerith was coming to understand something about Ronna too. Behind the girl's quite genuine kindness was an innate cruelty much like her father's.

Sensing a lull in Aerith's story, Tifa gently broke in. "Can I ask something? The Sector 5 House . . . Is that the same thing as the Leaf House?"

"That's the one. Actually, at the time, its official name was the Sector 5 Undercity Juvenile Care Facility, but everybody just called it the Sector 5 House. It didn't become the Leaf House until I was much older.

"Actually, the Sector 5 House had kind of a shady reputation. I had no idea at the time, but the owner used to cut deals with businesses in the slums. When the kids were old enough to move out, a lot of them were sold into lives of hard labor."

Tifa responded with a horrified gasp.

"Come to think of it, I guess that makes him a trafficker—just the kind of thing you used to worry about. The children didn't know anything, of course. And neither did the teachers or staff who actually spent time with the kids. When the orphanage finally changed hands, it was X who took over—the boy who beat up Marcellus. I heard he saved every gil he ever made and bought the place out once he was all grown up."

"Huh . . ." Tifa said, though clearly a bit disappointed. "I was just thinking about one of our Avalanche operatives. There was a rumor he donated a lot of time and money to the Leaf House, since that's where he grew up. I wondered if you might've known him back then, but it sounds like maybe not."

"You mean Biggs?"

"Huh?! So you *do* know him?!"

"Well, I never met him in person. But in my last few years in the slums, I heard the teachers and other kids talk about him a lot. They really looked up to—"

Aerith's voice shot up in volume as she cut herself off. "Wait a second! I can't believe I never put it together! X must be Biggs!"

"What? But—"

"X told me he was brought to the orphanage as a baby. Nobody knew his real name, so the staff members decided to call him X until they settled on something else. The name caught on with the other children, and by the time X was old enough to understand, he'd decided he liked it. But he told everyone that by the time he moved out, he was going to come up with the greatest name ever, and that's what the whole world would come to know him by. And the name he must've chosen was . . ."

Both Tifa and Aerith chanted in unison, "Biggs!"

In the wake of the scuffle at Elmyra's house, after Aerith's new friends from the orphanage learned that she was using a pseudonym, the children's reactions had run the gamut: some were ambivalent, others confused, and still others upset. But X's reaction was different. He took Aerith aside and shared the story of his own name, seeming to hope it might put her guilt to rest. We've all got a right to choose the name we want to go by, he'd said.

As Aerith recounted the interaction, she saw tears welling once more in Tifa's eyes.

"He always knew the right thing to say," Tifa murmured. She cleared her throat and asked, "Would you mind if I told Barret later? He'd be happy knowing the full extent of what Biggs did for you and the rest of those kids."

After Meguro and his children had left, Elmyra said she had some things to take care of and headed out alone. She returned about an hour later and gave Aerith a full report of what she'd accomplished.

First, she explained, she'd gone by the Sector 5 House to apologize for Marcellus's outburst and to inform them of Aerith's real name. She explained to the children that Aerith had her reasons for concealing her true name, but that she still hoped to be friends with them. Elmyra also expressed her hope that those in the orphanage's care could be instructed not to discuss Aerith with people outside the House.

"I'd made up my mind to be as truthful with them as I could, but the housemother was understanding enough not to ask why exactly you needed to go by another name. She also assured me that Jean has a good head on his shoulders. He'll know how to get the other children on board with keeping your secret. And after that, I went ahead and told a few of my acquaintances living just beyond the alley."

"Okay."

"I think we can trust everyone to stay quiet, but to be on the safe side, I made one more stop to speak with Butch. He and the other number threes will take turns stationing men at our home, in case Shinra or some other interested party shows up. I think that ought to have us sleeping soundly enough, don't you?"

Elmyra's plan seemed to be working out. For a brief time, the two spent their days in peace. Aerith got used to going by her real name at home and by Ronna whenever she was out, and she was slowly getting the hang of life in the slums too. Having a visitor in the house all the time wasn't so bad either, and she got to know each of the number threes quite well, along with some of the men they trusted most. Meguro continued to visit a few times per month, though he never again brought his children with him.

Somewhere along the way, Butch announced his intent to retire, and Carlo's name came up as a potential replacement.

And then in February, Carlo took it upon himself to plan Aerith's eighth birthday party. It was going to be a huge event. He'd promised that everyone of note in the family business would be there to join in the celebration, and Aerith had been so overjoyed to hear it, she ran right over to give Carlo a great big hug. She even had permission to invite her friends from the Sector 5 House. (Carlo insisted, however, that Marcellus and Ronna be there too, no matter how much Aerith pleaded otherwise.)

But for all the planning, the birthday party never came to fruition.

The evening before the party was to take place, Carlo and several of his men had arrived to begin decorating Elmyra's front room, only for Rodin to burst in with awful news.

Meguro had suffered a heart attack.

They'd found him collapsed at home, and though he was still clinging to life, recovery was uncertain.

In an instant, everyone had a new priority: since Meguro was the acting head of the family business, he managed numerous crucial responsibilities that now needed to be delegated out. Business had to go on, and the family needed to appear strong. A young girl's birthday party was the least of anyone's concerns.

To Aerith's horror, Carlo immediately announced that the party would have to be postponed—though at the time, she found some small solace in the fact that he hadn't canceled it altogether.

Still, it was hard to get excited about a party held on some other, ordinary day of the year, while her own special day would pass by unobserved. Aerith's enthusiasm about turning eight years old withered away, and as the adults rushed to and fro sorting out their grown-up concerns, she took to closing herself up in her room for long stretches of time, much of which was spent in tears. One moment, she'd find herself overcome with anger at Meguro and his stupid heart attack, and the next, she'd be paralyzed with guilt.

When the morning of her birthday did arrive, she went downstairs to find that Elmyra wasn't even at home. There was only a very plain breakfast on the table, along with a note explaining that her mother had left early to speak with Meguro.

Aerith retreated upstairs without eating. A while later, she heard children from the Sector 5 House at the door, asking her to come out and play. She ignored them.

Finally, around evening, Elmyra returned.

"Meguro's going to pull through," she said. "He's past the worst of it."

"Oh. That's good."

"But get this. He was still going on about how he wanted me to promise to take care of his children if anything happens to him."

"He said *what*?!"

"Marcellus and Ronna and you all under one roof. Can you even imagine? I guess you and I had better pray with all our hearts that Meguro gets better."

Elmyra chuckled warmly, and Aerith couldn't help but join in.

"That's the first time I've heard you laugh since this whole ordeal began," remarked Elmyra. "How about you and I head out to town this evening? We'll find someplace with a little more cheer and some good food to boot."

"Yeah."

"That's the spirit. Actually, I've already arranged a bodyguard for our little outing. He should be here any moment."

"Who is it?" asked Aerith.

The words had hardly left her mouth, when the doorbell rang.

"Coming!" she yelled as she rushed to the door.

In the fading daylight, the man on the other side of the glass was little more than a silhouette. Aerith threw the doors open, excited to find out which of the family's men would be accompanying them, only to meet with a stranger.

Or rather, the man himself was a stranger, but his jet-black suit was all too familiar.

Aerith's mind flashed back to the Shinra Building. The few times she'd been brought before Professor Hojo, there had always been a man standing just off to the side, wearing a suit and tie of just that type. And the one and only time Aerith had been taken in to see President Shinra, another man in a black suit had stood at the president's right hand.

Shinra had finally come for her.

On finding Aerith the one to open the door, the man was momentarily startled. He then smiled ever so slightly.

"So this is where you've been," he said, his tone gentle.

Aerith retreated a few steps and shouted, "No . . . Go away!"

She hurried behind Elmyra's legs, clinging to them for safety. Meanwhile, the man confidently strode into the house, hardly acknowledging Elmyra at all. When Elmyra shifted to keep herself between Aerith and the stranger, he simply leaned to one side, stooping low to address the girl at eye level.

"Aerith," he said. "You know you're not just any little girl. You're a descendent of the Ancients."

Elmyra cut him off. "Excuse me, but you can't just barge in here. This is *my* home. Who are you, anyway?"

"My apologies. I'm here on behalf of the company. That is to say, the Shinra Electric Power Company."

"Pretty young to be representing Shinra, aren't you? Have they started sending interns to take care of business in the slums? And I'm still waiting to hear who *you* are. Don't tell me you believed your little corporate name drop would leave me too shaken for words."

One corner of the stranger's mouth twitched, and the calm vanished from his eyes.

"Tseng," he replied brusquely. "Of the General Affairs Division."

"And you're here because . . . ?"

"At present, I'm only hoping to have a short chat with Aerith."

"I'm not gonna talk to you!" shouted Aerith. "I don't want to!"

Elmyra took a step toward the man and said, "I think there's been some kind of mistake. What was it you called her just now? An 'Ancient'? Who are the Ancients?"

Tseng straightened and looked Elmyra in the eyes.

"They were the original stewards of the planet whose boundless knowledge and wisdom shall guide us to the promised land."

He turned, gesturing thoughtfully as he continued. "Some believe the promised land to be a myth. Others, an allegory of sorts. But we take the words of the scriptures at face value and believe it to be quite real. Which is why Shinra would like very much for Aerith to help us—"

Aerith had been listening in horror. She knew what he was really after: he meant to drag her away from her new home. She wouldn't let it happen, though. There was no way this man or anyone else was taking her back to the Shinra Building.

"You're wrong!" she yelled. "I'm not an Ancient!"

"But, Aerith . . . even when you're all alone, don't you hear voices whispering secrets?"

"No, never!"

Aerith turned and bolted for the staircase, taking the steps two at a time until she reached the landing and the safety of her room. She slammed the door behind her and dove under the covers of her bed.

It wasn't cold, yet she found herself shivering uncontrollably. Her new home, her new friends, her new mother . . . Everything she'd managed to secure this past year threatened to vanish in an instant, like nothing more than a cruel, fleeting taste of what could have been. She squeezed her eyes shut, trying to drive off the debilitating sense of fear or at least keep it at bay. But the awful possibilities simply played out on the backs of her eyelids instead. She saw herself being dragged to her old room in Shinra HQ and confined there. She saw Elmyra being interrogated and tortured for keeping her hidden.

What could she do? How could she stop it? She wanted to know what else the man and Elmyra were saying, but the thought of heading back out to the landing to peek downstairs was far too terrifying. He might spot her and try to come upstairs. He might *already* be climbing the stairs, about to barge in at any moment. What if—

The door creaked open.

Aerith hugged the blankets tighter yet.

But when the words came, it was Elmyra's gentle voice she heard.

"We reached an agreement."

Aerith cautiously poked her head from the covers. Elmyra had entered alone; the man was nowhere to be seen. Her mother's eyes were wet with compassion.

"Oh, you poor thing. This must have been so frightening for you. Everything's okay now. He's gone, and he won't be bothering us anymore."

Elmyra lowered herself onto the edge of the bed, leaning close to cradle Aerith in her arms.

"Is it true what he said? Are you really an Ancient?"

In typical fashion, Elmyra didn't waste any time getting to the heart of the matter.

"We're actually called the Cetra," Aerith replied. "Well, I mean . . . Mommy was a Cetra. I'm only half."

Elmyra nodded thoughtfully. "That man Tseng seemed to suggest that Shinra regrets its terrible treatment of Ifal—of your *mother*. At least, they recognize it's their own fault she chose not to share the one piece of information they wanted most. So the company has decided to ask you for one thing, and one thing only. All they want is to know the location of the promised land. Once they have that, they'll leave you alone forever."

The promised land. Aerith had heard of it, of course. Ifalna had mentioned the name in passing a few times. But Aerith had no idea what it was or where it might be found. She couldn't give Shinra an answer, even if she'd wanted to. And that apparently meant they'd never leave her alone.

"I don't know," she sobbed. "I don't know anything about the promised land."

"Tseng assumed as much. But he seems to believe that even if you don't know now, there might come a day when you do."

"I don't want to leave. I like it here. I like being with you!"

"I feel the same way. That's why I made my proposal. I told him that, seeing as you and I are together every day, it'd be very easy for me to keep an eye out for any sign of change. If it seemed to me some new knowledge had awakened inside you, I promised Shinra would be the first to know. But in exchange, they had to promise not to come near you until that day arrived. Tseng contacted his superior and got a formal agreement then and there. So I'll give him one thing; he knows how to get things done."

"So I can stay?"

Elmyra smiled. "That's right. And what Tseng never has to know is that while I will be keeping an eye on you, it'll only be to watch you grow up as an ordinary, happy little girl."

The long, deep blare of a foghorn sounded through the cargo hold. Aerith glanced up at Tifa, who continued to listen intently as ever.

"Once Shinra knew where I was, there wasn't much point in hiding my name. So I started going by Aerith again. Not just at home, but outside too. And for a while, my life was again peaceful. The Turks kept their promise, steering clear of the house, and the Gainsborough family business was running smoothly again."

With a slight smile, she added, "That's not to say everything was easy. Mom and I had our little arguments. Things didn't always go as expected, and occasionally I just wanted to run to my room and cry. But that's all part of an ordinary life, right? And in a way, that's what I'd always wanted."

"Ordinary is good," Tifa observed, her voice heavy with emotion.

"But ordinary never seems to last, does it? Eventually, my whole world was thrown into chaos again, and wouldn't you know it, I had Marcellus to thank."

"Oh no . . ."

Elmyra and Aerith were at home, and Carlo had just come by to visit.

"Aerith," the man exclaimed with a smile as he walked in. "How's it goin'? I brought ya somethin'."

From his briefcase, he produced a small packet of candies. To Aerith, it seemed a slightly childish gift for a girl of the very grown-up age of ten. Elmyra seemed to disapprove as well—though her concern undoubtedly had more to do with nutrition. For the past several weeks, she'd been emphasizing again and again how sweets were enemy number one to healthy teeth.

At any rate, once the gift was in Aerith's hands, Carlo straightened and said, "All right. Now your mom and I have got some pain-in-the-ass grown-up stuff to discuss. How 'bout you take those upstairs and enjoy?"

"All right."

It was the usual flow of events whenever anyone of note in the family hierarchy stopped by. Aerith was rarely informed about what was going on anymore, and she'd noticed that Elmyra had become a little less open and a little more motherly, particularly when it came to matters deemed too serious for her precious daughter's ears.

Aerith made an elaborate show of heading upstairs, certain to close the door to her room with a very audible thud. Then, without missing a beat, she opened the door once more, this time quietly and just enough to slip back out into the hallway. She crept to the landing, judging each footstep carefully to avoid the old wooden boards that liked to creak.

". . . real problem," she heard Carlo say. "I mean, we're talking a major issue here."

His voice was anything but hushed.

"How closely have you been following Meguro's condition?" he asked Elmyra.

"I'd understood his heart's doing pretty well."

"Unfortunately, that's pretty much the *only* part of him that's on the mend. The guy's got three other chronic conditions I can hardly even pronounce, and hell, you've seen his weight. He started packin' it on after Ronna was born and ain't never stopped. Since his wife died, he doesn't sleep, and the only food he'll touch is either sticky sweet or deep-fried in oil."

"Believe me, I know. I tried to get after him about it. Now I'm wondering if maybe I should've tried harder."

"Yeah, well, you and the rest of the sector. If ya bring it up, he either shrugs it off or goes ballistic. Anyway, now he's talkin' about movin' somewhere he can get better treatment. Like, up-on-the-plate better. Seems to think he can manage the business just as well from a cushy mansion in the sky. Worse yet, he plans to drag one of the number threes along with him too. One of us poor saps is gonna have to commute up and down, relayin' his orders. You seein' the problem yet?"

"I know Meguro's more or less runnin' things these days, but as far as the rest of us are concerned, he's on the same level as you. Makin' plans to move topside, without even givin' you a heads-up? It ain't right. It's a fuckin' insult, is what it is."

"Pain-in-the-ass grown-up stuff. I couldn't have put it better myself."

Elmyra paused before continuing. "Look, I was only ever a part of this because someone had to stand in for Clay. I've been hands off for years now, letting Meguro run the show. The last thing I want is to get wrapped up in a power struggle. Fight among yourselves if you like, but leave me out of it."

"This business is how you put food on the table. Doesn't matter if you pretend otherwise. At the end of the day, you're a part of this."

Elmyra muttered a response that Aerith couldn't make it out. Even so, she could envision the deep sigh that would've accompanied it.

"And anyway, that's not the worst of it," said Carlo. "The real pain in the ass is Marcellus. Snot-nosed little punk ran away from home. *That's* why I'm here. Normally, I wouldn't give a damn, but Meguro's ordered the whole family to organize a search for the kid, including you. So there you go. That's what he sent me here to say, and now I've said it."

"Goodness . . . I haven't seen Marcellus for at least a couple years. He's gotta be, what, thirteen? Fourteen?"

"Somethin' like that. Old enough to take care of himself, that's for sure. Hell, I ran away when I was twelve. So I dunno why Meguro has to make such a damn fuss about this."

"There's more you're not telling me."

Carlo snorted. "Yeah, well, the whole sector knows Meguro's on his way out. Sorry to be blunt, but it's a matter of when, not if. There are plenty of interested parties who'd like a piece of Sector 5, and they sure as hell ain't sittin' on their asses. Word is Corneo's lookin' to expand his empire, and then you've got the Manson brothers way on the other side of the city, gunnin' for new turf. Meguro's heard the talk, and now he's got this idea in his head that Marcellus must've been kidnapped. Honestly, I think he's overreactin', but . . . I dunno. What's your take on all this?"

"If it was a kidnapping, there'd be a message. A list of demands."

"Haven't seen nothin' like that. Not yet, anyway. And the kid's been gone goin' on three days. Now, you ask me, nine-to-one odds he just ran away. But I guess we still gotta prepare for the worst-case scenario."

"Hmph . . . All right. I'll keep my eyes open too, for what good it'll do us. I live in the nicer part of the slums, in case you hadn't noticed. Not a lot of likely haunts for kidnappers around here."

"I know. We'll spearhead the search. You've got Aerith to look after, so all I'm askin' is for you to be aware. And if the kid *was* abducted . . . Hands off or not, to anyone lookin' in from the outside, you're as prominent as Meguro. And Aerith's your daughter. If I were a slimeball lookin' for a bargaining chip, I know who I'd try to kidnap. And I'm willing to bet you'd give the business up in a second if it meant keeping Aerith safe."

Carlo's final few comments sent Aerith scrambling backward, breath caught in her throat. No longer paying attention to her footfalls, she managed to get several loud creaks out of the floor in the process.

Elmyra called sharply from downstairs, "Aerith?"

When Aerith didn't respond, the woman sighed and said, "I know you're there, so you might as well come down."

Her cover was blown. She had no choice but to comply.

When she appeared on the staircase, Carlo asked how much of the conversation she'd heard.

"Nearly everything," she admitted sheepishly.

"It's all right. Nothing's going to happen to you," reassured Elmyra, though her voice seemed strained. "Doesn't hurt to be careful, though," the woman continued. "Maybe we ought to get out of the city for a while. The nurse that used to look after Gabriel lives in Kalm now. I'm sure we could arrange to stay with her until it's safe again."

"Yeah. That might be a good idea," put in Carlo.

Aerith's spirits fell. Over the past few years, she'd grown terribly self-conscious of the burden she represented. In agreeing to take care of her, Elmyra had made one sacrifice after another. Now Elmyra was going to have to leave her own home too.

"I'll arrange a car and a driver to get you to Kalm," said Carlo. "No, scratch that. *I'll* drive. It's been longer'n I can remember since I've been behind the wheel, but I'd rather see you there with my own two eyes. So get a bag packed tonight. I'll be here at dawn. Put on some good shoes and clothes fit for lots of walkin'. We'll have to hoof it from here to the gate."

Everything was moving much too fast. Aerith desperately wanted to slam on the brakes.

Carlo seemed to sense her distress and said, "It won't be forever. Once things blow over, I'll zip right over to Kalm to bring you two back."

He smiled and puffed out his chest. Elmyra put an arm around Aerith's shoulders and squeezed tight.

It was dark, and Aerith and Elmyra had both gone to bed, trying to catch at least a few hours' rest before their departure. They'd spent the evening packing their essentials in the small suitcase that Elmyra and Clay had used for their picnics.

However, Aerith was too wound up to sleep. Her mind flitted from topic to topic, and at some point, she found herself wondering where Marcellus was at that moment. Could he really have been kidnapped? Or had he just run away? It was the first time she'd thought about the boy in years, yet the sound of his voice and the things he'd said that day in the garden were as fresh in her mind as ever. She recalled the drops of lemonade spattered across the dining table and the dirt stains left on his fancy white shirt after he'd been tackled.

It was hard for her to picture his face, though. What exactly had Marcellus looked like? After the fight, there'd been the thin trail of blood down his chin, and she had a vague recollection of his round, pudgy nose and narrowed, mocking eyes . . .

When Marcellus's features finally did emerge from memory, a shiver passed through her from head to toe, and Aerith muttered to herself, "Right . . . how could I forget?"

Sudden light flickered at the edges of her drawn curtains. Aerith sat up in bed, curious as to its source. When the light flickered again, she slid from the covers and padded across the room. Pushing one curtain aside—ever so slightly, so as not to draw attention—she peered down at the garden.

There, right in the spot where Jean had pushed him to the ground years ago, stood Marcellus.

Aerith gasped. Then, in the next moment, she too was in the garden.

At her feet lay Marcellus, faceup and covered in blood.

"No!" she screamed.

Marcellus's eyelids lifted slowly, ponderously. He groaned with pain and reached one hand toward Aerith's bare feet, grasping tight when he found her toes.

Another shiver ran down Aerith's spine, and the scenery melted and shifted once more.

Now she stood suspended above a place she did not recognize. She saw a long wall that seemed to curve away forever to both sides. Tattered stretches of chain-link fencing stood here and there.

When Aerith glanced over her shoulder, she saw the city looming large and yet somehow distant. Beyond the wall lay an endless
expanse of cracked, dry earth, and she recalled a story her mother
had once shared about the badlands that surrounded the city.

"Help . . . me . . ." groaned a voice, and Aerith realized she'd
drifted down to the ground, where Marcellus once more lay at her
feet. This time she could see faint, shimmering currents of light
pouring out of his chest, and she knew at once that the radiant
flow was life. Somehow, she'd always known. Marcellus's life was
slowly slipping free, and it would not be long until he'd lost it all.

"Where are we?" she whimpered.

"Sector 6 . . ." he moaned. "Near . . . Near the gate . . ."

"What gate?" she cried. "I don't know this place. I've never been
to Sector 6!"

But she stopped herself, took a deep breath, and told him,
"Hang on. I'll find help."

Aerith turned and ran in the direction opposite the wall,
hoping it would lead her to the slums and a familiar landmark.
Something. Anything. Or if not that, then at least some*one*. She
could beg for help or maybe invoke the Gainsborough name if
nobody paid her any mind.

But no matter how hard she ran, the distant piles of scrap and
the undercity's ramshackle skyline weren't growing any nearer.
Before she knew it, her surroundings were shifting again, and
Marcellus was no longer behind her. Everything was gone, melted
away and replaced with an all-encompassing white haze that enveloped and blinded her. An awful crawling sensation spread across
Aerith's skin, and she could feel her own blood steadily coursing
through her body with each sickening heartbeat.

"Make it stop!" she cried. "Help! Mommy!"

Her own voice seemed to fade in and out, one moment distant
and the next a thundering in her ears. The whiteness deepened
to gray and then black, and at last, reality began to fade back in.
When Aerith's eyes remembered how to see, they told her she was
in her room, and that she'd somehow never left. She lay crumpled
against the floor beside the windowsill but struggled to her feet
and violently thrust the curtains aside.

There was nothing in the garden. Only the darkness of night, though that too had begun to flee as dawn crept its way into the sky.

She sensed someone in the hallway, and not a moment later, the door pushed gently open. Elmyra's head poked through the gap.

"You're already up. Good. Carlo should be here any moment. Get changed and hurry downstairs."

"Marcellus," Aerith blurted. "He's in Sector 6. Near the gate. He's hurt and bleeding. I think he's in a lot of pain."

Elmyra's eyes were sharp with suspicion, but Aerith held her gaze, confident she was doing the right thing.

"Fine," said Elmyra. "Let's tell Carlo."

They didn't have to wait long. Carlo arrived at dawn as promised, and though he urged them to depart immediately, Elmyra insisted on a moment to speak.

"I got a tip on Marcellus's whereabouts. He's somewhere in the outskirts of the Sector 6 slums, near the gate. I think he might be hurt, and he's almost certainly in danger. Kalm can wait. Find Marcellus."

Carlo furrowed his brow and asked, "Where'd you get this tip?"

"Don't ask how. Please, just trust me on this."

Carlo stared at Elmyra and then at Aerith with an impatient scowl. But he eventually turned to leave, and as he walked through the garden toward the alley, he did so with obvious haste.

Aerith stared at her hands, clenching and unclenching her gloved fingers.

"And that's how Marcellus was found," she told Tifa. "He was near the gate on the outskirts of the Wall Market, just like I'd seen. When Carlo found him, he was hardly breathing, but they managed to get him to a doctor, and in the end, he pulled through. And that was that."

"But *how*? It's all so . . . mysterious. I mean, I feel like I've been saying that over and over, but . . . I just don't know what else to call it."

"If you ask me, there's more to it than my heritage. I'm half Cetra, but I think another big piece of it was the environment.

There's something different . . . something *special* about the place where the Gainsboroughs built that house."

"And all the flowers? Are they part of that too?"

"I think so. Every year they just pop out of the ground, the same way my mom Ifalna used to pop into my room to see me. I think the only reason she could come so often was because the location made it easy for her to visit.

"But now I can't make the visions come no matter how hard I try. That might be because I'm only part Cetra, but I've got a feeling there's another reason too. I think more than anything, it was the innocence of childhood that allowed me to see those things. I guess I'm just more in tune with the city these days, and it's dulled my senses."

"It seems like such a huge part of yourself to lose."

"Yeah. Now that we're off on this new mission, I guess it might've been a handy skill to have."

The two women fell silent. Happiness was a fickle thing, as were the circumstances it demanded.

"Oh!" exclaimed Tifa. "So how did Marcellus wind up near the gate in the first place? Was he running away from home after all?"

"Yeah. Carlo's hunch was spot-on. Marcellus was angry about moving topside, so he snuck out one night and made for the Wall Market. He was wandering the streets, looking for a place that might offer him a job, when he had a run-in with some of Corneo's goons. He managed to get away, but by then he had no idea where he was. He kept walking and eventually found himself near the wall, face-to-face with a monster."

"Poor kid . . . I bet Carlo was the hero of the day, though."

"Yup. Even I was seeing him in an entirely different light. He'd transformed from a jerk who was always threatening Elmyra to a friendly, reliable old guy. Well . . . at the time, he seemed pretty old. Looking back, I realize he was probably in his thirties."

"What do you think he's up to these days?"

Marcellus was back safe. But the family business couldn't overlook the fact that his brush with death had initially been prompted by a run-in with Corneo's goons. The thugs were undoubtedly near the bottom of the pecking order, and they'd most likely only been out to cause trouble, rather than acting on orders. Still, better safe than sorry.

Carlo arranged for two of his subordinates, by the names of Banco and Zoot, to reside at the Gainsborough home until things settled down. The two were in their late twenties, and though friendly enough, they didn't strike Aerith as particularly capable of keeping anyone safe. Especially not if their potential assailants included neighboring syndicates.

The duo spent most of their time lounging about and gobbling up anything Elmyra cooked with big, childish grins. When Carlo stopped by every few days to check on them, he seemed all the more mature and reliable in comparison.

During one particular visit, Carlo was acting unusual. He'd readily agreed when Elmyra invited him to stay for dinner, but he insisted that she make her famous deep-fried meatballs. Even after Elmyra told him she didn't have the ingredients on hand, he begged and begged until finally she saw no way out but to go shopping. Carlo directed Banco and Zoot to tag along as her bodyguards.

Aerith had been at the dining table watching the exchange unfold. The moment Elmyra and her escort were out the door, Carlo turned to her.

"Aerith, I've been meanin' to ask you . . ."

His voice was overly sweet.

"See, there's this one thing that's been buggin' me. The day we found Marcellus, Elmyra knew exactly where to find him. But I just can't figure out how she woulda known."

"Oh . . ." Aerith tried to respond as casually as possible. "I don't know either."

She was doing her best to appear calm, but she doubted her act was very convincing.

"Huh. Well, turns out there's a rumor goin' around the family that maybe Marcellus *was* kidnapped after all. 'Cause, y'know, the ones who beat Marcellus up in the first place were connected to Corneo."

"Yeah?"

"But it gets worse. The buddy who gave me the heads-up? He says people are startin' to point fingers at Elmyra, like maybe she was pullin' the strings. The way Meguro's been makin' plans for the family business without her, it coulda been she wanted to send a message. 'Get yourself back in line, or things get ugly.'

"I don't wanna believe it, but I hafta admit, it kinda makes sense. How else would she've known exactly where to find Marcellus? You see where I'm goin' with this?"

"They think Elmyra *wanted* Marcellus to get hurt?" Aerith replied, aghast.

"Bingo. And to be honest, it puts me in a real awkward position. The rest of the family sees how much time I've been spendin' here since Clay died. Now they're startin' to doubt *me* too. Like maybe Elmyra and me are hookin' up—erm, *makin' plans* I mean, to sell the family business off to the highest bidder. So I'm thinkin' it's only a matter of time until Meguro comes for us."

A chill ran down Aerith's spine as she recalled how fearsome Meguro could be.

"What're you gonna do?!" she asked Carlo.

"Like I say, the key to it all is figurin' out *how* Elmyra knew. If we had a simple, believable reason, we could explain ourselves to the family. Not that it's gonna be easy to clear our names, but the truth would at least give us a fightin' chance. And if nothin' else, it'd help me feel a lot better about which side of this I'm on."

Carlo stared at her, the conflict plain in his eyes.

"So if you know *anything* about what happened that day . . ."

Aerith understood the implication well enough—at least, she understood the way he was looking at her. Right now, Carlo was a friend. But that could change very quickly.

Her mouth trembled as she tried to speak. The morning Marcellus was found, Elmyra had made one thing very clear: Aerith was not to tell *anyone* how she'd come to know of the boy's whereabouts.

But she had to do something. And if it was the only way to keep Elmyra safe . . .

"It was me," Aerith admitted. "I saw it in a dream. Well . . . not really a dream, but that's the only way I can think to describe it. I ran into Marcellus, and he told me where I could find him. I know it sounds weird, but it's the truth! Really!"

She expected to be met with disbelief. Instead, Carlo nodded thoughtfully.

"And these dreams . . . do you see a lot of 'em?"

"Not a *lot*, but . . . the one about Marcellus wasn't the first."

"Hm. And if it'd happened before, Elmyra would be quick to believe you."

Carlo straightened in his chair, grinned wide, and reached a hand out to pat Aerith on the head.

"You really care about her a lot, don't you?"

Aerith wanted desperately to know what was running through Carlo's mind. She'd told the truth. Would they be able to stay friends now, or was it not enough?

"What's gonna happen now?" she asked. "I'm scared . . ."

"Me too, kid. Me too."

When Elmyra, Banco, and Zoot returned from their outing, Carlo immediately stood and made for the door.

"Somethin's come up," he said. "Gonna have to take a rain check on those meatballs."

"Oh, for the love of . . . You sent me all the way into town, and now you're gonna—"

Elmyra cut herself off when she noticed Aerith sitting sullen at the table. She glanced back at Carlo, taking in his dour expression.

"What happened while I was gone?" she demanded.

"That idea about takin' a little trip to Kalm is soundin' better all the time. Lemme hire a car. Or if you're determined to stick around, I can arrange for Aerith to go alone."

"What's going on? Are we expecting an attack? Is it Corneo's men? The Manson brothers?"

"Neither. It's Meguro."

"Meguro . . . ? You're not making any sense."

"Ever since he got word it was you who provided the tip that led to Marcellus, there's this idea goin' round that maybe you're in Corneo's pocket. And that I am too. That's what everyone's sayin'."

"Who's saying?"

"Rodin, Marvin, Roger, Bauman, Louis . . . and, most important of all, Meguro."

"The entire family . . . ?"

Elmyra's eyes squeezed tight. Aerith wished she could see the thoughts running through her mother's head.

When Elmyra finally opened her eyes again, she stared at the center of the table, where sat the photo of Clay and Gabriel, then swept her gaze back up to Carlo.

"Where is Meguro now?" she asked.

"At home. His plan to move topside is on hold until the situation calms down. He's got his whole house locked down tight. Guys posted everywhere. Aw, Elmyra . . . Don't tell me you're thinkin' of going over there."

"Just to talk. I'll make it clear I want out. He can have the whole damn business for all I care. Gabriel's gone, and so is Clay. My husband's claim was never mine to begin with."

"Whoa, whoa, whoa! You can't be serious!"

"I've been thinking this over for a long time already. The only thing holding me back was concern about how we'd make ends meet. But we'll figure it out. Now's as good a time as any."

"It won't help clear your name. If anything, Meguro'll see it as more proof that you've flipped over to Corneo. Worst case, he might . . ."

Carlo hesitated, unwilling to finish the thought.

"I hear you. But this is something I have to do. Look after Aerith for me, will you? Just for a little while longer."

Carlo's shoulders slumped.

"And you, kid?" he asked Aerith. "You okay with this?"

"No!"

Aerith's voice came out hoarse. There was a lump in her throat that just wouldn't go away.

Elmyra smiled and reached a hand to stroke her cheek.

"This could take a while. I might not be back until late. You have dinner with Carlo, hear? And don't give him any trouble when it's time for bed."

"Don't go!" she shouted, but Elmyra's back was already turned.

She rushed forward, hand outstretched to catch hold of her mother's shirttails, but Carlo grabbed Aerith by the arm.

"Let go of me!" she screamed. "Mom, stop! You can't go!"

The front doors closed, and Elmyra was gone.

Banco and Zoot stood awkwardly in one corner of the front room, looking to Carlo for direction.

"Make us somethin' to eat," Carlo snapped. "Anything. I don't care."

"I *hate* you, Carlo!" shouted Aerith.

Sadness flickered in the man's eyes, but still he held firm.

"Your mother's right," he said. "We gotta do this the proper way. Someday you'll understand."

Aerith had no appetite come dinnertime. She'd hardly sat down before asking to be excused, leaving the omelet prepared by Banco completely untouched.

Upstairs in her room, she paced restlessly, worrying about Elmyra and hoping she'd make it back all right. Each time she passed the window she glanced out, only to find the garden still empty and the day growing darker. Each time she went by the door, she stepped out onto the landing to listen downstairs, but caught nothing more than fragments of idle chatter among Carlo and his men.

It was near midnight when she heard the telltale click of the front doors' latch.

"Elmyra!" Carlo cried out with joy. "Thank god you're alive!"

"If I wanted a hug, I'd ask for it," the woman snapped in return.

Aerith raced to the front room so fast, she nearly went tumbling down the stairs. She found Carlo standing by Elmyra's side, scratching his head awkwardly, as Banco and Zoot looked on with mischievous grins.

"Mom!" Aerith cried.

Elmyra hurried over and bent down to eye level.

"I'm home safe, baby. Sorry I made you worry."

Aerith, too overwhelmed for any further words, simply launched herself into her mother's arms. The hug carried enough force to knock Elmyra backward, but this time the woman uttered no protest.

"I used to be able to carry you around without breaking a sweat. When in the world did you get so big?" teased Elmyra.

She hugged Aerith back firmly, and for a while, they sat there on the wood floor, forgetting everything and everyone.

Eventually, Carlo couldn't wait any longer.

"And?" he cut in. "What did Meguro say?"

Elmyra gently lifted Aerith to her feet, then slowly clambered up herself. She smoothed the wrinkles from her clothes and responded, "He no longer suspects that Marcellus was kidnapped. More important, he *never* suspected you or me of having anything to do with it."

"What? But my source said—"

"Meguro knows us. We're not the type to go skulking around in the shadows. If we've got something on our minds, we say it straight."

"Damn that old fart . . . Thinks he knows us better than we know ourselves."

Despite the harsh words, Carlo was beaming.

He paused for a moment, as if grappling with some unresolved detail, and asked, "Then what the hell was all that talk I was hearin'?"

Elmyra crossed her arms. "Remind me who exactly you got your information from."

"It was Butch. Butch told me. Even now that he's retired, he's been goin' by to see Meguro every now and again. Says he likes to keep up to speed on the family business."

Elmyra didn't have to say anything. She raised her eyebrows and waited for Carlo to fill in the blanks.

"Whoa, whoa. You're sayin' *Butch* set me up?!"

Carlo groaned and clawed at his face. He began to pace about the front room, angrily muttering, "Shit . . . Shit! Just wait till I get my hands on that wrinkly old bastard!"

"Calm down," said Elmyra. "I haven't finished yet."

Carlo managed to stop fidgeting, but he continued to glower, and his nostrils flared with each breath.

"As to Butch's motives and how he plays into this, I can't say. You go ahead and dig into that on your own time. But Meguro gave me something to take care of before you leave."

She pulled a small box from her purse, which she handed to Carlo.

"What is this?" he asked.

On pulling the lid off and inspecting the contents, Carlo's rage dissipated to shock.

Elmyra replied, "Gabriel's signet. It was fashioned as a pair, the other half of which is in President Shinra's possession. That ring symbolizes the goodwill between the company and our family. When Gabriel died, the ring was supposed to pass to Clay. That chance never came, so Meguro's been holding on to it."

"But that means . . ."

"The signet belongs with the head of the Gainsborough family business. As do these."

She produced an envelope from her purse, which she also held out to Carlo.

"Deeds to all the properties we own, along with the original memorandum laying out the terms of our business relationship with Shinra. You'll also find all the licenses and certifications we require to operate, and last but not least, an amended agreement listing all current members—from the top all the way down to the number threes—complete with everyone's fingerprint in blood to authorize the changeover. The whole family's on board with this. We all believe it's the right move to make."

She waggled the ring finger of her left hand, wrapped in a tiny bandage stained with a splotch of red, and added, "I signed too, when I was over at Meguro's."

Banco exclaimed, "Boss! Is she sayin' what I think she's sayin'?!"

Elmyra nodded, again proffering the envelope to Carlo.

"Meguro's not planning to kick the bucket yet," she said. "But he's wised up to the fact that he's in no condition to run things. He's been calling the other officers in one by one for a while now, making the necessary arrangements to step down. The last thing he had left to do was make sure you're on board."

Carlo's mouth opened and closed wordlessly. His hand reached out to take the envelope but darted back away. All the while, he was mumbling to himself, saying, "Where is this comin' from?"

and "Hell of a lot to spring on a guy all at once," and "What'm I supposed to do here?"

Aerith, Elmyra, and Carlo's two subordinates waited patiently as the would-be successor of the Gainsborough family business made up his mind.

When Zoot couldn't take it any longer, he exclaimed, "You're the *boss*, Boss!" The others shushed him, and Zoot resumed the wait, though now sniffling and wiping the occasional tear of joy from the corner of one eye.

In the end, it took Carlo three full minutes to decide. He gently lifted the envelope from Elmyra's outstretched hand—which had impressively remained aloft without so much as a tremble—and slid it inside the black briefcase ever at his side.

After a moment's thought, he reached back into the briefcase and pulled out a pistol. Carlo checked the magazine and slid it back into place. He set the weapon down on the dining table with a thud that echoed in the pit of Aerith's stomach.

"Guess this means we won't be comin' around no more," Carlo said. "You're gonna have to take care of yourselves."

Aerith blurted, "You're leaving us?!"

It didn't make any sense. Elmyra and Carlo were clear of suspicion, and Carlo had agreed to take over the family business with Elmyra's and Meguro's blessing. Everything had worked out. So why couldn't Carlo keep coming to see them?

Carlo's mouth screwed up tight in a last-ditch effort to hold back tears. "Yeah. I am. If I keep showin' up at the house, nothin' changes. If you're out, it's gotta look like you're out. Otherwise the neighboring syndicates will still see you as prime targets, and we'll have done all this for nothin'."

He brought a forearm up over his eyes and said, "Aerith, you'll be a real fine woman someday. Elmyra, you already are. Keep it up."

His final words out, Carlo threw open the front doors, dashing into the garden as if unable to bear prolonging the farewell a moment more. Banco and Zoot exchanged glances and hurried to follow.

A moment passed, and the door again opened quietly. Without

a word, and without any hesitation, Carlo stepped in and embraced Elmyra in a firm, brief hug. When he stepped away, he sighed deeply, stared at his feet, and then darted back outside.

It was the last Aerith ever saw of him.

Another stretch of peaceful days ensued, almost to Aerith's disappointment. There was no backlash. No hint of any threat to Elmyra's or Aerith's safety. At first, Elmyra insisted upon keeping the pistol close at all times, but six months of uneventful days finally convinced her they were truly safe, and she took the firearm up to the attic to stash away. Aerith was relieved to have it out of sight.

Sometimes, she found herself wondering what Carlo was up to, and if in the end they'd had any run-ins with neighboring syndicates. Members of the family business had long stopped coming by, and little word of its activities seemed to reach their household. At least, Aerith never seemed to hear about it. She assumed Elmyra might have her own quiet channels, but if she did, she certainly never spoke of them.

Still, if there was one thing Elmyra couldn't stand, it was sitting idle. She loved to work, and with her duties in the family business gone, she adopted other, more prosaic pursuits: waitressing at a local café, or putting her cleaning and tidying skills to use at the orphanage and one of the local clinics. The money she brought in managed to keep them afloat.

What amazed Elmyra the most, she'd later tell Aerith, was the fact that a job was always waiting for her, no matter where in the slums she inquired. Even shops that were already fully staffed were quick to point Elmyra to someone else who needed help. People all over the neighborhood seemed to be looking out for the Gainsborough heir and her adopted daughter, making sure the two were never left wanting.

It seemed too good to chalk up to fortune, and when Elmyra began to pry into why the entire sector was so forthcoming, a pattern quickly emerged.

Everyone in the sector, it seemed, had a story about Elmyra's late father-in-law, whether a personal favor received or a kindness done to a close family member. The man had offered help to so many people, he was regarded as somewhat of a legend.

Most important were the livelihoods he'd secured for count-less families throughout the slums. While Midgar was still an end-less expanse of scaffolding, the city's networks of corruption were also taking shape. Worst off were the day laborers, having traveled from all over with promises of steady work, only to arrive and have to fight for spots on crews that paid a pittance at best. Seedy con-tractors had been quick to set themselves up between Shinra and the city's workforce, charging finder's fees and commissions, and claiming hefty cuts in exchange for guaranteed placements—any name or device they could come up with to siphon a few more gil away from the workers and to themselves.

But in one sector, at least, things would be different, thanks to one Gabriel Gainsborough.

Driving the unscrupulous and the extortionate out of Sector 5 was a long, bloody process, but eventually Gabriel saw that Shinra's money was again flowing to the workers as intended. With time, he earned the company's trust and managed to negotiate even better conditions. As the city neared completion, many of the la-borers were able to transition into life as business owners, opening up their own small shops with the money they'd saved. Even after the businesses passed from one generation to the next, the resi-dents of the slums were not quick to forget the way Gabriel had fought for their families' futures.

The stories left Elmyra stunned, and for days and weeks after-ward, Aerith would hear her murmuring to herself throughout the day, "We've all got a lot to be thankful for."

Upon reaching thirteen years of age, it was customary for children living at the Sector 5 House to begin working somewhere in the neighborhood. Aerith, having been aware of the custom for some time, had resolved to do the same.

But when her thirteenth birthday arrived and she unveiled her plan, Elmyra was quick to shut it down.

"Why can't I get a job?" Aerith demanded.

"I'm not saying I want to keep you cooped up at home. I'm just worried. That's all. You and I have been through a lot."

"That was forever ago!"

"I know, but . . . when you've had life turned on its head as many times as I have, it gets to you. Every time things seem good and I let myself get comfortable, it all falls apart. I guess it's just my luck."

Elmyra shook her head and let out a deep sigh.

"Listen to me. At this rate, I might as well be keeping you locked up like Shinra. Go ahead. Get yourself a job. But try to find something close to home, would you?"

"Thanks, Mom."

Her mother's confession was like a breath of fresh air; it reminded Aerith of their early days together, when Elmyra had always tried to keep her in the loop, and she'd felt certain she was welcome. At the same time, Aerith couldn't help but wonder how many times she'd been the one responsible for turning Elmyra's life upside down.

Aboard the ferry, Aerith sighed much like Elmyra had.

"And as it turns out, Mom was right to be concerned. I should've listened."

Tifa gasped. "*More* trouble?!"

Aerith responded with a firm nod.

Aerith had planned to look for a job all by herself, but Elmyra beat her to the punch: the teachers at the Sector 5 House needed an assistant, and apparently, Aerith was the perfect girl for the job.

It was curious, though. Once Aerith actually began working there, it seemed that "assistant" was more or less a fancy way of saying she'd be spending most of her time playing with the other children. It didn't really *feel* like work.

When she'd dreamed of finding a job, she'd imagined diving headfirst into something new. Yoko, who had turned thirteen a few months earlier, had already left the orphanage. Now she was renting an old home together with some friends, and she spent her days fashioning handmade accessories that she took to markets around the sector to sell. Jean and X worked in a scrapyard, rummaging for machine parts, getting rid of the rust, and selling them for repairs.

But when Aerith excitedly discussed her friends' jobs at home, and suggested that maybe she could try something similar, Elmyra only pursed her lips and emphasized that she was not, under any circumstances, to set foot outside Sector 5.

Aerith had had enough.

"You said you wouldn't keep me locked up like Shinra!" she shouted.

"Don't you take that tone with me, young lady. I'm your mother, and I'm trying to look out for you."

In truth, Elmyra appeared exhausted. Her jobs seemed to be wearing on her, and Aerith hated the fact that *she* was the cause. If Aerith had never shown up in Sector 5, Elmyra would have never left the family business. She'd still be in touch with Carlo and the others, and she would have never known the hardship of working odd jobs all over the sector.

Surely, deep down, Elmyra felt the same. She had to regret sacrificing so much to take care of a stranger's child. That must've been the reason behind all the oppressive rules, boundaries, and curfews. It was Elmyra's way of getting back for all the years she'd spent tied down by her obligation to Aerith.

Tifa grimaced. "Talk about trust issues."

"I know. I admit it. The fact that I was thirteen and already in full-on moody teenager mode wasn't helping. What I really needed was some kind of outlet to focus on, like you had with your training."

"Exercise is amazing for clearing your head. I really recommend it."

"Oh, I'm definitely planning to start a routine of my own. Eventually."

"In other words, never."

Aerith laughed. "*Anyway*, in spite of all my moping and second-guessing, I did keep showing up for work at the Sector 5 House. The little kids were so cute and fun to be around, and they really seemed to be getting attached to me. By the time I was fourteen, I'd stopped complaining, more or less, and it almost seemed like the whole situation at home was gonna blow over without incident. But then, as luck would have it . . ."

Aerith had just finished a day's work at the Sector 5 House. As she neared home, she spotted a small group standing right where the alley opened up onto Gainsborough property. They were crowded together with their backs to her, blocking the way, and they seemed to be observing the house and its garden with keen interest.

She saw two women and two men, among whom one of the males seemed vaguely familiar: though she couldn't yet see his face, she could tell he was fairly young, and there was something about his gorgeous, wavy blond hair . . .

When his identity clicked, she couldn't stop herself from exclaiming, "Rodin!"

The man turned with a smile on his face.

Now that Aerith was certain, she added, "What are you doing here?!"

"Aerith! Good to see you."

Rodin's reply was cheerful enough. Still, the apprehensive glances he shot his companions didn't escape her notice.

"You've gotten taller," he added. "How many years has it been?"

"Two? Maybe more?"

"Sounds about right."

She peered more carefully at the other three members of his group, now wondering if she knew them as well.

The other man—large of frame and looking quite grown up, save for his face—held up one hand shyly and greeted Aerith with a simple, "Hey."

Now that he'd also turned, she could see the eyes, the nose, the mouth . . .

"Marcellus?!" she yelped.

"Wasn't sure if you'd recognize me."

"Of course I do!"

In truth, he'd changed so much, it was hard to believe he was the same person she'd met years ago. He was tall now and quite heavyset—almost a carbon copy of his father.

"Actually," cut in Rodin, "it's great that you do, 'cause it will save us all some time. This little field trip was Marcellus's idea. He must've badgered me about bringing him here every day for a month, until finally I caved. He says he just had to see you again, and so here we are."

With each passing sentence, Rodin's tone grew more apologetic and uncertain. At the end, he backed one hesitant step away from Aerith as he motioned for Marcellus to take over. Meanwhile, Marcellus had been glancing restlessly at their surroundings, as if expecting someone else to show up at any moment.

After a long, awkward pause, Marcellus reached a hand to scratch his cheek a few times, blushed, and said, "Aerith . . . First, I wanna apologize. I said some awful things to you. I shouldn't have been mad at you about using my sister's name, and I shouldn't have called you a thief. I was a stupid kid, always angry at everyone and everything. Can you ever forgive me?"

Aerith did her best to smile. "All ancient history. Anyway, it's nice to see you looking so well."

Marcellus's face lit up. "Yeah! I am doing well! And I owe it all to you. That day I got chased out to the sector gate and ran into the monster . . . Well, I thought I was a goner. But just when I was sure it was all over, I had this weird dream about you showing up to save me.

"At least, for a long time, I thought it was a dream. I knew there was no way you'd be out wandering the edge of the Sector 6 slums. You were supposed to be safe at home in Sector 5. And even if you had been near the gate that day, you wouldn't have wanted to help me after the way I'd treated you. So it didn't make sense for it be anything *but* a dream."

He hesitated before continuing. "Still, it felt so real. And then, the other day when I was talking with Carlo, he happened to mention that you were the one who knew where to find me. Carlo himself couldn't really believe it, so he kept quiet about it for years."

Aerith tensed, unable to believe that Carlo had divulged her secret. Had he betrayed her after all?

Something told her it was better not to confirm or deny Marcellus's suspicions, or to give any answer whatsoever. She offered a weak smile and waited for the young man to continue.

"I started looking into it," Marcellus said. "I read everything I could find about visions and speaking with others across time and space, and I got to thinking, maybe our interaction that day had something to do with the lifestream. You know about the lifestream, right? It's supposed to be some kinda current inside the planet. A kind of spiritual energy."

"Oh. Huh."

Aerith did her best to feign ignorance.

"In fact, they say the lifestream's where we get mako energy from. What we're actually doing is—"

"Marcellus!" snapped the younger of their two female companions. "You know we're not allowed to talk bad about mako. I'll tell Dad on you."

Aerith had been so surprised to see Marcellus that she hadn't taken the time to look the two women over carefully. The girl who had spoken was no older than Aerith. As soon as their eyes met, Aerith knew at once who she must be.

"That's my brother for you," said the girl. "Once he starts talking, he never stops. Hey, Aerith. How have you been?"

Ronna!

"Good," Aerith replied. "It's nice to see you're looking well too. How's your dad?"

"Not great, but definitely better now that we're out of the slums. Until we moved, I never realized how smoggy it is down here. You wouldn't believe how fresh the air is up on the plate."

Aerith replied with a wan smile. Ronna hadn't changed much; she still had a way of making people feel bad without meaning to.

"And Carlo?" Aerith asked.

"Trying his best. He's staying on top of the business. Honestly, I wouldn't have thought he has what it takes to make it through something like the Sector 5 turf war, but he somehow managed to pull through."

"Turf war . . . ?"

The question left Ronna looking perplexed. "Do you seriously not know? I'm talking about the fighting, right after Dad retired and Carlo took over. Remember? Corneo's people swooped in, along with like a dozen others. Bunches of nobodies swarming Sector 5 hoping to stake a claim. By the time Carlo and his guys had driven them back, the streets were practically red with blood. Marvin, Roger, and Bauman all died in the fighting."

"What?!"

How could that be true? If there had been fighting in the sector, Aerith felt certain she would've seen it.

"Anyway," cut in Rodin, "that's all over now. The family business is safe. The other groups went back to where they came from."

He glanced around nervously and added, "We done here? You two got to speak with Aerith, and that means I've kept my promise. If you've got more to say, you can write her a letter."

"Elmyra will be back soon," ventured Aerith. "Won't you stay for tea?"

"Not a good idea. We're not authorized to be in the restricted zone. We really oughta get outta here."

"Restricted zone? What's that?"

"It stretches from here to the station," explained Marcellus. "Shinra set the boundaries when the turf war broke out. The zone was to remain conflict-free, and anyone who didn't abide by the rules . . . Well, let's just say Shinra promised to take care of them. So all sides steered well clear of the zone. It was the one thing everyone could agree on."

"What are they restricting people from?"

Her question seemed to astonish Ronna.

"What do you mean?" the girl demanded. "They're restricting access to *you*, duh!"

The comment sent Rodin's restlessness bubbling over into panic.

"Okay! That's it!" he declared. "I warned you two about saying too much. Now we *really* have to get out of here."

He hastily ushered his little group away from the edge of the Gainsborough property. As Marcellus passed Aerith, he promised to visit again soon, saying he'd really like to talk more about the mysterious events of the day he'd almost died. Aerith was careful to stick to a noncommittal response. Ronna invited her to come for a playdate up on the plate, and Aerith promised to discuss the possibility with Elmyra.

The group of four set off down the alley. But just before they turned the first bend, Rodin stopped and pointed to the fourth, unintroduced member.

"This is Amber," he said. "We're gonna get married soon. Give Elmyra the news for me, would you? Tell her I wish I could've made a proper introduction."

Amber remained silent. She stared at Aerith with narrowed eyes, and Aerith found herself wondering what she'd done to invite such obvious hostility. The woman certainly didn't seem familiar.

When Aerith returned home, she wandered over to a waist-high cabinet tucked in the back corner of the front room, on whose surface rested a single flower vase. She recalled that it used to seat a television and tried to think when the vase would have taken the TV's place.

When the memory returned, it prompted a small gasp.

It had been about a month after they'd cut all ties with Carlo and the family business. Elmyra had bumped into the cabinet while cleaning, sending the bulky TV crashing to the ground. She'd kept putting off purchasing a new one until finally it just never happened.

Was it a coincidence? Or was it one more subtle ploy to limit the amount of outside information making its way into their quiet household?

When Elmyra returned in the evening, Aerith told her of the encounter with Rodin and the others.

"Imagine that," her mother replied. "I haven't seen any of them in ages. Did they look well?"

The woman's expression, however, didn't quite match her words. She seemed guarded. Alarmed.

"Hey, Mom? Do you know anything about a turf war?" Aerith ventured. "And something called a restricted zone?"

Elmyra waved the questions off, clearly anxious to change the subject.

"I see they've been filling your head with stories," she said. "You and I live in a different world now. There's no reason for us to get worked up about the little details of Rodin and the rest of the family's lives."

"This house," Aerith repeated more firmly. "And this neighborhood. That's the restricted zone, right? And those boundaries were chosen because that's where I live and where I spend my day. That's why you made such a big deal of me not going far from home to look for work. You made a promise with Shinra, and now I have to stay in this cell they've set up for me."

Elmyra's eyes closed. She slowly shook her head from side to side.

"That's not how it went down at all. But can we please not talk about this right now? There was a crack in the water tank at the café today, and I had to spend all day mopping up."

More evasions. More excuses. More deceit. It set Aerith's blood boiling, and the next words tumbled out of her mouth before she could stop herself.

"If work is so exhausting, just quit already," she snapped. "It never bothered you to take Shinra's money before. What's stopping you now?"

After she'd said it, she immediately turned away, unable to look at Elmyra and see the pain her words had caused. Everything following was a blur. She heard her own feet running up the stairs, and she heard the door to her room slam hard. She didn't want to talk. She didn't want to think. She wished she could just disappear.

"I figured I'd finally crossed a line," admitted Aerith. "I really believed that was the end of my life in Sector 5, and the end of my time with Elmyra."

"But you were living with her when we met you," said Tifa. "So you must've made up. It all worked out in the end, right?"

After her outburst, the only thing Aerith could think about was how she needed to get away. She couldn't keep dragging Elmyra down forever.

Kneeling at the side of her bed, she dragged out the dusty old suitcase she and Elmyra had once packed for the proposed flight to Kalm. In the end, they'd never gone, and the suitcase had remained unused and forgotten under Aerith's bed.

She grabbed clothes from her dresser and crammed them inside, then carefully nestled her most treasured belonging among the fabric. And finally, after stuffing all the gil she'd saved up from her work at the House into one pocket, she lugged the suitcase downstairs and out of the house.

The darkness of the familiar alley gave way to the harsh streetlamps of the sector's main thoroughfare. A familiar shopkeep called out to her as she passed by.

"Hey, there, Aerith. What's got you out this time of night?"

Impulsively, she lied. "Just a quick trip to Sector 6."

"Oh, honey . . . Don't tell me you're thinking of—"

"Nothing like that," Aerith scrambled to say. "Nothing to do with Wall Market."

"Well, stay safe, all right? Elmyra'd be devastated if anything were to happen to you."

With a courteous farewell, Aerith left the neighbor behind. She continued down the main thoroughfare, reminded of her adventure with Ifalna so very long ago.

Which direction to the Sector 3 slums? her mother had asked the woman outside their freight car.

She'd even asked the station attendant who chased them down. *Could you tell us the way to Sector 3?*

Aerith recalled her surprise on discovering that they'd been heading in the opposite direction all along, and that her mother's requests were in fact a ruse to throw off any pursuit. It wasn't until after they spied the sign for Sector 5 that Ifalna gave any hint of where they were actually headed.

I heard a story once—one that I hope is true. There's supposed to be a church in the Sector 5 slums. Long ago, people would gather there to worship God, but now it sits neglected. Nobody visits, which would make it a perfect spot for us to hide for a while.

Thoughts of her and Ifalna's daring escape lifted her spirits, and her steps grew lighter and more confident. The walking and the thinking swept away the cloud of melancholy that had hung overhead since she set foot outside Elmyra's front doors. Aerith nodded decisively to herself that this was the right thing to do. This was the adventure she'd been meant to go on, its final leg left too long delayed.

The church, Aerith had heard, was more or less a straight shot from the Gainsborough home; all she had to do was head toward the station and keep going. It would take her well outside the restricted zone, and frankly, that suited her just fine.

Don't ever let go of that.

The way you find joy in everything.

The memories of Ifalna continued to flood back stronger and clearer every step of the way.

Tifa smiled knowingly. "That's how it goes after a big fight at home, isn't it? For a little while, it's like you've got all the confidence in the world."

"Exactly. You have to keep moving. You can't let yourself stop and think it over, because you know it'll all come undone."

"I couldn't have said it better myself."

"But this time, I saw the consequences. Because of me, someone ended up very badly hurt."

As soon as she'd made the confession, she could hear Tifa swallow nervously at her side.

When Aerith neared the station, a train had just pulled up to the platform. Judging by the time, it was the last one to wind its way down from the plate for the night.

She glanced at it only briefly, intending to walk by as quickly as possible. The Sector 5 Undercity Station was a piece of her adventure she could do without remembering. She didn't want to let her eyes sweep across that one particular stretch of road or that one particular portion at the base of the concrete platform. A part of her feared that if she did, she might still see her mother there, lying limp and burning with fever as her life prepared to slip away.

She was nearly across the plaza and safely out of sight when another thought struck.

Was she making a mistake?

From the moment she pulled out the suitcase, she had been framing the flight to herself as something positive, but maybe running away was in fact a horrible, hurtful thing to do. The gloom of that possibility sapped her excitement and determination, which suddenly seemed far more vulnerable than before.

Aerith saw that the restricted zone had existed not to keep her penned in but to keep her safe from harm. The moment she stepped beyond its borders, she'd be exposing herself to great peril. A huge, invisible wall seemed to rise at her feet, blocking the way forward. The bright lights of the station and its plaza begged her to stay, warning that the moment she trod beyond their reach, her future would be as dark and uncertain as the streets ahead.

A cautious, searching voice interrupted her thoughts.

"Aerith?"

She turned to find a man, impossibly big in both frame and features, standing with his back to the station. Large eyes. Large nose. Large mouth.

A gasp escaped Aerith, and the man continued. "I knew it was you. You're all grown up now, but I still knew. You're the spitting image of her. Of your mother, see?"

Faz. Aerith's mind raced. How was he here? Why? He still wore the massive white lab coat she remembered from her days in the Shinra Building. Did that mean . . . ?

"You've got the wrong person," she said, turning her head and quickly walking by.

She felt Faz lumber after her and knew she no longer had a choice: the dark streets beyond the station were the only way left open.

"Aerith, wait!" called the deep baritone. "It's not what you think!"

In truth, she wasn't sure what she thought. All she knew was that she wasn't about to stop and find out.

As she half walked, half jogged along the cluttered, pitch-black dirt road, her mind frantically worked through the possibilities. It occurred to her that Faz could be furious. He might be nursing a years-old grudge, ever since Ifalna used him to secure their escape and promptly abandoned him once free.

The thought of trusting him or even stopping to engage in conversation seemed absurd. Who knew what he might do if he caught her?

Meanwhile, Aerith's knowledge of the route to the church had been tenuous to begin with. Faz's pursuit, coupled with the dark of night, certainly wasn't helping. After a while, she looked about and realized she had no idea where she was or whether the church was still ahead. The street had narrowed to a small, lonely footpath, surrounded on each side by mountains upon mountains of scrap.

The sight of the rusted metal sparked a flicker of hope, and she called out into the night, "Jean? X? Are you there?!"

Her cries garnered no reply. Suddenly, the hope seemed silly. Even if this was the scrapyard the boys picked from, there was no way they'd be out working so late at night. Still, she called again, desperate to locate anyone else so as not to find herself alone with Faz.

Aerith's next step planted against something lumpy and soft. It threw her balance, sending her pitching forward. Her suitcase landed against the hard dirt with a heavy thud and a crack, as if the handle had partially broken loose.

Aerith groaned in pain, turning and feeling with her hands along the ground to identify the object she'd stumbled over. When her fingers found it, the surface was spongy and covered in slime, and she shrieked with understanding. It was a monster carcass.

The creature was not long dead. Its remains emitted a faint, unidentifiable whooshing noise. Fluids oozed over the dirt, clinging to the bare skin of Aerith's legs and fingers and causing a faint tingling that seemed to build slowly and steadily to an awful burn.

"It's okay," sounded a deep voice. "It cannot hurt you."

She realized that Faz had caught up to her and now stood on the other side of the corpse.

Still sprawled on the ground, Aerith stared up at him, seeing him as she had as a girl of seven: an impossibly large figure that dominated her entire field of view.

The hem of her skirt had ridden up high, and she hastily pulled it back down to her calves. Slowly, carefully, she slid backward, away from Faz and the corpse, watching for her chance to pull herself upright and bolt.

"How could you be so cruel?" Faz demanded. "You had me sick with worry. I cried every day, imagining you and your mother living in the gutters, on the run from Shinra. I'd almost given up hope when Amber came to tell me she'd found you."

"Amber . . . ?" Aerith repeated the name, not comprehending.

Except, she *had* heard that name somewhere, just recently . . . Yes. The other woman in the group when Marcellus had come to visit. Rodin's fiancée. *We're gonna get married soon,* he'd said.

She recalled how the woman had glared at her. Now it seemed she was connected to Faz in some way. But how?

Faz picked up on the confusion in Aerith's expression.

"You don't remember Amber?" he said. "That's not very nice. She helped you. She was there to make sure you were safe, at the Sector 4 Undercity Station. Amber. My friend."

Aerith gasped. The grumpy woman in the baggy, filthy coveralls. The one who'd snapped at her and Ifalna and refused to help them down from the freight car. *That* was Amber.

"When she told me she'd found out where you were living, I came as quick as I could to Sector 5. And the timing was perfect. Can you believe it? Any later, and you'd have walked right past the station. I think it must have been Ifalna. She was watching over us, guiding us so we'd be in the right place at the right time."

Aerith slowly pulled herself to her feet, now certain that something was very wrong.

Faz, for his part, backed two steps away from her, as if to prove he meant no harm.

"Are you going to the church?" asked Faz.

"Huh? How . . . ?"

"The church. I told Ifalna about it once. She seemed very interested at first. I offered to take her someday, but suddenly her attitude changed. She said it was a horrible, vile place, and she'd never think of stepping foot inside. But after the two of you vanished, I was trying to think of any place you might've gone. That's when I remembered the church. I went to check it a few times, just in case. I prayed when I was there. I hoped maybe God would help me find you. But God didn't seem to hear, so I stopped visiting. I guess maybe there is no god."

A low growl interrupted Faz, and the big man turned ponderously to one side, examining the darkness.

"Monsters," he remarked. "It's not safe here. Especially not at night. We should go somewhere safe. The church isn't far. Wouldn't you like to see it? It's much closer than going back to the station."

Aerith tried to peer over Faz's shoulder, but she could no longer make out any light from the station plaza. If the lab assistant was telling the truth, she'd run much farther than she'd imagined.

"Maybe it would be better if I—"

"Oh, Aerith . . . I hope you're not saying I frighten you more than the monsters. Is that how you really feel?"

She nodded, seeing no point in trying to hide the truth. Surely he knew already. He'd seen the way she'd fled and how she edged away from him even now.

"What if I lead the way?" proposed Faz. "I'll walk ahead of you, and you can hang back as far as you like. But if any monsters come up from behind, we must run, you understand? Run for all you're worth. The neighborhood watch doesn't conduct any patrols at this time of night, and I'm not nearly good enough of a fighter to handle the monsters myself. Just because I am big does not mean that I am strong."

Faz offered a faint smile and trundled past Aerith in the direction of the church. She watched as the pale white slab of his back melted into the surrounding night.

He was right, and she'd known it immediately. She would never muster the courage to retrace her steps to the station now that she knew monsters were about. Luck had spared her any encounters on the way in, but that was no guarantee of good fortune on the way back. Her only choice was to follow Faz.

"Watch your step!" the big man called, already quite some distance away. "There's another dead monster up ahead. Fresh, just like the first one. It wouldn't be very pleasant to feel it squishing under your boots."

Faz had claimed that the church wasn't much farther. Perhaps, Aerith reflected, she should have been more skeptical. They'd been walking so long, it seemed almost a certainty that he'd hoped to trick her into following.

It wasn't until they'd passed the third monster corpse—fresh, just like the others—that she finally spied a large, mysterious structure emerging from the darkness.

"I wonder who killed them," Faz mused aloud as he lumbered up the dozen stone steps to the structure's heavy double doors.

Aerith had never seen another building like it. She craned her neck, trying to take in the full extent, but the two towers at its front stretched up and up, their tops obscured by the black of midnight. They appeared to taper slightly, perhaps ending in spires, and Aerith wondered just how high they went, and how they might look in the daytime.

The doors creaked and groaned as Faz pulled with all his weight. When they were at last open, he slipped inside, beckoning for Aerith to follow.

Aerith cautiously climbed the steps. At the top, she was greeted by a familiar, sweet smell wafting through the now-open doors. The inside of the church was darker still, but she could just make out the wood slats at her feet, and there was a pale, mysterious glow coming from an uneven patch of floor at the far end of the chapel.

"Flowers," Faz explained, as if he'd known precisely where her eyes were focused. "They bloom right here, in the middle of the church. God or no god, this place must be very special."

Much as she hated to agree with anything the man said, the remark seemed accurate. Flowers were a rare sight in the slums, so any place they took root was a location quite worthy of note.

When Aerith took her first hesitant step into the chapel, she found herself enveloped with the same lovely fragrance that hung about the Gainsborough garden. The joy was laced with guilt, however, as Aerith began to think again of Elmyra; was her mother still asleep, or had she already discovered Aerith's flight? Perhaps she was searching the neighborhood streets at that very moment, terrified for her daughter's safety. Perhaps she was rushing to the Wall Market, tipped off by the neighbor Aerith had encountered.

"You should try to get some sleep on one of the pews up here, near the flowers," said Faz, interrupting her thoughts. "I will go wait by the doors until morning comes."

"Thank you," she murmured warily.

Sleep was the furthest thing from Aerith's mind, but she nonetheless wandered deeper into the church, settling down on one pew nearest the small, glowing patch of yellow flowers. A slow, quiet sigh escaped her lips, and for the first time in hours, Aerith's muscles relaxed, freed from the constant, insidious tension that had plagued her since afternoon. For a moment, it seemed like she might actually doze off, and she scrambled for some line of thought to keep herself awake.

How would things have gone if Ifalna had lived? If the adventure had gone as planned, and Aerith and her mother had made it to the church that day, how would their lives have played out? Would Ifalna have found a job to support them? What kind of work had she had in mind? How had she planned to cope when she herself admitted to having no understanding of the outside world?

Would the two have remained happy as Aerith grew? Or would they have bickered and fought? Perhaps every relationship between mother and daughter came with its share of bumps, whether tied by blood or not.

"Aerith?" Faz's deep baritone called. He sounded to be at the other end of the church, just as promised.

"What is it?"

"I still have the house. The one in Sector 3. Everything's exactly as it was. I kept paying the rent on it so it would always be ready."

"Oh. I see."

"Wouldn't you like to live there with me?"

Hoping she'd misinterpreted, Aerith chirped, "You mean . . . just the two of us? You and me living together?"

Faz didn't respond.

She called out his name and nervously got to her feet. When Faz finally did reply, she flinched at how close he now sounded. She turned to find him standing just behind her pew.

"Yes," he rumbled. "We'll finally be together, my love. My dear *Ifalna* . . ."

He chuckled softly, eyes staring blankly ahead. One giant hand reached out to Aerith, and he repeated, "Come, Ifalna. Let's go there now."

The thick, sweaty fingers were nearly upon her. Aerith panicked. She grabbed her suitcase, intending to flee, but before her feet would respond, Faz had already clamped down on her arm.

"Let go!" she screamed.

She whirled her free arm with all her weight behind it. The heavy suitcase slammed into Faz's cheek. The force of the blow snapped the already damaged handle, sending the body of the suitcase spinning off into the darkness. Stunned, Faz released his grip and retreated a few steps.

"How could you be so cruel?" he cried, but Aerith was already running, weaving between pews and down the aisle toward the exit. Faz vaulted himself over a pew and gave chase, surprisingly nimble for his size.

"Wait!" he called after her. "Ifalna!"

Aerith had no intention of hearing him out. Her feet scrambled over the rotting old wood panels. The church's imposing doors hung ajar. There were only a few more steps to safety. She had to get away, and . . .

And then what?

Surely Faz knew how to find Elmyra's home. Amber would have told him. Which meant that even if Aerith managed to navigate the pitch-black slums and return safely, it would only be a matter of time before Faz reappeared, armed with some plan to drag her away.

She refused to live in fear forever, or to put Elmyra in danger because of her own choices. She had to act. She had to do *something*. She needed a way to make sure Faz never found her . . .

Aerith burst into the dark, chilly night. She'd scrambled halfway down the stone steps when she saw someone else at the base and froze.

She couldn't believe it. How had Elmyra managed to find her?

The woman stood with one hand on a hip, dressed not in pajamas but rather her usual daytime attire, looking almost as if she knew Aerith had to be inside. Still, as her daughter descended the steps, her face flashed momentary surprise, followed by relief and what seemed a dozen other emotions. Finally, it hardened, firm and unyielding, and she barked, "Aerith. Move aside."

Aerith complied automatically, glancing back as she did so. Faz had emerged from the doors as well and was lumbering toward her.

On noticing Elmyra's silhouette, he demanded, "Who's that? Who's with you?"

The words had barely left his mouth before Elmyra's other hand whipped out to one side, fingers tight around some sort of weapon. It was hard to make out in the poor light, but Elmyra swung it hard, connecting with Faz's neck and sending the man to the ground with a deep cry of pain and a heavy thud.

When Aerith finally processed the nature of the weapon, she was stunned anew. Apparently, Elmyra had been scouring the sector for her runaway daughter with nothing but a broom in hand.

As usual, the woman didn't waste any words. There wasn't a single question about the man she'd just downed or why he was with Aerith at the church. Elmyra simply remarked, "Time for us to be getting home?"

"Yeah."

"Not forgetting anything?"

Aerith gasped. *The suitcase!* She recalled how it had gone flying off its handle.

Elmyra crossed her arms at her chest and said, "Whatever it is, you better hurry up and find it."

Aerith nodded. "I'll be right back."

She hurried up the steps and into the deeper dark of the church. She approached the flower bed, turning in slow circles, straining her eyes until finally she spotted the suitcase. The clasps had come undone, leaving the contents scattered about. Aerith scooped up armfuls of clothing, stuffing them back into the suitcase. But no matter how carefully she scoured the area, the one thing that truly mattered was nowhere to be found: the small cloth bag from her mother, with the white materia inside.

"What's taking so long?" an irritated Elmyra called from the entrance.

"My materia. I can't find my materia!"

She heard the woman mutter, "Oh, for goodness' sake . . ."

But a moment later, Elmyra was also crouched near the pews, assisting in the search.

"It's in a little pouch made of cloth," Aerith explained.

"I know."

Despite her panic, Aerith couldn't help but smile. Every achievement she was proud of, every concern she'd grappled with, every detail of her life—Elmyra knew it all.

Still, the fact that her mother had known to come to the church was baffling. As Aerith's hands continued to feel their way along the wood floor, she asked, "How did you know I was here?"

"Wish I could tell you."

"Huh?"

"The second you left the house, I was hopping out of bed to give chase. But just as I got to the garden and I was racking my brain about places you might go, an image came to mind, clear as day. I saw the church at the edge of the slums, and I knew that was where you'd be."

"How . . . ?"

"Like I say, it just floated into mind. Not that that's anything new. I've lost count of how many eerie experiences I've had ever since you showed up. And since I knew right where I needed to be, I figured I could spare a minute to go back, get dressed, and grab something to use in case I ran into anything I needed to wallop."

"And out of all your options, you went with a broom?"

"I'm not saying I was thinking with a perfectly clear head. But it did the job, didn't it?"

Elmyra pointed just beyond Aerith's shoulder and said, "Look."

Aerith followed Elmyra's finger back to the center of the flower bed, where the plants seemed to have grown even denser over the past few moments. Aerith scanned the spaces among the petals, eventually catching sight of the supple fabric of Ifalna's pouch.

Carefully parting the flowers so as not to step on any, Aerith tiptoed in just far enough to scoop up the pouch and examine its contents. Ifalna's materia was safe inside. And, though it may have only been Aerith's imagination, its soft, reassuring glow seemed a little brighter than usual.

Aerith carefully retreated from the flower bed, intending to announce to Elmyra that she was ready to head home. But when she turned, her breath caught.

Elmyra sat on the front-most pew, head bowed, eyes closed, hands clasped against her chest in prayer.

When Elmyra again opened her eyes, she noticed Aerith's stare, and her cheeks flushed slightly.

"I used to offer thanks like this, back when I was a girl," she explained.

"Offering thanks," repeated Aerith. "Is that different from praying?"

"It is today."

"Who'd you offer thanks to?"

"Whoever it was that told me where to find you."

Elmyra smiled just briefly. Then she was up on her feet, walking down the aisle toward the doors and calling, "Come on. Let's get you back home."

"Mom?"

"What is it?"

"I'm hungry."

Elmyra snorted. "Don't push your luck. You might think everything's hunky-dory again, but as soon as we get home, I'm giving you a piece of my mind."

"Yes, ma'am."

Both mother and daughter were so relieved to be reunited, they'd let their guard down. And by the time Elmyra made it to the church's heavy doors, it was too late.

Faz stepped out of the shadow of one door, knocking Elmyra away with a single, mighty kick.

"Mom!" screamed Aerith.

She tried to run to her mother's side, but Faz was bearing down on her. She dodged past his reaching hands and scurried over to where Elmyra's broom lay on the floor. Now armed, Aerith turned and began to whack the large man's arms and chest. But just a few strokes in, the handle split.

Aerith dropped the splintered remains of her weapon, shuffling backward in terror.

"Over here!" her mother called.

She ran blindly to her mother's side, not noticing the pistol— Carlo's pistol—until it was up, clutched firmly in Elmyra's two hands and trained right on Faz.

The lab assistant froze, glaring at the weapon.

"One more step and I shoot," warned Elmyra.

"Why don't any of you understand?!" thundered the big man.

He again lurched forward, and Aerith heard the pistol's report, saw the smoke from the muzzle.

Bam! Bam!

Two more shots followed, and then more, echoing through the chapel, overlapping one another until it was hard to say how many bullets had been fired. When the magazine was empty, the gunfire gave way to a string of dry, staccato clicks as Elmyra continued to pull the trigger in panic.

But Faz still lumbered toward them, seemingly unaffected. His white lab coat was streaked with dirt, but Aerith could see no sign of blood or gunshot wounds.

He muttered deliriously as he approached, saying "Ifalna . . . My Ifalna . . ." over and over again.

Elmyra's features twisted. She glared at the pistol, denouncing it a worthless hunk of junk. She flung the weapon itself at Faz, only for it to sail well above the big man's head.

"Mom!" Aerith shouted. "Just run! We have to—"

A concussive burst of noise cut her short, so loud and sharp it seemed to rupture the surrounding air. She couldn't understand what had happened until she turned her eyes back to Faz.

The big man had fallen to his knees, right hand clasped tight against his left shoulder, where a large and growing patch of red had formed on his white coat. Aerith realized he'd been shot but couldn't understand how or by whom. Aerith glanced up and down the walls and aisles of the church but spotted no one else.

"Let's go," Elmyra repeated, strangely calm given what had just occurred.

Faz finally collapsed, hitting the wood floor with such force, Aerith could feel it jerk beneath her boots.

She looked at him, fear replaced by pity, and mumbled, "I'm sorry . . ."

"Come on, Aerith. Hurry."

Elmyra set off at a brisk pace, stooping once to pick up the two halves of her broken broom.

Aerith murmured one final apology to Faz and scurried after, the broken suitcase clutched in her arms.

"Mom?" she asked. "Where did that bullet come from? Who shot Faz?"

"I don't know, but I can guess."

Elmyra shook her head and added, "It looks like the restricted zone just got a little bit bigger."

Understanding dawned, and Aerith scanned her eyes up and down the chapel once more, this time looking for crisp jet-black suits. She decided that tonight, just this once, a word of thanks might be in order.

"Ever see that Faz guy again?" Tifa asked with obvious concern.

"No, but there are times when I *think* I do—and I freeze up . . . till I realize it's someone else."

"I bet."

Even all these years later, Aerith's perception of Faz still wavered, stuck somewhere between horror and sympathy. She knew she did not want to see him again. But she also recognized that his fate was inextricably tied back to her actions and Ifalna's, and she'd begun to wonder if the only way to free herself from that tangled knot of emotions was to face the man once more. She wondered if the opportunity would ever come, and if so, what form it might take.

"I'm here if you wanna talk," Tifa added quietly.

Aerith was grateful, as always, for this particular companion's warm, thoughtful acceptance. It was easy to speak of her past when Tifa was the one listening.

"Well, actually," Aerith announced, already certain of the next thing she wanted to share. "I *was* kinda hoping we could talk business."

"Uh . . . What kind of business?"

"You know. *Business.*" Aerith paused and then added, "Boys."

"Oh, that kind."

A clang of metal interrupted their conversation. Both women checked that their helmets were on tight and quickly ran their eyes over their disguises. Next, they glanced at each other, each woman holding an index finger to her lips with a whispered "Shh!"

Heavy footsteps wound their way through the hold, passing along the far side of the tall stack of cargo next to which Aerith and Tifa stood.

Tifa silently slipped to the edge of the stack, ready to pounce on the intruder whenever he rounded the corner.

Seconds ticked by. Aerith's chest burned, and she realized she'd been holding her breath.

The footsteps came to a halt. Then the familiar voice of Cloud Strife called out, "It's me."

Tifa's face flooded with obvious relief. After a moment, she said in a playful tone, "Meeting adjourned—for now."

Just as she did so, Cloud rounded the corner, his own Shinra helmet cradled in one arm. He glanced at the two women, and his confused "Hm?" prompted smiles and stifled laughter from both Tifa and Aerith.

Picturing the Past

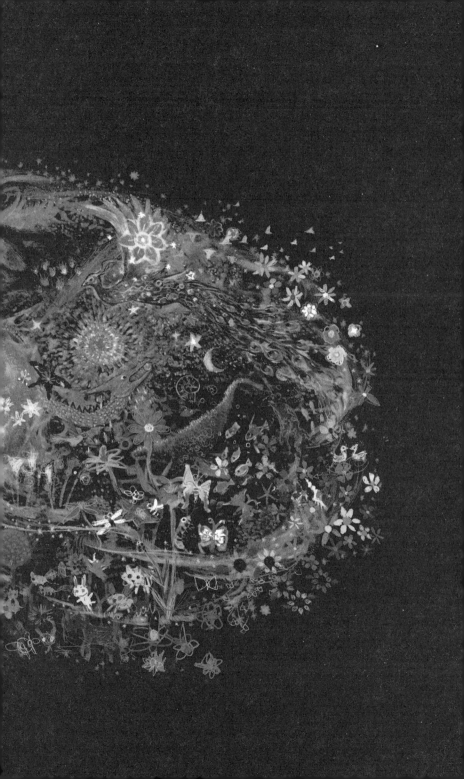

Mideel: Dr. Donovan

An endless expanse of green stretched out beneath me. It was exactly like the picture I'd seen in a magazine as a kid. The helicopter slowed, and the pilot barked at me over the comm as he prepped for landing. Half of the money up front. "In case you don't come back," he explained. Not that I could blame the guy. I nodded and forked over the cash.

They say Mideel's not a destination for the faint of heart. The terrain is unstable, and the lifestream flows just beneath the surface. The second my boots hit dirt, my chest tightened, and I found myself wishing I could be anywhere else. In other words, it was pretty much what I'd expected.

As the planetologists tell it, the lifestream is the physical manifestation of one stage of existence. In fact, that's the basic premise on which the whole field is built. When a person dies, the body returns to the soil. The soul, however, returns to the planet. Reunited with the lifestream, it courses along in the never-ending flow, circling the world until eventually it settles inside a new organism to begin life again.

Modern society isn't so romantic. To the nonbelievers, the lifestream's just a substance, though a useful one. Harnessed as an energy source, it's called mako, and it powers civilization as we know it.

The only problem is: if the planetologists are right, when mako's gone, it's gone for good. Every time you flick a switch, you're burning through a tiny bit of the planet's life force, and it's never coming back. Makes you wonder what kind of future we've got in store. Personally, I try not to think about it. Mako and all its conveniences are hard to give up. But every once in a while, when I catch sight of one of the reactors in the city's skyline, I can feel the weight of the guilt that's always hanging over me.

God, I wish I could go back to before. I would've liked to grow up without knowing a damn thing about any of it.

I learned what I know of planetology from Ifalna. The woman had an old-school grace, with sharp, almost regal features. That's how I remember her anyway. Last time I saw her was fifteen years ago, and I'd been all of nine at the time. I can still hear her voice in my head.

"We're all connected to the planet through the lifestream," she'd said one day when Aerith and I had been arguing. "You're connected. Aerith is connected. And I am too. Think about what that means. If everyone in the world shares a bond with the planet, then we're all connected to each other. Like tiny drops of water coming together to form a mighty river.

"Which means that when we fight, we're fighting against ourselves. Both you and the planet are happier when you try to get along. So, now that you know that . . . is there something you'd like to say to Aerith?"

Ifalna was kind. Gentle. Always smiling, even though she didn't have much to be happy about.

Ifalna and her daughter, Aerith . . .

When I think back on the two Ancients and the time I spent with them, that's when the specter looms largest.

The quiet hot springs town of Mideel sits on the largest of a chain of lush islands far to the south of Midgar. The residents call it a town, but even "settlement" would be a stretch. The first building I laid eyes on was the local clinic, so that's where I started. A medical facility meant records. Leads.

The physician, a man by the name of Donovan, was cordial

enough. He looked to be in his mid-thirties, with a gaunt face and sunken eyes. Funny how doctors are never in great health themselves.

I pulled out the photo of Geddie Bach. The good doctor immediately replied that the man was no resident of Mideel. I could've told him that.

I threw out a few details to see where it got me. Geddie would have passed through the area fifteen years ago. Were there any records of him receiving treatment at the clinic?

Dr. Donovan retired to the examination room, and I heard the sound of moving boxes and rifled papers. I spied a bench that had seen better days and sat down to wait.

Every so often, I'm grateful for my uniform. There isn't a Shinra-fearing town on this planet where the sight of cobalt blue doesn't open doors and loosen lips. The company has business everywhere. Nobody's surprised when a trooper shows up asking questions, and most people answer obediently, regardless of their personal feelings for Shinra.

The doctor was compliant, too, though his search sure as hell wasn't fast. I was beginning to wonder if he'd lain down for a nap when the door finally opened.

"I'm sorry," he said. "I went twenty years back but found no record of any patient by the name of Geddie Bach."

"Thanks anyway," I said, unable to hide my disappointment.

The doctor offered a sympathetic smile. "That's not to say the man never passed through these parts. If he was in good health, he might've never had a reason to come to the clinic. It might not be a bad idea to ask around. Maybe the older townspeople can tell you more."

"I'll do that," I replied.

But as I lifted myself from the bench, the doctor dropped a name.

"Glen Reiner."

". . . Excuse me?"

"I do have record of a Glen Reiner. The time frame matches. He was treated here fifteen years ago—in fact, he was the only patient on record that year who wasn't a native of Mideel. The chart mentions that he was a Shinra trooper, just like you."

My pulse raced.

"Could I see the chart?" I asked.

The doctor nodded, holding out a manila folder he'd brought from the back. Inside were the treatment records for a Glen Reiner.

"Not to pry, but I'm guessing you're here in an *unofficial* capacity?" asked the doctor.

". . . Yeah."

"I never saw you, and I never gave you that chart. You snuck into the clinic after hours and found it all by yourself. Got it?"

I nodded, and Dr. Donovan briskly turned on his heel, heading back to the examination room.

Knowing I'd never get another chance, I called after him, "Is there anything else you remember about Glen?"

"I wouldn't know your Geddie or Glen or any other patient from fifteen years ago. I've only been in Mideel for three."

Apparently, everything I was gonna get from the clinic was already in my hands.

I flicked through the pages of the chart. Fifteen years ago, a villager spotted a man shambling aimlessly through the nearby brush, disoriented and babbling incoherently. The stranger was identified by the Shinra-issue dog tags around his neck. Glen Reiner, twenty-five years old. He was diagnosed with a torn ligament in the right ankle and mid-stage Type III mako poisoning, including symptoms of severe memory disruption. After half a month in the clinic, a passing cargo chopper offered to airlift him back to Midgar. The discharge papers included a hastily scribbled signature from the chopper's pilot; I made it out to read "Jack Klein."

I was already planning my next move. However, I'd made the trek out to the edge of the world; I figured I might as well speak to the other locals before I left.

I flashed the photo of Geddie Bach around. Not a soul claimed to know the man. One wrinkled old villager did recall a Shinra trooper laid up in the clinic once upon a time, but neither the photo nor the names—Geddie *or* Glen—seemed to ring any bells.

The chart did name the man who carried Glen from the brush

to the clinic, but that was a dead end: the villagers informed me he'd passed away some time ago.

Fifteen years is a hell of a long time. Enough for nine-year-old me to grow up into a man of twenty-four, soon to have a kid of my own. I'd found all I was going to find in Mideel, and it was time to get back to Midgar. The pilot I'd hired was all too happy to oblige.

When we touched down, I went straight from the heliport to HQ, where a friendly face and a few slipped bills bought me the next bit of info I'd need.

The official word was that Glen Reiner ate lead on a battlefield in Wutai, date of death only three days after his flight back from Mideel. That's one hell of a dedicated soldier, to shamble back onto the front lines while still in the throes of mako poisoning. And that's one hell of a commanding officer to put him there. Something didn't add up.

But I wasn't after Glen Reiner. I was looking for a man named Geddie Bach, who up and vanished fifteen years back. Geddie would've been in Mideel—I was dead certain about that. My search had instead turned up evidence of Glen, a soldier I'd never heard of and whom the company reported KIA, despite highly unlikely circumstances.

A soldier who just happened to be in the same place at the same time as Geddie: Mideel, fifteen years ago. There was a connection here. I could feel it in my gut.

They say the lifestream bridges time too. It connects people of the past with those in the future. Maybe they're right.

If so, it might mean I was guilty of even more than I thought.

Sector 7: Jack Klein

Jack Klein was easy enough to track down. Even the pilot who flew me in and out of Mideel had heard of the guy. Klein's flying days were over, but he still lived in company housing in Sector 7.

He turned out to be a cranky, swollen-faced old bastard. I paid him a visit the following weekend. It wasn't even noon and he already reeked of booze.

Klein was cagey to begin with, and more so when I told him I was looking into something that happened fifteen years ago.

"You're in the service," he snapped. "You know how it is. Some things are on a need-to-know basis."

Fortunately, a bottle of the corner shop's finest vintage turned the conversation around. That, too, was a tip I'd picked up from the pilot who flew me home.

"I ain't a snitch," Klein said. "But I've been told I'm a talky drunk. Get enough in me, and sometimes I start sayin' things I shouldn't."

"Fifteen years ago," I repeated, "you lifted a soldier from Mideel with a serious case of mako poisoning. His name was Glen Reiner."

"Oh, I did, did I?"

I waited.

When the bottle was half-empty, his tongue started wagging.

"Back then, nobody knew shit about mako or how to properly handle the stuff. Saw a whole lot more poisoning cases than you do now. Anyway, when you found a guy who you knew wasn't gonna make it, there were these lab coats in R & D who would take 'em off your hands for a little scratch. I always knew I was bein' paid to keep quiet 'bout the whole thing, but it creeped the hell outta me. I mean, they spun it as an open call for 'volunteers' to help test out new treatments, but bullshit never smelled so sweet. There ain't a shred of compassion across that whole damn division."

Klein grimaced, as if admitting that he wasn't exactly a beacon of compassion himself. "Yeah, I remember Glen Reiner. When I scooped him outta Mideel, the guy was so far gone, his legs could barely hold him. All wobblin' around with every step like he's about to pass out drunk. Typical mako poisoning. We weren't no friends, but it still broke my heart to see him a husk of the man I sent in."

"Hang on. Are you saying you're the one who flew him into Mideel in the first place?"

"You didn't know? Then what the hell are you here for?"

That was how I first learned of the Special Geological Survey

Initiative. The way Klein spoke of it, I could tell he considered his involvement to be the highlight of his career.

The initiative only existed for a brief window, fifteen years ago. The surveyors were enlisted men and women who volunteered for the program and found themselves reporting directly to President Shinra. Selection itself came with a sizable bump in rank, and if the surveyor successfully completed his or her mission, the promised rewards were enormous.

"There were risks, of course," said Klein. "Likelihood of mako exposure was high. Dangerous levels. Possibly fatal. 'Cause that's exactly what they were searchin' for, see? Natural reactor sites.

"Here's the kicker, though. President Shinra must've been out of his goddamn mind, because the only clue he gave the poor bastards was a photograph of some unknown landscape taken at some unknown location. Hell, it wasn't even a proper photo. It was a *drawing* that someone had pointed a camera at. The surveyors were bein' asked to find the exact spot shown with nothin' else to go on."

I swallowed. My throat was drier than a well in Corel.

"Rumor was that the president had some shady geomancer doin' the drawings." Klein laughed, a short, sharp exhale.

He grabbed the wine bottle and held it between his knees, hand tight around the glass neck like he was in his cockpit, gripping the cyclic.

"The surveyors themselves were a ragtag bunch. Men, women, troopers of all ages. Only thing they shared was a dream; this was their big shot to break free of a two-bit life.

"All they had to do was believe that the scenery in their pictures was truly out there, somewhere in the wide, wide world. And boy, did they. On the back of each photo was a set of coordinates. Not exact coordinates, mind. If Shinra knew where to find the places, why bother with the surveys? No, they were just a best guess provided by some glasses-wearin' desk jockey from HQ's upper stories."

Klein pulled back on his imaginary control stick.

"I lost count how many times I loaded up with a new set of hopefuls, flying 'em to spots all across the planet.

"No landings. That was understood. I wasn't about to risk losing my bird to a monster attack out in bumfuck nowhere. Or worse, to a stray squad of Wutai bastards. The surveyors wore chutes; when they were happy with the site, they jumped. They had ten days to scout out the area. On the eleventh, another chopper would be there with a rope to haul 'em up, *if* they showed."

Klein sighed. "The number of 'em I ever saw again . . . now *that's* one I can still count. Ain't none of 'em boastin' about some fountain of mako they found. Just haggard faces thankful to be home alive.

"As for the rest, well, these weren't friendly places. Plenty of monsters to do you in for."

He paused to take a swig of wine, seeming to forget that he'd just sent his imaginary copter spiraling out of control.

"Felt bad for the ones that didn't make it. I mean, I liked 'em all well enough. They had guts. Dreams. Wanted to make better lives for themselves. You don't see much of that in the city, and especially not up on the plate. Midgar wears you down. Makes you soft."

I swallowed again, throat still dry, and asked, "What kind of pic . . . What kind of *photo* did Glen have?"

The old pilot's eyes glazed over. "The only reason Glen Reiner stuck out to me was because of his photo. The night before we took off, he and I nearly came to blows about where I'd be flyin' him. As far as I saw it, his picture was some rocky bluff straight out of Cosmo Canyon."

"Cosmo Canyon?" I parroted, taken aback.

I knew the place, of course. It was a tiny settlement a continent away, perched among rocky, arid wastes that lay far to the west. They say Cosmo Canyon holds deep significance for planetologists.

"I had two drop-offs that day. The first one was headed to a spot just south of Fort Condor, after which I *assumed* I'd be droppin' Glen off in the vicinity of Cosmo.

"At the time, I was based outta Junon. I'd checked the charts and decided to hit up Fort Condor first. Smooth flight, smooth send-off. The first surveyor went out the side, and then it was just me 'n' Glen."

Klein paused to look me up and down, as if hesitating over whether to continue.

"The smug bastard leaned forward and handed me a sheaf of

paper folded in half. I opened it to find a set of coordinates in Mideel, along with ten thousand gil, all in crisp notes."

He shook his head. "At that point, I figured why the hell not. If he wants to go on a wild chocobo chase and answer to the president for it when he returns, let him."

The wine bottle was now empty.

"Extraction was somebody else's problem. So to be honest, after I dropped Glen off, I forgot all about the guy and got on with my usual duties. Shinra had me flyin' cargo all over the planet. If it was inhabited, I'd been there.

"Imagine my surprise when I drop a shipment off at Mideel's clinic and find Glen in a hospital bed. Frankly, on the day of his jump, the guy acted like he'd never deployed a chute before. He pulled the cord so late, I half figured he ended up a red stain on the jungle floor. But there he was, alive and breathing, and that's somethin' to be thankful for, mako poisoning or not."

And yet you decided to sell the guy to Research and Development, I thought bitterly, but I held my tongue.

I pulled out the photo of Geddie: a young man of about twenty-five at the time, clad in a lab coat and possessing average, forgettable features.

"Just to be sure. Do you recognize the man on the right?"

"Sure. That's your Glen Reiner right there." Klein snorted. "Another one of them lab kooks, huh? Shoulda figured. Glen didn't seem the soldier type."

I left Klein in his cups. A deep sigh escaped me when I was out the door.

The photograph of Geddie was still in my hand; I stared at him, standing there in the past, smiling brightly in his white lab coat. Beside him was a nine-year-old boy. Me.

Sector 7: Silvina Kelly

Shinra has housing scattered all across Midgar for its army. Most units are old and cramped, the smallest not much more than a broom closet with a bed for some young, single recruit. A spouse or a kid will get you a larger place, but it still ain't gonna be pretty to look at.

Meanwhile, the civvies have it good. Corporate employees get cozy little homes in perfectly planned suburbs. Suits before boots, I guess.

Anyway, Shinra brass must've been drowning in complaints, because at some point, they instituted a new program: any trooper, even a private straight out of basic, was eligible to apply for a spot in company housing. It was mostly lip service, of course. The odds of winning a spot were so low, you might as well play the slots and hope for a jackpot.

But it wasn't impossible. Silvina Kelly was one of those rare individuals to beat the odds.

My luck's not half bad either. I didn't land a spot in employee housing, but I did land Silvina.

When I got home that night, I found her at the sink, brushing her teeth.

"How'd it go?" she asked.

"Not bad. I think I made some serious headway."

"You did, huh? Well, now you've got me on the edge of my seat. Come on. Out with it."

"Ah, baby . . . You don't wanna hear this. It's not a story of blue skies and sunny days."

"I'll put up with a storm cloud or two on our way to a brighter future."

A brighter future. I sure hoped it would be. Maybe when all this was over, the nightmares would stop. I'd quit thrashing and yelling in my sleep, and Silvina would finally be able to get a good night's rest.

"All right. I guess I'd better start with Mideel then."

I stood at her back, my arms gently curled around her sides, hands cradling the swell of her belly. It wouldn't be long now. If I was serious about a future with these two, I needed to square away my past.

Silvina's big, round eyes held on mine in the bathroom mirror. They were full of laughter. God, she reminded me of Aerith. If Aerith were still alive out there, this was exactly how she'd look.

The Shinra Building, Fifteen Years Ago: Aerith

Aerith was a resilient child. That's what my mother said, anyway, and I think she was probably right.

Running around in those cramped living quarters, Aerith and I had our fair share of bumps and bruises. There was always an arm bashing the edge of the desk or a shin slamming against a corner of the couch. When the unlucky appendage was Aerith's, she never cried out in pain. Her smile would vanish, though, and that's how I'd know she was suffering. It was the same way she reacted whenever her mom was late coming back from the lab.

A few times, I saw her lose her cool. I remember her yelling at the door once, just after Geddie Bach had walked out.

"Stupid Geddie! I *hate* him!"

"Aerith, you mustn't say such things," Ifalna gently chided.

"But he does awful things to you! You came back bleeding today!"

Ifalna *was* bleeding; I had to give Aerith that. The elder Ancient had returned with white bandages about her wrists, already stained red where the fresh wounds were beginning to leak through. She often came back looking exhausted, but that day, her eyes seemed almost hollow.

"It's all *Geddie's* fault!" declared Aerith. "He did that to you!"

"I promise you, Geddie had nothing to do with this. He has no reason to hurt me."

"But every day, he's the one who comes to take you away!"

"Geddie's just doing his job," I said, with the kind of confidence only a nine-year-old can muster. "If he weren't here, it'd be somebody else showing up at the door each morning."

"But . . . !"

Aerith cut her own protest short, diving facedown onto the couch and burying her head in the cushions. My own mom sighed, figuring this argument for a lost cause.

"Ifalna," she ventured, "our shift's almost over, but . . . if you'd like us to stay and look after you, we'd be happy to do so."

Ifalna flashed a weak smile. "That's very kind of you. But I'll be fine."

"All right . . . We'll see you tomorrow, then. Aerith, I hope you'll be in a better mood come morning."

Aerith didn't reply. As Mom and I filed out of the room, I glanced back to find the girl's head raised from the cushions, watching us go. She silently scrunched up her nose, puffed her cheeks, and stuck her tongue out.

At the time, you couldn't have dragged the words out of me, but I was smitten. To me, Aerith was one in a billion. My first brush with love.

The corridor outside their room turned an abrupt corner, beyond which we found Geddie at his plain, unassuming desk. When he wasn't escorting Ifalna to and from the research lab each day, that's where he stood, carefully noting the comings and goings of anyone in contact with the two Ancients. Geddie wore a white lab coat, just like everyone else on the floor who wasn't a soldier, but Geddie was no scientist. He was an ordinary guy hired to do an ordinary job for Shinra's Research and Development Division, just like Mom and me.

He greeted us casually and asked, "Heading home?"

I replied first. "Yeah."

Geddie was a decent enough guy. I had nothing against him. At the moment, he was a glorified doorman, but from the way he talked, you could tell he had his sights set higher. Mom liked to say he was a real go-getter, and that I could learn a thing or two from him.

"Welp, work's gonna be real fun tomorrow," complained Geddie. "Think Aerith's gonna yell at me again, or am I in for the silent treatment?"

"Just part of the job," sighed Mom. From the way she said it, I could tell the reassurance was meant for her own sake as much as Geddie's.

"What makes it especially hard," replied Geddie, "is the fact that she's so darn *cute*."

He winked at me. I kept my mouth shut, praying no shift in my expression had given me away.

Mom glanced over with a little smile, too, but when she spoke again, it was to Geddie. "I feel for the girl. Of course she's going to lash out. Her mother's coming home in bandages, for goodness' sake. Honestly, I'm starting to wonder what in the world is going on in that lab of theirs."

"Don't ask me. You know how it is around here. Even if I knew, I wouldn't be able to tell ya." Geddie let out a small sigh. "The lab assistants are getting squeamish, though. They seem to think Professor Hojo's going too far."

Everybody even remotely involved with the lab knew who Hojo was. The man ran Shinra R & D. I'd encountered him two times in my stint as Aerith's playmate. I prayed there wouldn't be a third.

"Anyway," continued Geddie, "that's not even my biggest problem right now. There's this friend I grew up with, see? He enlisted in the army, while I came to work here in R & D. But get this: the other day, he tells me he's being promoted. A big bump in rank and pay, and all he had to do was sign up for some special, hush-hush operation. I mean, how unfair is that? I'm practically beating myself up for not deciding to enlist too."

"Military life is hard," counseled Mom. "Be thankful you've got a nice, quiet job right where you are."

"You make it sound like I don't *want* to work hard," grumbled Geddie.

"I'm sorry. That's not what I meant."

"Look . . . if you hear about any good openings, would you let me know? Shinra or otherwise. At this point, I'm willing to look outside the company if it'll kick my career into high gear."

"Nothing wrong with transferring to another division. But stick with the company, Geddie." It was the same advice I'd heard from Mom a million times before. "You're better off working for Shinra than somewhere else, 'cause at the end of the day, Shinra controls the world."

Sector 7: Silvina Kelly

Silvina lay facing me on the bed, fast asleep. I listened to her gentle snores and reached a careful hand to her belly. Inside was my baby. *Our* baby. The three of us were connected via the lifestream, bonded to one another for eternity as mother, father, and child.

I'd do whatever needed to be done to make sure those bonds were pure. I wanted us to start fresh, with nothing dragging us down.

Military Housing: Joann Liu

I awoke with a new line of attack in mind. I wanted to get started immediately, but Silvina made me sit and eat, saying it wasn't an appropriate hour to go paying house calls. From the way the hands on our clock crawled 'round, I would've sworn the damn thing was busted. Finally, they read nine, and I shot off to see Jack Klein once more.

The corner shop wasn't open, so this time cash had to suffice. Klein snatched the bills from my hand, and I had a name: Joann Liu.

Another quick stop by HQ netted me an address. I thanked my lucky stars and paid off my contact. I was about to meet the *other* survey member from that day fifteen years ago—the one who'd hitched a ride to Fort Condor alongside Glen Reiner, aka Geddie Bach.

Liu lived in officer housing—fairly plush, at least by military standards. She was a short-statured woman of about forty, with a physique that made it plain she didn't skimp on PT. If I had to guess, she was the type who was strict with herself and stricter with everyone else.

She wasn't gonna answer any questions until she had my rank and station. Her voice was sharp, like a needle on my eardrum.

"You're not a *Turk*, are you?" she demanded.

It struck me as a strange thing to ask. Her eyes regarded me with quiet suspicion, and I realized that if I wanted anything out of this encounter, I was gonna have to share some details. I hesitated, unsure where to begin or how much rope to let out. If I gave away too much, the whole investigation could blow up in my face.

I decided the key points to keep quiet on were Aerith and Ifalna.

My time with the Ancients was a secret I'd probably be taking to the grave. Mom had made me swear not to talk about it. Hell, I hadn't even told Silvina about that part of my life.

"It's completely personal," I assured Liu. "Something for my own peace of mind. Nobody else has to hear about it."

It was just a bit of baggage I needed to clear up before my kid was born—and that meant the clock was ticking. I explained that there was a guy who'd looked out for me when I was young. He'd vanished, and when I tried to look him up as an adult, I was told he'd died fifteen years ago. But when I asked *how*, nobody could give me a straight answer. So now I was trying to track down people he'd known, to see what they could tell me.

"His name was Glen Reiner," I said, holding out the photo of Geddie Bach. "This is him before he died."

When Liu displayed no sign of recognition, I continued with my story, pretending not to notice.

"You knew Glen, didn't you?"

She didn't answer, so I fed another coil.

"Fifteen years ago," I repeated. "The Special Geological Survey Initiative. A chance for the bravest of the brave to make a name for themselves. The day Glen Reiner shipped out, there were three people aboard the chopper: Glen, the pilot, and—"

"And me."

Liu gave a quiet snort and flumped down on her couch. I looked around but didn't see any options for me to sit.

I guess she likes to keep her visitors standing.

"The pilot's name is Jack Klein," I said, continuing the tale that had led me to her. "He told me you and Glen seemed pretty chummy that day in the chopper."

Liu snorted again. It seemed to be a habit of hers.

"And let me guess," she said. "The kid in the photo is you?"

"That's right."

"Then I expect you probably know that the guy you're standing by is named *Geddie*, not Glen."

". . . Yeah. I do."

"You gave his name as Glen when you showed me the photo 'cause you wanted to see how I'd react."

"You got me."

"Hmph. Well, you're gonna have to start by telling me just how much you know about—"

The tail end of her demand was cut off by a bang against the wall at her back, loud enough to make me jump. Someone had either slammed a fist against the wall or rammed the other side. Liu, however, didn't even flinch.

The apartment's front door opened directly into the living room. That was where we were sitting . . . or where one of us was sitting, anyway. Off to the right was a small kitchen, complete with a dining table for two. I saw a couple other doors: one to my left and another straight ahead. Most likely, they each led to a bedroom.

Bang. Another one. The noises were coming from the bedroom at Liu's back. Someone was in there.

"Settle down, Lilisa," Liu said, her voice not unkind.

Lilisa . . .

Lilisa . . .

I *knew* that name. I wasn't sure from where or when, but I did. I worked my way back through my memory logically, methodically, until a cold, sinking feeling told me that my subconscious already had the answer.

This was a name I didn't *want* to remember.

I'd been handed a trace of my past that I normally kept locked in a drawer in a dusty corner of the far reaches of my mind. Worse, the damn thing was as fresh and vivid as the day I sealed it away.

A Memory: Lilisa

We were in Aerith's room. Normally, Mom would've been there too. But at that particular moment, it was just Aerith and me.

Aerith had set down her paintbrush and was slumped listlessly in her seat. She didn't seem in the mood to talk, so I let her be. I was more worried about Mom, anyway. One of R & D's specimens had escaped from its cell, and Mom had been ordered to assist in the search.

"I'm sick of drawing," complained Aerith.

"I know."

You've said it a million times, I thought.

Looking back, I should've shown some sympathy. But at the time, I was just a kid.

I did manage a little encouragement, in my own way.

"Geddie will find a way to help. We just have to be patient."

Two weeks had passed since I slipped Geddie the special drawing. I'd expected things to escalate quickly, but the days dragged on as usual. The only difference was that Geddie wasn't at his desk anymore, and the other lab assistants had begun taking turns ferrying Ifalna to and from her quarters.

"You're right," said Aerith. "Sorry."

She'd picked up on my irritation, and now I had her walking on eggshells. I felt like an asshole.

The door opened, just enough for one of the lab assistants to poke her head through. This one was young and fairly new.

"Have you finished drawing?" she asked.

"She's *working* on it," I insisted, suddenly protective of Aerith. "It's not some stupid doodle she can finish in a few minutes. Give her some space, would you?!"

The lab assistant scowled and stormed into the room, leaving the door wide open behind her. All I could think about was the specimen on the loose.

"Close the door!" I screamed.

But it was too late.

A black shadow burst in, shoving past the white-coated lab assistant, who toppled to the floor with an astonished cry.

My eyes locked on the shadow. I was the only thing standing between it and Aerith. Except, I wasn't holding my ground out of bravery. I was just too damn scared to move.

The shadow, I quickly realized, was actually a woman. She was clad in some sort of black robe, and her eyes darted furiously about the room. When they landed on Aerith, she let out a shriek and pounced. White knight that I wasn't, I dove the hell out of the way.

"You!" the woman screeched. "You're Aerith! You're the reason he's dead! Do you have any idea how many people you've sent to die?! It's all because of you and your pictures!"

Hate and fear filled the intruder's crazed eyes. Her pale hands locked tight around the seven-year-old girl's delicate neck, and all I could do was watch. I thought for sure this was it. Aerith was going to *die*.

In the end, the encounter wasn't nearly so final.

Out of the corner of my eye, I saw the lab assistant struggle to her feet. She fished a syringe from her pocket and jabbed it into the crazed woman's neck, where it remained lodged like a dagger. The robed woman shrieked again, but her knuckles loosened and her arms fell slack, and then she was slumping forward, pinning Aerith against the wall with her weight. Aerith's eyes, big and round and full of terror, locked on mine. I cast my own gaze downward, unable to bear the shame of my cowardice.

I found myself looking at the intruder's feet. The hem of her robe was frayed to shreds, leaving bare her sickly, waxlike skin. Near her ankle, I spotted a tattoo scrawled in black ink.

24.

The lab assistant shot a glance up to a security camera installed in one corner of the room.

"I need a team in here!" she shouted. "Lilisa's been subdued! Get her back to her cell!"

Another *bang* sounded on the other side of the living room wall.

Liu shook her head. She leaned close to the wall, shouted, "Quiet, Lilisa!" and settled back down on the couch with closed eyes.

"Lilisa and I went through basic together at the tender, stupid age of nineteen. Back then, she wasn't like that. I mean, she didn't talk much, but it wasn't because she couldn't. She was just shy.

"Mako poisoning," Liu continued, eyes still shut tight. "That's what changed her. R & D put her in a hospital bed and helped her past the worst of it, but . . . Well, let's just say there's been a lot of banging on the walls these past fifteen years."

A low, animalistic wail had begun shortly after Liu's sharp admonishment, and it crescendoed now into an almost human sob.

Liu sighed. "Maybe it wouldn't be so bad, knowing there's someone else out there who's heard my side of the story."

Her eyes snapped back open and locked on to mine.

"And I figure there might be a few pieces to this puzzle that you can fill in."

Joann and Lilisa, Glen and Geddie

Joann Liu and Lilisa Meg entered service on the same day—as did one Glen Reiner. The three trained together as new recruits, but that wasn't the only thing they had in common. They'd also all grown up in the slums.

That final point caught all of them more shit than they deserved, but Lilisa had it especially hard. Whenever she screwed up during training, a certain instructor liked to chalk it up to her background. One day, she returned to the barracks still fuming. Anger trumped good sense, and she stormed back out to confront the instructor, only to find Glen already in the guy's office, protesting the treatment of his fellow soldier.

From that day on, Joann, Lilisa, and Glen were fast friends, spending most of their free time together.

Enter Geddie Bach.

Geddie, it turned out, was close with Glen; they'd been neighbors growing up. Glen began inviting his old buddy to hang out with his new friends, and pretty soon, the little trio had a regular fourth. That was how the three recruits and one Shinra R & D employee ended up spending nights and weekends together, cooking meals, drinking, and talking of their dreams for the future.

When Joann dreamed, she dreamed big. Right from the start, her sights were set on brass, and a salary to match. Someday, she'd remark with a laugh, she was gonna be issuing orders to Heidegger himself. It was half a joke and half not.

Glen was just as ambitious. Every time Joann talked of a future glory, he was right there to claim he'd accomplish as much and more.

Their brash initiative seemed to spur Geddie on too. He began to speak of promotions and real responsibility at work, and of learning to play office politics so he could get ahead.

Lilisa, on the other hand, was content simply to wear a uniform.

She'd come from a particularly poor background even among grounders, and life was grand enough now that she had no need to worry about food in her belly or a roof overhead.

When word spread about opportunities to be had in a brand-new unit reporting directly to the president, Joann could barely contain her excitement. A lack of upfront details about the so-called Special Geological Survey Initiative did sprout some concern, as did the alarmingly generous rewards and the consequent risk they implied. But in the end, her wildfire ambition razed a path straight to the sign-up desk.

She arrived to find Glen already handing in his application. The two shared a laugh; they'd both thought themselves very cunning, never mentioning any interest in the program among their little foursome of friends. But given Joann and Glen's professional drive, they'd always been bound to sign up.

They were both accepted, as well. Then came the waiting. They could ship out at any time, they were told. They were to be prepared to drop everything and go at a moment's notice.

Joann redoubled her training, adopting a strict regimen from sunup to sundown, though still allowing herself to enjoy the company of her friends in the evenings. Glen was always there to share a drink and a bite to eat; sometimes Geddie or Lilisa joined in, too, and occasionally both were there, bringing the old group together just like before.

Finally, the call arrived for both Joann and Glen: they'd be shipping out the following morning.

In the meantime, they were expected at Shinra HQ, where a rally was to be held for all surveyors about to depart.

When President Shinra himself stood to address the surveyors, Joann had stars in her eyes. The initiative was no longer just a way to get ahead in life. She was among the few and the proud: a select group whose efforts would reshape civilization as we know it.

Joann wasn't the only one. By the time the president's address was over, the whole crowd was swept up, fully committed to the mission that lay ahead.

In filed the Turks, handing out small, ten-centimeter-square photographs, one per surveyor.

When Joann received hers, she studied it for a long, quiet moment. It was a very peculiar thing; as far as she could tell, it was a photograph of a painted landscape. On the back of the photo was a handwritten set of coordinates.

Those coordinates, President Shinra explained, indicated the individual surveyor's mission site. Each surveyor was to be transported to the listed coordinates by chopper, at which point they'd parachute in and attempt to find the precise location depicted in the photograph. They'd have ten days to do so, after which they were to rendezvous for extraction at the drop site.

Discovery of the location in question was worth 50 percent of the purse advertised at sign-up. If the location proved to be a suitable site for construction of a mako reactor, the full 100 percent was to be awarded. And if the site was exceptionally rich—a trove of mako the likes of which President Shinra had long dreamt to find—the payout jumped to 220 percent. That's the kind of money you could live out the rest of your days on, never having to lift a finger again.

Honestly, the atmosphere of the meeting was such that the surveyors would've geared up right then and there, even sans any promise of gil. Glory to the company and all that jazz. That's how worked up President Shinra had them. They sure as hell weren't in any state to be making rational decisions.

In any case, once the rally was over, there was another, more personal party waiting. Lilisa had had the day off, and she spent it in her apartment cooking up a half-dozen mouthwatering dishes, planning to hold a little send-off for her friends. Joann was the first to arrive, followed by Glen, who brought Geddie along to complete the usual group.

Soon the drinks were flowing and everyone was having a good time, reminiscing about times past and letting imaginations run wild about the adventures ahead. The mood was light and happy, a lot like a birthday party. At least, that's how it was until Lilisa got a little too tipsy and burst into tears.

"Please don't go," she begged Glen in particular. "Something awful is going to happen. I just know it. You have to stay."

She clasped his hands in hers and added, "I'm in love with you."

The abrupt confession stunned Joann at least as much as Glen.

When Glen finally regained his composure, he tried to talk her down. "It's all right," he said. "I'll be back. I promise." As he spoke, he eyed Joann and Geddie, desperate for help.

Joann announced, "I think I've had one too many," and headed out to get some air. She was all too happy to exit the awkward scene—not least because she wanted to avoid starting another of her own. In Joann's eyes, Lilisa had crossed a line. The four were friends, but the scope of that friendship fell well short of interfering with one another's dreams. Glen was aiming high, chasing bigger things. Lilisa had no right to hold him back.

That said, it was a conversation she and Lilisa could have later in private. No reason to ruin the party and spoil everyone's last night together.

Joann stationed herself at one end of the foyer running the length of the barracks, where she stared out a partially open window at the giant plume of smoke rising from the nearest reactor. Cool evening air blew in, a welcome change from the stuffy atmosphere left behind.

She couldn't have said how long she'd been standing there when she heard Geddie's hoarse, panicked cry calling her back. When she turned, her blood chilled. Geddie lay facedown on the threshold, body halfway out in the foyer. When she rushed over to check on him, she saw the short, sharp tremors running through his body. It was some kind of seizure.

"Geddie?!" she cried. "Answer me!"

She hadn't recognized *why* he was shaking, but she knew it was bad. Her next thoughts were of their two other friends still inside, but training kicked in and she doubled back first, pounding on the door of a neighbor, who only needed one glance at Geddie before he ran to find a medic.

When Joann finally made it back inside the apartment, she was hit by the stench of vomit and worse. Glen and Lilisa lay facedown in their own filth, exhibiting the same short, sharp spasms as Geddie. She called their names and shook their shoulders but got no response.

Joann was on the verge of panic when she heard a weak, shaky voice at her back.

"Lilisa . . . She . . ."

Geddie had pulled himself to his feet. He stood with one shoulder leaning heavy against the doorframe.

"She must've . . . slipped something into the food."

The warning out, he collapsed once more. Still, for Geddie at least, the spasms seemed to have passed.

It was ages before the medic arrived. When he did show up, Joann recognized him as another recent recruit stationed in the same barracks. He was young, but he moved quickly and confidently, first checking on Glen and Lilisa, who were now unconscious. Geddie, though weak, seemed to be recovering. The medic didn't share his diagnosis aloud, but Joann overheard him asking to be put in immediate touch with the Research and Development Division at HQ.

From there, things moved fast, and the details were hazy. A whole crew of men and women in white coats had descended upon the apartment within a matter of minutes. The first ones to arrive carried Glen, Lilisa, and Geddie off on stretchers. The researchers left behind divvied up the apartment, cleaning up the vomit and examining the half-empty beer bottles and half-eaten plates of food. Everything was tested on the spot, systematically, with some kind of reagent.

"Got a positive over here," she heard a man say, clearly not pleased by the discovery. "Mako. Just as we feared."

That particular researcher had been in the kitchen, testing food in one of the serving dishes.

Joann spent the next hour and change in the hot seat, interrogated first by the R & D scientists on the scene and then by damn near half her chain of command once they'd caught wind of the hubbub.

Was the mako introduced into the food by accident, or was it put there intentionally? If the former, whose fuckup was it? If the latter, what was the agenda? No details were shared with Joann about whether her friends were all right. It was just one rapid-fire question after another about the mako and how it got there, questions Joann was unable to answer.

At long last, another trooper arrived with orders from higher up, and then all the researchers and corps were filing out of the apartment, leaving Joann alone and bewildered in a room that now reeked of skunked beer and spoiled casserole on top of everything else.

Lilisa must've slipped something into the food.

Geddie's words echoed in her skull. She tried to make sense of the claim. Had Lilisa poisoned the food to try and keep Glen from leaving? Was Lilisa capable of that sort of thing? Joann didn't want to believe it, but love could drive a person to do crazy things.

When Geddie finally returned to the barracks, it was close to midnight. The Shinra scientists had him on a cocktail of drugs that seemed to be doing the job; he claimed to be feeling a lot better.

"They tell me my symptoms were pretty mild. I'm still a little nauseous, but I think I'm gonna be all right."

"What about Glen and Lilisa?" she asked.

Geddie's eyes fell. "The doctors can't get them stable. When we were on the stretchers, I could hear the lab assistants calling out their names, but neither of them was responding."

"Geddie . . . I need to know. What happened after I left the room?"

"After you left . . ." He hesitated, his brow now furrowed. "I remember hearing the oven timer go off. Lilisa had mentioned she had a casserole cooking. But the ringing didn't even seem to register in her mind. She was too focused on Glen, begging him over and over not to go.

"Glen was desperate to change the subject. He said he was dying to try the casserole, but Lilisa wasn't going to budge. I was afraid the thing was going to burn, so I went to the kitchen to take it out. I brought it out to the table, and Glen sat down right next to me, scooping up a big helping. The casserole was still bubbling, but he was shoving mouthful after mouthful down his throat, saying it was the best thing he'd ever tasted. That seemed to improve Lilisa's mood, and she grabbed a bowlful herself.

"I've got a tongue that'll burn on warm milk, so I didn't start eating until a few minutes later. By the time they were showing symptoms, I'd only had a few bites. I guess that's why I got off easy."

Geddie paused before adding, "It was a damn good casserole. Would've never guessed there was mako in it . . ."

"You're *certain* it was the casserole?"

"Well, that's the only thing we ate that you didn't, right?"

Military Housing: Joann Liu

"Tell me," said Liu, "you ever heard of mako slag?"

"Of course."

It was a term for the residue that built up when a mako-driven internal combustion engine failed to completely burn its fuel. The stuff could hang around in a vehicle's internals for weeks, a toxic surprise for anyone stupid enough to start poking around in the engine compartment without protective gear.

"Lilisa was posted to the army's mobile infantry division. She was mostly in charge of maintenance and repairs."

Liu raised an eyebrow at me as if to say, *You see where I'm going with this?*

She hopped up from the couch and walked to the kitchen, where I heard her pour herself a glass of water. When she came back to the living room, she sank back into her seat.

"There's still one thing I don't get," I said. "How did Geddie end up as part of the Special Geological Survey Initiative? You two shipped out the morning after all this went down."

Liu nodded.

"Oh, it was a flagrant breach of regulations. If word of what he and I arranged ever leaked—even now, fifteen years on—they'd knock me out on my ass faster than you can say 'court-martial.' And yet here I am, sharing all the details with a total stranger."

"I won't tell another soul."

"I know ya won't. Not that I'd really give a damn if you did. My heart doesn't belong to the military. I'm only here for the money, and I've been thinking for a while now that maybe it's time for me to get back to the slums."

"I'm not sure what you're getting at."

"This is a calculated risk. After I'm done scratching your back, I'm hoping you'll scratch mine. Something tells me you'll be able to answer a few questions that have bothered me ever since this went down."

"I'll tell you everything I know," I replied immediately. Maybe *too* quickly, even. I was scared to death she'd see right through me.

Liu turned to look at the door leading to Lilisa's room. She stared at it pensively for a time, then gave a thoughtful nod.

"That night, after Geddie got back, he told me he didn't want Glen to lose his one big shot. If Glen wasn't gonna be able to go on his survey op, then Geddie was determined to go in his place. He'd come back successful and share the news with Glen to help spur his friend's recovery.

"Geddie was so committed to the idea, he'd even slipped into Glen's hospital room to lift the dog tags from his neck. He showed them to me, so I knew it was true. The only problem, Geddie said, was that he needed me to back up his story. My help was crucial if he was going to pass as Glen from the time we shipped out to the moment he jumped.

"Now, you tell me, how the hell would *you* feel hearing something like that?"

"Couldn't say. I guess my first reaction would be to wonder if Geddie's up to the task. He was no soldier. He was going in blind, without a lick of training."

In truth, I'd have had a few choice words to share with anybody trying to turn a close friend's death to their own benefit. But I didn't say as much to Liu. And it was good I didn't, because Liu's reaction sure as hell wasn't the one I would've predicted.

"I was moved half to tears, goddammit," she said. "It was the most noble, selfless display of friendship I think I've ever seen. Geddie was ready to put everything on the line just to keep Glen's dream alive."

Of course, when I took a moment to reflect on it, it made sense. If Liu had felt otherwise, she wouldn't have gone along with Geddie's story. And if she hadn't helped Geddie, we wouldn't be in her living room talking it over.

"Geddie's one lucky bastard," she added. "We found Glen's pack still in his room, untouched by R & D, with the photograph he was assigned tucked safely in one pocket."

Joann and Geddie

Members of the Special Geological Survey Initiative were to as-
semble for departure just outside Shinra HQ, in Sector 0. Hoping
to avoid any encounters that could expose their scheme, Joann
and Geddie (posing as Glen) waited until the last possible second to show up. They slipped onto the back of a truck driven by
a fresh-faced trooper who looked about as clueless as they come.
Four other surveyors were aboard the truck, but through a stroke
of good luck, none of them had ever met Joann or Glen.

After a smooth ride to the heliport, Joann, Geddie, and the others all piled aboard Jack Klein's bird for a transit flight to Junon.
Once there, the other four disembarked, heading to other helicopters with flight paths plotted out to get everyone to their drop
coordinates as efficiently as possible. Only Joann and Geddie remained aboard Klein's craft.

During the flights, the two had their helmets on, making it easy
enough to obscure Geddie's identity. They made a show of friendly,
familiar banter in front of the pilot, and Joann spent a good portion of the flight sharing "expert tips" for a truly flawless parajump.
The explanation conveniently included exaggerated descriptions
of absolute basics like how to put the chute on and where to find
the cord. Geddie hadn't even laid eyes on a parachute outside of a
book, but he still managed to whisk Joann's concerns away with his
determination and passion for the mission ahead.

Military Housing: Joann Liu

And then they'd reached the drop site south of Fort Condor,
and Joann had made her jump. For her, that's where the story of
Geddie Bach went blank.

"Now it's your turn," she said to me.

"All right."

I got right into it, sharing the details of the remainder of
Geddie's flight exactly as relayed by Klein. I figured there wasn't
anything in there that needed to stay secret from Liu. I explained

how Geddie begged Klein to take him to a different destination. How he'd waited until he was alone with the pilot to offer the bribe.

In the back of my mind, I couldn't help but wonder what would've happened if Geddie had found himself assigned to a different pilot that day. Would he have bribed someone else as easily as Klein? It was hard to say. Maybe Geddie was prepared to resort to other methods if tossing gil didn't suffice.

"But in the end," said Liu, "Geddie didn't find anything at all, did he? I heard he was extracted from Mideel with a bad case of mako poisoning."

"Yeah. Klein handed him over to R & D for . . . treatment."

"Pretty ironic that he'd meet the same fate as Glen."

"Tell me," I said. "Whatever happened to Glen? The *real* Glen."

Liu was quick to oblige. "Among the surveyors, I was one of the lucky ones. I didn't find the spot in my photo, sure, but I did come back alive and healthy.

"About two weeks after I got home, Lilisa was discharged from R & D's care. A couple of Turks brought her over to my place, probably 'cause they didn't have anywhere else to take her. The way they told it, she'd had a real bad case of mako poisoning. Lilisa had eventually regained the ability to walk, but R & D said not to expect much more of a recovery than that.

"When I asked the Turks about Glen, they filled me in on what happened. R & D had tried everything they could. Apparently, Professor Hojo himself stepped in to oversee treatment near the end. But it just wasn't enough.

"So Glen was dead, and now the Turks were asking me if I was willing to square things away for both him and Lilisa. I figured it was the least I could do for a couple of good friends. I cleaned out their apartments, threw out what I could, and hung on to a few personal effects.

"Lilisa's parents had already passed, so there wasn't anyone for me to notify. As for Glen's, they didn't say much when I gave them the news. His mom and dad seemed to have made peace with the possibility already. Their boy was a trooper, and the country was at war."

"Hang on," I interrupted. "You told them he died in combat?"

"That was the standard line for anyone who didn't make it back from a Special Geological Survey op. If anything, it was better for the surviving family. It meant they'd be eligible to collect benefits."

"But that didn't apply for Geddie."

"As far as the rest of the world was concerned, Geddie vanished into thin air. And as I understood it, his only living relative was his mother. His father had already passed away."

"I see . . ."

Liu loudly slapped both palms against her thighs and announced, "Well, that does it for my side of the story. Now it's time for you to hold up your end of the bargain. I've got questions, and my gut tells me you've got answers."

I didn't recall promising Liu anything, but I waited to hear what she had to say.

"The day of our flight, Glen was supposed to drop just outside Cosmo Canyon. I saw his photo. Those were the coordinates he was assigned. But you say Geddie convinced the pilot to change course for Mideel.

"Why? Did Geddie have a second photo? Or some kinda tip? What had him so convinced he'd find an assload of mako in Mideel . . . ?"

Liu was posing questions, but they were directed as much to herself as to me. I could tell she was still sorting though possibilities, thinking out loud.

"And if he *did* have solid intel suggesting a site in Mideel," she continued, "where did he get it?

"Hell, what was with that intel in the first place? Why were the Turks handing out photos of *drawings*? Where did they come from? Who made 'em? What possessed President Shinra to base an entire operation around a bunch of artwork?"

I excused myself to use the restroom, closed the door, and quietly slipped out the window.

The Shinra Building: Aerith

Aerith and Ifalna lived in a room in Shinra HQ, somewhere among the upper stories. I never learned which exact floor. Mom told me we weren't allowed to know, and I had no reason to question it.

My eyes and ears were open, though, just like any kid. I saw how the place was constantly swarming with men and women in white lab coats, their eyes bloodshot and their feet stumbling as they went about their duties on the brink of exhaustion. Geddie once told me the entire operation might as well have been running on zero sleep. There were troopers too—not armed to the teeth, but there all the same. Geddie said they were there for our protection, and I believed it. The adjacent floors housed Shinra R & D's ever-rotating menagerie of monsters, and to no one's great surprise, monsters tend not to be in the best moods when they're poked and prodded for days on end. Occasionally, one or another would lash out violently enough to break free of its confines, and then our whole section of the building would go on lockdown. Needless to say, there was always a certain tension in the air.

Mom was in charge of tending to the daily needs of Ifalna and her daughter. She'd been chosen for the job partly because of me: I was the right age to make a good playmate for Aerith. Mom didn't tell me until years later, when I was old enough to handle the money responsibly, but Shinra had even been paying me a bit for the trouble.

Every morning at ten, Geddie showed up to escort Ifalna to the lab. While she was away, it was Mom's responsibility to clean the room and take care of the laundry, and mine to keep Aerith occupied.

I wasn't complaining. There were worse ways to spend the day as a kid. Aerith and I would show off stupid little dances we'd made up the night before or just run in circles around the room. Aerith loved playing hide-and-seek, despite the fact that there are only so many places you can hide when you're stuck between four walls. We added an extra rule that whoever was hiding could make a funny face when found; if you could make the seeker laugh, it didn't count that you'd been discovered, so you still won that round. I dunno if you can still call it hide-and-seek at that point, but it was easy enough to play, which made it a pretty good standby when we couldn't think of anything else to do.

Aerith's usual spot was behind the couch. She'd lie on the ground faceup, like a doll accidentally left behind by a busy toddler. Her eyes would be wide open, rolled up and to the side, with her tongue sticking out in the opposite direction. I must've seen that face a million times, but it never failed to get a laugh out of me. And when I laughed, Aerith laughed too.

That's the kind of girl she was: sweet and innocent, always smiling, never weighed down by the reality of her circumstances.

At least, that's how she was before the drawing began.

I remember it like it was yesterday. We were taking a break from the billionth round of hide-and-seek, and Aerith was doubled over giggling because of some vapid story Mom was sharing: an *extremely* overexaggerated tale of how I once came across a monster near home and carefully backed away. The way Mom told it, I bolted from the scene like I was scared for my life, and I'd been moving about five times faster than she'd ever seen me run before.

"Wow! *Five* times faster!" exclaimed Aerith. "Your legs must've been moving so fast, I bet they got all tangled up! Am I right?!"

I rolled my eyes and was about to respond, That's *what you got out of the story?*

But before I could, Aerith was on her feet, furiously pumping her legs in place and asking, "Like this? Am I close?"

"Triple that, and you'd *almost* have it."

Normally, I wouldn't encourage Mom's ridiculous embellishments, but when I saw how much Aerith was enjoying the story, I decided to go along with it.

After another few seconds of running in place, Aerith abruptly froze and turned to stare at me wide-eyed.

"What kind of monster was it?" she asked. "A bomb? A cactuar? A goblin?"

Aerith began listing off every monster she'd ever heard of.

"It wasn't anything cool like that, all right?" I snapped, my irritation back in full force. "It was like . . . like a wererat, but shrunk down in size."

"That's just a normal rat!"

"It was a *monster*, okay?!"

"How do you know for sure? What about it was different from a regular rat?"

"Its tail was at least *twice* as long as a normal rat's. And the end was all coiled up like a corkscrew."

Now I was just winging it.

"What's a corkscrew?"

"That thing for opening bottles. It's all twisty and stuff. You know, a corkscrew."

I drew loops in the air with my finger.

"No?"

"Oh, geez. Um . . ."

I scanned the room for a piece of string, figuring I could wrap it around my finger or something.

Mom smiled and announced, "Hang on. I'll be right back."

She popped out of the room and returned shortly. Except, instead of a piece of string, she came back with a notepad and a pen.

"Go on," she urged. "Let's see this rat of yours, corkscrew tail and all."

I was in too deep to back out now, so I snatched the pen and pad from Mom's hands and took a seat at the desk, where I began sketching out my giant, imaginary rat, whose tale was now five times more twisted than its supposed tail.

"Kinda like this," I said, presenting my creation to Aerith.

"Ooh . . . !"

She stared at my drawing intently. *Too* intently. I mean, calling it a drawing was being generous. It was more or less a circle with five lines for legs and a tail.

"Hang on," I said. "I can do better."

I flipped to a new page and started over. I hadn't been expecting her to take it so seriously.

But Aerith's second reaction was even worse than her first.

"Grrr . . ."

It was like a low growl. The kind of thing you'd hear from an angry lion. Without any warning, she leaned in close and yanked the pen and pad from my hands.

"Hey!" I blurted out, half-angry and half-confused.

But Aerith's mind was already a million miles away. The pen

swiped one anxious, precise stroke after another, all across the page, point pressed so hard the whole pad buckled.

I saw a person's face. And then trees, and flowers. Animals, or maybe monsters. I wasn't sure. Mom and I looked on in silent awe. Aerith kept adding one object after another, until the surface was more ink than paper.

"Ngh!"

Aerith let out a grunt. She seemed to be in pain, but she didn't stop drawing. As far as I could tell, she *couldn't*.

My mother glanced up at one corner of the room.

"Emergency," she said, voice quavering. "We need assistance. Now, please!"

That was how I first learned of the surveillance cameras that were watching Aerith's and Ifalna's every move, day and night.

A moment later, Geddie burst into the room, along with a whole gaggle of white-coated lab assistants. Last to enter was Professor Hojo. He proceeded immediately to Aerith's side and peered intently at the picture, ignoring the girl completely. Aerith's eyes remained fixed on the page. The pen kept moving. To me, it looked like she'd been possessed.

"What is it, my dear?" cooed Professor Hojo. "Do you *see* something? Some image inside your mind?"

The girl nodded.

"Yes," she said. "I . . . I can see it. And hear it too. There's a roaring, like . . . like a rainstorm or a great big river."

Professor Hojo chuckled softly—a creepy, mad-scientist sort of chuckle. I didn't like where any of this was going.

"Aerith," he said. "You've awakened."

He continued to chuckle.

Mom's face had gone pale. "I'm so sorry," she mumbled. "I didn't mean for any of this to happen . . ."

Looking back, I don't think it was me she was apologizing to.

The Slums: Joann and Lilisa

The string of days I'd taken off to wrap up my past were all used up. I was back to real life, working nights like always. I'd finished one particularly tiring shift and was making my way home in the morning, feeling like a salmon returning to spawn as I fought against the surging current of nine-to-fives.

When I got to the house I shared with Silvina, Joann Liu was standing outside.

"If I'd known you had a broad in there, I would've waited for you outside work," she said. "C'mon. We're goin' for a walk in the slums."

I could tell she wasn't going to take no for an answer.

"How'd you find my place?" I asked, hurrying to keep pace. Her brisk gait surprised me, given her short stature.

"Same way you found mine. I gotta admit, I was surprised to see just how much info the company keeps on us—and how much of it is up for grabs for anyone willing to flash a few gil." She chuckled. I sensed a warmth in her demeanor that wasn't there during our initial encounter.

"There's something different about you today," I remarked.

"Yeah. You're probably right. I took some time to think about our conversation. I decided maybe it's all right for me to have hope."

She smiled and added, "It's been a long time since I felt this free. And I owe that to you."

I wasn't sure how to respond, so I didn't.

"What I mean is, I saw you trying to come to terms with your past, and I decided maybe there's something to that."

Liu turned a sharp corner. Now we were on the street leading to the station. I had to concentrate just to keep up with her.

"Glad I could help," I said. "I'd been feeling kinda bad about the way I skipped out on you."

"You should feel bad. I bared my soul back there, you know? Gave you the whole truth, but you didn't even have the balls to answer a few questions."

"Sorry."

"I'm not here for an apology. I came for answers." Her voice was stern now. The smiles and laughter were long gone. "Where'd Geddie get his photo of Mideel?" she asked. "And who was drawing those pictures? I know it won't change anything now, but I gotta hear it, for my own peace of mind. And don't worry. I'll take it to my grave."

I kept my mouth shut, following Liu in silence. A minute or so later, we were at the station, where I was in for another surprise: Lilisa was there, standing in a corner near the gates. She weaved unsteadily from side to side, and passersby shot her cold, cautious glances.

"There's one little detail I didn't share with you yesterday," Liu said. "About the present day, that is. Lilisa and I take a lot of trips to the slums."

I was starting to think that every time this woman opened her mouth, I was racking up a debt that was going to be real hell to pay off.

Liu and I sat beside each other on a bench in the train car. Most of the other seats were full, too, but the only passenger standing in the aisle was Lilisa. I figured the other passengers were coming off graveyard shifts like myself. They worked in the city all night, then went back to their homes in the dim gray of the slums as soon as the sun came up. Poor bastards.

I'd never had the awful fortune to live in the slums, but I'd done three peacekeeping tours with Public Security. It hadn't left me with a very positive impression of the place. I dunno. Maybe that bias comes built-in when you're born topside. You spend your life doing everything you can to keep from falling down below, 'cause once you're off the plate, it ain't easy getting back up.

That's what you're taught, anyway. They drill it into you from the time you're a kid: the slums are a place for the dregs of humanity.

Liu seemed to pick up on the fact that I was on edge.

"Don't worry," she said. "No one's gonna fuck with you while you've got that uniform on. Sure, they'll jeer and let off some steam, but they're not stupid enough to start throwing punches."

"Sure hope so," I said.

"Even down in the slums, everyone dreams of scoring a company job. They like to bray about the evils of Shinra, but it's never more than empty words. We were the same way."

We.

She was talking about herself, Lilisa, Glen, and Geddie. Because of their upbringing, the four shared a certain bond I'd never understand.

"'Course, I also promised myself that if I ever made it topside, I'd never step foot in the slums again. Funny how things never go quite how you imagine, isn't it?"

The train came to rest at the Sector 7 Undercity Station. Lilisa lurched and weaved her way out the doors, and we followed. The flow of disembarking passengers clearly showed the way to the central slums, but Lilisa was going the opposite direction. She seemed to be headed for a junkyard filled with old, broken-down railcars. I glanced at Liu, eyebrows raised. She nodded and told me the locals commonly referred to the place as the "train graveyard."

Lilisa staggered on, squeezing through gaps between dilapidated cars and occasionally climbing aboard one to walk its length to an exit on the other end.

"Where is she taking us?" I asked.

"Couldn't tell ya. It changes every day. I just follow to wherever she takes me. If she gets lost or climbs aboard one of these things and finds out that it's a dead end, I help her get back on track. If any thugs show up and give her a hard time, I take care of 'em."

Liu grinned. "I guess you'd say I'm her bodyguard."

"How aware is she of what she's doing?" I asked. "You said it was mako poisoning, right? I'm no expert, but even I can see her brain's pretty much fried."

"Oh, she had it bad, all right. But there are a few of us—people taking care of friends and family in similar condition as Lilisa—who suspect these little 'walks' might not have anything to do with the poisoning at all. We're inclined to chalk it up to whatever hush-hush treatment it was that R & D provided. The lab coats made them this way. That's the theory Glen's mother subscribes to. She says she found weird scars all over her son's body, like he'd had some kind of surgery."

"Huh?"

My mind was filling up with more than a few new questions.

I started to ask, but Liu hissed, "Shhh!" and stopped short, pointing a finger at a clearing ahead.

Several figures stood in the open space, wearing the same black robes as Lilisa. I counted six or seven. None of them seemed to be doing anything in particular. They just stood there aimlessly, each facing a seemingly random direction, but all with their heads tilted upward. I followed their gazes but couldn't see anything but the grimy steel girders lining the underside of the plate.

Liu indicated two of the robed figures standing slightly apart from the rest.

"That one's Glen," she said. "And that one's Geddie."

"Wh—?"

I couldn't even get the whole word out, I was so shocked.

"It was about five years ago. Glen was shuffling to and fro in the slums, and just by chance, his father found him and took him home. When Geddie's mother heard the news, she became convinced that her son was still alive too."

Liu paused, then said, "No. I guess really she never accepted that Geddie was dead in the first place. Maybe that's part of being a parent."

I wasn't sure I agreed.

"And then, it was like someone up in the sky was listening and heard a mother's desperate prayers. Not that I buy that sort of crap, but . . . one day, Geddie just kinda showed up at home. That was four years ago.

"Wasn't just Glen and Geddie either. In the slums, it's not too uncommon to hear about residents going missing, like they've vanished into thin air. Suddenly, a bunch of those long-lost individuals were showing back up. Some had been missing for a couple years or so. Others had been gone as long as fifteen.

"All of 'em in the same state as Lilisa. And the creepiest part is that they all had tattoos. Somewhere on the body, there was always a number."

"Numbers, huh?" I replied. "Yeah, that sounds like the R & D I know. People, animals, monsters . . . They're all just specimens. So what did the company have to say about all those sudden reappearances?"

"Shinra issued some half-assed apology about mistakes in KIA reports due to the chaos of the war. But that only covered the combatants. For the others, they claimed most had been undergoing long-term treatment at Shinra facilities, and a policy change meant that anyone who didn't wish to continue treatment could ask to be discharged."

"They're claiming *this* lot checked themselves out of the hospital?" I waved a hand in the direction of the black-robed figures. "I'd sure like to know how they managed that. I mean, just look at them."

Liu snorted.

"Personally, I think the whole division oughta be locked up, starting with that bastard Hojo. But the parents of some of these people feel differently. They see a son or a daughter that's still alive instead of dead to mako poisoning. And if they're happy to have their kid back home no matter the condition, I don't think it's my place to convince them otherwise. Yours, either."

Accept it and move on.

That seemed to be Liu's message.

I walked into the clearing and carefully sidled up to one of the robed figures Liu had pointed out. I peered under the hood to find a gaunt face with hair and beard left to grow untamed. But it was Geddie Bach, all right. I had no doubt of that.

"Geddie?" I ventured, but the man provided no response.

I tapped him lightly on one shoulder. At that, he turned slowly, lazily, to gaze in my direction.

"It's been a long time, Geddie."

His eyes showed no sign of recognition. I could tell there was something more at work than a gap of fifteen years.

"I didn't mean for . . ."

I trailed off. Nothing I said was reaching him. I sensed someone at my back and turned to find Liu.

"For years, I really believed Lilisa poisoned our food," she said. "Her feelings for Glen seemed a reasonable enough motive, and she had the means to get her hands on the right substance. But your visit got me thinking again, and now I've got a better answer."

"Which is . . . ?"

A few possibilities were whirling through my mind. First and foremost, I needed to work out what Geddie's and Glen's survival meant for me. Second, how was I going to worm my way out of the questions I knew Liu was about to ask next? How much responsibility did I bear for the shattered state of this little group of friends, and would I ever get the chance to atone for my actions?

"Where do I go from here?" I asked Liu.

"You gotta pick up the pieces one by one," she replied. "Don't worry. You have time. As you can see, they aren't going anywhere."

The train ride home was far less crowded than the ride in. Lilisa was able to sit, and she did so, taking a spot next to Liu. She seemed exhausted by her journey. Her head rested on Liu's shoulder, and Liu held a palm against the other side to help keep her steady.

I sat at Liu's other side. At one point during the ride, she reached an arm around my neck and pulled me in close. It was a lot less tender than the way she was holding Lilisa.

"Here's my theory," she said. "I think there *was* mako in that casserole fifteen years ago. But Lilisa didn't slip it in there. Geddie did.

"With his job granting him free access to R & D facilities, it wouldn't have been hard for him to get ahold of some highly toxic mako derivative. And I think the purpose of his crime—yeah, that's right, I said *crime*—was to secure a seat on Klein's bird. For whatever reason, he believed he had a lead on the fabled trove of mako President Shinra was after. All he needed was a means to get to it.

"I dunno what kind of rose-colored future he had in mind for himself once he found the site, but I think he was so determined to come out on top, he was willing to do anything to make it happen, even if it meant taking advantage of our friendship . . . and Lilisa's love for Glen."

Liu's arm squeezed tighter. It was getting hard to breathe.

"Please," I gasped. "Let go."

She continued as if she hadn't heard. "The only thing I can't put my finger on is *what* drove Geddie to those lengths."

Her hold grew tighter yet.

"So I asked myself . . . what business could a kid like you have with a nobody like Geddie Bach?"

"What was it you started saying to him back at the clearing?" she asked. "What was it you didn't mean to happen? Huh? I'm betting you wanted to apologize. You didn't mean for him to end up shambling around the slums as a husk of his former self."

I kept my mouth shut.

"My money says there was a kid painting those landscapes the Turks photographed. And I'm starting to think that kid was *you*."

"Yeah . . . No. I mean . . ."

"Better start talking."

She eased her arm from my neck, but I could tell she was ready to clamp down again if I so much as shifted my weight.

"It was a girl," I croaked. "Her name was Aerith."

I told Liu everything. The way I'd spent my days with Aerith. The story about the rat and the corkscrew tail and the pad of paper and the way it was killing her and the plan I cooked up to try and keep her safe.

In a span of hours, Aerith's drawings were the only thing anyone in R & D was talking about. It wasn't much longer before President Shinra himself came down to watch her work. He was particularly interested not in the people or animals, but rather the vegetation, the rock formations, the backgrounds . . . He asked questions about how she came up with the things she drew and what made them important.

Aerith ignored him at first, but when he continued to press, she begrudgingly shared that the images just floated into mind. Sweeping landscapes full of tiny details would flash into existence and linger there, refusing to go away.

The answer seemed to please President Shinra a great deal.

At my side in the train, Liu sighed. "Right. And next came the Special Geological Survey Initiative."

"Bingo. The president is a believer. As far as I can tell, he really thinks the Ancients possess some mysterious power capable of bringing boundless prosperity to all. My guess is that when he saw Aerith's drawings, he interpreted them as mankind's chance at greatness finally coming to hand."

"And what about you? Do you believe there was something special about those drawings?"

I'd long ago realized that Aerith wasn't a normal kid. She seemed to see and hear things that I never picked up on. But at the time, I didn't dare tell anyone that she was different. I didn't even allow myself to dwell on the realization. I felt certain that if I pointed out the things that made her special, the lab assistants would drag her off someplace far away, and I'd never see her again. Ancient or not, all I wanted for Aerith was to live a normal life like me.

I cleared my throat. "The day Aerith started drawing those pictures, something inside her changed. She quit smiling. She didn't eat much anymore. The stupid little dances stopped, and all the books she used to read over and over sat unloved on their shelf.

"The seventh day after I drew that shitty picture of a corkscrew, I was told I wasn't allowed to see Aerith anymore. Mom kept going to work as usual, but I was left at home with nothing to do.

"Mom tried to explain. She said Professor Hojo had decided upon a different direction for his research—a direction in which I played no part. Mom told me to go play with the normal kids in our neighborhood instead. That's exactly how she put it. 'The normal kids.' Those words stung hard. I sat at home, crying by myself for days.

"But after a week of R & D's new direction, they reversed track. One evening, out of nowhere, they sent for us—not just Mom, but me too. As we made our way to the Shinra Building, I had a real bad feeling about what we were gonna find. And I was right. Aerith was there, but just barely. She'd wasted away to skin and bones, like a sick puppy out on the streets. When we used to play together, she'd always worn her hair in an immaculate braid. Now it hung loose and tangled, and her clothes were stained with ink and paint.

"And there was another change that bothered me even more. One entire wall of their room was covered in paint: a giant mural showing landscapes and people and weird creatures I'd never even dreamed of."

The Shinra Building: Aerith

We were in the hallway, right outside Aerith's room, when my mother knelt down to look me in the eye.

"They want you to convince her," she said. "You have to get Aerith to start drawing again."

I was sitting next to Aerith at her desk.

"Did you draw all this?" I asked, pointing to the mural.

She nodded, and the room's lights caught the streaks of tears slowly drying on her cheeks.

"I did, but President Shinra and the professor . . . They say they don't like this one. They only want me to draw *places*. The drawing doesn't need to be big, they say. But it has to be a place."

"You don't want to?"

"It's not that I don't want to . . . It's . . . I *can't*. I don't see any more."

"Why not just make something up? Like . . . draw a bunch of places from your imagination. Places you *wish* were real."

Aerith's eyes widened at the suggestion. She shook her head violently. "No. *No way*. It has to be a real place," she insisted. "If it's not, somebody could *die*. That's what the professor said."

It wasn't until after I'd grown up that I understood what she meant. The survival rate among surveyors must have been dismal. But the fact that Hojo would look a seven-year-old girl in the eye and tell her that people's *lives* were riding on her actions made me sick to my stomach.

In any case, I didn't know any of that back then. I was a kid. All I could focus on was how annoyed I was about once more being dragged into Aerith's latest problem. It wasn't like there was anything I could do to help.

"Then I guess you gotta try harder," I said, shrugging my shoulders. "Good luck with that."

"Didn't you hear me? I can't!"

"Okay. Then tell them you're done drawing."

"I just want to see my mom. That's all. Why won't they let me see her?"

I should have been angry at Shinra. Instead, I kept digging into Aerith.

"Fine. Then listen carefully. I'm gonna tell you what to draw, and you gotta draw it exactly. If you can do that, I promise it'll be the last picture you ever have to make."

"You'll make them stop? How?"

"I can't tell you yet. But if this works, you have to do whatever I say, okay?"

She stared at me with those wide, round eyes. They seemed to bore their way into my soul. Finally, I couldn't stand it anymore and had to glance away.

"Okay," she said. "I'll do it."

I don't think she agreed because she believed in me. I think she did it because she was at the end of her rope. She'd been defeated. Her one friend in the world turned out to be a puppet at Shinra's beck and call.

Sluggishly, she pulled out a new sheet of paper and arranged her pens and brushes at the desk.

I sat next to her and whispered into her ear.

"An island there.

"Now, fill it with lots of trees.

"Make them tall. Real tall, like a two-story house.

"The leaves should be giant. Each one as big as you are; and fill all the branches.

"The trees should be packed tight. So tight, you can hardly walk between them.

"Dark green. Darker. And make the trees even a little taller."

It was something I'd seen in one of Mom's magazines. I kept directing Aerith until the picture was done, and then I pushed the emergency call button. I knew Geddie Bach would be the one to respond.

When he appeared at the door, I handed him the picture and said in a low voice, "She says this is the one. She summoned the last of her strength to make this picture, and she says it's the clearest, most vivid one she's ever seen. But that's it. She says the power and the images in her head are all gone now, and she can't draw anymore. She wants to know if you'd please explain that to Professor Hojo."

Geddie stared at me for a while and then at the picture.

"All right," he finally concluded, not taking his eyes from the paper. "I guess I'll break the news to the professor."

His words felt absentminded.

"This is Mideel, isn't it?" he asked.

"Beats me."

He continued to scan the picture carefully for a while before walking in to confront Aerith.

"This picture you drew. It's a place in Mideel, right?"

Aerith looked at me blankly. I nodded to her, ever so slightly. I didn't care what she said. I just wanted Geddie out of there as soon as possible.

She took my cue and nodded decisively at Geddie.

"I knew it!" the man exclaimed. "I've seen this before! It was in a magazine or something, and . . ."

"You'll make sure it gets to Professor Hojo, right?"

"Yeah," Geddie promised. "Of course."

In the end, Geddie somehow managed to keep the picture's existence entirely to himself. And because of that, Glen and Lilisa were now milling around like zombies, devoid of happiness or dreams, and Liu had lost her two closest friends.

Two weeks after I gave Geddie the picture, I came face to face with Lilisa.

"She burst into the room and started strangling Aerith," I explained to Liu. "The girl was too terrified to speak, but I saw the way she looked at me. She blamed me. She'd been begging me to help. To save her. And instead, I dove out of the way. Even after Lilisa was sedated, I was terrified. I ran from the room, leaving Aerith to fend for herself."

As I retold the story, tears welled in my eyes.

"Seems your guilt finally pushed you to act."

I nodded slightly, innocently, in that same manner Aerith had nodded when I urged her to lie.

Liu heaved a sigh. "Let's zoom out for a sec. The person responsible for the way Lilisa and Glen are now is Geddie. You might've provided Geddie a reason to act, but the fact that he actually did is all on him. You didn't know what he'd try when you handed him the picture, and you weren't aiming to get a couple of strangers poisoned.

"And as for R & D, plenty of lives have been lost to their meddling. I'm not about to lay the blame for any of that on you."

"Th-thank you." I managed to respond.

I wasn't sure gratitude was the response this called for, but I couldn't think of anything else to say.

"At the end of the day, there's nothing I can say that'll ease your guilt. And frankly, I don't think you ever gave a damn about my side of the story."

"That's not . . ."

I trailed off. Liu was right. She'd seen that for me, Lilisa, Glen, and even Geddie were only the periphery.

"There's a plaza out in front of the Sector 8 Station. You ever been there?"

I furrowed my brow, unsure what Liu was getting at.

"No. I've never spent much time on that part of the plate."

"A flower girl sets up shop there. Pretty sure she goes by the name Aerith."

Sector 8: Aerith

When I stepped out of the Sector 8 Station, it was nearly evening. Sure enough, there was a flower girl in the plaza. She had a basket on one arm, and she smiled kindly at everyone who passed her by. The color of her hair was right, and her wide, bright eyes seemed like they could be the same ones from my memory.

Still, I wasn't sure.

I watched as a customer purchased a flower from her, then headed off, saying, "Thanks, Aerith. See ya tomorrow."

Apparently she had regulars. And her name *was* Aerith, just like Liu had said. But was this the Aerith I'd known?

She watched the customer disappear into the crowd. When she turned back around, she caught sight of me. No surprise there; my uniform made me stick out like a sore thumb. Not to mention that a Shinra trooper's stare was usually enough to grab anyone's attention. I pulled off my helmet and walked in the flower girl's direction.

As I drew nearer, certainty sank in. It was the same Aerith, all right. She watched me with a vague, uncertain smile, but when we were close enough to talk, the expression vanished from her lips.

She had to know who I was.

Aerith glanced about her surroundings and drew a half step back.

"Hey. Aerith, I . . ."

I didn't know where to start, but I blurted out my name, and then the floodgates were open. I started talking about everything. I recounted every single memory I had from childhood—the fun times, the boring times, the times I'd cursed myself for not being brave enough to help her, the times I'd wallowed in despair over what a shallow friend I'd been.

When the surge subsided, I added quietly, "Sorry. I . . . I guess I've just always wanted to apologize. I felt like I *had* to, or else I'd never be able to get on with my own life. And . . . hell if I know why, but I went about it in the stupidest, most roundabout way possible. Instead of searching for you, I had myself running around in circles, spinning like a corkscrew until . . ."

Throughout the whole confession, Aerith stared at me, her expression blank.

Finally, she cleared her throat and said, "Um . . . I'm sorry, but . . . I think you have the wrong person."

"What are you talking about? You're Aerith. Your mother is Ifalna. She's an Ancien—"

Her face stiffened, and I finally understood.

I was a memory she had no desire to dredge up again. I was one trace of a past she was better off without.

"My bad," I said, voice catching in my throat. "Guess I was mistaken."

I pivoted away and headed in the direction of Sector 7, wanting to leave that painful encounter behind as quickly as I could. But when I reached the edge of the plaza, I stopped and turned to catch one last glance. Aerith was looking my way.

And for the briefest moment, I was sure I saw her eyes dart up and to the side, and her tongue poke out in the opposite direction.

When I got home, Silvina greeted me at the door. She didn't look a thing like Aerith. For the first time in as long as I could remember, the great, heavy mass of guilt that had grown alongside my love for my partner and the mother of my child was gone. I felt sure it had been swept away for good.

About the Author

Kazushige Nojima was born January 1964 in Sapporo, Japan. A writer and video game creator, he has been involved with the making of numerous game titles, primarily in the capacity of scenario writer. His credits include the main scenario writing for *Final Fantasy VII*, *Final Fantasy VII: Advent Children*, *Crisis Core: Final Fantasy VII*, *Final Fantasy X*, *Final Fantasy X-2*, *Kingdom Hearts*, and *Kingdom Hearts II*. He is also the author of the novels *Final Fantasy VII: On the Way to a Smile* and *Final Fantasy VII: The Kids Are Alright—A Turks Side Story*. A fan of heavy metal music, he owns an extensive electric guitar collection, though he is unable to play the instrument particularly well.

About the Translator

Stephen Kohler is a translator of narrative fiction, games, and comics, including such titles as *Witch Hat Atelier*, *Magus of the Library*, *Final Fantasy XV: The Dawn of the Future*, and *NieR:Automata—YoRHa Boys*. He lives in western Japan with his wife and daughter.